Also by Bruce Macbain

Odin's Child: Book One of Odd Tangle-Hair's Saga

Roman Games: A Plinius Secundus Mystery (Book 1)
The Bull Slayer: A Plinius Secundus Mystery (Book 2)

The Ice Queen

A novel

BRUCE MACBAIN

Blank Slate Press | Saint Louis, MO

Blank Slate Press
Saint Louis, MO 63110

Copyright © 2015 Bruce Macbain

All rights reserved.

For information, contact
Blank Slate Press at 4168 Hartford Street, Saint Louis, MO 63116
www.blankslatepress.com
www.brucemacbain.com

Blank Slate Press is an imprint of Amphorae Publishing Group, LLC

Manufactured in the United States of America
Cover and Interior Illustration: Anthony Macbain
Cover Design by Kristina Blank Makansi
Set in Adobe Caslon Pro and Viking

Library of Congress Control Number: 2015916957

ISBN: 9781943075140

To Carol with love and gratitude

The
Ice Queen

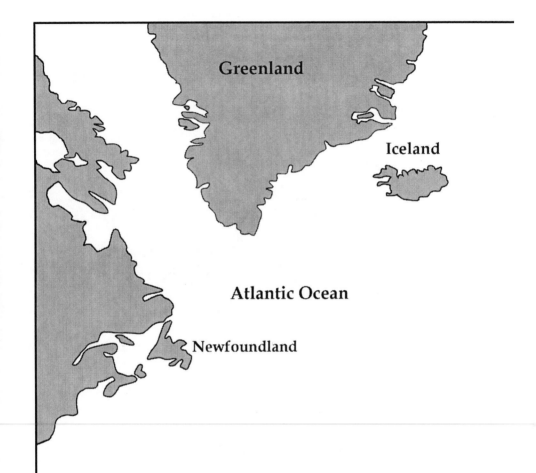

Greenland

Iceland

Atlantic Ocean

Newfoundland

The Viking World

Genealogy of the House of Rurik (simplified)

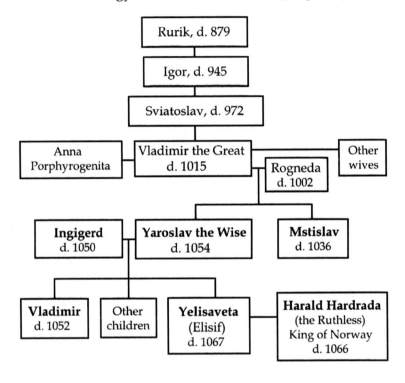

Royal Family of Norway (simplified)

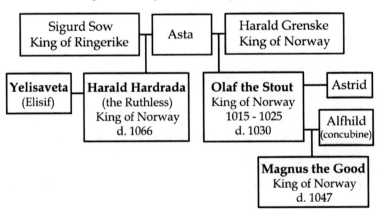

CAST OF CHARACTERS

- Churillo Igorevich: Putscha's dead father
- Dag Ringsson: a Norwegian noble, Harald's mentor
- Dmitri: priest, chaplain and tutor in Yaroslav's household
- Dyuk Osipovich: mayor of Novgorod
- Eilif: Jarl Ragnvald's son, commander of Yaroslav's druzhina
- Einar Tree-Foot: an old Jomsviking, Odd's companion
- Eustaxi: Mstislav's son
- Feodosy: abbot of the Caves Monastery
- Harald Sigurdsson (later called "Hardrada/ The Ruthless"): a prince of Norway, half-brother of Saint Olaf
- Ingigerd: Yaroslav's wife
- Kalv Arnesson: a Norwegian jarl
- Kuchug: Mstislav's bodyguard
- Leonidas: a Greek sea captain enslaved with Odd
- Lyudmila: Putscha's mother
- Magnus (later called "The Good"): a prince of Norway, the son of Saint Olaf and a concubine and foster son of Yaroslav
- Mstislav Vladimirovich: Prince of Chernigov, Yaroslav's brother
- Murad: a Turkish slave dealer
- Nenilushka: Putscha's daughter
- Olaf "The Stout": King of Norway, later canonized
- Putscha: Ingigerd's dwarf
- Ragnvald: jarl of Aldeigjuborg, cousin of Ingigerd
- Stavko Ulanovich: a Rus slave dealer
- Teit Isleifsson: deacon, later priest, of the cathedral at Skalholt in Iceland
- Thordis: nursemaid to Yaroslav's children
- Tyrakh: khan of the Pechenegs
- Ulf Ospaksson: a Varangian Guardsman
- Vladimir (Volodya) Yaroslavich: son of Yaroslav and Ingigerd
- Vorobey: a holy man in Yaroslav's household
- Vyshata Ostromirovich: a Rus boyar
- Yaroslav Vladimirovich "The Wise": Prince of Novgorod, later Grand Prince of Kievan Rus.
- Yefrem: bishop of Novgorod
- Yelisaveta Yaroslavna (Elisif in Norse): daughter of Yaroslav and Ingigerd
- Yngvar: a Swedish adventurer, Ingigerd's nephew

PROLOGUE

Here begins the second book in the saga of Odd Tangle-Hair.

A year ago, Bishop Isleif, my father, brought me to the old heathen's tumbledown farmhouse to record his reminiscences of young Prince Harald, who, as all the world knows, became king of Norway and has been dead now for over a decade. Odd, so he says, served the prince as his skald in Gardariki and in Golden Miklagard when they were both young men. But, of course, the fellow is boastful. How much of anything he says can be believed? What is certain is that he returned to Iceland after an absence of forty-some years—old, ragged, and emaciated. Since then he has spoken to no one, though his neighbors whisper that he has a fortune buried under his floor and that he worships demons, as his father once did.

The result of this visit was that I, who recoiled even from the heathen's shadow, was forced to spend seventeen days and nights alone with him, scribbling madly to record the details of his bloody and godless life. At last, fearing for my sanity, I fled the house while Odd lay sick and delirious with fever. But by then he had worked his devilry on me. I fell prey to dreams of battle and lust, and to deadly curiosity about forbidden things. I saw myself caught in the web of that man's life, with all its carnage, lewdness, and idolatry—at once repulsive and alluring.

Now, once again, I am ordered by my kindly, unsuspecting father (who is about to depart for Rome) to return and, if the old hermit is still alive, to hear more of his saga.

I am sorry to say that he seems to have recovered his health. This

morning he took my arm and drew me into his dusky hall. The man re-
sembles his house: weather-beaten, uncared for, squat, broad-shouldered,
ruinous in places but still solidly founded.

Without preamble, he has sat me down firmly on the bench and has
begun a great bustle of unrolling my bundle of second-quality parchment
on the table, mixing my ink, and trimming my quill for me—all done with
a practiced hand. While he is thus occupied, I recall to mind the events
which have brought us to this point in his saga.

In the year AD 1029, Odd was a youth of sixteen. His father, Black
Thorvald, a gloomy, soul-sick man, had filled the boy's head full of ancient
poetry, rune-lore, and tales of Odin, Thor, and the other demons of old.
As the result of a brawl at a stallion fight, Odd's family found themselves
at feud. Their enemies attacked and only Odd escaped from their flaming
house—the very one in whose ruins we sit now—and fled Iceland in a
stolen ship to seek his fortune as a viking. His chief companions were
young Kalf Slender-Leg (a good Christian boy who nevertheless was
devoted to Odd), and Stig No-One's Son, a rootless vagabond who taught
Odd the art of seamanship and became something of a father to him.

But this Odd Thorvaldsson is, by his own admission, a man of dark
moods and uncontroable rages, who cannot keep friends for long.

Arriving in Norway, they found themselves in the midst of civil war.
Blessed King Olaf was fighting to regain his throne and convert the
heathens, who were still thick in the land. Kalf chose the better side, Odd
the worse, and there was a painful break between them.

The following Spring, Odd and Stig and their shipmates sailed out
to go a-viking in the Varangian Sea. Along the way, they were joined by a
bloody old heathen, Einar Tree-Foot—a man who had lost a leg, an eye,
and a hand in the wars of his viking youth. He promised to guide Odd
and his crew to riches; instead, they were captured and enslaved by the
barbarous Finns. At last, Odd was able to rescue his men and escape with a
casket of stolen silver—oh, he is clever and brave—that must be admitted.
Well, he's an Icelander, isn't he? But again, as so often before, his wild
temper threw away what his shrewd head had won.

Their ship was dismasted by a storm and their hard-won silver washed
overboard. On Einar's advice they decided to make for Aldeigjuborg on
the shore of Lake Ladoga where they could lay over for the winter. As
they toiled at the oars, rowing slowly up the Neva, they were overtaken

by a large and splendid dragon ship, which bore down on them as if to sink them if they didn't steer out of its path. Standing in its prow was none other than Prince Harald, Saint Olaf's brother—the very man whose story I was sent here to collect from Odd's lips. A wise captain would have given way. Not Odd. Stubbornly, he held his course steady, despite Stig's countermanding order. At the last moment, the men obeyed Stig and a collision was averted. In a fury, Odd flung himself on his old mentor and Stig knocked him down. When his anger had cooled, Odd knew he had been in the wrong—for he isn't a stupid man, far from it, and somewhere in his shaggy chest there lurks a good heart, if he would only listen to it more often. But now there was a wall of hate between these two old friends, which neither seemed able to cross. It was a pitiful and divided crew that finally docked in Aldeigjuborg's harbor.

That day Odd encountered Harald and his men in the street and a fight was narrowly averted by the smooth-tongued courtier, Dag Hringsson. He invited Odd to dine with them that night in the hall of Jarl Ragnvald, governor of the town. There, Odd learned that Harald was on his way to Novgorod to enlist in the retinue of Prince Yaroslav the Wise and his consort Princess Ingigerd. The princess, however, dreaded his arrival and would do anything in her power to prevent it. Odd and Harald discovered a mutual love of poetry, and Harald ended by enrolling Odd in his band as his personal skald.

The next day, however, Odd was approached by the slave dealer, Stavko Ulanovich, who handed him a purse of gold—a bribe from Jarl Ragnvald, on behalf of his cousin Princess Ingigerd, to spy on Harald and, if possible, to assassinate him. Both sides, Odd tells us, thought that they owned his allegiance. In fact, neither did.

Odd has arranged my writing materials on the table, with candles all around to ease my eyes. He has tossed off two or three horns of ale. (I have brought a barrel of it with me.) He has begun to pace to and fro as the words pour out. I am his prisoner again, or, to speak more truly, his prisoner still, for the intervening six months have vanished. I know he will mock my Faith. I know he will stir and tempt me into seeing the world through his eyes. I know all this and yet I cannot resist him. Again he wraps me in the web of his life, making me go where he leads, while my quill scratches furiously on the page as though Satan himself were guiding my hand.

With these words, Odd Tangle-Hair takes up his saga...

1

A touching family scene

The fever that I had felt coming on struck me with full force around evening on the day that I parted from my crew. First I was burning hot and soaked with floods of perspiration. On the fourth day came an ague in which my limbs trembled and my teeth chattered with cold. Following this, the fever returned and continued to alternate with chills every fourth day. All in all, I was desperately sick with this quartan fever for nearly a month. My nineteenth birthday came and went while I tossed in delirium.

Unluckily for me, Jarl Ragnvald owned a Greek physician of whom he was very proud—one of those frauds whose entire art consists in draining a man of his blood just when he needs it most. The leeching alone would soon have killed me if I had not finally thrown off the fever by myself.

When at last my sight cleared, it was to behold the Jarl's face—cold-eyed and wry-mouthed.

He was vexed. I was not earning my twelve golden ounces lying sick abed in Aldeigjuborg. He informed me that Harald and Dag, despairing of my life, had gone on to Novgorod weeks ago. "Your man here, the cripple, will feed you and clean you up. He hasn't left your side these twenty days. I swear he has a stronger stomach than I."

I lay naked on a bed of rotting straw in a tiny, airless cell in the loft of his hall. A stench of sweat and urine invaded my nostrils; it was coming from me.

"He isn't my 'man'," I answered weakly, "he's a warrior of the olden time and a shipmate of mine."

"If you had a ship," Ragnvald sneered.

"You've had rough weather, Captain, but you're topside-up again now." Einar Tree-Foot's face swam within my view. "I told that leech if you was to die I'd have a bucket of his own blood from him; he left in a hurry," the Jomsviking chuckled. "Will you drink some broth and beer?"

"With thanks, Tree-Foot. Then I want a bath and my clothes—the new ones Dag gave me—and I'll feel fit enough to travel. I'm as eager to leave this place as the Jarl is to see me go."

"As to your clothes," said Ragnvald drily, "my physician advised burning them—contaminated by the miasmatic vapors, he feared."

"By the what?"

"Hard to explain to the ordinary man."

"Yes, well just send someone to market to buy me others."

"No time for that, I'm afraid. The boat I've hired for you has already delayed as long as it can, and there may not be another going up before next spring. We'll be icebound here before the month is out."

He called for a servant, who hurried in, flung a bundle of threadbare rags on the floor, and rushed out again holding his nose.

"You'll find these adequate."

How he was enjoying this! He could barely keep from smiling. He had purchased my honor, as he thought, and so could afford to humiliate me in this petty way, and, through me, Harald.

When I had eaten a little, dressed, and crept on shaking legs down the ladder to the hall, he took me aside and gave me my orders:

"You understand, it is not that infantile braggart, Harald, whom we have to fear nearly so much as Dag Hringsson, his advisor. The man was born a plotter. Likely he intends to murder Magnus and hire soldiers for a march on Norway—exactly as King Olaf himself once did. This or any other schemes that you become aware of, you must instantly report either to Stavko Ulanovich or to my son, Eilif, who has the honor to be Captain of the Prince's druzhina—his hird, as we would call it in Norse; you'll pick up the lingo soon enough.

"You will also use your powers of persuasion to turn Dag and Harald aside from any such acts. And if persuasion fails—well, a skald stands closest to his lord in battle, and in the hunt, and when he sleeps, or bathes, or dines. There are a hundred ways that death can come to a man—you wouldn't stick at that would you? Naturally, there will be more money from time to time, as long as we are satisfied with your performance. And, my friend, don't try to play a double game with us—not if you want to grow old in the enjoyment of your ill-gotten wealth."

I smiled evilly and nodded, for I imagined there was little chance of my leaving this place alive unless the jarl was perfectly sure of my obedience.

Soon afterwards, standing on Aldeigjuborg's wharf, I scanned the waterfront, searching for the Viper. But she was gone.

With a sore heart, I saw her in my mind's eye plowing the white-maned sea with Stig at her helm. Einar read my thoughts and was silent for a change. Then we jumped down into the waiting boat.

The vessel was what they call a strug in the Slavonic tongue—a dugout, carved from a single, gigantic tree trunk. This one measured some forty-five feet long and eight abeam, with room for forty rowers and much cargo. Her crew were all Slavs and only their skipper could speak a few words of bad Norse.

They were going up to Novgorod, he told me, to deliver, in addition to myself, some books and a packet of letters to Yaroslav and his consort.

For the next seven days the oarsmen toiled against the swift current of the muddy Volkhov, which links Aldeigjuborg with Novgorod, a hundred miles to the south. Lulled by the monotony of the scenery and the drone of the rowers' song, I passed most of my time asleep; though whenever I awakened, Einar was always beside me, ready with a portion of cold porridge and warm beer.

By the time we came in sight of Novgorod, I was nearly my old self again and itching to use my legs.

We reached the city around dusk on a gusty, late autumn day. The wind blew an icy chill off the river, but, wrapped in a fur, I stood up in the prow, eager for my first sight of the place. On my right hand, the lofty onion-domed spires of a church; on my left, five long jetties running out from the shore with ships of every size and description tied up to them. And dead ahead of us, a wooden bridge, decorated, like all things in this wooden city, with fantastic carving and bright splashes of paint.

Gliding beneath the bridge, we docked beside the last of the five piers, from which a path led up to the gateway of a high stockade, built almost on the water's edge. The skipper, gesturing, shouted: "Dvor Yaroslavl;" and seeing that I didn't comprehend, added "Knyaz!" and louder still, "knyaz, is 'prince', yes?"

Shouldering the bundle of books and letters, he scrambled onto the dock, and followed by Einar and me, marched through the gate and up a log-paved road to the house.

The Rus use the word 'dvor' for any dwelling, great or small, set within its own fenced yard. This particular yard was very big, a miniature farm really, where cattle, horses, and goats cropped the last yellowing stalks of summer grass. The house itself, set well back from the palisade, sprawled over a wide area. It was two stories high and built all of logs, except at one end where it adjoined a tall stone tower. Like most Rus houses, the ground floor was reserved for the animals and slaves. Around its second story ran a porch with ornate posts and railings, which was approached by a steep stairway.

To be truthful, these were the very first stairs I had ever encountered. Not wanting to appear a fool, I approached them with a show of confidence, determined not to look at my feet—and stumbled on the topmost step with some injury to my shin, my palms, and my pride.

Not a good omen, I thought ruefully, and covered my embarrassment with cursing.

At the top of the stairs we entered a vestibule where closed doors faced us on every side. As we stood uncertain which way to go, there reached our ears the shrill cry of young voices. Next instant, one of the side doors banged open and through it tumbled a rowdy gang of half a dozen children of both sexes and of every size from a very small boy to a willowy girl of about thirteen, who was taller by a head than all the rest. With her pointed nose and chin, and a single thick plait of yellow hair hanging to her waist, she reminded me with a sudden pang of my murdered sister, Gudrun Night-Sun—except that Gudrun was only an Iceland farm girl, while this one was nobly born, and she knew it.

"Nenilushka," said the girl, "we shall be the warriors of Rus, but you must be a Pecheneg horseman from the steppe because they are squat and ugly just like you."

The one addressed laughed idiotically, showing a jumble of teeth. I had thought her at first to be a child like the others, but at second glance saw that she was a dwarf; easily in her twenties, to judge by her face, yet whooping and galloping about on her stumpy legs as though there were no difference at all between herself and the children.

"And you can have Magnus on your side too—he's also a squat ugly thing."

The others giggled.

I was curious about this Magnus Olafsson, of whom I had heard so much. I saw a pale, lank-haired boy of about eight, with arms and legs as thin as straws, who stood apart from the others, smiling hopefully. I would never in five lifetimes have guessed him to be the offspring of that blood-soaked, broad-chested, square-headed king. I recalled what Jarl Ragnvald had told me: King Olaf had visited Novgorod more than a year ago to beg money and arms for his ill-fated bid to regain the throne of Norway. He had brought with him little Magnus, his son by a concubine, and then left the child behind to be fostered by the prince and princess. Ingigerd loved the boy fiercely, excessively—as she had (perhaps?) loved his father—and she was determined to place him on the throne of Norway. Thus he stood in the path of Harald's ambition—and knowing Harald, I didn't give much for the boy's chances.

The girl went on assigning to all the children their parts, calling each by name: Volodya, a very handsome boy of ten or eleven, who even in play looked serious; and Anna, a waif of eight or nine, and the two littlest boys, both sturdy, grinning imps. They all, even Volodya, obeyed her without hesitation.

Just then, bustling through the open door, came a little, quick old woman, clutching to her bosom a very dirty baby. The baby howled and struggled to get free until she crammed a piece of honeycomb in its mouth. Still holding it, she made a lunge at one of the smaller children, then at another, and another, while they laughed and danced out of her way, singing, "Thordis, here, catch me—old Thordis, over here—!"

The laughter stopped abruptly when a pair of double doors at the farther end of the vestibule swung open. Through them strode a woman, tall and richly dressed in a wide-sleeved gown of red brocade trimmed with marten. Behind her I glimpsed part of a room and a number of men in it, all be-furred and be-jeweled, and all standing.

Old Thordis began at once to wheeze apologies: "Forgive me, Princess, they're too much for me; they'll kill me soon, see if they don't."

"Dear thing," the other replied, "we've a houseful of strong young

9

servant girls for that—it's just your own stubbornness that keeps you at it. Here, put Vesevolod down and catch your breath."

The infant so named had by this time covered itself entirely with honey and, as it crawled about on the rush-strewn floor, picked up so much of the straw that it soon resembled a scarecrow more than a human child.

"That's better," said the princess. "And now, you—" She turned on the children and all warmth deserted her voice. "Why aren't you at your lessons?"

The others, with sheepish looks, drew closer to the girl. Except for Magnus: he crept to Ingigerd's side (for it was certainly she) and put a shy hand in hers.

"Do you know that you have interrupted a meeting of my council with your racket? So much that I and my boyars cannot hear ourselves think! You will apologize now to Nurse, and to these men"—she beckoned the grandees out of the room behind her—"and to me. Then you—Yelisaveta, Volodya, and Anna—will return to Father Dmitri and ask him to give you extra lessons tonight for a penance. And you, Nenilushka,"—addressing the dwarf girl—"go at once to your father and tell him to give you three hard blows across the back with a rod—and I will ask him later if he did."

While Yelisaveta pouted, Volodya, serious and handsome, took a step forward, bowed to the boyars, to his mother, and to Thordis, the nurse, and said in a voice that had neither pleading nor defiance in it that they should consider him alone to be the cause of the mischief and on no account blame his brothers and sisters, nor especially, the dwarf, who only did what she was told. He gave this speech first in Norse and then in Slavonic.

"Princely spoke," murmured Einar beside me.

"Aye, Tree-Foot, he'll make a king, one day."

The boyars beamed and could hardly leave off kissing the lad; and old Thordis kissed him, too, though he tried to fend her off.

But Yelisaveta's eyes flashed with anger. "First of all, Mother, they aren't your boyars, their father's. And second, I'll do no extra penance— living here at all is penance enough for me!"

"Little bitch!" cried Ingigerd. "You think so? I could send you somewhere to live that would be far less pleasant than this! Don't tempt me."

"You don't frighten me with that, Mother. I'm already condemned to be married—that's all decided, isn't it?—and so I can't be stuck away in a convent, though I shouldn't mind it at all if it meant never seeing you again!"

Without warning, Ingigerd struck her daughter a cracking blow across the face, then another and another, and the girl hit back wildly with her fists until young Vladimir forced himself between them. Yelisaveta was crying hysterically by now; he took her by the arm and pulled her away. The little 'uns and the dwarf, all sniffling, followed them out, Magnus last of all.

The old nurse sighed and shook her grey head as if to convey that this strife between mother and daughter was nothing rare.

The princess, white-lipped with anger, noticed us at last, and before I could speak, snapped, "Why d'you stand there like gaping fools! Does it take three men to carry a parcel? Put it down and get out. Here, boatman, for your trouble."

At a sign from her, one of the boyars took a coin from his purse and tossed it at us. With that, Ingigerd turned back to the council chamber, the boyars following at her heels, and the last in line pulling the doors shut after him.

The skipper, his flat Slavic face breaking into a wide grin, exclaimed, "Wooman," followed by the word, "knyaz!" and then a booming laugh. Pocketing the coin and still laughing and shaking his head, he sauntered out the door, leaving Einar and me alone in the empty vestibule.

"Saucy bit o' stuff ain't she?" remarked Einar with a twinkle in his one eye.

"What, the daughter or the mother?"

"Not them—the nurse! Did you not see her eye on me all the time? And her old enough to be a granny! Women love Einar Tree-Foot, I don't know what it is."

"I'm sure I don't either. Let's find Harald."

✝

After much wandering through empty rooms and corridors and inquiring of the few souls we met, only one of whom could speak intelligible Norse, we managed at last to understand that the Giant was nowhere about; that, in fact, the dvor was empty save for women and children and the servants. Prince Yaroslav and his Swedish druzhina, five-hundred strong, plus Harald with his hundred and twenty Norwegians had marched west three weeks ago to collect tribute from the Chudian tribes. They weren't expected back before the first hard frost, in about a month.

It became obvious at the same time that no one had the least idea who we were. However, we made ourselves at home, scavenging for food in the kitchen and stowing our few belongings in an empty room.

Presently we heard the boyars bid a noisy farewell to their princess and gallop off to their own dvors. We saw no more that night of the High and Mighty Ingigerd or her affectionate daughter.

2

MY LORD NOVGOROD THE GREAT

Early the next morning we paid a visit to the market. Novgorod was a center for merchants of many lands and its marketplace rang with the cries of Greeks, Arabs, Persians, Jews, Saxons, Swedes, Danes, and Finns in addition to its native Rus and Slavs.

Here a couple of chained bears were prodded into dancing; and there a grinning, slobbering idiot rolled himself on the ground, twisting his arms and legs into knots while the crowd threw coins; elsewhere, a mountebank juggled torches while another swallowed fire. And through the midst of it wound a noisy procession of minstrels—a dwarf blowing on a trumpet, a youth beating a drum, and others rattling tambourines, all blending their music with the cries of the vendors at their stalls.

After taking in these marvels and along the way purchasing some decent clothes for the two of us, I decided to look up Stavko. I intended, sooner or later, to tell him the truth: that he and Ragnvald should cease to consider me their spy. But in the meantime there was much that I was curious about, and he struck me as a man who knew many useful things.

Inquiring for him, we were told that the establishment of Stavko Ulanovich, Slave-dealer to the Gentry, could be found on Ilya Street as you mounted Slavno Hill, directly behind the marketplace. While we made our way there, I explained to Einar how the slave-dealer had invited me to his tent in Aldeigjuborg the day before I fell ill, given me Ragnvald's gold to spy on Harald, and told me to meet him again in Novgorod.

His shop-house was the typical two-storied building of logs with a shingled roof. Einar and I mounted the steps to the second floor, where the beautiful Egyptian girl, Jumayah—the same one who had summoned me to his tent in Aldeigjuborg—answered our knock.

Inside, the steamy lamp-lit interior heavy with perfume, the low table, thick rugs, and heaps of silken cushions, and the naked women lying upon them, reproduced exactly the scene of our first meeting, as I had just finished describing it to Einar.

We found Stavko, on his knees in a corner of the room, grunting in the act of love with one of his properties—this being, as he had told me, his invariable morning regimen. We waited politely for him to finish.

He gave the girl's behind an affectionate pat, pulled up his voluminous trousers, buttoned his caftan and advanced on us with a smile on his round, pug-nosed face. His bulging eyes gleamed, his greasy braids, weighted with lead balls, swung as he moved. He planted wet, thick-lipped kisses on my cheeks.

"Odd Tangle-Hair! My friend! I am delighted to see you well again—though, look at you—how thin!" He pinched my cheeks and arms with those fingers so educated in the feel of flesh.

I introduced Einar, who had begun to make noises in his chest like a sea-lion at mating time as his one eye scanned Stavko' smerchandise.

"Yarilo, god of war, has dealt harshly with you, eh, old fellow?" said Stavko to him, noticing the Jomsviking's loss of leg, hand, and eye.

To this, Einar replied by lifting the skirt of his tunic, beneath which unmistakable life stirred, while he remarked that he wasn't so badly off for parts as many men his age.

The slaver, taking this as an invitation to show us his "dears," clapped his hands, and the women approached and stood before us, their eyes empty and their arms at their sides. There wasn't even one that I remembered seeing just a month ago. Business, it seemed, was thriving, and the tender Stavko must be suffering a broken heart a day as he took reluctant leave of each cherished pet.

"Look your fill, sirs," cried he, chuckling and salivating with his words as he habitually did. "You, at least, have gold to spend, friend skald, heh?"—with a wink and a nudge at me.

"Not much, I fear, and my friend has none." (I had given nearly all the gold to my crew to refit the Viper.)

"Ah? So? In that case it would be my pleasure to extend you credit."

There was no one I wanted less to be indebted to. And, to tell the truth, my recent illness had left me still somewhat enfeebled where my spear was concerned. Just as well, I thought, in dealing with this slippery fish, not to be too distracted by his wares.

"Kind of you to offer, Stavko Ulanovich," I replied. "As soon as I have silver from my lord Harald I promise to spend it here."

Einar shot me an anguished look at the prospect of so long a wait, but Stavko passed it off with a shrug, and purred: "Well, how else can I help you then? Have you seen anything yet of our city?"

"Exactly my purpose in calling on you."

"Excellent! Then I am at your service. Pyotr, see my ladies behave, and if we have customer, sell him Zabava if you can—I'll go as low as a quarter grivna for her." These words were addressed to a sullen young man whom Stavko introduced as his nephew.

As we went out the door, the slaver said to me in a low voice: "I had hoped to see you alone, my friend, as we have certain private matters to discuss, yes?"

"I have no secrets from Einar Tree-Foot."

"No, no, it can wait. Now,"—he stood on the top step and threw his arms wide—"permit me to introduce you to Gospodin Velikiy Novgorod, as we Rus call him: 'My Lord Novgorod the Great'! Oldest, freest, handsomest of all cities in Gardariki! Ten thousand live here and every single one quick with fists. We are excitable people! Here, walk with me to top of hill; from there you can see everything."

We mounted the crowded street, passing beneath the eaves of narrow shop-houses that overhung it on either side. Here, in the artisan's quarter, every trade imaginable was practiced, from locksmiths to leather tanners, and from shipwrights to smelters: each craft claiming a certain length of street front for itself, and marking it, like a dog his tree, with its own peculiar smell. I noticed at once an unusual aspect of the town: there were no wheeled carts or wagons to be seen at all, but only sledges, whose runners glided easily over the polished planks of the pavement.

From the top of the hill the city lay spread out below us, divided in halves by the Volkhov with its single bridge. On the farther bank rose the citadel, dominated by the wooden spires of Saint Sophia. To the left of it, said Stavko, was the poorest part of town; it was called Lyudin End.

"Lyudi," he explained, "means Black People—black with dirt of honest toil, and, though they are most despised of men, we know that Christ loves them best. Now, look to right and see Nerev End, where boyars—nobles—have town houses."

"But why," I asked, "does Yaroslav keep his dvor here on the low ground by the marketplace instead of on the citadel or among the mansions of his boyars?"

"Answer to this question not so simple." He frowned in thought. "Come, we stroll down through town while we talk."

We descended the hill by a different way, which brought us to an open area on the farther side of Yaroslav's dvor. This also was a market square; it was called Gotland Court and was the center of Swedish commerce in the city. Here the Swedes had their guild hall and warehouse. Here, too, within shouting distance of the palace, were the five long barracks that housed Yaroslav's druzhina.

To spare you more of Stavko's wretched Norse, I will cast his story in my own words, as follows:

Some years ago, Yaroslav had rebelled against his father, Grand Prince Vladimir of Kiev, and had recruited Swedish mercenaries for his army. Unfortunately, he found them hard to control. Citizens were beaten and robbed, wives and daughters raped. Matters led finally to an uprising led by the boyars. In a day of bloody fighting, most of the Swedes were massacred.

Unfortunately for Yaroslav, it was just then that a message reached him from one of his sisters in Kiev, informing him that their father had died and that one of his half-brothers had seized power in the city and was bent on butchering all of his rivals. To defend himself from this new threat, Yaroslav had no choice but to plead with the boyars and people to uphold his side in this new civil war. Amazingly, they did. Of course, in return, the boyars exacted a high price—nothing less than a blanket exemption from the laws of the city. The prince had no choice but to pay it.

After this, Yaroslav built himself a new dvor and chose its site precisely in order to be near the Swedish community, or what remained of it after the massacre. He was still determined to rely no more than he could help on those arrogant and unruly nobles. He turned again to Sweden and now sued for the hand of Ingigerd, the daughter of the king. In her retinue came her cousin Ragnvald and hundreds of fighting men. With their help, Yaroslav defeated his half-brother.

In the years since, the prince had come to rely more and more on his Swedish mercenaries (although whether they were his, as opposed to hers, that is, Ingigerd's, was a tricky question). The boyars, for their part, had kept the peace, but were still resentful. Like nobles everywhere, they lived for glory and booty, but the prince made little use of them, preferring to rely on his Swedes instead. Even more than this, the boyars resented being dictated to by Ingigerd.

At this point in our conversation, we crossed the bridge and mounted the slope of the citadel. There we found ourselves gazing up at the cathedral.

"Ah," sighed Stavko, crossing himself. "Is beautiful, yes? Built all of oak without a single nail and no tool but axe."

We were not alone as we stood before the great carved doors. Lying on the ground all around us was a pitiful collection of paralytics, drunkards, lepers, and lunatics, all clad in filthy rags.

"Christ cares for those whom the world casts off," the slave-dealer piously murmured. "Here they find refuge; is a good thing, yes?"

"A very good thing," I agreed.

But Einar, who had been uncommonly quiet all this while, snorted with disgust: "Are there no honest thieves among this vermin? Did you see Einar Tree-Foot lying about on the doorstep of Svantevit's temple begging alms? You did not! Einar Tree-Foot stole what he wanted like a man! Piss on the lot of 'em, say I!" (He seemed to have forgotten that if I and my crew hadn't wandered down a certain dark alley in Jumne Town, he would have been torn to pieces by a mob of angry Wends, who caught him with his hand in Svantevit's offering bowl.)

These unfortunates had now begun to creep, crawl, and stagger towards us, uttering piteous cries and reaching out their bony hands for alms. Stavko, with an expression of alarm, hurried us away. At that moment, we heard the loud pealing of a bell coming from the market side across the river. Up and down the street people stopped and turned toward the sound, while in the houses shutters were thrown open and heads thrust out. From all sides people poured into the street and soon a river of them was streaming toward the bridge.

"Assembly bell," said Stavko, betraying some annoyance. "No doubt a prank. Bell rope is there for any drunken fool to pull who wants to make spectacle of himself. Ignore it, friends, let us continue walk."

I gave Einar a questioning look. What weren't we supposed to see?

From up ahead of us, with a jingle of harness and the clatter of hoofs on the paving logs, there came in sight a troop of horsemen, forcing their way through the mob and making likewise for the bridge. At their head rode a handsome man whose black beard rippled over his scarlet-clad breast. Stavko, like everyone else, snatched off his hat and bowed low as the figure passed. If I hadn't known otherwise, I would have taken him for the prince himself.

"Thinks himself nearly as great," said Stavko under his breath. "Dyuk Osipovich, Mayor of Novgorod. He leads boyar faction; is no friend of ours."

"In that case, friend Stavko, we must certainly follow him."

The crowd bore us along while Einar, hanging on my shoulder, struck out viciously with his crutch at every hapless Novgorodets who jostled us. Once across the bridge we found ourselves back near the spot from which Einar and I had set out that morning: in the market next to the palace, or, more precisely, in a long cleared area between the two, big enough to hold many hundreds of people.

"The assembly meets on Yaroslav's doorstep?"

"Prince and his loyal subjects prefer it so," Stavko answered coolly. "Troublemakers may say what they please, but they know who listens."

"Is there so much rebellious talk, then?"

"We are turbulent people," he shrugged. "If prince is bad, into mud with him!' is common saying of ours."

"Is that likely to happen now?"

"Oh no, is all just talk and grumbling. With Yaroslav and druzhina away, boyars think to frighten Princess Ingigerd. How little they know her spirit! She will stamp foot—they will run away like mouses!"

I had for some time been puzzled by this attitude of his. "Stavko Ulanovich, you yourself are not Swedish—"

"Me? I am Rus! As pure-blooded as any."

"Then how is it you're so warm for Ingigerd and her countrymen?"

"Business," he shrugged. "Swedish merchants encourage trade and we all profit." True enough, and yet I couldn't escape the feeling that there was something else, some more personal reason that he was not telling me—perhaps because he didn't know it himself. Was it possible that this man who dealt in women's flesh—bought and sold, owned and used it as he pleased—was it possible that he longed to believe in a woman stronger than all those others, stronger, in fact, than himself? A woman who could own and command him? Was the slave-master offering the princess his humble adoration?

We listened for a time, while Dyuk the Mayor and other boyars took turns haranguing the crowd—mostly in Slavonic, in which I could only detect occasionally the name of Ingigerd. But at every mention, it was greeted with groans and catcalls from all over the audience. This, said Stavko, was merely their hired claque. Looking about me, I wasn't so sure.

Leaning close to my ear, he interpreted: "They are proposing law to limit number of Swedes and other Northmen in city, levy head tax on them, forbid them to own land."

"What will happen if it passes?"

"Impossible! Prince, too, has friends among boyars, and princess knows very well how to use them."

Suddenly and without warning fists began to fly all around us and we found ourselves pushed and pummeled on every side at once. "Dear me," said Stavko, "it seems we're voting already." We were alternately yanked apart and dashed together again in the heaving crowd. "—forgot to explain—vote with fists—turbulent people—bridge!"

It was that very place towards which the crowd carried us. First Stavko and then Einar disappeared in separate swirling battles. Now I was on the bridge, and giving as good as I got.

Great One-Eyed Odin! It felt fine after so many weeks of sickness, idleness, fretting, and regretting—just to hit a face! Life pounded in my veins. It was great fun until some troll lifted me off my feet with one hand around my neck and the other on my belt, held me for a moment over his head, and lightly tossed me.

I bobbed in the freezing river, gasping for breath, while scores of other bodies plummeted all around, sending up geysers of water.

Then with a wave and a cry of thanks to all My Lord Novgorod's peculiar citizens, I struck out for the shore.

3

AN INTERVIEW
WITH THE PRINCESS

Einar and I stumbled into each other on the bank, both of us bruised and wet but otherwise sound. Stavko got a blow on the forehead, which kept him in bed for three days, nursed by the lovely Jumayah. The fist fight—vote, that is—on the 'Swedish question' was inconclusive, he told us when we went to call on him. He was quite sure nothing more would happen now before Yaroslav's return.

As the following days succeeded each other, time began to weigh on me with nothing to do but roam about the palace. I soon knew every corner of it.

The lowest story of the building served as store room, stable, and slaves' quarters. The second story, reached by the outer stairs, consisted of a wide vestibule (as I have already said), which gave onto a banqueting hall large enough to feast a hundred men at one time. In the middle of one wall sat a pair of carved and gilded thrones for Yaroslav and his princess.

As in all Rus houses, there was no open hearth for cooking or warmth, but instead, a huge clay oven decorated with tiles, which occupied one whole corner of the room. As the nights grew colder, we spread our bedding out beside it and even on top of it. Beyond the great hall on one side was a big kitchen, while on the other there extended a maze of little rooms linked together by corridors. Some contained beds in which four or five could sleep side by side, but others were bare. On every wall of the great hall and of the smaller rooms, too, I found painted scenes of hunting and war, or sometimes row upon row of bright red cockerels and other birds, or again, twining vines and flowers.

As I think I have mentioned, the only part of the palace which was built of stone was a tower three stories high that was entered by a door leading off the hall. Here, I was told by a servant, the princess and her children had their private quarters and I was warned to stay out.

To conclude my description of the palace, I must say that it was not very clean—and I speak as a plain Icelander, not some fastidious Greek. Bones and the debris of old meals lay in corners where they had been thrown and forgotten; broken crockery was everywhere (for the Rus, when they are drunk, love to break things), and the floors here and there were puddled with beer or piss.

On my wanderings I caught occasional glimpses of Ingigerd coming or going, always to the sound of rustling brocade and the tramp of many feet: deep in discussion with a circle of men, and followed by a train of servants, pages, and by a sleek greyhound bitch who was never out of her sight.

The children, too, I saw sometimes, scurrying here and there, accompanied by dwarf, nurse, or tutor (though never by their mother). The older ones were much taken up with their lessons. This servitude was invented by the great Vladimir, their grandfather, who valued learning highly—not alone for the royal children but for those of the boyars as well, and for girls as much as boys. Yaroslav, his son, took after him in this respect (if in no other) and was reputed to be the greatest scholar in the land—a prodigy who could read books in five languages. Needless to say, his own children were kept hard at it. Even little Anna, who could not have been more than eight, I watched laboring for a whole morning with her stylus over a strip of birch bark, engraving their peculiar letters on its soft pulp.

When not occupied with schooling, however, they went where they pleased, ignored by the grownups, wheedling food from Cook in the kitchen, or playing the sort of noisy games I had first seen them at. Even the baby, whose name was Vsevolod, crawled everywhere on his fat knees, brushing with disaster in a hundred different forms, noticed at the last moment by Nurse, snatched away, spanked, scrubbed, or fed with honey, set down again, and again forgotten.

And sometimes I would see Magnus sitting alone on a corner seat in the vestibule, gazing out of a little window that overlooked the river.

I spoke to him once when Einar was with me. He was greatly impressed with the old Jomsviking's wounds and his bloodcurdling stories, and would not let us go. Anyone could see that the boy was lonely. Orphaned, cut off from his home, resented by Ingigerd's children because of the very intensity of her love for him, the reasons for which he could not fathom. And now, on top of all, threatened by Harald, who was enough to scare anyone, let alone this little mite.

It was not hard to feel sorry for him, even though he was a petulant, moody, and unappealing child. We had been talking together a long time before he asked innocently who we were. With some hesitation I confessed that we belonged to Harald's retine. Instantly he turned his face away and would not say another word.

✝

The following day I received a summons to wait upon Princess Ingigerd.

It was delivered by a dwarf—a man past middle age whose ungainly little body supported a large and noble head, perfectly formed and covered with crisp, silver curls. I had seen him already among the princess's attendants. He walked with a swagger, as much as his misshapen legs would allow, and stuck out his barrel chest like a bantam cock. He was richly dressed in fur-trimmed cloak, yellow-dyed boots, and a ruby earring in one ear. An enormous bunch of keys on a big ring jangled at his waist as he bustled along, and he was never seen without his weapon—a wooden short sword, quite cunningly carved and painted, which he wore stuck in his belt. His Norse was even worse than Stavko's. "Gospodin," he said, using the Slavonic title by which anyone of the warrior class or above must be addressed, "come tower."

His message delivered, he stalked away, not deigning to look back to see if I followed.

We mounted the spiral staircase to its second story and entered an antechamber where several young women sat gossiping and laughing while they worked at their needles. The grand little man scowled at them and they fell silent at once and began to stitch with great concentration. Halting before an oaken door on the farther side of the chamber, he knocked with a wrought iron knocker which had been placed at a height convenient for him.

A woman's voice bade us come in.

We found ourselves in a large room whose furnishings consisted of a tall chest against one wall, a couple of chairs and a table, a broad bed, and the indispensable oven. On the wall above the bed, a row of gilded icons reflected the light of candles. Otherwise, the room was lit only by a splash of afternoon sun that filtered through the mica panes of a high window. Beneath the window sat Ingigerd. She was speaking in rapid Slavonic to a secretary who scratched away furiously on his strip of birch bark. She looked up as we entered, and the dwarf spoke a few words to her.

"Thank you, Putscha," she answered him in Norse. This was a courtesy she rarely omitted, to speak only Norse in the presence of Northmen. "I may need you later."

He bowed himself back into the angle formed by the wall and the clothes chest and shrank into its shadow. He had a little stool there that he sat upon, so that his head did not show above the chest, but the effect was exactly as if he wore one of those magical caps that old stories tell of and had vanished into thin air. When I thought of it later, it struck me how remarkably easy it was to forget he was there at all.

"Sirko, stay!" This was to the greyhound bitch that had bounded forward to growl at my feet. Obediently it retreated to her side and sat on its haunches, panting, its muscles trembling under its glossy hide. Another word of command sent the scribe away; he closed the door softly behind him.

"Odd Thorvaldsson," she addressed me, "you must think us very rude, but there are always outlanders coming and going here and no one knew who you were until Magnus mentioned it to me. Accept our apologies." She motioned me nearer. "Come sit beside me, I want to talk with you."

If she recognized in me the shabby spectator of her recent battle with her daughter, she gave no sign of it; and I didn't remind her.

I have not yet described Ingigerd. Her forehead was broad and high, her grey eyes large and slightly protruding—which added to the impression they gave of seeing very deeply into things. Her lips were full, her teeth clean, and her breath sweet. It was a face both less and more than beautiful: no feature of it perfect, yet in a room full of pretty women it was she you would notice first and remember longest. Though she was somewhere between thirty and forty, and the mother of five children, she was still slim, as high-strung women often are. Her worst feature, some might say, was her hands, which were big for a woman, with long strong fingers. Like any married lady, she covered her head with a kerchief to hide her hair from all but her husband. Her head cloth was white linen, held in place by a circlet of gold.

"Princess," I began at once—I had been rehearsing this speech—"before any words pass between us, there is something that must be put right."

"Oh?"

"You think you are speaking to a hired spy in your service, for I suppose your cousin lost no time in sending word to you about our 'arrangement'."

She colored just the slightest bit and looked at me intently.

"I won't deceive you; I am no such thing."

Reaching into my purse, I took out two gold ounces—all that remained of the sum Stavko had given me—and held them out to her.

"You will find ten coins missing: nine of them went to my old crew to refit our ship. With a half of one I bought a slave girl from Stavko and let her go"—she cocked an eyebrow slightly at this—"and with the other half, less a little silver, I bought the clothes you see me in. I do not feel obliged to you for what I spent, and I herewith return the rest."

Since the time I'd first set eyes on her, I had, without precisely knowing why, made up my mind to do this.

"How very convenient, to spend a great deal of someone else's money and yet feel no obligation." The voice was lightly mocking, not angry. "No, don't protest. I agree with you. The money was given in a bad cause and used—I don't doubt—in good ones. You owe me nothing."

"Thank you, Princess. I hoped you would say so."

"Ragnvald is a loyal friend, but a man of no subtlety. Have no fears on that score, I shall ask nothing dishonorable of you. Putscha?"

The dwarf emerged from his dark corner, took the coins from my hand and vanished again. As I happened to gaze after him, I was startled to see a man's face looking back at me from the wall.

Ingigerd, following my glance, began to smile. "It's a mirror. You mean to say you've never seen your reflection before?"

"Only in the eyes of others, Princess."

"Well, and what do you think of it?"

She unhooked the polished bronze disk from its nail and put it in my hands. A troll with a gaunt face, deep-set black eyes, a mane of black hair and ragged beard glowered back.

"As I feared, not very handsome."

"No," she looked mock-serious, shaking her head, "not very. I think I can guess your nick-name, let me try. Black-Beard. No? Dark-Brow, then. No again? Curly-Hair."

"Close enough, Lady. Odd Tangle-Hair, at your service."

"You can smile! I was beginning to fear you never would. Well, Odd Tangle-Hair, tell me how you've been spending your time with us so far."

"Seeing the town with Stavko."

"With whom?"

"Stavko Ulanovich, the slave-dealer. A very warm supporter of yours—"

"Oh, yes, of course. Him. A useful little man if you can bear his manners."

(What cold repayment for his devotion, I thought.)

"We attended the assembly and found it most entertaining." I ventured this with a smile, at the same time touching a bruise on my cheek that was still livid after a week.

But the princess was neither sympathetic nor amused. "Yes, I know all about that. Because the town militia fight like old women and the boyars would rather doze beside their ovens than take the field, we are forced to rely on mercenaries—thank God we have the wherewithal to pay for them. I only wish we could afford more!"

I shrugged with feigned bewilderment. "I couldn't follow the argument very well—your name was mentioned ..."

"I should feel neglected if it weren't. The woman, the outlander, the Catholic. So easy to make me the butt of all their little grievances. Only let some poor Swedish soldier take an apple from the market without paying for it, and it's my fault. They prefer to forget that my husband began enlisting warriors from my country before he ever married me, just as his father, the great Vladimir of whom no ill can be spoken, did before him. But don't worry, I know how to deal with these malcontents, and they know it!"

I'd only meant to test her a little, not provoke her to rage. "I believe it, Lady," I said quickly. "That you are no ordinary woman, I've seen and heard already."

"Have you?" She relaxed a little, leaning back in her chair. She was silent for a few moments, as if weighing what she would say. "As a girl at my father's court I had absolute freedom to speak and act as I pleased. And I made it plain to my husband-to-be that I would accept no less here. Are you a man, Odd Tangle-Hair, who believes a woman's only business is with her distaff and loom? For if you are, we shall never be friends."

"I'd not looked for that favor in any case, Princess."

She waved this aside and said, "Let us be frank and honest with each other, it saves so much time. For instance, what exactly do you know of me?"

This was sailing near the wind. Choosing my words carefully, I replied that her intelligence and piety were ever on her cousin's lips, and that I understood her to have been a friend to Olaf of Norway, whose death I happened to have witnessed—

She put her hand on my arm with a suddenness that startled me. "You knew him?"

"Purely by accident. Harald has probably told you already—"

"Harald has said little about anyone but himself. You tell me."

And she made me narrate the battle and Olaf's death from start to finish in every grim detail: the leg chopped off, the neck nearly severed, the fight over his corpse in which it was dragged this way and that until it nearly came apart. By the time I was done, her cheeks were wet.

"Your feelings are strong, Princess," I said. "And since we're being frank, I will say that I find it curious—to be so warm for a man you'd never seen in the flesh before a year ago?"

"But you saw him! You felt his courage, his strength, his passion for the Faith. The whole northern world rang of it. So, when he came to us at last, seeking refuge from the Danes who had driven him from his throne, I knew what to expect—and I was not mistaken!" She passed her hand over her eyes. "He had already sought my hand in marriage—did you know that? Years ago he had sent his skalds to my father's court, and they praised him in such language that I would have married him gladly; but my father, who was his enemy, forbade it. He favored a more advantageous match, here in Gardariki. Well. All for the best. It was God's hand at work. As Princess of Novgorod, I could see that Olaf got the money and soldiers he needed to regain his throne. But then so soon to see him go! And then to learn of his death! But he left with my husband and me a part of himself—Magnus, his son, to foster like our own. An obligation we will honor— with our blood if need be."

She swallowed hard and looked away.

What an extraordinary speech. These were the words of a woman in love. And though she was careful to say 'we', I suspected that Yaroslav had little to do with it.

In a moment she was herself again. "Tell me now about this Harald whom you serve, for I have hardly been able to form an impression of him; no sooner does he arrive than he goes off on campaign. What is he like? Is he a man or only an elongated boy?"

"He is fast becoming a man, Princess, and a hard one to deal with."

"And why do you attach yourself to him?"

"It serves my own purpose and costs me little."

"Little so far."

"What do you mean?"

"You expect to rise with him; very well, but you must be prepared to fall with him, too, unless you're the kind of man to whom treachery comes easily. Are you?"

"My empty purse should answer that."

"Yes, of course," she laughed. "Putscha?"

Again the dwarf materialized at her elbow.

"Odd Haraldsskald, I will put you to a test. You will need money for women, and drink, and so forth before your lord returns. Will you do me the favor to take back one of these gold ounces—just one, mind you—as a gift of simple friendship and nothing more? For we are agreed you would not take it otherwise."

"I will take it with gratitude, Princess, and repay it when I can."

"Repay? Ah me, what does he say? Does he mistrust me still?" She put on a sad expression though her eyes belied it. "Take it under what terms you like, then, and I vow that Harald is a luckier man than he knows to have you in his retinue. And now I have work to do. Putscha, see my friend out and bring back the scribe."

"Princess?" I said.

"Yes?"

"It's nothing—I feel like a fool asking."

"What, for heaven's sake?"

"Since I walked in your door I've smelt wildflowers or heather, I could swear it, though there's none about."

"You smell this." Smiling, she motioned to the dwarf, who brought from her table a vial of blue glass. She unstoppered it and held it under my nose. "Distilled from the crushed petals of roses, a flower you've never seen, I think. I put a few drops of it on my body every day. It comes all the way from Golden Miklagard, where they have the skill to put a field of flowers inside a little bottle, and it cost my husband a stack of kuny—of marten pelts—this high." She held out her arm at shoulder level. "How he moaned! Do you like it?"

"I—yes." It reminded me, in fact, of those delicious scents that clung to the girls in Stavko's establishment, but I thought it best not to say so.

"You're blushing! Whatever for?"

"First the mirror, then this. I have much to learn."

She laughed—not as people do when they show you up for a bumpkin, but gently. "I should be the one to blush, Odd Tangle-Hair. At this rate, you'll soon know every secret we women have. Where do you come from that they have neither mirrors nor scent? You're not Norwegian?"

"An Icelander, Princess."

"Ah? And you didn't like it there?"

"I liked it."

"But—?"

"There was some trouble. I had to leave."

"The old story. You men are never happy unless you're murdering each other. Well, I hope you will like it here with us, Odd Tangle-Hair. And now, my friend, good day."

✝

I took a solitary walk that afternoon and held conversation with myself. I had been prepared to dislike Ingigerd for any number of reasons. But I found her a very different woman from the one I had imagined. A woman of fierce loyalties, passionate, intelligent. A woman who did not marry, I calculated, until she was far into her twenties, and then only by order of her exasperated father. Was it because she secretly loved a fierce viking, who sent her poems?

Despite all the blather about his virtues, this affair was passing strange. Perhaps, just because she had never seen him in the flesh, she could turn him into a figure of fancy that no other man—certainly not her husband—could hope to live up to. Could Olaf himself live up to it when they finally met? What really had happened between them? Had they consummated their love, or had she offered herself and been spurned? Olaf's piety was, by all accounts, as excessive as his bloodlust. But clearly her whole existence centered on him. Only now she had transferred that passion to little Magnus.

Often in the days that followed, having nothing else to occupy me, I found my thoughts going back again to my conversation with the princess.

I asked myself why Fate had so arranged things that at every turning I encountered Bloody Olaf: first the living man, then his corpse, then his memory. I of all people. It was decidedly unfair. I'd had to endure a year of my friend Kalf's mooning over him while I bit my tongue and kept silent. Now must I hear it all over again from Ingigerd? I almost felt as if his ghost were stalking me.

What was the man's secret? How had he fired the passions of these otherwise level-headed people? Was it possible that Kalf, Ingigerd, Dag, and so many others were wrong and I alone was right? I nearly began to doubt myself... but, no! Olaf, the terror of pagans, gouger of eyes, chopper off of hands, was my natural enemy. The broken bodies he left in his wake could just as well have been mine, or my father's, or Glum the berserker's, or Einar's. No. Let him haunt me to the last day of my life, let him infect the whole world around me with this strange enthusiasm, he would still not have my willing prayers!

And I remembered, too, I was not completely alone. There was one other—I was convinced of it—who shared my hatred of Olaf, although for other reasons. His half-brother.

If young Harald could learn to lie so smoothly, well, by the Raven, so could I.

These were some of my thoughts.

At other times they revolved around Ingigerd herself. I'd expected some mannish monstrosity in woman's dress. I found instead a woman full of charm and pleasantry—laughing sweetly, smelling of flowers.

Yet deep-minded. One who would not give up all her secrets in a day. What other loves, hates, ambitions, longings lurked behind those wise grey eyes? I made up my mind to try what I could learn.

An interesting puzzle, I said to myself. At the time it seemed no more to me than that.

4

the brothers
vladimirovich

The blare of war-horns shattered my sleep. I leapt up and rolled off the oven. The servant girl I was sleeping with caught me by my shirt and saved me from breaking an arm.

With Einar and a crowd of servants, wives, and children, I ran to the porch that overlooked the courtyard to see what the matter was. The sun, rising at our backs, had just cleared the roof of the palace and bathed everything below in the golden light of dawn. There was nothing yet to see, but the horses caught the smell of their brothers on the wind and trotted round and round the palisade, whinnying.

Our ears caught the distant rumble of men's voices singing a marching song, mingled with the clatter of hoofs and the tread of boots. Soon there came into view the tips of spears and two fluttering banners, both emblazoned with the trident emblem of the House of Rurik.

Then through the gate, hastily unbarred, rode a troop of heavy cavalry in spiked helmets and long mail hauberks, armed with lances and bows. Behind them marched a column of foot soldiers, battle-stained and dirty but singing away lustily, until the spacious yard was filled with them.

Yaroslav, as I'd been told, had gone to make war on the Chuds, accompanied by his brother Mstislav, who had joined forces with him on the march, and by Harald, whose good luck it was to arrive just as the prince was setting out. Here they were back again, weeks before they were expected, and to judge from the dozen or more sledges heaped with precious furs now being dragged into the courtyard, the campaign had been a great success.

Ingigerd, with a fur thrown around her shoulders against the morning chill, pressed past us and descended the stairs to the courtyard, holding in her hands a goblet of mead. One figure detached itself from the knot of horsemen and rode toward her.

"Yaroslav Vladimirovich, by God's grace all is well with us here," she declaimed in a voice that could be heard to the farthest rank, "though your people hunger for your wisdom, which no one, I least of all, can emulate." Standing by his stirrup, she proffered the goblet, which he took and drained.

Hurrying after the princess came Father Dmitri, the family chaplain and tutor, all bows and smiles. Three deacons followed him, carrying the big icons that ordinarily hung above the throne in the great hall.

Yaroslav dismounted, knelt, and kissed each icon as it was held out to him, while addressing it by name: Saint George (his patron), Saints Boris and Gleb (who in life had been his half-brothers, murdered in the blood-letting that followed their father's death), and lastly the Theotokos—the Mother of God—whom he kissed most reverently. The warriors who filled the yard uncovered their heads and echoed his prayer of thanksgiving for the preservation of his City and himself.

From kissing the icons, he stood up to embrace his wife and kiss her tenderly on each cheek and on the lips. If a woman's back and shoulders could speak, Ingigerd's delivered an oration on the theme of frigid submission.

Then Mstislav threw back his head and laughed like a clap of thunder. "By the Devil's mother, Inge, it's good to see you again!"

Yaroslav, smiling weakly, yielded to his brother of the booming voice, who swept Ingigerd up in a huge bear hug and planted woolly kisses on her.

Where Yaroslav's embrace was chaste and careful, Mstislav's was a tornado. But her unyielding spine continued to speak—to shout—the same text as before.

"My children?" asked Yaroslav, finding himself with no one else to kiss. "Where are my sucking pigs?"

The 'sucking pigs' were produced at once, hastily dressed and faces washed, shepherded down the stairs by their old nurse, Thordis. They stood in a row, from shortest to tallest, and Yaroslav kissed each in turn gravely on the brow and called down God's blessing on them. Coming to his pretty Anna, his manly Volodya, and his darling Yelisaveta, he asked them in a most solemn tone if they had been good children and obedient to their nurse, their tutor, and their mother?

"Yes, Papa," Yelisaveta lied for them all.

Mstislav, done with smothering Ingigerd, now directed his boundless joviality at his nieces and nephews. Where their father had blessed them, their uncle tossed them, spun them around, crushed them to his fur-clad bosom—especially Vladimir, calling him Young Falcon, and declaring, "Soon it'll be your turn, Eaglet, to go a-warring with us, for, damn my head! No young man who's worth anything can exist without war, eh? What sort of a Rus would he be who never once slew pagan! You're worthy of our father, Vladimir, whose name you bear, for by Christ, he slew many a pagan!"

Young Volodya looked as if he thoroughly agreed with his uncle's view.

"You, Father What's-Your-Name, tutor." Mstislav dragged Dmitri to him by the front of his cassock. "Let these young pups be free of lessons for today. Damn it all, how often do they see their uncle?"

Yelisaveta, Volodya, and Anna whooped and threw their arms around him, and he enfolded them all in one great embrace. A stranger coming upon this scene could pardonably have made the mistake of thinking that these were Mstislav's children and that Yaroslav was only some elderly bachelor to whom they had just been introduced. Not that Yaroslav didn't love his children—he did, fiercely. But even with them, he could not overcome the timorous shyness that thwarted his relations with everyone.

Neither brother, though, had much of a greeting for Magnus, who, as always, hung back from the rest. Ingigerd drew him to her and put her hand on his head.

Meantime, Vsevolod, the littlest 'sucking pig', or 'falcon', or 'eaglet', whom his uncle had absent-mindedly tucked under one vast arm, reached that pitch of excitement that he pee'd on Mstislav's armor. He was hastily given back, howling, into Nurse's arms.

Then the two brothers, handing their horses over to the grooms, mounted the steps to the porch, where I and the other members of the household stood watching.

On horseback, and seen from a distance, Yaroslav looked the part of a warrior and prince; but at closer hand one noticed the clubbed foot and the limp, as well as the shortness of his stature, the roundness of his shoulders, the mildness of his face, and overall, the awkward movements of one who plainly felt uncomfortable, even slightly absurd in helmet and armor and massive sword belt and scabbard.

Other warriors in the front rank dismounted and followed the two princes up the stairs. Harald, taking the steps two at a time, led the pack.

I stepped in front of him.

"What?—Tangle-Hair! You're alive, you bloody beggar! I almost didn't know you! Don't they feed you here? The fever, of course! Christ, it's good to see you! How long have you been here? You're all settled in? Ah, you should've been with us!"

He looked triumphant, a whirlwind of energy and high spirits.

Dag, right behind him, began apologizing: "Look, old fellow, I hated to leave you with Ragnvald but your ferocious friend here"—with a glance at Einar Tree-Foot—"seemed to have everything in hand so—"

The fever was nothing, I assured him. It was boredom I was dying of at the moment.

"No fear of that now!" laughed Harald. "Now you'll see things happen!"

"What sort of things? Tell me."

"No," said Dag, with a twinkle in his eye, "let him be surprised. Odd Tangle-Hair, your curiosity must wait a little longer."

And, grinning both, they would say no more.

A feast was announced for sundown. The butchers and the cooks got busy; heralds were dispatched all over the town, bearing invitations to various important personages; the druzhiniks, dismissed to the barracks or to their houses, were instructed to wash and change their clothes, and reassemble at the appointed hour.

Yaroslav and Mstislav enjoyed a steam bath and then spent an hour together in St. Sophia's church, thanking God for their victories. (Mstislav, in his way, was every bit as pious as his brother.) Harald, Dag, Einar, and I passed the day in drinking and trading impressions of our Rus friends.

5

The Boy
At Dinner

When the festive board was finally laid, you would have had to listen closely to hear it groan; by which I mean that the vittles were adequate but not what you would call princely. The meal consisted mainly of tough mutton and black bread. The prince himself, because he had painful teeth, had to be content with a little boiled chicken minced up fine, some cabbage soup, and mushrooms—the latter provided by his 'sucking pigs' who had spent the afternoon mushrooming in the woods beyond the town and had returned with full baskets. Yaroslav was an expert on the subject of mushrooms. He picked through their baskets carefully, naming all the different varieties and exclaiming on the delicious qualities of each.

The majority of his army—Rus, Slav, Swede, Norwegian, and Pecheneg (a troop of the latter serving as Mstislav's personal guard)—caroused in the barracks in Gotland Court. Only some fifty of the most favored dined with the prince in his hall.

Nearest Yaroslav sat his wife and brother. Seated next to Ingigerd was Yefrem the Bishop, a sleek, well-oiled man, whom I had not seen before, but would see much of hereafter. Farther down sat Dyuk the mayor. Next to him was Eilif, Jarl Ragnvald's eldest son, who held the post of captain of the druzhina. Eilif was about thirty years old, short and coarse-featured (though I should be the last to hold that against anyone). In fact, he bore a strong resemblance to his parent, although compared with the jarl, he was slower of tongue and duller of eye. Opposite these sat Harald, Dag, and myself.

Harald had already introduced me to Yaroslav as his skald and the prince gave me a warm greeting. Not so Ingigerd. Her greeting to him and Dag was frosty. And to me also, even though she had been so affable at our first meeting and in the days that followed whenever I encountered her. This stung me. It seemed unfair in her to make me an enemy, just when I had decided that I liked her. (It never even entered my head that she might be acting coolly toward me in order not to compromise me with Harald and Dag.)

The feast proceeded with an unstinting flow of ale and mead—in this respect, at least, Yaroslav was not miserly. And he himself drained as many cups as anyone.

Toast after toast was drunk to the Holy Orthodox Faith, may God preserve it! A great amount of crockery was flung about. There were brawls, in the midst of which some men puked and others keeled over. I felt I might do either one, as I tried to match drink for drink with these Rus. Einar Tree-Foot slipped in beside Old Thordis on the bench, and, as far as I could see, made himself quite entertaining.

Yaroslav, too, became ardent after downing half a dozen goblets of mead, and pulled Ingigerd onto his lap and kissed her several times.

While we feasted we were entertained by the palace dwarfs, who performed feats of tumbling and stilt-walking. The head of the troupe was that same Putscha whom I have already described. With him was Nenilushka, his daughter.

(On the subject of these dwarfs, I should explain that they are not the same as the dwarfs one hears of in stories, those tireless miners who delve in the earth for gold. Nor are they of the Lappish race, whom I had met on my travels. They are not, in fact, a race different from ourselves at all, but merely sports of nature. The Rus keep them as pets, and a man or woman will do anything, no matter how shameful, in a dwarf's presence, as though it had no more sense than a dog or a piece of furniture. As far as I could discover, however, their feelings are no different from ours.)

The dwarfs performed their handsprings and vaults with great skill— Putscha especially, who was able to support a pyramid of the other three on his shoulders. Seeing him stripped to the waist, I was surprised by his muscularity; there was considerable strength in that little body.

A feast is an ideal occasion for studying one's hosts. Drunk, they will show you more of themselves in a few hours than in a week sober. And so I took this opportunity to observe the brothers Vladimirovich.

Yaroslav had a homely face with a rather large nose; his graying hair was cut in a bowl, his beard spade-shaped. He wore rings on all his fingers as well as other costly jewelry, and yet his clothes were plain and even threadbare. He was a man, I concluded, who liked to boast his wealth, while at the same time caring little about his person.

Mstislav presented (as I have already said) the strongest contrast to his brother. About the same age as Yaroslav, he enjoyed a great reputation for boldness in battle and generosity to his retainers. (His druzhiniks, it was rumored, ate with silver spoons where we had to be content with wooden ones.)

This night he wore a bear-skin cloak, one pearl earring of great size, and a necklace of wolf's teeth—and not just any wolf but a particularly crafty old fellow, whom he had patiently tracked to its lair and dispatched with only a knife. His trousers, to use a poetic figure of the Rus, were as wide as the sea, and his boots had arches so high that a sparrow could fly underneath them. He was a stupendous drinker and seemed always, as I observed in the days to come, to be somewhere between drunkenness and sobriety.

"Ale!," he bellowed and, impatient to be served, strode over to the vat, thrust his whole head in, and brought it up with the foaming liquid dripping from his hair and his long moustaches. "Hah! Ha, ha! Drunkenness is a blessing sent by God, eh, brother? 'Strong drink is the joy of the Rus, they cannot live without it.' I'm quoting our father's very words."

I found it hard to believe that he and Yaroslav were sons of the same father, but they were—and in a family not noted for brotherly love. In the past they had fought each other to a draw over who should possess their father's capital of Kiev. The result was that Yaroslav had promised not to move his court there for so long as Mstislav lived. To make certain of it (for Yaroslav would not have been the first in that family to break an oath), Mstislav installed himself as Prince of Chernigov, from where he could keep his eye on Kiev, only a few miles distant.

In the five years that had passed since then, the two brothers—considering their bad beginning—had got on pretty well with each other. It was their custom to exchange yearly visits in the summer or fall, taking it in turn to play host, and to assist each other in military ventures.

But if Yaroslav was content with their arrangement, his wife was not. Ingigerd, I began to see, despised her husband for a weakling and cherished a bitter hatred of Mstislav. And he, knowing this perfectly well and being a man of high good humor, missed no opportunity to provoke her.

"Brother of mine," he cried, throwing an arm round Yaroslav's neck, "let us drink to brotherhood! To the bond between brothers—between men, damn my head!—that no woman ever has, nor ever will comprehend."

Yaroslav, pinioned in this embrace, with some difficulty got his cup to his lips. They drank and Mstislav flung his cup at the wall shattering it to splinters (it was made of colored glass, from Miklagard, and must have cost a good deal—there were only a few on the table). Yaroslav, drinking from its twin, seemed on the point of doing the same, but had second thoughts and set it down carefully.

It must have been hard, I thought, for Yaroslav the boy to have grown up with a brother like Mstislav.

"Now Inge, my darling girl," Mstislav teased her, "why such a sour face? Heh? Are we not friends? Damn my head, if this brother of mine hadn't married you, I think I'd have done it myself! What's the old saying—'If there were only one scheming woman on earth, every man would claim her for his wife'? Hah! Ha, ha, ha!"

"What a blessing, Mstislav Vladimirovich," she answered softly, without looking at him, "to have so keen a wit. Take care on whom you exercise it."

The Prince of Chernigov hadn't any exceptional wit, really. He struck me rather as a sort of great bearded child, who could pass from laughter to tears and back again in a twinkling. In the course of the evening I saw him weep when he remembered that his youngest son had been gored to death by a bison exactly a year ago to the day; yet a few moments later he was roaring with laughter at the antics of Putscha.

These particular antics were not a part of the dwarf's performance but were the gyrations of the frightened creature as he slapped at his coat, which some druzhinik had set fire to. Comical as this was, it would not be worth mentioning except that it had an interesting result.

"You, whatever you call yourself," Ingigerd turned savagely on the prankster, who was so drunk he hardly knew where he was, "if you ever assault gospodin Putscha again I will have your privates cut off and thrown to my dog for a tit-bit, since they're too small to make a meal of."

There was plenty of laughter around the table at the drunken man's expense; but Mstislav, already vastly amused, laughed till the tears ran down his cheeks. "'Gospodin' Putscha!" he gasped. "'Gospodin' to a dwarf with a wooden sword? What a joke, heh? Ha, ha!"

In the meantime someone had the goodness to throw a pail of water on Putscha.

The drunken offender stared at Ingigerd stupefied. Doubtless, he'd never been spoken to so roughly by a woman and it took a few seconds for the insult to penetrate his fuddled brain. When it did, he lurched to his feet and made a violent grab for the dwarf, who fled under the table to his mistress's side. The man's friends, while laughing, did their best to restrain him.

"Eilif Ragnvaldsson, I want that man beaten with a rod," cried Ingigerd, who was now very angry, "and fined the cost of two coats to replace my dwarf's ruined one! Now, you there, take him away!"

Now the laughter stopped. The Swedes looked questioningly at Eilif, their captain.

Eilif scowled at his plate in silence.

Is he afraid to punish his own men? I wondered. He's not his father's son, that's for certain.

"Eilif, do something, for Christ's sake!" Ingigerd hissed at him between clenched teeth. Only those of us quite close heard her. There was a painful silence, then: "Do as the Princess says!" he growled at the offender's companions.

At this, Mstislav roared, "Brother Yaroslav, does your captain of druzhiniks wear a dress? By Christ, I'll never bring my wife under this roof. Give her ideas!"

The offender, screaming oaths at the top of his voice, was dragged away.

On many a druznik's face was written scorn for their so-called captain. I exchanged glances with Harald and Dag; they saw it, too.

But this was only the beginning of Eilif's humiliation that night, for Yaroslav chose this moment to make a speech:

"Boyars! Druzhiniks! Attend me!" He hadn't a strong voice. "Please, silence if you please. Yes, well, now—I say, now—ah, has come the happy moment for distributing rewards from the tribute we have levied on the Chuds. We took over a thousand kuny in sable and marten pelts of the best quality, which we shall trade next summer in Miklagard for silks, and wine, and, ah, perfume?"—a bashful look at Ingigerd—"and, ah, so forth. Yes."

Yaroslav was the only man I ever met who could make the Norse tongue sound puny. It was a Norse, besides, that was salted with Slavonic words which were in general use at court. One of the first I learned was kuna, which, from meaning marten pelt, comes also to mean money because pelts are the common currency here.

"First, then, as is fitting," the prince resumed in his faltering voice, "to gospodin Eilif Ragnvaldsson, the captain of my druzhina, thirty kuny!"

Eilif, who had not shifted his gaze from the table this whole time, acknowledged his reward with a grunt.

"To gospodin Steinkel Valgardsson, fifteen kuny. To gospodin Kolchko Vasilkovich, fifteen kuny—" Yaroslav read on while he squinted at a strip of birch bark which he held close to his face.

Throughout a long list of honored warriors, I kept glancing nervously at Harald, thinking that surely he would not be passed over entirely, but growing more worried as every name was mentioned but his. But he sat relaxed with a faint smile on his lips; Dag too.

"Finally, to gospodin Harald Sigurdsson, half-brother to King Olaf of blessed memory—to him I give the sum of fifty kuny, and a fine sword, and a country estate at Menovo with the produce of the villages of Menovo and Ovseevo, and hunting privileges in the lands around them."

Mstislav, who had been half-dozing for some while, opened his eyes wide and stared in astonishment at his brother. All through the hall there was a hush. An estate worthy of a boyar!

After the first hush of surprise, there began a buzz of voices up and down the benches. Eilif's eyes, riveted on Harald, blazed with hatred: the hatred of a cowardly, indolent, and stupid man, a man who could barely rouse himself to perform his duties or discipline his men, but who could be stung into hitting back viciously at a rival.

"And, in God's name, druzhiniks," Yaroslav struggled to be heard above the rising clamor, "I pray you, do not think it strange that I heap such rewards on a mere youth—and one whom I did not even know above six weeks ago. You all saw him on campaign—how sparing with his own men, how ruthless with the enemy! Despite his tender years, his sagacity is as prodigious as, er, his size! And as to that, why, I do not hesitate to call him a Goliath—but a Goliath who fights for God and not against Him! Eh? Ha, ha!"

"Thanks to this young man alone," he pointed his finger at Harald, "we have brought home a haul of furs greater than any of us had thought possible, and in a month's less time! While some of us were content merely to take what was offered"—this with a sidelong glance at Eilif—"it was Harald's excellent idea to seize the youngest baby in each homestead we passed by—but only pagan babies, I assure you—and put a noose around its neck. We had only to hang a few of them before their parents' eyes and it was wonderful how quickly they discovered stacks of pelts and other precious things that they had forgotten they owned. And so I feel that I do no more than reward him from his own earnings!

"In short, I hope to persuade Harald Sigurdsson, already dear to us for his brother's sake, to seek his fortune in our service with, er, advantages to us both." He ended on a rising note, making it sound like a question.

Harald rose to acknowledge the honors heaped on him, but the only people cheering, I noticed, were myself, Dag, Harald's standard bearer, his steersman, and the few other Norwegians in the room.

Eilif, with an animal cry of rage, pushed himself from the table and rushed from the hall. Ingigerd reached out a hand to stop him but he tore past her. And it cannot have improved his spirits any that Yelisaveta, sitting at the children's table, was heard to laugh out loud as his back disappeared through the door.

I was as glad for Harald as he was for himself. How soon Dag's prophecy of his brilliant future seemed to be coming true, and beyond our wildest expectations! And as Harald's fortunes rose, so rose mine. I cheered and pounded the table louder than any, and he and I downed a goblet of mead together with our arms around each other's shoulders.

But Harald wouldn't have been Harald if he could have let it go at that.

Mstislav, roused from his half-doze, was feeling energetic again. He was very strong and loved to show off, and no sooner was the awarding of booty concluded than he called for a horseshoe to be fetched and, with all eyes on him, bent it until it broke in two.

"Ho hum," said Harald, leaning back from the bench with his hands behind his head and an insolent smile on his face. "I could do that when I was twelve."

"Heh? What's that? I thought I heard the peeping of a chick," said Mstislav. "Little chick, t'was only a dandelion chain that they told you was a horseshoe, ha, ha!"

There was laughter all around the room from those who had just discovered in their breasts a twinge of resentment at this young upstart's fantastic good luck.

"Strong you may be, little chick—are you, perhaps, a wrestler too?"

"Aye, Lobster-Face," answered Harald, "and one that's never been beaten. What about you?"

"Mind how you talk to your elders and betters, chickadee!" Mstislav was growing warm. "When I warred against the Kashogian folk and the battle was going against us, I challenged their chief to a wrestling match—and there's many a man here who can testify to my words—no holds barred and only one to walk away. He was a big man and fast, but, by God, I crunched his neck for him!"

"Now, brother, I want no killing in my hall." The tone of Yaroslav's voice made it sound more like a plea than an order. On our side Dag was trying to distract Harald.

"A friendly match, brother," replied Mstislav. "Only a friendly match to settle the point. The winner to be that man who can lift the other off his feet and throw him onto the table top. Are you game, little chick?"

Harald was on his feet in an instant, unclasping his belt and pulling off his shirt. Mstislav, downing a last great gulp of ale, did the same. The benches were cleared and a space made in the middle of the hall.

Harald, of course, was taller and younger. But Mstislav was much the wilier. As for drunkenness, I guessed the honors were about even, though the Rus with his fiery face showed it more. As they circled and feinted, watching for an opening, the druzhiniks and others in the hall laid bets and shouted encouragement to one man or the other. But most cheered for Mstislav because he had many friends here.

The combatants dashed in, grappled, broke away, dashed in again. Soon both were panting and the sweat ran in rivers down their backs. But Harald was having the worst of it.

"Enough!" cried Yaroslav from the sidelines. "In God's name call it even."

"Never!" Harald gasped.

Again he rushed at Mstislav but clutched only empty air. This old fox knew tricks undreamt of by Harald. They grappled again, snorting like a couple of bulls, each trying for a hold. And this time Mstislav, lightning-fast, slipped under Harald's arm, got behind him, applying a hammer-lock with one hand while he gripped his trousers with the other, shoved him to the edge of the table, kicked his legs out from under him, caught him around the knees, lifted him over head, and dropped him square on his back amidst the dirty plates, gnawed bones, and half-filled goblets.

Mstislav turned away, let go a war whoop, and raised his arms above his head in sign of victory.

And Harald? My Harald, my lord, the someday King of Norway, who would raise me with him to fame and fortune if he didn't get himself killed first? Harald snatched up a carving knife that lay on the table and flung himself at the Rus.

The Pecheneg bodyguard, shouted a warning. Mstislav turned and crouched. Harald's blade missed his neck by an inch. As their bodies collided, Mstislav rolled backwards and sent Harald flying head over heels onto the floor. The bodyguard stood over him, his saber raised for the death stroke.

I threw myself on top of Harald as he lay helpless. Dag and some others piled on, too, and together we shielded him from the blade and pinned him to the ground.

When he realized he was overpowered, he quit heaving and grunting, let go of the knife, and asked to be let up.

I looked to Dag. Dag looked to Mstislav, who nodded. Cautiously, we released him.

Dag, very pale around the gills, attempted a laugh and said, "Too much drink for a young head. Harald begs your pardon, Prince Mstislav and—"

"Shut up! I'll do my own begging!"

Dag's mouth snapped shut instantly.

"Mstislav and Yaroslav Vladimirovich," said Harald, still breathless from the struggle, "I do ask your pardon. Please blame my action on the hot-headedness of youth."

This must be his stock answer whenever his temper got him in trouble; he had used it on me the day we nearly fought in the streets of Aldeigjuborg. Would it work again here?

Mstislav, beet red and scowling, stared for a moment out of his big,

43

bulging eyes. Then cracked a smile. "Hah! I like this young man."

By this time the drink had taken its toll on us all. My own head was going round and round. Harald, at least, had been true to his word in this respect: I wasn't bored anymore.

And so—not a moment too soon—the night drew to a close.

6

YELISAVETA PLAYS A GAME

"She feared no one but Almighty God and Him only moderately," said Yelisaveta Yaroslavna, sitting on a stool in the kitchen with her arms around her knees. She was holding forth on her favorite subject: the life of her great-great grandmother, the formidable Princess Olga.

Two days had passed since Yaroslav's feast. It was afternoon and the girl, done with her lessons and feeling hungry, had repaired to her favorite haunt, which also happened to be mine. We sat warming ourselves by the big bake oven, nibbling on a fresh loaf and drinking kvass.

Yelisaveta had reached that age when she was not supposed to talk familiarly with strange men, and her nurse ought to have been more vigilant. But the old lady's attention was elsewhere. Einar Tree-Foot, wearing a nearly new shirt and a nearly clean rag over his eye socket, was curdling her blood agreeably in a far corner of the room.

"Olga was wife to Igor," said Yelisaveta, looking serious, "who ruled all the Rus in those days; not his only wife, for he was a pagan and had many, but she was the one he loved best.

"When Igor was murdered by the Drevlyans—they were a savage tribe who dwelt deep in the forest north of Kiev—Olga plotted her revenge. Now the Drevlyan chief, who was a great stupid oaf named Mal, wanted to marry her. She pretended to accept his offer and invited his ambassadors to come to Kiev. But, when they arrived there, thinking themselves so grand and all, she ordered them to be seized and buried alive right before her eyes!

"Then she asked Mal to send another embassy—I've said he was stupid. And when they came she invited them to have a steam-bath, the way you're supposed to with visitors. But when they were all inside, she locked the door, and set the bath-house afire and burned them all up!

"Next, still pretending that she would marry this blockhead, she went with all her boyars and druzhiniks to pay him a visit. And Mal was so happy, he put on a great feast for her. But when all the Drevlyans were drunk, she told her druzhiniks to murder them all, and went round, herself, to each warrior, spurring him on!

"After that, she ruled Kiev all by herself for ten years, until her son grew up. It was then that she became a Christian—the very first of the Rus to do so—and she held to the Orthodox Faith for the rest of her days, no matter that her son and nearly all the Rus people kept on being heathens for years and years.

"And the most wonderful thing of all she did was sail to Constantinople—Miklagard as you Northmen call it—to visit Constantine Purple-Born, the Emperor of the Greeks. And he was so smitten with her beauty that he bowed low before her, he and all his courtiers and eunuchs besides, and begged her to be his wife and live with him in his splendid palace, which is built all of marble and has a golden tree in it with a golden bird that sings!

"After that, she died and went to heaven and became a saint. I pray to her quite often, you know, because she knew how to punish her enemies." Yelisaveta paused and looked at me gravely. "I have enemies, you know." Then she bit sharply into the loaf and washed it down with kvass.

The expression of her face, as she told this tale, was striking. I couldn't help thinking how like her mother she was, and how natural, therefore, that they should be enemies. For indeed they were, bitterly and without truce. Almost daily, the palace echoed to their loud wrangling over the smallest trifles.

"Would you like to be a queen one day, Elisif Jarizlafsdottir, in a country far away, and punish your enemies as much as you please?"

Harald had come in silently, stooping under the low doorway, and stood behind her as she finished speaking.

She turned in surprise. "Oh, it's you! You shouldn't creep up on people that way, you'll give them a fit. What did you call me?"

"Elisif. Elisif Jarizlafsdottir—your name in plain honest Norse. These

Slavonic names of yours tie my tongue in knots. Only I will call you Elisif, and then only in private."

Looking down on her from his great height, Harald seemed more than ever gigantic. But, though her forehead barely reached his chest, she answered him, "Indeed! And who said you might call me anything at all in private? Especially seeing as my mother hates you."

"Does she? Then we have something in common." He reached up and with his knife cut a slice of meat from one of the hams that hung from the rafters overhead. "For you, sweet Elisif." He handed her the morsel.

Her cheeks turned red; she was plainly uncertain how to behave toward this prodigious boy-man. She said petulantly, "There you go again; who ever heard of such a name? If you must call me by it, write it out for me."

Now Harald was at a loss. Like most people, he had never cared a jot for writing, but suddenly, before this educated girl, he was abashed.

"What, can't you?" she asked with wide-eyed innocence. She wasn't going to let him off easy.

"I, ah, have not had leisure to master your Rus letters."

"Oh, I know the Roman letters, too, and the Greek ones. Write it any way you please."

"Gospodin," I broke in, "it's for just such things that you have a skald. Permit me."

"Yes, dammit, yes, of course!"

I cut off a sliver from one of the fire logs next to the oven and scratched her name on it in Roman letters (I had amused myself by learning them during my winter in Norway). And then—just to show off, I admit it— wrote it in runes as well.

"What a clever fellow you are!" She cocked an eyebrow at me. Up til now she had paid me little attention. "Where did you learn that?"

"Well—"

"Too clever sometimes," Harald glowered at me and shouldered himself between us. This was his show and I was spoiling it. I smiled and stepped back. How little it took to make him jealous!

"There's one or two Northmen here that are always talking about the runes," Yelisaveta said. "I've overheard them. Once I heard one say how they can make a person fall in love against her will. Will they do that to me?"

She swept back her long hair and tilted up her face to him. There was no mistaking the finely calculated lowering of the eyelids.

"They will, pretty Elisif," he answered; "they will indeed. Throw the sliver into the fire now if you would be free of me. Isn't that the way of it, skald?"

Thor's Billy goat! I thought. He's serious. Does she know that? Surely, with her it's nothing but a game to provoke her mother. And not only her mother, for I had happened to learn just the day before that it was Eilif Ragnvaldsson to whom she was betrothed. Whether Harald knew this, I was not certain.

She tucked the sliver carefully inside her bodice, between her small pointed breasts.

Old Thordis, just then happening to look up and seeing her little pigeon between us two vultures, flew squawking to the rescue and drove us from the kitchen.

"Harald," I said when we were beyond the door, "can I give you a word of advice?"

"No."

And he walked away.

And what wise counsel I could have given! Dag himself would not have been more eloquent. We were here, I would have reminded him, to make friends, not enemies; and where we found enemies, not to embitter them more. Money. Troops. An alliance. And then home to Norway! (Or, in my case, Iceland.) These were what we sought; not affairs with betrothed young ladies that could only lead to trouble. Was this a skald's fate, I wondered morosely, to see clearly and be ignored? An incident that occurred soon afterward made me more worried still.

✝

Mstislav had introduced to the court a new game which he called by the foreign word shatranj. The board and pieces, together with some notion of the rules he had gotten from an Arab traveler. Many of us younger folk tried to learn it and spent the long nights playing against each other for modest stakes.

On one particular evening we were all gathered around the board. Harald and I had played to a draw. Volodya had taken on Magnus, when none of the others would play with him, and had beaten him—but gracefully and with good manners. (It always impressed me that this boy, who as eldest son might have had the best reason for disliking his mother's pet, was the only one of Yaroslav's children to behave at all kindly towards him.)

Then Yelisaveta challenged Harald.

They were both good; and they played eagerly, deploying their men swiftly at first; then, with great deliberation, hunching close over the little board until Harald's lips almost brushed the hair of her head. No need to speak. The thrust and parry of the game took the place of words. That same joy showed on Harald's face as when he played at poetry—which is also a game of intricate rules and subtleties. In Yelisaveta's green eyes was the pure thrill of combat. The men and boys in her life had fought, or would fight, real wars on real battle fields. Only on this little field could she match herself with them. Here she was their equal.

We happened to be in one of the ante-rooms off of the great hall, with the door shut to keep out the cold. It banged open suddenly, revealing Eilif in the doorway. The wind rushing in made the candle flames tremble.

"Yelisaveta Yaroslavna, come into the hall and drink with me." He had the fiery face and thick speech of one who has drunk deep already.

"Later, if I feel like it."

"Now! Leave this childish stuff to the children."

"Am I one of the children, Eilif?" said Harald in a sarcastic voice.

There followed a silence, while the two players studied the board and the rest of us watched Eilif grow redder in the face by the moment.

"Yelisaveta, are you coming or not!"

When an enemy's brows knit together and his mouth turns down to the degree that Eilif's did, a prudent man will just loosen his blade very slightly in its scabbard. I touched my side and remembered, with sinking heart, that I had no weapon on me—nor did Harald—while the captain of the druzhina was wearing both sword and dagger. Distracted perhaps by Eilif's presence, Harald made a careless move on the board.

"Eilif, shut the door," said Yelisaveta. "You may stay on either side of it for all I care." She spoke without looking up, while her slim fingers advanced a bishop and removed Harald's rook from the board. "Check," she said.

Eilif was baffled, and honestly pained; you could see it in his face. He took two steps into the room and stood glowering at them.

Harald moved his king out of danger—you must understand that the whole object of this interesting game is to render that piece unable to move in any direction—but Yelisaveta pursued.

"Check again."

Harald frowned.

Eilif saw this and his face brightened a little. If this thorn in his flesh was going to be defeated, and by a girl, that was worth watching!

"Eilif," she said sweetly, "I'm sure if you tried very hard you could learn the rules. It's the same thing as when you command your druzhiniks, except that these little soldiers don't laugh at you when your back is turned.—Check again, gospodin Harald." She removed his queen from the board.

Gods! I thought. What reckless game is she playing? She wants to infuriate them both. She wants them to fight!

The joy drained from Harald's face. He drank angrily from a flagon that was by his elbow and, after furrowing his brow for a long while, advanced a pawn, slapping the piece down hard on the board. Eilif leaned nearer, screwing up his eyes with the effort of comprehension; and the rest of us—I, Volodya, Magnus, and two boyars' sons—also pulled our chairs close.

The pawn was taken. Yelisaveta's horseman rode to the attack.

Now Harald squeezed his king between thumb and forefinger as if he would punish the little monarch for blundering into this hopeless position. He pushed him violently there, and there, and there; but everywhere the way was barred. He interposed another pawn, but this warrior, like its brother, fell before Yelisaveta's attack.

"Shahmat," she said. "I fear your King is dead."

Harald worked hard to force a smile. Although he could never bear to lose at anything, he was doing his utmost—because this was Yelisaveta—to hold on to his temper.

And he might have succeeded had not little Magnus, with more bravado than sense, said cunningly, "Why, Uncle Harald, this makes the second king you've lost in as many years; you really ought to be more careful." (His meaning being that Harald had lost his first king on the field of Stiklestad, as though he had let Olaf die to suit his own purposes.)

Knocking over table and board and sending the pieces flying, Harald lunged for Magnus' throat. The boy hung like a rag doll in his huge hands, twisting helplessly, unable even to scream.

Here, like an answer to his prayers, was all the excuse Eilif needed. "Your back!" I shouted.

Harald crouched and spun as Eilif's blade whistled over his head. Its point slit the cheek of one of the boyars' sons who was too slow in getting out of the way. Dropping Magnus, Harald grabbed a chair to defend himself with. Volodya, seizing the chance, dashed in bravely and pushed Magnus out of the room.

In less time than it takes to tell it, Harald's back was up against the wall and the chair in splinters as the captain of the druzhina, wielding his sword with both hands, rained blows on him from every side. No one—certainly not I—had the hardihood to step between Harald and that lethal windmill.

So this is how it ends, I thought. Good-bye, Harald, good-bye fortune.

But Yelisaveta shrieked, "Eilif, you filthy coward! Cut him and I swear by Christ Almighty I'll slit your throat on our wedding night!"

This warning had the unmistakable ring of sincerity to it. Eilif paused in mid-stroke. A mistake. In the blink of an eye Harald thrust the splintered chair leg in his enemy's face and drove his knee hard into his balls. As Eilif doubled over, Harald gripped his sword arm and cracked it at the wrist. Eilif rolled about on the floor, groaning.

Yelisaveta's face was flushed and her breathing came quick; and there was in the way her glittering green eyes watched Harald something like exhilaration, or triumph, or the first stirrings of passion.

"Hold, in God's name!" cried Yaroslav, appearing suddenly in the doorway with Volodya at his side, and Mstislav and Dag close behind them.

Needless to recount all the various conversation that followed. It was pretty quickly agreed by everyone except Eilif (who was speechless) that Magnus was most to blame for making a remark that Harald was bound to resent. As for the rest of it, no one was dead, so that was all right, but Harald and Eilif had better steer clear of each other from now on and consider their feud at an end. That was an order.

But, of course, it wasn't as simple as that. Harald had been on the point of murdering young Magnus and doubtless Ingigerd was hearing it from the boy's trembling lips at this very moment. Here was no cause for celebration.

And soon things took an even nastier turn.

7

PERUN OF THE
SILVER FACE

The sun glowed like a copper penny in the mist. It was a bleak morning in October. "Best weather in all the world for hunting!" swore Mstislav.

Our horses stood in the stable-yard, exhaling plumes of steam, while the grooms put on the bridles and tightened the saddle girths. The huntsmen struggled to hold back their wolfhounds, boarhounds, elkhounds, and mastiffs—nearly a hundred dogs in all—that yapped and strained at the leash.

We were at Yaroslav's estate at Rakom, a much larger residence than his dvor in Novgorod. Here he kept his stables, kennels, and mews.

"Ho!" bellowed Mstislav, striding about. "The sweet smell of horses and sweet cry of hounds!" He had already taken a quantity of ale on board and his face was red and jolly.

His brother, by contrast, looked uncomfortable. Yaroslav hunted the same way he went to war, earnestly and dutifully—because it was expected of a Rus Prince, but with no real joy in the thing. He sat a horse well, though, and you soon forgot about his deformed foot.

We were a large party which included Bishop Yefrem (not in his priestly garb, of course), several boyars with their retinues, and favored druzhiniks of both royal brothers.

Eilif was absent, still nursing his hurt pride and fractured wrist. Only four days had passed since his fight with Harald.

Einar Tree-Foot, too, had begged off with the excuse that he found riding too hard on his old bones—which surprised me because it was the first time I'd ever heard that tough old man plead his age for any reason.

Ingigerd was not the only woman among us (a few boyars' wives were present), but she was the only one dressed as a man—in a coat and trousers of forest green, with boots of crushed leather, a hunting knife in her belt, and her hair, without its matronly head cloth, plaited in one long braid wound around her head.

In Iceland it is not absolutely unheard of for a woman to dress up as a man, though it can be grounds for divorce if the husband objects. In Gardariki, too, it caused tongues to wag. Bishop Yefrem looked askance and held conversation with his beard, in which the words 'God', and 'ordained', and 'differences between the sexes' could be heard pretty clearly.

Yaroslav, feeling that his wife needed some defending on this score, blurted out, "In God's name, Bishop, take off her trousers and you'll find her still as the Almighty made her!"

Yefrem, in some confusion, thanked him but declined. Of all of us who overhead this exchange none laughed louder than Ingigerd herself.

We mounted up. The princess rode a dappled grey mare with harness and saddle of green leather and green ribbons braided in its tail and mane. A groom held her stirrup while gospodin Putscha knelt down and made his back into a step of exactly the right height for her to put her booted foot upon.

(Of the Rus horses, I should say that they are short-legged and shaggy, very like our Icelandic ones. I chose for myself a black stallion that reminded me of Grani, my beautiful horse that had been maimed in the stallion fight at Thingholt—the cause of my family's doom. It hardly seemed possible that that was only three years ago.)

Our way took us first through the little village of Rakom where the 'black people' in their rough coats and bark shoes doffed their caps as we trotted by. Once past the village, we cantered across a stubbly meadow, then slowed to a walking pace as we came to the dense wood on the other side.

I had never hunted much (there being no large game in Iceland) and was an indifferent rider. Harald, too, was a novice—he sat his mount awkwardly, and the animal seemed absurdly small for him though it was the biggest in the stable. The Rus, on the other hand, all of them, even Putscha on his pony, rode as if they were sewn to the saddle.

The forest around Novgorod is full of marshes, shallow lakes, and myriad little streams, but an early frost had hardened the ground so that we could gallop where we pleased. We struck down by the river and held our course that way, riding south towards Lake Ilmen through stands of pine, dark with the shade of overhanging boughs, and oak trees, covered trunk and twig with a glittering sheath of ice.

"My dear, you're not too cold?" Yaroslav inquired of his wife, who rode beside him, just ahead of me. "Your mittens—where are they? In God's name put them on, your little hands will soon be frozen! And pull up the collar of your coat, never mind that it hides your pretty neck. That's better. You women, ha, ha! You women!" He chuckled and shook his head. After a pause, he resumed. "I wonder, shall we find the lake frozen clear across? No, of course not; no, you're quite right. I was thinking, my dear, we should stop tonight at the country house of Dyuk Osipovich—yes, yes, I know, My Love, but he has offered and I can't very well refuse him, now really, can I? And we'll finish up at your estate on the lake, does that please you? I thought it would—one's own familiar things around one, there's nothing to compare with it! Ah, if only God sends herds of animals across our path—enough to satisfy even Mstislav—then we shall soon be home again, soon home again with our dear little ones around us. I'm praying for it, believe me."

With such conversation did fond Yaroslav beguile his Lady. While she favored him at intervals with a nod.

When the woods gave way again to open land where we could ride several abreast, Dag, Harald, and I rode alongside the couple, and the conversation became general and quite merry.

Dag was at his wittiest and Ingigerd laughed at every sally. Even Harald managed a few awkward pleasantries, muttering them into his bosom so that he would not seem to be addressing her in case she chose to ignore him. But, on the contrary, she answered him very pleasantly.

I suggested to Harald that we play the game of kennings, challenging her and Yaroslav to guess the meanings of the knotty phrases that skaldic poets employ: 'Fjord elk' for ship; 'wound dew' for blood, and the like. Her delight and wonder at our cleverness knew no bounds.

What a number of faces this woman wears! I thought to myself. With her daughter, severe; with her husband, aloof; with me, at first, charming, but afterwards, cool; with Harald, until now, not even that. Yet here, dressed in men's breeches and a coat too large in the shoulders, she seems, strangely enough, most girlish and gay. And which of all these faces is truly hers—or, have we even seen the true one yet?

The prince's forest teemed with game of every kind and it was decided to hunt a different sort of beast each day. And so it went: on the first day, boar; on the second, wolf; and on the third day, bison. This is an animal I had not seen nor even heard of before. It is like a bull but shaggy, with its head covered by a mass of wool, and a woolly beard hanging from its chin. The Rus hunt it on horseback with the bow, which they have learned to do from the steppe dwellers.

Mstislav's Pecheneg bodyguard—a silent, watchful man named Kuchug—brought down one, galloping alongside it with the reins in his teeth and shooting it until it bristled with arrows. Mstislav wounded one, but his horse stumbled and it got away. And Yaroslav actually killed one, though he gave the credit to Saint George to whom he had prayed as he loosed his arrow. Bishop Yefrem killed one too and was quite happy to take the credit for himself.

That evening we lodged at Gorodische, an estate of Ingigerd's about three miles from Novgorod by the shore of Lake Ilmen where the Volkhov leaves it.

Our three day excursion had taken us round the lake and we were nearing our starting place. Harald, out of his element, with no opportunity to shine and nothing to show for his pains, had gotten more irritable every day until now he was sunk in a very black mood. After picking at his dinner, he wrapped himself in his furs and went quickly to sleep, or pretended to.

The rest of us stayed up, stretching our legs to the oven, while Mstislav, as he worked the burrs out of his wolfhound's coat, entertained us with stories of hunts gone by and dwelt lovingly on each of his narrow escapes from death.

The next morning Ingigerd went out of her way to be charming to Harald, asking him how he had slept and refusing to be put off by his mumbled replies. She declared her intention to go hawking that day, for Lake Ilmen, she said, was home to thousands of birds. "That is the quarry I prefer, gospodin," she said. "Am I right in guessing that you're as bored as I am with all this chasing after bison, wolves, and pigs? Let the others go their own way—what is it to be today, husband, elk? Wild horse? Well, never mind, but please do me the favor to come with me, gospodin Harald.

Dag and Odd too, unless they would find a woman's company tedious. I keep a well-stocked mews. Come choose whatever bird you like."

Harald could not very well refuse her pretty invitation, and Dag and I, after an exchange of wary looks, agreed also. Yaroslav, I thought, looked as though he would much rather be coming with us than keeping his brother's company for another day. But Ingigerd had quite pointedly not invited him.

The mews was a long, dimly lit shed that smelt of feathers and droppings.

"Speak softly," she whispered. "Make no sudden movements. Their nerves are as taut as bowstrings."

On perches along both walls they sat—perfectly still until they sensed us. Then a current of excitement ran through them, audible in shrill cries, in the fanning of wings, in the tinkling of the bells on their jesses. Pairs of glittering eyes followed us in jerky movements. It was a thrilling feeling to be in the dark, unprotected, amongst these sensitive killers.

"You may choose among eagles, gyrfalcons, goshawks, sparrow hawks," Ingigerd said in a low voice, "but the best are my little peregrines."

I recalled how Harald had bought gifts for the royal couple in Aldeigjuborg: a falcon for him, a reliquary for her. Funny that he had got their tastes exactly backwards.

Pulling on a horsehide gauntlet, she took a small brown bird on her fist.

"My favorite. She has the courage of an eagle, this one. I fly only females, they are the great killers—larger, stronger, braver—oh, much braver—than their mates. See the thighs, how muscular they are. It's not strength of wing alone that counts in a falcon. Come, now, and choose."

Dag and I followed her advice and chose peregrines. Harald chose an enormous eagle.

Outside, the morning light was dazzling—the weather having improved over night. We mounted our horses (Putscha, as always, performing the office of footstool for his mistress) and the grooms handed up our hooded birds onto our gauntleted fists.

"Hold the jesses between your fingers, so," Ingigerd said, indicating the strips of leather that hung from each leg. "That way you won't lose her."

We left Gorodische and cantered over the stony ground by the lakeside, followed at a discrete distance by three mounted servants, leading a pack horse with food and drink for the day's excursion.

Ilmen is a big lake. Ice had formed already round its edges. In a few weeks more you could drive a sledge and team straight across it.

As we slowed to a foot pace, the princess instructed us how to let the right arm 'float' so as to cushion the jolting of the horse's gait, which falcons dislike. Meantime Sirko ranged ahead of us, sniffing out quarry. That dog, I reckoned, with its delicately shaped head and body so lean you could count its ribs, had a keener intelligence than all of Mstislav's brawny mastiffs put together.

We rode four abreast, talking of this and that. Somewhat to my surprise the name of Olaf was never mentioned, not even when the subject touched on religion, as it did when we passed by the ancient cult center of the Slavic thunder god, Perun.

This was a close, thick, shadowy grove by the lakeside, full of gnarled trunks and twisted boughs. Dead fowls hung from the branches there and, dimly seen among the trunks, stood a wooden post carved in the rough likeness of a man. Sirko bounded into the trees, barking excitedly. She had found an unexpected quarry.

Men shouted and unseen bodies plunged away through the underbrush. Harald and I dismounted and went in a little way with our swords drawn, but we found nothing except a maggoty goat's carcass several days old lying at the foot of the idol.

Harald shoved against this idol with all his might, straining until he was purple-faced, but he couldn't budge it. It was easy to read his thoughts: Olaf, by the grace of God, had thrown down idols by the score, just by touching them, by merely commanding them. And could he not throw down even one? In the end, he had to be content with hacking up its face with his sword, and we made our way back to the others.

"Perun," said Ingigerd, as we resumed our ride, "was their name for Thor and this was his place. The original statue was huge, so I'm told; its face made of beaten silver with a moustache of gold. But that was fifty years ago, before Saint Vladimir abolished the old religion and broke up the idols. Even so, the country folk here have made a new one which they sacrifice to in secret. Dvoeverie we call it: 'double faith'. It persists not only in the countryside but even in our cities. Last year my husband hanged a dozen sorcerers in the town of Suzdal alone; we could hang many dozens more and still not root them all out."

Here, I thought, was the obvious place to unite the praises of Olaf to those of Vladimir—the two champions of the new religion in their respective countries. Oddly, though, no one did. Perhaps Harald, Dag, and the princess felt reluctant to shatter this momentary truce by mentioning that man's name, whose legacy set them at each other's throats.

To fill the silence, I remarked that the old gods seemed to be everywhere in retreat.

"True," said Ingigerd, "and yet, the heathen devils do not give way easily, do they?"

"I am of the opinion, Princess, that we ought to be free to choose the devils we prefer."

"Are you? What an extraordinary idea," she laughed. "But I suppose we must make allowances for a skald—poetry and deviltry being much the same thing."

Dag was doing frantic things with his eyebrows to get my attention; Harald was giving me puzzled looks.

"Gospodin Odd,"—she regarded me now quite seriously— "for some reason it amuses you to play at being a heathen, but I doubt whether you have seen very much of heathenism, really. I have. Despite my father's sternest efforts to forbid it, the old religion still flourishes in Sweden. To this very day the blood sacrifice is performed every ninth year at the great temple of Odin in Uppsala—not a mile from our hall."

"I've heard of it," I replied. "I once knew a Swedish berserker who was initiated there as a boy." (Poor Glum—I hadn't thought of him in a while. Blasted by Thor's hammer while he stood on the pitching deck of my ship. Was he in Valhalla now, matching his frenzy with One-Eyed Odin? I mightily wanted to believe it.)

"Do you know what happens there?" Ingigerd pressed on. "They hang nine men by their necks from the trees that grow in the sacred grove. Nine men and nine males of every other sort of animal—much as was done here in Perun's grove once upon a time—and they let the carcasses hang there till they rot. This is no idle rumor. I and my brothers were taken there as children to see this wickedness with our own eyes. I will never get the smell of the place out of my nostrils. Now, Odd Tangle-Hair, think carefully, for I know you are a young man who thinks about things. Are these really the devils you would have us be free to choose?"

"Princess, I would not willingly hang anyone. But were you not boasting only a moment ago of the twelve that your husband hanged in Suzdal?"

"But, in God's name—!"

"Precisely."

"Heigh ho!" cried Dag, breaking in upon us with a desperate laugh. "Can't we talk of something less gloomy on this fine morning?"

Our conversation was ended more effectively by Sirko at that moment dashing into the midst of a flock of cranes that were hidden among the tall reeds by the side of the lake. Red-headed and dagger-beaked, they rose up with a great clatter of wings.

Instantly all else was forgotten in the excitement of the chase. Ingigerd, unhooded her falcon and made three swings with her arm, letting go the jesses on the third and launching the huntress into the air.

The little peregrine soared upwards on knife-blade wings until she was only a speck in the sky. Then, choosing her target, she dove, falling like an arrow, while below we earth-bound creatures held our breath. But at the last moment she missed the mark, while the cranes continued to gain altitude.

"Now," breathed Ingigerd, "now show us your heart, little one."

To strike a second time she must get above her prey again, at the cost of enormous effort, for even one steep climb is enough to tire a falcon. The cranes were moving out of our view now in a direction away from the lake. Ingigerd, laying her head on her horse's neck, spurred it into the trees, heedless of branches and pitfalls, shouting encouragements to the bird. We raced madly after.

Again the falcon climbed and dove, and high above us there was a silent explosion of feathers. The dead crane, all legs and neck, fell to ground, the falcon descending after her.

Reining in our horses, we found her perched on the crane's body, which was easily six times her size, beginning to pluck at it with her beak. Sirko stood guard beside her in case the other cranes returned, seeking vengeance, for catching her on the ground, they would kill her.

Ingigerd, with careful movements, stroked the peregrine's back with one hand while she deftly hooded it with the other. Then, opening the crane with her knife, she cut off a bit of the flesh and fed it to the bird.

"I won't fly her again today, she's exhausted. You've done an eagle's work this day, pretty one."

After that, Harald, Dag, and I each flew our birds with good success at grouse and wild goose. As the afternoon light began to fade, we handed over our falcons to the servants.

"Let's go back again by the shore," said Ingigerd, "though it is not the straightest way to Novgorod. The lake is very beautiful at sunset. The loons call to their mates and, if we're lucky, we may hear a nightingale sing. The Rus grow sad and weep whenever they hear one," she smiled.

The setting sun splashed fire on the clouds, while we rode, not talking much, but listening to the conversation of the birds, and the lapping of the water, and the scrunch of our horses' hoofs on the pebbly shore.

We were skirting Perun's grove again and Harald turned to me and said he wasn't sure what a nightingale sounded like but he thought he heard—

What he heard was the whistle of a sling bullet. The first one flew wide but the second hit his right shoulder. He slid to the ground, writhing in pain while his horse reared and plunged away. Out of the shadowy grove figures leapt at us, their faces hidden behind grinning leather masks such as mummers wear, and shouting, "Perun! Perun!"

One seized my horse's bridle, another dragged me from the saddle and struck me a blow with a cudgel at the base of my skull that laid me out senseless. When I came to, the clangor of steel on steel rang all around me. I struggled to my feet, drew my sword, leapt into the melee.

"The princess!" shouted Dag to me. "Find her, watch her!"

But I had no chance to obey. One of our attackers came at me with a spear. I dodged his thrust and drove my blade into his side, then skewered another between the shoulder blades. Dag took his place beside me— leaping, whirling and striking everywhere.

But Harald was having the worst of it. It was like the bloody field of Stiklestad all over again. Just as on that day, he stood with his feet planted wide apart and wielded his long sword with two hands. But he had more assailants to contend with than either Dag or I, and as fast as one fell another took his place.

We cut our way to him and the three of us fought back to back. Soon seven or eight of the enemy, about half their number, lay dead or dying on the ground, their masked faces smiling as though death were a pleasure to them. The cries of "Perun!" grew thinner.

Finally, they'd had enough.

Three of them kept us in play until the others could drag their fallen friends out of sight; then those three broke off and dashed after their comrades into the trees.

We sagged against each other, gasping for breath. I felt my skull where I'd been clubbed, and hoped it wasn't cracked. It hurt like anything. From the ground nearby came a moan; Ingigerd raised herself on an elbow and called to us. Sirko, quivering in every muscle, stood guard over her. Helping the princess to stand, we saw on her forehead a red swelling and a smear of blood.

"A stone," she said, touching the place and wincing.

"You're very lucky," replied Dag, "it only grazed you. And none of them came near you to finish the job with steel?"

"I suppose they shrank from killing a woman."

"But Princess, you are dressed as a man."

"Well, then, God has been merciful! Would you rather I'd died?"

"Oh, on the contrary, Princess, your death, alone in our company, would be most awkward for us."

"Filthy heathen animals!" she shifted ground abruptly. "Obviously, the ones we surprised this morning, waiting in ambush for us. When my husband catches them he'll nail their heads to these trees, I swear it by Christ's Body!"

"Villagers of the neighborhood, you think?" Dag asked.

"What else?"

"Why were they masked?"

She shrugged. "Part of their devilish cult."

"Aha. But still, rather too well armed for peasants, wouldn't you say?

"Well then who, pray?" she rounded on him sharply.

"I'm sure I don't know."

While we talked, the servant lads came cautiously out of the trees some distance behind us, leading their horses and still carrying the hooded falcons.

"Why didn't you help us, you dogs?" growled Harald, shaking a fist at them.

"Leave them be," said Ingigerd, "they don't understand a word you're saying."

"Useless, then, to ask them what they might have seen," said Dag to no one in particular.

"What should they have seen, Dag Hringsson? If you have a thought, please say it plainly."

But at that moment Harald groaned and toppled over like a felled tree. The right side of his tunic was sticky with blood and a dark stain was spreading. Under the tunic, there was so much blood we couldn't find the wound.

"Spear," he grunted. "Went in deep."

"Not as bad as the one you got at Stiklestad old fellow," said Dag lightly. "Just you lie still now—you'll be all right." But to me he showed a grim face.

"He can't sit a horse," said Ingigerd, going to her grey, which stood nearby trailing its reins. "I'll ride to Gorodische and send back help."

But Dag was quicker and seized the bridle before she could mount.

"I can't allow you to do that, Princess, not with the woods so full of pagan marauders."

"I don't fear those dogs."

"Really? I wonder that you don't. I fear them, I confess, and I will feel much safer if you stay with us. Much safer. It's nearly dark now and I don't think they'll risk the chance of killing you by mistake."

"Who do you mean—the pagans?"

"Why, of course. Who did you think I meant?"

"Let go of my bridle, damn you!"

They stared hard at each other but Dag didn't flinch.

"Very well," she said at last. "You may be right."

She'd been beaten in this test of wills. It must have been an unaccustomed feeling.

"Thank you, Princess. Now, tell one of your boys to ride to Gorodische and return with bandages, and a sledge and team. The other two must ride straight to Novgorod and inform the prince what has happened, and ask him to tell Harald's hirdmen to row up to Gorodische at first light tomorrow. He's to say the order comes from me. I want Harald taken to his own dvor at Menevo without delay, and in his own ship."

"And if my servants are waylaid by the heathens?"

"Then, Lady, we will stay here and defend ourselves as best we can until we're found."

She issued curt orders in Slavonic to the youths, who saluted and galloped off.

And we four sat in watchful silence as night spread over the lake.

8

A COUNCIL
OF WAR

In due time we were fetched back to Gorodische and Harald put to bed in Ingigerd's own chamber. And the next morning his dragon ship arrived and tied up to the landing slip. One hundred and twenty Norwegians poured over the side, demanding angrily to see their young chieftain. Almost unnoticed in this crowd were Yaroslav and Einar Tree-Foot.

"What a business, what an outrage!" lamented the prince as he leaned anxiously over Harald's prostrate form. "Eilif and the whole druzhina are out scouring the countryside at this very moment. He insisted on it himself and rode out before it was even light—uncommon early for him. He'll pull their roofs down over their heads, have no fear."

Yaroslav, prepared for any eventuality, had brought along both a priest and a physician—the latter being, like Jarl Ragnvald's, a Greek from Miklagard. But Einar shoved his way to the front, and swore, by the Raven, that no one knew more about blade wounds than a Jomsviking. After some dispute, he was allowed to take charge of the patient.

"Boil me six onions cut up in a little water," he ordered.

A serving woman was sent in haste to prepare this dish. While we waited, he studied his patient. The blood had by now been washed away, revealing a black-encrusted stab wound about three fingers wide.

"The question is," said Einar tugging his beard, "are his guts pierced? Those other giblets don't matter a fart in the wind so long as the guts ain't

pierced. If they are, start digging his grave. Now, youngster, drink this."
The onion soup had arrived; he held the bowl to Harald's lips.

"Someone count to a hundred slowly. By the Raven, must I do all!"

Yaroslav being, by everyone's admission, the best educated among us, offered himself for this service.

As the count neared its end, Einar bent over the wound. "Easier when she's fresh, but it can't be helped," he muttered, and with his fingers pulled apart the crusty flaps of skin, ignoring Harald's groans. A trickle of bright red blood began at once, but Einar put his nose next to the wound and sniffed.

"Can't smell a thing; he'll live," was all he said, straightening up. He left it, as a task beneath his interest, to the Greek to patch up the wound.

That very afternoon, by Dag's order, Harald, swaddled in furs, was laid gently on the deck of his ship. I took the helm and put her about. We rowed past Novgorod and downriver another ten miles to Harald's dvor—the one he had been given by Yaroslav. He had visited the place once already and purchased some slaves for it, including one lovely young girl that Stavko let him have for a song.

✝

That evening Dag and I sat beside Harald in his bed-closet, with the door shut, and held a council.

"Sunsets!" Dag swore. "Nightingales! And the whole time leading us into an ambush! The first time we passed Perun's grove must have been to alert their lookout; she didn't take us that way just to argue religion with Odd here—which, by the way, my young friend, had better not happen again. Personally, I don't care if you dance naked under the moon, but keep it to yourself. This is a Christian court, as you may have noticed, and talk like yours has a way of getting to the wrong ears."

"Yes, Dag, all right—but an ambush? You're not serious."

"Never more. Why—you think she isn't capable of it? No, dammit, everything fits. Have you ever seen a battle with no dead left on the field, not so much as a single weapon dropped? Believe me, I looked. They left nothing behind that could be traced to them.

"And then back comes Eilif the next day without a single prisoner to show for his efforts, but with five wounded of his own, and claiming to have won a battle with the 'pagans', after which he hanged all the survivors, says he, and burnt down their village. Which I don't doubt—the hanging and burning—to make it look good. But those casualties were none other than the men we wounded, being smuggled back into town."

"And all this was done for the purpose of killing Harald?"

"And you and me, yes. And they damn near succeeded."

"You're forgetting the princess was wounded too."

"A sham. Self-inflicted. For a heathen, friend Odd—if that's really what you are—you seem strangely anxious to pin the guilt on them. Or does the fair Ingigerd's guilt disturb you even more? Don't set your foot on that path, my friend, it's a slippery one."

"Don't worry about me."

"I worry about everyone."

At that point Harald, who was so weak he could barely talk, gritted his teeth and raised himself up on an elbow. "I blame you for this, Dag Hringsson!" he said between clenched teeth. "You persuaded me to take refuge in Gardariki—refuge, you said. And what do I find but swords drawn against me! I'm as sore wounded as I was on the field of Stiklestad and it's your fault! Now, I want that woman dead—you hear me? I want her palace burned to the ground, I want her head brought to me on a pike, and Magnus's head with it! I've got six score Norwegians here ready to die for me, and every one of them a match for five Swedes. Now, you see to it, goddamn you, or it'll be your head on a pike, you hear me ... ahh!"

He fell back, clutching his belly; fresh spots of blood showed through the bandages.

Dag leaned forward and said in an earnest voice, "You're right, my friend, I underestimated her. I blame myself. I simply didn't expect her to move so soon. Now listen to me carefully, Harald. I wouldn't have brought you here if I didn't think the prize was worth the hazard. What happened today won't happen again. From now on we guard you well—a dozen of our best men with you at all times—waking, sleeping, shitting, drunk, sober. But as for Ingigerd, we smile and do nothing—no violence, no threats, no accusations—nothing. We bide our time. She has enemies; I know who they are. More important, we have a friend. Yaroslav. He favors you already, soon he won't be able to do without you. He must realize that he put his head in a Swedish noose the day he married that vixen. She and her relatives have just about stolen his country from him. And that's where we come in. We're the lesser of two evils, and not just to Yaroslav—the boyars will see it that way too."

"Then let's waste no time," I said. "I'll pay a visit on the mayor and arrange a parlay. It's a skald's job."

"Good. Do it at once," said Dag. "But disguise yourself somehow. Ingigerd has eyes everywhere."

Harald roused himself again. "I've never heard Dyuk Osipovich speak Norse. How are we to parlay with him?"

"I've been hard at work on my Slavonic," I said. "I'll manage."

"You—" he said with an expression that seemed to convey equal amounts of wonder and exasperation. I didn't like his tone of voice. We looked hard at each other.

After an uncomfortable moment, Dag resumed. It would take time, it would need caution. But when the moment was right we'd settle accounts with Ingigerd, Eilif, Ragnvald, Magnus—the lot. "But hit back wildly, Harald, like a blind man dueling, and we lose everything. As for our Norwegians, they must continue to believe in the pagan ambush for a while longer; I want no brawling with the Swedes, not yet."

"How do we explain the bodyguard to them?" he asked.

"Your dignity requires it, that's all. You're practically a boyar, aren't you?" Dag folded his arms and leaned back against the wall, his handsome face frowning. "Now you know what you're up against and you know my plan. If it doesn't suit you, say so and you'll see the last of me."

There was a long pause—too long. Harald gave him a sullen nod.

✝

That night I sat up late, chewing over the events of the past few days. The last thing I wanted was for Harald to be killed—on his success rested all my hopes. And I was more than half persuaded that Dag was right about Ingigerd, and that, having failed once, she would try again. And with what result? If she didn't succeed in killing Harald, he would surely kill her, whatever Dag said. The leash that held him in check was growing more frayed every day; sooner or later it must snap.

The thought of Ingigerd's death sent an unexpected rush of feeling through me, and left me with my heart beating fast.

A second thought came on its heels. Why, in the ambush, had I only been knocked down? Why had I escaped death, unless my attacker's purpose was not to harm me but to keep me out of harm's way? And, if so, on whose orders? Who cared so much that I should live?

That night, as if Perun of the Silver Face still watched from his Russian sky and muttered some warning to me, it thundered.

9

the holy
fool

Not long after our return from the hunt, Mstislav and his warriors set off in their log boats up the Volkhov, bound for his capital of Chernigov. Without his booming voice, the dvor seemed unnaturally quiet. The stillness was soon made deeper by a blanket of snow that smothered everything. A damp cold gripped the country and, though the palace ovens blazed day and night, still the walls were icy to the touch and we wore our fur coats to bed.

The cattle and horses that grazed in the prince's yard were brought inside now and lodged on the ground floor, where they and the slaves burrowed for warmth in the same straw. Snorting, lowing, bleating— all the various conversation of animals—together with their warm and comfortable smells rose through the floorboards to our quarters above.

By the end of November the rivers and lakes had become one great highway of ice reaching from the Varangian Sea to Lake Ilmen and beyond. As the ice sealed Novgorod off from the sea, it opened it to the land, for a horse can pull a sled over snow and ice at twice the speed that it can pull a wagon over a dry road. Thus, farmers from far and wide brought their goods to market more easily now than earlier in the year. Whatever cattle they hadn't the fodder for, they slaughtered, and on any day you could see in the market place heaps of rock-hard carcasses stacked with their legs sticking up in the air.

Four-footed beasts of a less welcome sort appeared in the city too.

Packs of wolves and wild dogs, driven by hunger, prowled the streets, even in broad daylight, killing livestock and the occasional child.

Dag and I were constantly on the alert for any new threat against Harald. Our warriors stood guard around his bed day and night while he recovered from his wound. But nothing untoward happened. Instead, life in Yaroslav's dvor settled down to a routine.

We rose every day before sunrise, following which the prince and princess, with others of the court, would hear mass sung in the cathedral of Saint Sophia. Following mass, the prince and his boyars would busy themselves with various affairs of state. At midday we sat down to a sizable dinner, the company consisting of the prince and princess and the senior druzhiniks, as well as an elderly sister of Yaroslav's and a great number of cousins who lived off his bounty.

After dinner, it was our habit to nap for an hour and then seek our own pleasures for the remainder of the day. Often we spent the time out of doors, riding, sledding, and skiing for exercise. It wasn't long before Harald was able to join in, although I think he was in more pain than he would admit.

Yaroslav, however, generally spent this time shut up with his books— he owned twenty-two volumes, more than I would have guessed existed in all the world. For this reason, he was known as 'The Wise'. Whenever he tired of solitary study, he would seek the company of priests and monks, to whom he was devoted. He delighted in posing biblical conundrums to the bishop, which, so I was told, frequently confounded that holy man.

At sundown we ate supper, which, in this frugal court, consisted mostly of the leavings from dinner. However, there was generally some sort of entertainment worth attending. We might have music played on tambourines and pipes by a troupe of wandering entertainers; or else Boyan, one of the Rus druzhiniks, a truly inspired man, would strum his gusli and sing heroic lays in the Slavonic tongue, which I was beginning by now to understand more and more of.

As the weeks went by, Harald began to spend much of his time in the company of Yaroslav, observing at close hand his manner of ruling. He would ask him questions, which the old man—delighted to find a willing audience—would answer in the most tedious detail, on everything from taxation, to the minting of coin, to the drafting of laws. All this Harald was storing up for the day when he would reign over Norway: for he was determined to be not only a king but a very thorough king.

Once a week the prince gave up his afternoon of study to meet with the Duma—the council of boyars. In this council sat (or, more correctly, stood) all his senior men whether Rus, Slav, or Northman. Harald, who had not yet received the title of boyar, although he paraded himself like one, was permitted as a special favor to be present at its meetings and also to bring me along. He needed me with him because of the babble of languages. Even among the prince's household, Slavonic was the preferred language except when talking to Northmen. (Yaroslav's children floated easily between the two tongues, using sometimes one, sometimes the other, and often combining them in a jargon that only they understood. I thought it doubtful that their children would speak the old language at all.)

I was making good progress in Slavonic, but Harald, like the typical Northman—even including Dag—had learned just about nothing of it. He spoke Norse to everyone alike, whether they understood him or not, only shouting louder when he met with incomprehension. Because meetings of the Duma were conducted mainly in Slavonic, I served as his interpreter.

It was in the Duma that we began to grasp how great a role Ingigerd played in everything that went on. She sat at her husband's side and never hesitated to give her own opinions, and attack those of others, whether the subject was hiring fresh levies of mercenaries, endowing a monastery, arranging a royal marriage, or even conducting a military campaign.

And boyars who would have knocked their own wives head over ass for a lot less presumption than that, often wound up grudgingly taking her advice because it was the best. Among themselves, however, they wondered aloud why the prince never beat her for her impudence. The conclusion was that either he feared her or loved her excessively: either way a disgraceful condition for a man to be in. It was even whispered about that she used spells, taught her by her old nurse or some local witch, to un-man her husband and make him submissive to her. In fact, it quickly became plain to us that no one at court had much admiration for Yaroslav. His crippled foot, his piety, his bookishness, his stinginess, and, last but not least, his wife were all counted against him. There wasn't a man in the druzhina but would rather have served under jolly and generous Mstislav if he could.

Here we saw our chance to undermine Eilif and indirectly attack Ingigerd, his patroness.

Harald was granted membership of Yaroslav's druzhina, but at the same time insisted that Dag and I and the one hundred and twenty Norwegian warriors who had come to Gardariki with him were his druzhiniks, to be kept separate from the others.

Harald had no sooner arrived in Novgorod than he bargained with Yaroslav over our conditions of service, insisting that each of us should have a slave woman to sleep with; should receive the unheard of salary of five ounces of silver each month; and should be given for rations a gallon of ale, four pounds of bread, a pound of meat (except on fast days), a half a pot of honey, and ten ounces of butter every day. Further, he asked that a new hall be built for us, larger and better made than any one of the five barracks halls that housed Eilif's men.

Yaroslav the Pinchpenny groaned, but agreed to it all. Why? Because, just as Dag had predicted, he was beginning to see in Harald the counterbalance to Eilif, whose surly incompetence was growing more intolerable every day. And the son of Ragnvald could do nothing but chew his lips in futile anger while he watched his authority over his men, little enough to begin with, collapse under the weight of one humiliation after another.

It was in this atmosphere that I conducted our secret negotiations with the mayor, as I had proposed to Dag and Harald. He and many of his fellow boyars deeply resented Ingigerd's power because her Swedish clique dominated their city and their prince. It was decided, then, that they would marshal support for Harald in the Duma.

Our plan bore fruit almost at once. A gang of bandits under a chieftain named Solovay had harassed the countryside for years. The druzhina, under Eilif's indifferent command, had made a show of chasing him, but always without success. Now Dyuk and his friends in the Duma urged that Harald be given a chance at him and Yaroslav leapt at the idea, ignoring, for once, his wife's objections.

Fifty of us on horseback tracked the bandit through snowy woods for a week, ran him to ground at last, and in a battle fought in a swirling snow storm captured him and brought him back alive. For his crimes, the man was publicly flayed and his skin nailed to a tree.

Suddenly Harald's name was on everyone's lips: villagers brought him gifts of trussed hares and geese, wealthy merchants invited him to dinner, and I composed a long poem in honor of his victory. It was all happening just as Dag had promised. Harald's star was rising, to the great satisfaction of us all. At about this time—hard as it was to believe when you looked at him—Harald celebrated only his sixteenth birthday.

I should say here plainly that there was much I admired and even envied in him—his ambition, his single-mindedness, his gift for leadership and skill at arms. I wished mightily to have more of those qualities myself. But, for all that, I knew that I could never be his friend.

He was, for one thing, dangerously unpredictable—alternating arrogance with bouts of despondency. Oftentimes he talked as though there was nothing in the world he couldn't do, and expressed a deep belief in his own luck: he could not lose a battle, no ship could sink under him, no horse could stumble. But there were other times, most often when he had spent the day drinking, when he would be irritable and gloomy and would pace the floor all night, tortured by the thought that Eilif, or Magnus, or anyone at all, might be preferred to him. At such times, the smallest setback or embarrassment (as I shall narrate later) would send him into a wild rage, during which it was neither pleasant nor safe to be around him.

(You may say, remembering my own outbursts on various occasions, that I am not the man to condemn Harald. The fact is, I found myself becoming less temperamental the more I was with him, owing to a feeling that one of us, at any rate, must be in control of himself.)

Harald was especially hard on the women he kept. I saw the bruises on them—not that this sort of thing stirred much comment. Once one of them came to me in terror of her life and I kept her with me until he cooled down.

At bottom it was anger and deep resentment and a sneaking feeling of unworthiness that drove Harald. His need for constant praise was more than I could cope with, and after a time I began to despise the hackneyed verses—even when they were deserved—that I churned out at his command.

✝

My growing estrangement from Harald was not the only thing to vex me during those winter days of 1031.

One day, not long after our return from the hunting expedition, Dag came looking for me in the palace kitchen, took me aside, and informed me in a low voice that my 'interesting views on religion' had recently come to the prince's attention—thanks, no doubt, to Ingigerd. But worse than that, Father Vorobey had charged me with being possessed by a demon. Yaroslav had told Harald, Harald had told Dag, and now here was Dag to tell me: something must be done.

I have not yet mentioned Father Vorobey.

He was what the Christmen of Gardariki call a starets, a holy fool. He lived in a tiny hut behind the palace, crammed with icons and tiers of candles that burned day and night. His matted hair and beard hung to his waist, his feet and chest were bare in every kind of weather. He lived on nothing but water and black bread, and he clanked when he walked on account of the chains which he wore under his ragged cassock. His age might have been anything from thirty to sixty. And he never washed.

Though he spent most of his time in prayer, he had the run of the dvor and would pop up at the most unexpected times and places—sometimes to stare in silent ferocity at whomever he chanced to meet, at other times to dance about, howling like a berserker, and then, just as suddenly, vanish. Yaroslav was in awe of the man and consulted him about his dreams and all sorts of other matters.

Vorobey and I had our first encounter just a day or two after my arrival in Novgorod. As Einar and I were prowling about the palace, getting the lay of it, he sprang upon us suddenly in a deserted corridor and commenced to leap about, pointing at us—or was it only at me?—with his bony finger, while screaming some incomprehensible gibberish.

I was dumbfounded, never having seen such a thing before. But Einar, nothing daunted, shouted his war-cry and advanced on the fellow with his sword drawn, whereupon the lunatic fled. We had seen nothing of him since and I had just about put him out of my mind.

But he, it seemed, had not forgotten me.

My demon, so he insisted to the prince, was the size of a small child, black, with hoofs and a long tail, and sat upon my left shoulder, making hideous faces at all who came near it. In the holy fool's opinion it was a heathen god—possibly Volos, though he couldn't be quite sure on that point. (Like most Christmen of my acquaintance, he believed that the old gods were real enough, but that they were creatures of evil—demons, in fact—who had tricked mankind into worshiping them.)

"So you see how it is, my friend," said Dag in his most engaging manner. "God only knows why Vorobey has picked on you, but I warned you there'd be consequences sooner or later, and now you really have got to face it. Christmas will be here before we know it and the whole druzhina hears mass on Christmas day. And the prince simply will not permit heathens with demons on their shoulders to spoil the proceedings. You must be exorcised and that's flat."

"And what must I do to be exorcised?"

"Whatever Vorobey says; he's the expert."

"And what then? Must I be baptized too for Harald's sake?"

"Not while the water in the font is solid ice," he smiled, "but in the spring—at Easter—yes, I think you'd better be. Would that be so very bad?"

"I will not do it."

"Dammit, Odd, I wouldn't ask if it weren't important! You've become an embarrassment to Harald; we can't have that."

"Ah. And why doesn't Harald tell me this, himself?"

"I don't know, I suppose he thought it might sound better coming from me."

"He thought, or you did?"

"Odd, this isn't getting us anywhere. Will you do as I ask?"

"I can't, Dag. My father worshipped the old gods—"

"*Everybody's* father worshipped the old gods! Times change, and we must change with them."

"It's different with me somehow—he's a part of me still. Maybe I am possessed. Do you think I am?"

"By a stubborn streak as broad as Thor's belly, if by nothing worse. Now look, Easter's a long way off. For the moment it will suffice to have you exorcised and prime-signed. Will you do that much for me?"

I recalled that my brother Gunnar had let himself be prime-signed when he began to trade with the Christian merchants on the coast of Iceland, because many of them pretended that a heathen's word wasn't to be trusted (as if theirs were any better). In itself it was a small thing— yet I hesitated.

"This Vorobey—he says the demon on my shoulder is Volos? What is Volos god of?"

"How the devil should I know that?"

"Because you know everything, Dag. Tell me."

He shrugged. "Oracles and poetry, I seem to recall someone saying."

"Poetry! Then just as Perun the Thunderer is their way of naming Thor, by Volos they must mean Odin."

"I suppose, if you want to look at it that way—"

"This starets sees truer than I gave him credit for! I am a poet and Odin is my god. I made up my mind to that a long time ago."

"Well, why don't you and Odin just have a good chin-wag about it then, and let me know what you decide!"

"Dag, don't get angry. I know this is important to you and Harald and all of us. If it is Odin, he'll give me a sign. And if he allows me, I'll do as you ask. There, I've said it."

"Well, I thank you for that much anyway," he sighed. "We'll talk again?"

"Surely."

He started to clap me on the left shoulder, as he often did; stopped, and made a wry face instead at the imp who squatted there.

✝

That night, before I went to sleep, I prayed for a dream, and I awoke in the middle of the night with the feeling that I had dreamt, though I could remember only a fragment of it. I was back in Iceland, a little boy again, and my father, looking stern but not unkind, was offering me his knife and a bundle of sticks, holding them out to me. That was all there was. But the meaning of it was plain.

Dressing quietly in furs, hat, and boots, and taking with me a lamp and a knife, I climbed over the bodies of my sleeping comrades and went outside. The moon was near full and the snow glittered like glass as I headed south along the river bank, leaving the city behind me. Across open fields I tramped until, at last, I came to a little copse of birch and rowan that grew by the riverside.

Fixing my lamp in the notch of a tree, I cut from one of the rowans sixteen slivers of living wood and scratched on each one, as well as I could in my mittens, one of the sixteen runes of the futhark. Then, putting the slivers in my hat, I shook them while I asked Odin to tell me by means of a sign whether I should obey Dag's command.

I drew one slip out and held it close to the guttering flame. It was 'yr', the last rune in the third aett, signifying the wood of the yew, which has the power to bestow wealth, favor, and protection: the best of all signs! Who can comprehend the mind of a god? But like it or not, I must accept his judgment, and my father's. I would do as Dag asked.

The next morning found me kneeling before the altar in the church of Saint Sophia. The prince and princess, the bishop, Dag, and Harald were there; Einar, too, keeping his gimlet eye fixed on Vorobey, while that man, with the most bizarre grimaces and gestures, stalked round and round me.

"Away with thee, O unclean demon!" cried he. "Take fright, leave, flee, depart! Depart to a waterless desert and untilled land where no man dwells!" Oh! it was making hideous faces at him and screaming blasphemous words. And, look there! it had jumped down from my shoulder and gone in my mouth, hoping to hide inside my belly. This was one of the cleverest demons, swore the starets, that he had ever matched his strength against.

"Out in the name of Christ!" he cried again, now gripping my shoulder from behind and pounding my back with all his might. "Volos, I command thee! Go from this man, from this house, from this city! Ah, listen, d'you hear its screams? It's in agony for we know its name! Out, Volos, out I say!"

I was the one who was in agony as he continued to thump my back and shake me until I thought my head would fly off my shoulders. Kneeling on the ice-cold floor with nothing on me but a white shirt, I began to shiver and suddenly sneezed.

"See, see! It flies from his mouth—d'you see it?"

Yaroslav ducked as though it were coming straight at him, and he and the others hastily made their cross.

"There it goes, ha, ha, ha!" laughed Vorobey shrilly, while pointing to the ceiling and pretending to follow it with his finger. "It's looking for the way out, for it hates churches! There you wicked, unclean thing, d'you see the door—there, out with you now! See? He's going—he's gone!"

The Holy Fool made a farting noise with his lips and pantomimed kicking the demon's ass. Then he mopped his sweaty forehead with his sleeve and sank upon his knees. "Volos is vanquished," he said in a portentous whisper, "the victory is God's. Praise Him with the sound of the trumpet, praise Him with psaltery and harp!"

The prince beamed at Vorobey, and the two men mumbled prayers together for some minutes, until the starets, leaping up suddenly and barking like a dog, dashed away out the door.

For myself, I do not believe that anything flew from my mouth, nor did I ever fear that Black-Browed Odin would be bested by such a creature as Vorobey. But I kept those thoughts to myself. Dag clapped me on the shoulder—without hesitation this time—and so did Harald: both of them, I thought, looking a little embarrassed; after which the bishop prime-signed me by touching my forehead with oil and making the cross over me.

And that, for the moment, was that. I can't say I felt any different for the experience, and almost my first act was to break one of their commandments. For it was on the very next day that Putscha came swaggering up to me to deliver a summons from Princess Ingigerd to attend her at her estate on the shore of Lake Ilmen.

10

I OBSERVE AN
OLD CUSTOM

A fog hung low overhead, caught in the skeleton fingers of the passing trees. My sleigh horse trotted briskly along the bank of the frozen Volkhov, and the jingle of his harness bells was the only sound to be heard in all that silent landscape. The cold was sharp enough to cut your ears off.

Putscha would say only that his mistress was enjoying a few days' solitude at Gorodische and that I was requested to drive out an hour before sunset in a sleigh which he would provide. I was to tell no one where I was going and I was to come alone, or I would find the gate shut in my face. To all my questions he only shook his handsome head and kept his lips shut tight.

The possibility of a trap occurred to me at once. Finding Harald too well guarded, she and Eilif had decided to get at him through me. I nearly told Putscha to take himself off and tell his mistress that I was not a man to be summoned here and there at anyone's whim. On the other hand, I thought, what kind of an adventurer is it who declines the adventure when offered? So I accepted.

As daylight faded from the sky, I arrived at her gate and drove my prow-nosed sleigh up the path that led to the house. As a groom ran up to take my horse, the door at the top of the stairs opened and Ingigerd stepped onto the balcony.

"Thank you for obliging me, Odd Tangle-Hair; come up and warm yourself."

Inside, I asked her pointedly the reason for my invitation.

"Yes, of course, you're curious," she said with a very pretty smile, "but first, there's a small ceremony to be gone through. It's a custom of the Rus to offer a visitor a steam bath when first he arrives. If I'm not mistaken, you've been owed this hospitality for some time now."

"Princess, my welcoming bath was a dunking in the Volkhov. And since then, I've not waited for an invitation, but have bathed every Laugardag as all Icelanders do."

"Still, it's a custom worth upholding. Will you humor me?"

A servant came up behind her and draped a robe of silver fox skins around her shoulders. She already had her boots on.

The bath was some hundred paces from the house: a little log cabin with two doors in its front, a water barrel next to the wall, and, nearby, a bonfire where two men were heating a pile of stones.

The Rus have taken up the steam-bath from the Finns, who once were numerous in this part of the country. This bathhouse so much resembled the sauna at Pohjola, where brave Ainikki lost her life, that the sight of it stirred a rush of memories and sent an arrow of pain through my heart. Yet, to my surprise, I found that I could not clearly see Ainikki's face any more. Had all those things really happened? Had there been such a girl and had I loved her? The thought of her now held only the sweetness of a half remembered dream.

"Are the stones ready, Blud?" Ingigerd's voice broke in upon my thoughts. Her Slavonic had a charming Swedish lilt to it.

Blud was an ugly brute with frostbite marks on his cheeks and a hatchet in his belt. He looked up from the fire and answered that they were.

"Excellent, then begin."

Blud and his companion, using wooden spades, levered three big stones onto a gridiron to which carrying poles were attached on either side. With the sweat running down their faces from the terrific heat, they carried the stones inside and tipped them into a trench that encircled a wooden platform in the center of the little room. They made several trips before all the stones lay in the trench.

"Go in, Odd Tangle-Hair," said the Princess. "Hang your clothes on the pegs just inside and mount the platform. Blud will see to the rest."

'Blud seeing to the rest' was what had me a bit worried. Yelisaveta's

story about how her great-grandmother, Olga, had burned up the
Drevlyan ambassadors in just such a steam-bath presented itself vividly
to my mind. I saw no latch on the outside of the door, but it was only
necessary to wedge a log against it and I would be trapped. Not for the
first time, the fear of being burned alive stirred in my bowels.

Nevertheless, I squared my shoulders and stepped inside, trying my
best to look at ease.

"There's a lamp burning so you can see to undress," the princess called
after me. "Do be careful of the stones. Enjoy your bath."

The door closed behind me.

I put my ear to it. Did I hear a noise? But this was absurd, what could
she gain from my death? I went ahead and undressed.

I had no sooner sat down on the platform than water, poured in
from outside, sluiced through the trench and over the hissing stones. Steam
erupted all around me, filling the chamber, and, despite my nervousness,
I felt myself yielding to the heat. Rivers of sweat ran down my sides; I
stretched out full length on my stomach and let a pleasant torpor creep over
me.

As usual, Tangle-Hair, I admonished myself, you've let your
imagination make a fool of you.

Like most steam-baths, this one was divided lengthwise by a
partition, making two compartments, each with its own door, so that men
and women could bathe together without seeing one another. On the
other side of the partition I thought I heard the door creak open. Another
bather? But the men brought all the stones to this side. "Who's there?" I
called in Norse and then in Slavonic.

No voice answered, but I was certain I heard breathing and the sound
of someone brushing against the wall. Blud with his hatchet! My muscles
tensed. I rolled from the platform, felt carefully for the edge of the trench
with my toes, for I was blind in the steamy darkness, stepped over it, and
followed the glow of the lamp to the wall where my clothes hung.

We men fear ridicule so much more than peril that twenty Bluds
would not have made me run out the door clutching my clothes in my
arms. I only wanted my sword. Thus armed, I crept back to the platform
and strained my ears to listen.

For a few heart beats, nothing. Then he brushed against the partition
again at the back of the chamber. A moment later I heard him draw a

breath—not on the other side but on mine. There must be a door I hadn't seen, or maybe a gap between the partition and the back wall.

Crouching by the platform, I tightened my grip on Wound-Snake's hilt, though sweat made it slippery in my hand. If I can't see, neither can he, I thought. He thinks I'm on the platform. When he strikes with his axe, I'll know where to thrust.

I held my breath and waited.

"Odd Tangle-Hair, where are you?"

A woman's voice? I reached out a cautious hand. It found a bare ankle, slid up a smooth calf. At the same time, I smelled the rosy scent of her perfume.

"What in the world are you doing down there?"

"Yes, well, I, ah, dropped something. It's not important. I say—it is you, isn't it?"

"Whom were you expecting?"

"Why didn't you answer me when I called out?"

"I wanted to surprise you."

"Well, you have succeeded, Princess."

"Come and lie down again."

Tossing aside my sword where I hoped it wouldn't be noticed, I obeyed. Ingigerd climbed up behind me and knelt astride my hips. Warm thighs embraced me, and strands of her unbound hair brushed my back. Her strong, long-fingered hands began to knead my neck and shoulders, then worked slowly downward to my waist and hips.

After a time she whispered, "Are you ready?"

"Yes!"

"One moment, dearest."

The slash of birch twigs across my buttocks came as something of a shock. I'd misunderstood her question.

She continued to whip me, laying on with a will, stroke after stroke, inflicting quite genuine pain—and yet, a pain that aroused me to an unbelievable degree. Impossible to wait longer! I rolled on my back and reached for her arms, but she slipped away, ran to the door and threw it open. For an instant she stood on the threshold, silhouetted against the twilit sky; then, without a stitch of clothing on, ran out.

I leapt after her, catching her round the waist before she'd gone many steps, and we fell together in the snow. She lay on her back and I upon her; her golden hair spread out around her like the rays of the sun, whose glowing center was her face. Her skin was slick with sweat and hot against my own.

"We'll soon feel the cold's bite," she laughed, and, sliding from under me, dashed for the house.

Up the stairs, down a passageway, and through a door I chased her—then stopped short when I saw that the room we'd entered was not empty. Three of her serving women plus Putscha, whom I thought I had left behind in Novgorod, huddled round the oven, warming themselves. They looked up as we burst in.

"Bless me, Lady," one of the women giggled, with a sly look at me, "I'll wager this 'un can do the job and then some. A good night t'ye both!"

Followed by winks and laughter, we passed through a door opposite and shut it behind us.

"You trust your servants pretty far, Princess," I said, still breathless from our exertions.

"I do—and now you must call me Inge, if we're to be lovers."

"Beautiful Inge—" I took her in my arms and tried to kiss her, but again she wriggled free.

"You're too hasty, young man! There are the decencies to be observed."

I watched in astonishment as she proceeded to drape kerchiefs over the icons that hung on the wall over her bed, and especially the large one of Saint Irene, her patroness. The woman would stand stark naked in front of Putscha's eyes but not this painted saint's! Next she removed the little silver crucifix from around her neck and said:

"Now that you're almost a Christman, my dear, you must learn to respect the things you previously scorned."

"I meant to ask about that, Inge. Was it you who denounced me to your husband?"

"Indeed it was. I whispered in Father Vorobey's ear, too."

"Why?"

"Well, God forbid that I should fornicate with a pagan!"

"Ah, of course, I see that."

In place of the crucifix she hung a little chamois bag, tucking it between her white breasts; it rustled faintly as she touched it.

"A charm against conception," she said. "A wise-woman of the neighborhood made it for me."

"Heathens have their uses then?"

"Ah, you're a clever one," she laughed, "far too clever for me! But now," she said, coming to my arms, "let us do the thing!"

By the gods, for a mother in her middle years she was still a magnificent woman! Breasts that could yet turn their pretty, pink noses upward, a stomach just nicely rounded, and below it a thatch of hair like spun copper. And she 'did the thing' as I had never known it done before; pulling me onto her, filling her hands with my hair, kissing my lips and neck, and moaning to spur me on. She reached her climax quickly but prolonged it for what seemed like minutes, as I thrust manfully away.

At last she lay still, breathing lightly, her eyes half-closed.

We lay together quietly for a time until, touching my lips with her finger, she said: "Please, dear Odd, don't misunderstand me. You're a lovely boy—no, don't start in again about your black hair and eyes—I mean it, a lovely boy; your face so serious, and so transparent. I'm trying to say that I could easily give my heart to you, if I had it to give. But I have loved only one man in my life—you must know who I mean. You may think me a fool to love a dead man, no doubt you're right. I didn't choose to; it happened, that's all. But, you see, there's no room for love between you and me."

It was only as she spoke the word that I could put a name to my feelings and realized that I had been in love with her from the day we met.

"If not love, then what, Inge?"

"The desire of flesh, nothing more. Will you have me on those terms? Say yes or say nothing, I won't hear words of love."

"Yes."

"And nothing more?"

"If it must be."

"Then that's settled." She nestled her head under my arm.

"But, Inge,"—a sudden doubt assailed me—" doesn't your religion condemn this desire of the flesh? Mustn't you confess it to Father Dmitri, your chaplin?"

She looked at me as though I'd lost my mind. "Confess? To Dmitri? I should say not! I am a daughter of Eve, through whom sin came into the world. Like all Eve's daughters I am weak and sinful by nature. And besides, I have been a dutiful wife and born my husband children. What more can he expect? I must be the woman I am. God and blessed Olaf will forgive me."

"As to God, Inge, I can't say, but I've met Olaf and, if I were you, I shouldn't like to run into him in the next world; there never lived a less forgiving man."

"You godless wretch," she answered, "how dare you talk like that." But she was laughing as she said it and rolled on top of me, covering my face with kisses. Which roused us to combat once again.

We decided to excite each other this time in less accustomed ways, and in so doing I could not help but see the inside of her thigh. Four long parallel scars ran the length of it. The gashes that produced them must have been frightfully deep. She explained that she'd once owned a bear cub with whom she loved to play, but that one day, without warning, it turned vicious and clawed her. Luckily, she always carried a small knife on a chain around her neck, which she was able to plunge into its eye and brain. She was eight years old at the time.

I found this a sobering thought.

Our second bout finished, she called to one of the women to bring us a tray of honey cakes and walnuts and a flagon of green wine. We ate and talked of this and that, chuckling over Einar Tree-Foot and Old Thordis, who, swore Inge, would be much improved in her temper if my friend bedded her.

When our hunger was satisfied, she lay my head in her lap and said, "Tell me everything about yourself, dear Odd, I want to know all about you."

I told her the bits I was proud of and she responded to each with looks of astonishment, or amusement, or sadness, or whatever the words suggested.

At last, after a night of talking and dozing and still more love-making, it began to be morning and I readied myself to go. (She had sent her women to fetch our things from the sauna; I noticed, with a blush, that my sword had been found and replaced in its scabbard.)

As I was pulling on my boots, she sat by me on the bed and, smoothing my hair, asked me if I intended to tell Harald where I'd been. When I hesitated, she took my face between her hands and said, "My dear, we both have masters—if I must deceive mine, you must also deceive yours."

"By no means will I deceive Harald as long as I accept his silver," I replied, full of righteousness. "On the other hand, I consider it neither his business nor anyone else's whom I make love to. Will you be content with that answer?"

"More than content," she answered meekly, and planted a chaste kiss on my cheek.

I drove back to Novgorod in the grey dawn of a gusty morning. The tossing clouds and swirling snow made a fit backdrop to the confusion of my thoughts. I could hardly believe what I had just done. Bedded a princess! A woman without peer in all the world. I had an urge to shout it aloud to the hills, I was that pleased with myself. Ah, but no. For Harald must never hear of it.

Here was the lie. Not deceive Harald while sleeping with his deadliest enemy? What troll-talk! And yet, if my answer satisfied Inge, as it seemed to, couldn't it satisfy me too—at least for a little while? Oh, but it was impossible, I must either tell him or never see Inge again. But to lose her! No, I couldn't think of that—not so soon, not with the smell and feel of her still so new.

And hadn't I handled myself well? A whole night of love-making and conversation and I hadn't made a fool of myself once (if you didn't count the steam-bath) nor betrayed Harald in any way I could think of. Nor would I betray him.

Yet in my heart I knew I was no match for this woman, fifteen years above me in age, and in experience older still. Thor's belly! What did she want of me?

Vaguely worried and perplexed, yet at the same time enormously excited, I drove straight to our barracks in Gotland Court and threw myself down on a bench to sleep.

✝

When I awoke my thoughts were no clearer, but I longed already to be with Inge again. She forbade me to call my feeling love. All right, then, it was a thing wholly of the body, but no less urgent for that. In my indecision, I yielded my will to hers and let her decide for us both.

In the weeks that followed we met constantly, in front of whole battalions of blinkered saints. Sometimes at Gorodische, sometimes in another lodge she kept near the village of Lipovo, sometimes, so help me, under Yaroslav's own roof. When I protested of the danger, she replied that she liked it best when it was dangerous.

She was a master at arranging trysts. There was a maple sapling that grew behind the dvor next to the men's latrine. She would send Putscha to tie a bit of thread to one of its twigs in such a way that no one who wasn't looking for it would notice it. A red thread signified that I was to ride out to Gorodische; a white one, that we should meet that night in her bed chamber in the tower; finally, a green thread meant that I should look under a certain stone at the foot of the sapling for a message, written in a cipher of her own invention. She took extraordinary delight in all this complicated business; I think it excited her as much as the love-making itself.

As for her servants, all of whom knew about us, she swore that they were absolutely loyal, and I could only believe her, though I wondered whether it was love or fear that made them so. Moreover, if it should ever be necessary to explain my absences to Harald or Dag, I was to say that I had spent the night at Stavko's house in the company of his ladies. That genial slave merchant was forewarned to support my alibi.

In the course of our meetings, I never found Inge precisely the same woman two days running. Sometimes she would be preoccupied with weighty matters of state, making me feel rather like an ignorant child. At other times she was a child herself—coaxing, pouting and playful. She loved any sort of surprise or secret, and was forever giving me elaborately wrapped trinkets and making me guess the contents before I opened them. I soon ran out of places to put the things where they wouldn't attract attention.

It was after bouts of love-making that she revealed more of her past to me. Novgorod and Yaroslav, she said, had been hateful to her from the first moment she arrived. Her husband's dullness and lack of energy drove her wild, his city bored her. The only things that made life bearable to her were wielding power and taking lovers. Yes, she had taken them before from among her husband's druzhiniks (what boyar's wife had not?), although even that pleasure was spoiled by the knowledge that she could parade them naked past his window, if she'd a mind to, and he would notice nothing. "And they call him 'The Wise'!" she laughed bitterly.

One night, my curiosity got the better of me and I decided to take the wolf by the ears: "Did Olaf bed you?" I asked casually as we lay naked under the covers, sipping from a goblet of mulled wine.

She struck the goblet from my hands, sending it flying across the room. "Don't speak his name! That man was holy—a living icon—don't even think what you just said!"

This sudden ferocity stunned me, but it answered my question. I was more certain than ever that Olaf in the flesh had been more of a disappointment to her than she could afford to admit. She had a gift for love and the only man she truly loved would not take the gift. Somewhere that must have left a deep wound. I wondered then and often again, whether when I, or Yaroslav, or any other man lay with her, it was his untasted kisses that she imagined she felt. Furthermore, she had transferred her passion for the father to his son, the shy and sickly Magnus; even professing to see Olaf's rugged features in every line of his wan little face.

On a different occasion, still mindful of the ambush that had nearly claimed Harald's life, I asked her straight out if she would go so far as to kill in order to protect the boy.

Instead of the furious outburst, which I half expected, I got a look of innocence that would have done credit to a virgin. "Are you asking me for a declaration of war, my darling? You men kill all the time and generally for no good reason at all, but with men there is always so much posturing and shouting and swearing and insulting to be got through first. A woman is different. Like the falcon, who does not make a speech before she strikes, a woman goes swiftly and quietly to the task at hand."

"And that's what you're planning for Harald, is it—a quick and quiet death?"

She laughed and covered me with kisses, which had the effect intended of distracting me from further conversation.

Even had the ambush never happened, I would have been a fool not to suspect her motives in taking me into her bed. But as the weeks went by and she made no attempt to wheedle even the smallest confidences out of me, suspicion surrendered to manly pride. After all, why shouldn't she desire me for myself? In bed I was young and able, in conversation not dull. Indeed, she seemed to find virtues in me that I never even suspected, and I began to think better of myself than I was used to.

Einar Tree-Foot, however, would not let me off so easily. He was the only man in Novgorod I dared confide in, because he had no other loyalties and, for all his cackle and conceit, he knew how to keep his mouth shut when it mattered. I was glad I'd taken him along—though I didn't always like the advice I got.

"Will you let an old man give you a word of warning?" he said one day when we happened to find ourselves alone.

"You will anyway, Tree-Foot, what is it?"

"Harald may be Dag's fool, but you're mine, and I worry about you."

"Why, because of Inge? Then you worry about nothing."

"Maybe, maybe not. You know that Thordis and me keep company. Now, I won't have it thought of her that she talks behind her mistress's back no more'n I talk behind yours. Still and all, not everything must be said in words. Tangle-Hair, you're like a man trapped in a pit with two wolves who want to tear each other to pieces—the wolves in question being named Harald and Ingigerd, just in case you don't take my meaning—and all I have to say is, look sharp that they don't tear you up instead. That's all the advice Einar Tree-Foot has to give you. I wish it was more."

"Thanks, old friend, but not needed. I'm quite equal to looking after myself."

Einar Tree-Foot snorted.

11

A Lovers' Quarrel

Harald, his face flushed with drink, lurched to his feet at the head of the table and proposed, "Yelisaveta!"

"Yelisaveta!" we answered, tipping back our mugs of ale and setting them down again with a bang.

That pleasant young lady was not, however, among the company; nor was her father, nor her mother—to whom we had already drunk 'Health' and 'Damnation' in that order.

It was early in the month of Yule and Harald was playing host in his new dvor to me and his dozen bodyguards for a day of sledding, fighting with snow-balls, getting drunk, and enjoying his latest purchases from Stavko's establishment.

Dag was noticeable by his absence: there had been a coolness between those two for some time now. As for me, I would far rather have been abed with Inge than damning her in Harald's company, but there was no putting him off this time. As the sun sloped toward evening, we had done the first two items on his list, were in the midst of the third, and anticipating the last.

But it was not to be.

At that precise moment one of those pretty slaves ran shrieking into the room.

"What the devil's wrong with you?" snarled our chief, with his usual good manners.

Not knowing a word of Norse, she could hardly be expected to tell him. But she motioned to the bed-closet and we all followed.

She had been turning the straw mattress and found something rather nasty stuck to the bottom of it—she pointed at it from across the room, not daring to go closer. It was a flat piece of wood, about three fingers wide and the length of your forearm. A brown mess of dried blood covered both it and the mattress around it.

"Odd! Odd, for Christ's sake!"

"Right behind you, Harald, don't shout. Here, let me get a closer look."

Despite the encrusted blood, the rune signs, large and deeply carved, were easy enough to read.

"They're sickness runes," I said. "It's a spell to bring the wasting sickness on you."

"Get it out! Get it out of here!"

He wouldn't touch it any more than the girl. It was up to me to peel it from the stiffened cloth and carry it over to the oven, while the others dove out of my way as though I were walking with a bar of red-hot iron.

"Don't stand there, damn you—get the mattress!" Harald flung the trembling the girl at the bed.

We consigned the rune-stick and, with some difficulty, the mattress, too, to the flames; but Harald continued in a remarkable state of agitation—not that anyone treats this sort of thing lightly, mind you. He shouted up his whole household—the stable hands, the kennel master, the falconer, the cook and her assistant, the jack-of-all-work, the girls he kept for fucking and other household chores, the whole pack of them—and proceeded to rant at them, slap them, and shake them till their teeth rattled, although most of them couldn't understand him.

Those who did, pleaded that they knew nothing about it. The mattress had not been turned in a week; the thing could have been put under it any time since then. No, they'd seen no strangers about the place. In God's name he couldn't think that any of them—

"Eh, what else should I think?" Harald fairly screamed at them. "One of you sneaking dogs is guilty and if I don't find out which one, I'll butcher the lot of you, see if I don't!"

Leaving them all quaking and the girls in tears, he next began to rush from room to room, sweeping crockery from shelves, pulling odds and ends out of cupboards, turning clothes trunks upside down in a search for other horrors. When he was through, the house looked as though a hurricane had swept through it, and all he had to show for his efforts was a cracked cup with a bit of mold and dust and cobweb in it.

"D'you see this? Do you see this?" He waved it under my nose. "Ashes of a burned cat, isn't it, Tangle-Hair? Or a baby! D'you think it's a baby?"

I thought it nothing of the sort but agreed anyway. It was not safe to contradict Harald at times like this.

He flung the cup at the wall.

"That bitch! Does anyone deny it's her? Eilif and his bully-boys couldn't kill me and she knows there'll never be a second chance now that I'm on my guard. So it's magic now! By God, I smelled witchcraft on her the first hour I met her!"

"Harald," I protested, trying to persuade myself as much as him, "nothing's more unlikely. Think back. You heard how she talked about the hanging of those heathen sorcerers, she's dead against 'em."

"You take a lot on faith, Tangle-Hair, if you swallow all that. You believe she grew up next door to Odin's bloody great temple at Uppsala and never did more than stick up her pretty nose at the smell? But we'll pay her back in her own coin. You shall carve a runestaff and slip it under *her* mattress."

For an instant I thought, Great Odin, he knows I sleep with her! But I managed to say calmly, "How should I find my way to Princess Ingigerd's bed chamber? And anyway, the runes themselves are nothing without the singing of spells over them, and that I know nothing of; no more than your assailant does, I think, for you look healthy enough to me."

But already he'd stopped listening and was off on another tack.

"Thjodolf!" he called to one of the bodyguards. "Drive the sleigh to town and come back with a priest—any priest, I don't care who—and holy water, he's to bring holy water, d'you understand? Hurry!"

He never stopped pacing the whole time until the sleigh returned bearing Father Dmitri.

To make short of a long story, the priest was told to sprinkle all the corners of the house with holy water while commanding the evil spirits to begone in Christ's name; and when he was done, Harald swore him to secrecy. Needless to say, Dmitri rushed off at once to tell everyone he knew and the incident became the topic of much conversation during the next few days.

Despite the cleansing of his house and all the reassuring things that I or anyone else could think of to say to him, Harald continued for more than a week in one of those black despairing moods that would overcome him whenever he felt himself thwarted or threatened. The men who were detailed to stay with him night and day looked half-mad themselves by the time the fog lifted.

I, however, had little time to devote to Harald's troubles; for I suddenly had plenty of my own.

A few days after the episode of the runes, I was summoned by Putscha quite openly one evening to call on the princess in her chamber after dinner. This surprised me for, as I've explained, her usual manner of inviting me to a tryst was by means of the colored threads.

This time, however, love was not her object. I found her in a spitting fury.

"Haraldsskald, what is this?" She thrust a cylinder of birch bark in my face before I was half through the door.

I knew without unrolling it what it was; I had written it. For some time, you see, Harald had been composing love poems (rather good ones, in fact) to Yelisaveta—or rather Elisif, as he always called her—and reciting them to her whenever an opportunity offered of getting her alone for a few minutes. But such chances came seldom, as Inge was, by now, well aware of his interest in her daughter and was doing everything possible to have the girl watched and any encounters with Harald swiftly terminated.

I hit on the idea of writing the poems down. And so lately I'd been inscribing them and passing them on to the other children to give to their sister on the sly. In the same way her answers were returned; answers which grew steadily more ardent and which were reinforced by the glances that passed between the two at meals, even though Inge made sure that they sat too far apart to speak.

"Do you know what it says, Haraldsskald?" Her voice was cold and accusing—a voice that made even boyars wince. I saw at once that I must not give in to it.

"Do you?" I asked.

"I'm not the scholar of the family, godammit, but I know my abc's!"

'Often in my dreaming
see I thou,
my gold-ring-Gerd,
my Gefn-of-Jewels,
winding and twining
thy white bracelet trees,
like a true wedded wife's,
around my body.'

—she read aloud in a voice that dripped venom. "I doubt she can understand half of it, such fantastic rubbish!" She flung the scroll away. "Father Dmitri found it among her school things and brought it straight to me. I had the children's room searched and found others. I found this, too, Haraldsskald." It was the sliver of wood with 'Elisif' scratched on it in Roman letters and in runes. "I know nothing of that heathenish writing, I'm happy to say; perhaps you can tell me how my daughter comes to have such a thing in her possession."

While I explained that it was only a harmless joke of Harald's, the thought nagged at me that her first question, if she really was ignorant of runes, surely ought to have been not, Why does she have it? but What does it say?

"Inge," I protested, "you've no cause to be angry with me. As you keep reminding me, I am Harald's skald, which you knew from the beginning, and I've done no more than a skald's duty."

"I did not expect that your duty included betraying me, you puffed up little sneak!"

"Betraying you! If anyone, I've betrayed Harald. Inge, listen to me—"

"You will call me Princess. I'm not Inge to you anymore."

"I most humbly beg your pardon, Princess, but you're talking like an ass. You told me yourself that Olaf sent skalds to woo you until your father forbade it? And with what result? The memory of Olaf has made you an unhappy woman ever since."

"At least, I was a woman, Yelisaveta's a child."

"Aye, *your* child. She's your daughter, like it or not, with all your fire and defiance. Fighting with her will only bring about the opposite of what you want. If you'll take my advice, let her see Harald as much as she pleases and I guarantee she'll find him unbearable within a month."

"What a smooth-tongued rogue you are. She'll find herself in his bed long before that! Carry this message to your master, skald. I will not tolerate his tampering with my daughter. He is nobody and the son of nobody. He is not worthy to take off her left shoe—tell him that. And tell him that if necessary I will send her to Pskov, where her uncle, Prince Sudislav, will keep her under lock and key until she marries Eilif in the summer. In the meantime, I will guard her more closely than ever; more closely even than Harald has taken to guarding himself these days. Tell that to your master, skald. Now get out."

Two spots of red burned in her cheeks.

"Inge, sweet, look at me"—I tried putting my arms around her—"this needn't make us enemies. We can still—"

"Putscha! Summon men to take this boy from my chamber if he will not go by himself!"

That made me angry. "Boy? Boy! I've been man enough for you up till now! No need to call for help, Princess, I'm leaving."

The heat of my feelings astonished me; no woman had ever affected me like this before. I spent the rest of the night drinking myself stupid and talking to no one, not even Einar.

After that, the days stretched into weeks of misery. To avoid seeing Inge, I took to spending all my time at Harald's dvor (without, of course, telling him why he was suddenly favored with my constant company). It was Yelisaveta herself who got word to him that her mother had found them out, had gone out of her mind with rage and given her the worst beating of her life, and that he was please! please! to write no more poems for the time being.

Harald laughed when he read me the note—it was this that brought him out of the funk he'd been in ever since the runestaff incident; he gloried in the sense of power that it gave him to drive Ingigerd mad.

I began to fear I was going that way myself. To take my private revenge on Inge, I jumped into bed with my slave woman (who'd been having pretty light duties up until then), plus all of Harald's (he was generous that way), and when I came to the last of them started in again; but done in anger it left me empty and unsatisfied.

I tried persuading myself that I was glad to be quit of the business: no more sneaking about, conspiring, fearing discovery every day. Yet day and night the same scene came again and again to my mind—a scene where Inge fell sobbing into my arms, pleading for forgiveness, and begging me to come into her bed again. And, oh how I wanted to! I was sick with the pangs of love.

12

CHE PIG
FARMER'S SON

Christmas morning.

I stood in the church with Harald and Dag and a great crowd of boyars and druzhiniks together with their families; stood for four interminable hours while the cold numbed my feet and crept up my legs. In Gardariki the Christmen think nothing of praying for three or four hours at a stretch and they have no benches in their churches. If only to keep the blood flowing, they are constantly in motion—crossing themselves, bowing, kneeling, standing again—and all the while smiling, whispering, and signaling to their friends.

Despite the discomfort of it, it was a spectacle worth seeing: The rumble of bass voices droning in the dark hollow of the church so as to make the floor hum under your shoes; the peopled walls alive with painted saints in the flickering candlelight; clouds of perfumed incense drifting in the air while the bishop and his minions, in brocades stiff with golden thread, performed their secret magic at the altar.

Yaroslav, too, appeared in full regalia with his sons beside him, all of whom, even to the baby, wore the golden torques of Rus Princes around their necks. And Ingigerd, standing with her daughters in the women's gallery, glowed like one of her own icons in silken gown and necklaces of topaz, amethyst, and pearl. Damn the woman!

The feast that followed marked an end to the six weeks of fasting which the Christmen observe before their god's birthday. Meat appeared once more in the marketplace and there began an orgy of eating and drinking throughout the city that lasted till Epiphany, twelve days later.

In times gone by, when Grand Prince Vladimir reigned in Kiev, the whole population of the town, rich and poor alike, it was said, were treated to a banquet in the palace. But Yaroslav was too tight-fisted for charity on such a scale. It was only the usual mob of furred and booted boyars, rowdy druzhiniks, and even rowdier monks that sat down to dinner with the prince and his family.

Still, this was a goodly number of guests, who in one sitting consumed (I was told by Cook) fifty-six roast pigs, fowls innumerable, an arm's length of sausage per man, and thirty casks of mead and ale.

In honor of the season, the floor and tables in the great hall were strewn with new straw; sheaves of wheat from the autumn's harvest were placed in all the corners; and a huge Christmas candle, its butt stuck into a loaf of Christmas bread, was set in the center of the table.

A few places down and across the table from me sat Inge. Laughing and radiant, she was devoting herself entirely to her husband and Eilif. Since it was out of the question that either of those two had said anything the least bit amusing, I concluded that her gaiety was put on for my benefit; she knew without even looking that I was watching her. Damn and damn her again!

Beyond Inge, on Eilif's other side, Yelisaveta sat. The young princess had never looked lovelier, what with gold rings plaited in her hair and her brocaded gown trimmed with ermine. But she was unhappy and didn't care who knew it. While Eilif, her betrothed, launched clumsy pleasantries at her like rocks from a catapult, Yelisaveta frowned at her plate or else turned round to feed morsels to her dwarf, Nenilushka, who took the offered food between her teeth like some pet animal.

Across from me sat Harald, so far separated from Yelisaveta (as was the rule now) that the two could not even see each other, let alone speak. He too scowled at his meat and ground it between his teeth as though it were his enemies' flesh and bones.

And this was only the beginning.

Two things happened in the course of our dinner that pretty well squelched the festivities.

The first concerned Father Vorobey, who always put in an appearance at the Christmas feast. As the hour progressed and he did not appear,

Yaroslav grew worried. The starets had not been at mass that morning either and no one, in fact, could remember seeing him since the week before last. Finally, the prince went himself to look for him in his hut, and found him—kneeling before an icon of the Virgin with his hands raised above his head in an attitude of worship.

It was only when Yaroslav ventured to touch him that he perceived the man was frozen hard as a rock. Apparently his supply of fuel had run out during the night while he was lost in meditation.

In tones of sorrow Yaroslav reported his bizarre and melancholy discovery to us. He hoped, nevertheless, he said, to prevail upon God to restore life to his holy fool, and the bishop hastened to assure him that nothing in the way of beseeching would be left undone.

We had scarcely recovered from this first blow to our spirits, when the second and by far the more serious one occurred—though it began innocently enough. The Christmen have a custom of giving each other gifts on Christmas day. Accordingly, while we ate, small presents from Yaroslav were handed round the table to each of us, Thordis acting the part of the babushka, or old woman, who customarily delivers them. In every case they were either glass beads, or copper-gilt brooches, or some other cheap trinket.

"Einar Sveinsson as goes by the name of Tree-Foot," said Thordis stopping beside him. "Nor not only something from the prince but a little bit of a thing from me as well, which hoping it won't be took amiss." Her old cheeks covered with blushes, she thrust two small packets at him and fled to the farthest end of the table.

Einar unwrapped the first packet, which contained a tarnished brass belt-buckle from our generous prince and provider. On opening the second he let out a merry cackle and held up for all of us to see—an eye-patch, made of red silk and embroidered all around the edge with golden thread. Not waiting a moment but whipping off his customary soiled rag, he put the patch on, adjusted it just so, and hobbled—one might almost say danced—directly down to where his lady-love stood and, before she could flee again, delivered a loud smacking kiss upon her lips, which caused the children to shriek with delight.

When the uproar had died down a little, Ingigerd said sweetly, "Thordis dear, if you can walk without your knees trembling—and I shall certainly forgive you if you can't—come here to me now for there is one more present I would have you deliver."

The nurse obeyed, some whispered words passed between the two women, and Inge placed an object in her hands.

"To Harald Sigurdsson," said Thordis, "with the compliments of Princess Ingigerd and may you always think of her when you look at it." This speech she mumbled very rapidly and, setting the thing down at his elbow, beat a swift retreat. You would suppose she knew what was coming.

The object, whatever it was, was in a cloth bag tied at the neck with a drawstring. With a wary look, Harald undid it, reached inside, and brought forth a silver pig—small enough to just fit in the palm of his hand and cunningly formed in every detail.

"Why—?" he began. Then turning it over he saw that it was a sow with teats.

"Happy Christmas," called Eilif with a grin all over his ugly face.

Great One-Eyed Odin, I remember thinking, here's the end of us for sure!

I was very nearly right.

Eilif and Inge, you see, were openly ridiculing Harald's inferior birth. He and his half-brother Olaf, you may recall, had the same mother, but while her first husband, Olaf's father, sprang from the Ynglings—the ancient royal line of Norway that boasted the god Frey as its progenitor— her second, whom she married many years later, was only a minor kinglet named Sigurd Sow. He had earned this ignoble nickname by caring so little for his dignity as to work side by side with the laborers on his farm, even to slopping the pigs with his own hands. Here, then, was Inge's revenge on Harald for trying to usurp Magnus' place as Olaf's heir and in daring to court her daughter. For, concubine's son though Magnus was, the Yngling blood ran in his veins but not a drop of it in Harald's.

"Suee, suee, suee!" Eilif cried, cupping his hands and yelling down the length of the table. There was scattered laughter, though most of those present hadn't the least idea what any of this was about. They only saw Harald's fist, white-knuckled, close around the pig.

Of course, he should have laughed too—that's what Dag would have done. If the enemy had sunk to such childishness as this, it was as good as an admission of their impotence. But Inge and Eilif knew their man better than that, and he didn't disappoint them.

"Eilif Ragnvaldsson, I keep pigs on my farm too," said Harald in a voice tight with anger, "nor am I ashamed to feed 'em with my own hands. And d'you know what I shall feed 'em with, Eilif? You! And the princess can call me 'sow' all she pleases while I feed you to my pigs!"

Dag tried to quiet him but, as usual, without success. Harald only got louder as resentments that had festered for years found their voice at last.

"You fancy Olaf's blood more than mine, do you, Princess? Why, when I saw it flow at Stiklestad it looked no different from other men's—no different from mine! Admire his blood, is it? Almighty God, his blood was cold as ice-water, for the man hadn't a human heart in him at all! But maybe you know that, eh, Ingigerd? Maybe you found that out for yourself, eh? Come, Princess, we know what he was like: selfish, cruel, stupid; if that's how saints are made, then I reckon he is one!"

It was exactly what she'd hoped he would do. Every Norwegian face in the room wore an expression of shock.

Clutching the pig in his huge fist, he rose and came along the bench towards her. She stood to face him—fearless, though he towered over her. Eilif, the coward, kept to his seat behind her, doing his best to look innocent.

"Princess," said Harald, "it's a fine gift you've given me—too fine for a farmer's son. You would have spent your silver better, Lady, to hire more assassins, more heathen witches! That's your style, isn't it?" He drew back his arm. "So I give it back to you, Princess, to remember me by—"

Harald flung the pig in a downward direction at Inge's head but she dodged to the side and instead it struck Eilif square on his forehead. The whites of his eyes rolled up and he slid senseless to the floor. The pig, rebounding, skittered along the table top and came to rest in front of Yelisaveta. She, with a flair for gesture worthy of her mother, picked it up and touched it to her lips.

Immediately Eilif's Swedes, those who were at table with us, leapt to their feet—not that they gave half a damn for their captain but the honor of the druzhina was at stake. Of swords and axes there were none, thankfully, for on Christ's birthday we were forbidden to come to the table armed for war, as we usually did. Still, there were lots of knives about.

What saved us was Yaroslav, for a change, behaving almost like the master of his house.

"Harald Sigurdsson, in God's name, have you gone mad? Shedding a man's blood on this day and breaking the peace of Christ? No, gospodin, it can't be tolerated. Now I shall ask you to, ah, to take your men and leave this hall at once. D'you hear me? Nor show your face again until I give you permission. There. There you are, sir."

To my great relief—for I figured he was quite capable of battering Yaroslav too in his present mood—Harald obeyed. Our men, reluctantly leaving behind their roast pork and sausage all but un-tasted, fell in behind him and we stalked out of the banqueting hall in silence. As I turned to go, I saw a smile on Ingigerd's face. Short of producing a bloody riot, this had surpassed all her expectations. She had dealt her enemy a death wound this time.

When we had Harald alone in one of those little rooms nearby the hall, Dag was not slow to tell him why:

"Idiot! What do you think has kept us afloat at this court? Olaf! That king, whose name you made so free with, happens to be our only piece on the board—without him we have no game at all! Nobody but Ingigerd cares if you're a bloody Yngling or not. You are brother to a saint! You fought at his side. To save his precious life you shed your blood. That is why our Norwegians follow you instead of Magnus. And what do you do? You mock him, you insult his memory! God in heaven! She set a trap for you and you fell right into it! Does nobody here use his brains but me!" He paced around the room, pounding his fist into his hand. I'd never seen him so angry.

But Harald put an end to our little discussion with a bellow of rage and frustration, "Out of my way or I'll break you! I want no more advice from you or anyone!"

Assuming that 'anyone' included me, I stood back and gave him a clear path to the door, where he was headed. So did Dag at the last moment, or I'm sure Harald would have torn an arm off him at the very least. As it was, Dag looked crushed. Our game was finished. It had been a piece of folly to begin with. Ingigerd had only to find out Harald's weak spot, stick in the knife and twist it; he had done the rest all by himself. Damn the woman!

Harald rode off to his dvor, no doubt to beat the servants bloody and have a good brood. Dag and I pushed our way through the mob of Norwegians who crowded round us in the vestibule, shouting angry questions, and hastened off to an ale house in the town, where we too could brood, like black-hearted Loki, over the ruin of our world. Not wanting to spend the night either at Harald's, or in the barracks, or the palace, we wound up sleeping there.

By the next morning, however, Dag had regained his spirits somewhat. Harald had been victimized, dammit; insulted most intolerably! What man of spirit would not have taken offense? Prince Yaroslav was a fair man and must already be regretting his wife's low attack on the most enterprising of his officers. We must get to Yaroslav, he said decisively, without a moment's delay.

Unfortunately, we couldn't, thanks to Father Vorobey having picked this inconvenient moment to die. Yaroslav, to my amazement, was quite serious about restoring him to life. For three solid days and nights, stopping only for a little sleep and nourishment, Yaroslav badgered the Virgin Mary to carry his prayers to God, while the bishop (whom I always suspected of despising the Holy Fool) laid on the incense and the music. Meanwhile the grumblings of the Norwegians grew louder as their chief continued to hide from them. Finally, Yaroslav had to admit defeat and ordered the carpenters to prepare a coffin for Vorobey which would fit his unusual posture—it proving, by this time, impossible to straighten him out. (I barely controlled the urge to suggest that they mount him on the palace roof until the spring thaw; what a striking masthead it would have made!)

The funeral at last concluded, we were admitted to Yaroslav's study where we found the old man weary and depressed.

I won't try to recount all our conversation, which was halting and disjointed, as the prince seemed barely able to concentrate on our words. Dag mentioned Ingigerd's name but Yaroslav silenced him with a gesture of annoyance. Plainly, he would hear nothing against her. All right, we decided, ignore Ingigerd, concentrate on Eilif. That line of attack succeeded beautifully. Yes, of course, Yaroslav agreed, the whole business was Eilif's fault and he must be made to pay. Messengers were dispatched at once to summon Eilif and Harald to an audience, and the one to Harald was instructed to say that he would find the outcome very much to his liking.

The captain of the druzhina was first to arrive, with a nasty purple lump on his forehead. Mind you, he'd only just gotten rid of the splint on his right wrist a week or so before. The question, I thought, was not so much whether Harald or Inge would prevail in the end but whether Eilif would live to see it.

To be brief, Eilif was found guilty of provoking a fight on the Lord's birthday and condemned to pay Harald twenty times the weight of the pig, an amount equal to forty grivny, in silver. Harald's spirits lifted instantly as Eilif's plummeted, and he went straight from the palace to the Norwegian barracks, where he found most of his men sitting about the place idle, disgusted, and truculent. But here was Harald at his best. Stick him in front of some fighting men and no one had to tell him what to say. Ingigerd had thought to divide him from his men, to whom Olaf's name was sacred, but she made the mistake of underestimating his enormous natural talent for talking to simpletons—which is surely the greatest part of being a successful commander.

Leaping up on a table and calling them his fellow soldiers, he looked them squarely in the eyes and swore he hadn't said any of the things they'd heard him say, and offered to lay his hand on a red-hot anvil if his word wasn't good enough for them. Without giving them too much time to think that over, he promised to divide amongst them the entire amount of silver owed him by Eilif, because it was they who had been insulted, as much as himself, and damned if he would let some bloody Swede get away with that! And didn't they wind up cheering themselves hoarse and carrying him round the barracks on their shoulders!

But there was still worse to come, from Ingigerd and Eilif's point of view. Dag that very night came up with an inspired idea, the sort of thing only he could have thought of, and instructed me to mention it to Harald. His advice would get a better hearing, he knew, if it came from me, which, after all, was what I'd been enlisted for in the first place.

The result was that after dinner the following day Harald asked Yaroslav's permission to speak to the assembled court. In the hearing of all the druzhiniks, both his Norwegians and Eilif's Swedes, he proposed the dedication of a church to Saint Olaf, to be built entirely from contributions and to be a place of worship for all the Catholic Scandinavians in Novgorod. If the prince and princess would give his project their blessing, he himself was ready to lay down a hundred pounds of silver on the spot to start it going.

Bishop Yefrem turned a lovely shade of purple—being Orthodox, you see, and hating the Catholics—but he suffered it in silence.

As did Ingigerd also. From the expressions that crossed her face, I could just about guess her feelings: first, astonished mirth at the very nerve of him; then dismay as he seemed to be actually getting away with it (the table pounding of the druzhiniks, including even the Swedes, was thunderous); and last, cold fury as the realization dawned that she could not afford to oppose him and, in fact, must publicly congratulate him for these pious sentiments.

Hating her as I did—oh, yes, I had hated her for weeks now, did I forget to say so?—hating her as I did, I delighted in her twitching lips and stumbling words. At last this proud and foolish woman had taken a fall!

All in all, the tables had been turned very neatly. Not only was Harald not divided from his men—quite the contrary—but Ingigerd and Eilif came out of the affair looking very bad. For Eilif it was a disaster. Offering a scurrilous insult to Harald in the first place, then letting himself be floored without striking a blow, and, to top all, being fined forty grivny for his pains—it stripped him of the last shred of authority. Oh, he went on posing as captain of the druzhina, but from that time on he had no influence with the men at all, and they, held in check by neither a prince nor a captain whom they respected, soon got completely out of hand.

As for the famous silver pig which started it all, taken and hidden by Yelisaveta and passed from child to child, it finally came back to Harald, who showed it off to everyone as if it were a badge of honor. Altogether, very neat.

Curiously enough, it was the very next day that, happening to visit the palace latrine and happening, for some reason, to glance at our 'message tree', I saw a red thread tied to its twig.

You recall that I just said I hated Inge? My heart leapt to see that red thread! Leapt as if nothing else mattered in all the world but her; leapt and went on leaping the closer to Gorodische I came, for I commandeered a sleigh and set off on the instant.

To my knock the door flew open and Inge, my lovely Inge, threw herself into my arms, buried her head against my chest, and through her tears told me how miserable she had been and how we must never, never quarrel again, and without a second's delay drew me into her bedroom and began to pull off my clothes, and as we made love and she neared the climax, cried, moaning, that she loved me.

Well, I mean to say—how often do one's daydreams come true?

✝

The next day I will always remember for pure, free, careless joy. Never mind what came afterwards—I would not part with the memory of it for anything. I drove our sleigh over dazzling fields of snow, with Inge, swathed in ermine, on the seat beside me—red-cheeked, snow crystals on her lashes, laughing as we tore along at a breathless pace, and Sirko raced beside us. Afterwards, we dined at her lodge on caviar, goose, and venison, and in the evening drank wine and made love. During the whole time we never spoke the names of Harald, Eilif, or Yelisaveta. As it drew towards night, I took my leave of her with many kisses and set off homewards. (She would remain at Gorodische one more day, we decided, for appearance's sake.)

As I entered the Norwegians' barracks, Dag sprang upon me as if he'd been watching out for me all day long, and asked me, in a tone I didn't quite like, to take a walk with him.

"Just how long have you been romping on the princess's belly?" he asked straight out. Never a one to mince words, Dag.

"What? Don't be absurd. I don't know what you're—"

"Save your breath. It was a suspicion and you've just confirmed it. You're a bad liar, Odd, it's one of the things I like about you."

"How did you guess?"

"One notices things—especially when the lovers have quarreled."

"Who else knows?"

"Do you think you'd still be alive if anyone else knew?"

"I see. And what do you plan to do now, tell Harald?"

"Oh, I like you much too much for that, but you must earn my silence, Odd. Ingigerd will try again to kill him and keep on until she succeeds. I don't underestimate either her malice or her resources."

"Nonsense! I know she'd like to see his backside going away, but you haven't a speck of proof that she ever tried to kill him."

"Jesu! What a performance she must be putting on for you, I'd love to see it. But the facts, my friend, are otherwise, whether you care to face them or not. Now, setting aside your tender heart, I have to know what she plans to do next."

"If you're asking me to spy on her—"

"Asking you? I'm telling you. It's that or face Harald—who will not be pleased."

This was bluff. Harald would raise such hell that all Novgorod would know about it by morning, which was the last thing Dag wanted. We'd all have to pack up our kit and leave.

"Then, tell him and be damned! I haven't betrayed the smallest confidence. She asks me nothing about him."

"How would you even know, you innocent! Can you account for everything you've said to her? Every word—what he likes to eat, whom he sleeps with, the hours he keeps, who guards him at night."

"No, nothing!"

He stopped to look at me long and hard. "Give her up, Odd."

"No."

"What d'you think—that she loves you?"

"What I think is none of your business."

"You are a stubborn lad, as I begin to see."

"I could have told you that."

"It won't last, you know. Sooner or later Harald or Yaroslav will find you out; either way it'll be the end for you, and probably for us all. What am I going to do with you?"

"I should have me killed, Dag Hringsson, if I were you. There's nothing else for it."

He let out a sigh that hung frozen, a little cloud of ice, in the air.

"It may come to that. In the meantime do me, at least, the favor of keeping your mouth shut and your ears open. You owe me that much. And for the rest, God help us." He turned abruptly and walked away.

Poor Dag. What a task he'd cut out for himself: making Harald and me—his two trained bears—dance the steps he gave us. I saw weariness in his eyes and the beginning of fear. Fear, I think, that he was building on sand and that the first strong tide would wash us all away.

13

i become
a sinner

The coming of spring to Novgorod is announced by the river with sudden loud cracks, as the solid center breaks up into jagged floes, and softer clicks as the floes dissolve in a myriad tinkling pieces—bobbing and whirling away downstream between the ice-bound banks. When the last ice is gone, then the boatmen go down to their vessels, which have lain stuck fast in the river all winter, and haul them out to careen and re-rig them.

Now the rain comes in crashing thunderstorms that wash the snow down in torrents from the hillsides and make the river overflow its banks. It's a rare spring that sees no houses swept away in low-lying parts of the town. Even the ground floor of the palace is often awash, although they have installed gigantic pipes made of hollowed tree trunks to drain it.

Rain and melting snow turn the ground into such a quagmire of sucking mud that a horse or man will sink in it up to his knees. Not until mid-May do the fields dry out sufficiently for the 'black people' to get on with their planting.

The spring is an unhealthy time of year as well as an uncomfortable one, with pestilence and fevers common. I was spared a second bout of my fever, but many others in the town fell sick. Magnus, just past his ninth birthday, fell ill and for a while looked like dying. Ingigerd, haggard and red-eyed, kept vigil at his bedside until the crisis was past.

Yelisaveta said bitterly, not caring who heard her, that her mother would not have wept half so much over one of her own.

Easter, and the day of my baptism, were not far off. Einar had decided to be baptized with me and was looking forward to it, for the reason, he said, that he wanted a new suit of clothes. Why, he'd known a man once that was baptized four times just for the white clothes they gave away!

As the day approached, he and I, together with some warriors newly arrived from the heathen parts of Sweden, were ordered to take instruction in our new Faith under the tutelage of Father Dmitri. Hollow of cheek, long of nose, and thin of hair, he took his place before us in one of the palace rooms, leaning upon a lectern, while we sat before him on rows of benches.

We were but rude, simple men and had no idea what a great deal of explaining we were in for.

Right at the start he ambushed us with the three gods who were One, and the Son who was half god and half man. But soon, seeing some of us begin to stretch and others to yawn, he paused to assure us that as soon as we were proper Christmen, God would answer our prayers.

I was overjoyed to hear this for I had a number of prayers all ready— the chief of them being that Yaroslav should never catch me in bed with his wife. Some others in the audience, impatient of waiting for the glorious day, began to shout their prayers aloud, much to the priest's dismay, seeing that most of them had to do with 'sticking a sword into that bastard Svein', or 'getting their hand up Grushenka's skirt'. We got merrier and merrier, with each of us trying to outdo the prayers of the others, until the priest could scarcely be heard above the din. Only after shouting and flapping his arms for some time, was he able to recapture our attention for his next topic, which was the Creation of the World.

He read us the verses about God creating the world and placing Adam and Eve in the Garden, and added that all this had taken place exactly six thousand five hundred and thirty-nine years ago in the month of September.

"Now really," said I, raising my hand, "I'll believe the six thousand and so forth if you like, but how can you know it happened in September?"

"Easily explained, my son," he replied, looking down his long nose at me. "Didn't Eve give Adam an apple? All right, and aren't apples picked in September?"

Well, everyone laughed and I felt like a fool, so I kept quiet for a while.

From describing the Beginning of Things he skipped right to the End. In the Last Days, he said, mankind would be beset with continual wars and plagues. Antichrist would appear on earth. At the same time there would come four Kingdoms of Beasts and the giants Gog and Magog would fight against the true Christmen in a great battle at a place called Armageddon. After this, Christ would descend from Heaven, for the second and last time, to pass judgment on us all. Thereafter, the wicked would spend eternity in Hell, with molten pitch, sulfur, lead and wax being continually poured on their heads. But those who enlisted in Christ's druzhina—here he lifted up his eyes—would have eternal life in Paradise.

"Doing what?" one fellow in the back wanted to know. "D'you mean fighting all day, as they do in Valhalla, and, when you're killed, coming to life again next day to fight some more?"

"Good God, no!" He'd meant no such thing. "Paradise—," he said, "Cherubim and Seraphim—throne of God—harps—"

"Pah!" the questioner spat. "You call that life?"

There was much laughter at this, but the priest, scowling and wagging his finger at us, warned that we were already living in the Last Days! For how else to account for the Infidel Arab enslaving half of Christ's earthly empire, and what could that portend but the beginning of the End?

That put a stop to the merriment.

But we Norse, I thought to myself, have no need of Christmen to teach us about the end of things. Why, change a few details and it's the same story my father used to scare me with when I was a boy and we took those long rambles together in the night: Ragnarok—the doom of the gods—when Loki, and the Giants, and Fenris Wolf storm the towers of Asgard and bring them crashing down. And since our religion is plainly much older than theirs—for Odin the All-Knowing walked the earth long before Jesus—it must be from us that they got the story and now pretend they thought of it themselves!

As I turned this over in my mind, a wave of memory surged through me with such intensity that for a moment I felt again the chill of those long-ago nights and my father's rough hand on mine. Fear and longing filled me both at once and suddenly I shivered with the uncanny feeling that he was near me. Strange how this priest's words stirred feelings in me just the opposite of what he'd intended.

Having given us a proper scare, Father Dmitri proceeded to instruct us how the White Christ would save us from our wickedness, and how even a fool could see that he was the True God, because didn't it say so right here—and here—and here? And he began to read us some verses of old prophecies. But it was all such a jumble of foreign names and obscure arguments that we pretty quickly got confused; especially when he said that these prophets, by whom he put such store, were all Jews, but that the cursed Jews themselves refused to believe a word it!

I won't tire you with all the rest of our first day's lesson. He told us about how Jesus commanded us to love our enemies, so that if a man hit you on the one cheek you were to offer him the other also instead of splitting his skull for him as he damn well deserved. One grizzled warrior asked sarcastically, "What's Yaroslav paying us for, then—to kiss his enemies?"

That plainly was a hard one for Father Dmitri. He started to say one thing, then started to say another, rolled his eyes in despair and raced on to the subject of miracles.

Making the blind to see and the lame to walk, and even raising folk from the dead—why, Christ and his druzhiniks had done all that just as easy as anything—not to mention those many saints who came along afterwards right up to our own day.

But here I couldn't keep myself from asking, "Excuse me, but what about Father Vorobey? He was still as cold as yesterday's mutton after three days trying to resurrect him."

That seemed to be another hard one for the priest, and he could see that we were getting restless, being active men not accustomed to sitting for very long at a time, so he went straight on to the Crucifixion.

Now this story, too, the Christmen have stolen from us. Again, my thoughts flew back to Iceland and I heard the sound of my father's voice shouting these words of Odin All-Father's to the echoing hills:

> *Nine nights hung I on the wind-whipped tree,*
> *Whose root sinks deeper than man's knowing.*
> *I, Odin, by a spear transfixed,*
> *A sacrifice to Black-Brow'd Odin:*

Myself to myself.
They gave me neither bread nor drink,
Yet down into the depths I looked,
Down, down I reached and grasped the runes,
Screaming, grasped them, flung them up
And then fell back.

Well, you can see the similarity at once, except that Odin, through his suffering, gave us the runes and, with them, poetry and divination, while the White Christ, so far as I could see, gave only a license for one half of mankind to persecute the other half.

But to come back to Father Dmitri's lecture, he was describing the murder of Christ by the Jews with such liveliness and emotion that suddenly Einar Tree-Foot could stand it no longer.

"By the Raven," he cried, jumping up and brandishing his sword, "none would've dared touch him if my Jomsvikings had been there!"

Instantly the room exploded into shouting and stamping, and many others drew their swords and swore that, by the gods, let 'em just see some Jews anywhere about and they'd send 'em away holding their heads!

Well, the scene got wilder and wilder until, at last, Father Dmitri just gave up and fled the room, hugging his book to his chest.

That night a mob of Swedes ransacked and burned some shops near the market, which were said to be owned by Jews. The flames spread quickly and came so near the palace that there was panic inside and everyone rushed about with buckets, wetting down the roof and walls. Even so, it was only a sudden change in the wind that saved the dvor from going up in flames.

Yaroslav was as frightened as anyone. He shouted for Eilif to take charge and do something, but, when they located the captain of the druzhina, he was lying drunk in bed with a slave woman. His rival then was sent for. Mind you, they might easily have found young Harald in the same condition as Eilif on any given night, but his luck saved him once again: he was reasonably sober and not otherwise occupied.

He called out the Norwegians, half of them armed for battle and the other half with buckets and blankets. The rioters were dispersed in short order but our best efforts could not prevent the fire from raging out of control. It leveled the Market Side all the way from Carpenters' Brook to the Mound, destroying four churches and sixty houses before it was done—and that, despite the red roosters that all Novgorodtsi paint on their doors to protect them from the ever-dreaded flame.

Two days later, Yaroslav, backed by Harald's strong arm, cashiered thirteen of the ringleaders without pay and banished them from the city. No matter how justified might be a Christman's hatred of the Jews, he lectured them, arson could simply not be tolerated in a city built of wood.

At the same time he rewarded Harald with the gift of a fine silver-inlaid battle ax and extra rations for our men. And I commemorated the event with a poem in which I devised kennings for 'fire' more elegant and obscure than any ever heard before. As for Eilif, he didn't show his face at court for a week.

After things had had time to settle down a bit, we were recalled to our catechism. This time Father Dmitri, carefully avoiding anything to do with the Jews, spoke about Saint Vladimir and the conversion of the Rus, concerning which I had heard something already from Stavko.

"Now Vladimir, my children," the priest began, "was, in his early life entirely given up to lust, for he kept eleven hundred concubines—far surpassing the number that even Solomon had—and was married to five wives. One day, however, God put it in his heart to renounce his heathen ways and seek a new religion. Now, being ignorant of all other religions, he did not know how to choose one and so he sent his four most trusted boyars on a long journey for the purpose of investigating the various religions of men.

"They traveled first among the Volga Bulgars, who are followers of Mohammet, but returned, saying that they found no joy among them, in particular because strong drink was forbidden by their holy law. Vladimir was appalled. 'The Rus', he said, 'cannot live without strong drink'.

"Next, the four envoys visited the Germans, who are Papists, but returned saying, 'Their churches are cold and there is no beauty amongst them'. Last of all, they journeyed all the way to Miklagard, which is both New Rome and New Jerusalem, and whose Emperor is God's viceroy on earth. And this time, when they returned to Kiev, they could scarcely tell of the wonders they had seen, for words failed them. 'When we entered the Cathedral of the Holy Wisdom', they told the Grand Prince, 'we did not know if we were on earth or in heaven. Surely God dwells there'. Vladimir believed them and on the spot chose the holy Orthodox religion for himself and his people.

"Soon after making his decision known in Miklagard, he received in marriage Anna Porphyrogenita, daughter of the Emperor Romanus and the sister to the Emperor Basil. Never before in the whole of history was a foreign prince so honored as Vladimir was, and all because he embraced the True Faith. Immediately, he sent away his concubines and his other wives, cleaving only to Anna, and he and the whole population of Kiev were baptized together, rejoicing and praising the Lord, in the river Dnieper. This was in the year six thousand, four hundred and ninety-six from the Creation, or, as the Papists call it, Anno Domini 988.

"After that, Vladimir easily overthrew the demons, whom some of the people in their ignorance still worshiped—Svarog, Dashbog, Stribog, Khors, Yarilo, Lad, Volos, and Perun—especially Perun. Him he ordered to be tied to a horse's tail and dragged to the river while men walked alongside flogging the idol with sticks.

"Then in Novgorod, too, the idols were overthrown, whipped, and flung into the river. And the people, seeing how feeble were these gods, who could not even defend themselves, went joyfully to be baptized in the Volkhov."

"All, Father Dmitri?" I broke in. "All of them joyfully? None held back?" I hadn't come to the lesson intending to quarrel, but anger suddenly flared up in me.

"Well, I mean to say, no, of course not; there were some so depraved by superstition that they hung back."

"What was done about them, Father Dmitri?"

"They were dragged down by the scruff of the neck and thrown in! Why, d'you think they deserved better? Did God ask Lucifer politely if he would be so obliging as to leave Heaven? No, gospodin, he did not. He commanded St Michael, the general of his host, to take the Evil One by the heels and fling him into the pit, him and all his fallen angels! And should we do less wherever we find Satan? Does that answer your question, you, whoever you are?"

"He's Harald the Norwegian's skald," someone in the audience called out.

"Well, he should know better, then, shouldn't he?" said Dmitri. "Anything else you want to know, my inquisitive friend?"

Inwardly I thought, What have we done that we should be plagued by the Vladimirs and Olafs of this world? But to his question I answered,

"No, Father, nothing else." What was the use of talking? They would have it their own way in the end.

Smoothing his ruffled feathers, the priest continued: "And so we Rus hold Grand Prince Vladimir in pious memory and we treasure his relics—his foot, his skull, his jaw bone—all are preserved in the Cathedral at Kiev, or in other places, and their power is great."

It always amused me to hear Vladimir's name spoken with such reverence at court, seeing that Yaroslav had been in open revolt against him at the time of his death (out of resentment, so it was said, to the wrong done his mother when the Grand Prince took a Greek princess to be his single lawful wife). It was only the old man's death that prevented a bloody civil war between father and son, Kiev and Novgorod.

"And now, my children," Dmitri concluded his sermon, "before I release you, for I can see the hour is getting late, I deem it most important to remind you of how blest, how fortunate you are to be baptized into the Holy Orthodox Faith and not the accursed Church of Rome. For you must understand that the Latins are heretics, who believe that the Holy Spirit proceeds from the Father and the Son instead of from the Father alone; they are baptized in only one immersion of water instead of three; they do wrong also to take the Host in an unleavened wafer instead of in bread as Christ instructed us; they despise the flesh in that they require their priests to be beardless like eunuchs and deny to them the blessings of marriage—with the result that they all take concubines instead!

"Why, it is even said of them by no less an authority than that learned monk of Kiev, Feodosy of the Caves, that they eat lions, wild horses, asses, bears, and beavers' tails, and are unclean in all their habits. This same Father Feodosy instructs us to avoid their communion, nor eat or drink from the same bowl with them; but if we must, out of Christian charity, give a Catholic food from our bowl, we must wash it out immediately afterwards and ask God's pardon.

"And now, my children, go and pray earnestly to God, asking him to make you worthy of this sacrament—its day is fast approaching—from which you will arise new men in Christ."

✝

Father Dmitri sent us away to pray and meditate. And I did meditate.

I had been all through this in my mind before now. My mother had been Christian and so had Kalf Slender-Leg, the dearest friend of my boyhood. I could say nothing against them. But I had seen also how lustily these Christmen could hate—and hate not only the heathen or the Jew but each other! I'm a good hater too, but I don't lie and call it Godliness. No, I will receive their baptism because it is a writ of entry into the great world, where I must make my way. When I am among them I will swear 'by Mary' and 'by Christ' as they all do. But I will not believe what they teach; and, in the secret place of my thoughts, I will still pray to Odin All-Father and the other gods of olden time—if only so that I may not affront my poor, mad father's ghost.

†

Came the day.

Dressed in our gowns of snowy white, we stood barefoot in a line before the font, ready to 'put off the old Adam and put on the new', as Father Dmitri expressed it. Thanks to his efforts, we were all able to recite our Creed, if not much else. We had each been given a new name, too: mine was John, for the saint whose feast day this happened to be. (Fortunately, it was not generally the custom here to call someone by his baptismal name—Yaroslav's, for instance, was George; Ingigerd's was Irene—so that I could continue to be 'Odd' to my friends.)

Dag, with great good humor, stood godfather to Einar. Yaroslav, as a way of doing honor to Harald, insisted upon being my godfather, which, necessarily, made Inge my godmother—adding incest to adultery in the tally of her sins—and mine. Yesterday I had only been a damned fool; from today I was a damned fool and a sinner.

When it came my turn, I faced west, spat three times while renouncing Satan and all his ways, was thrice immersed in water, dabbed all over with oil, and became in the eyes of the world a Christman—and so sank into the chasm which opened at my feet.

I mean that chasm which lies between the old ways and the new, between heathen and Christman, barbarian and city-man; a chasm that I have wandered in for many years now, nor have I hope any longer of finding my way safely to one precipice or the other.

14

BETWEEN
TWO WOLVES

Easter eve.

The cathedral was filled to overflowing. The service lasted hours. We knelt, we rose, we knelt again; we crossed ourselves times without number. The gilded icon screen glowed in the light of a hundred tall candles and the air was heavy with the smell of wax. At the altar, priests came and went, each performing his mysterious office, while the choir chanted: the high clear voices of the boys, the booming bass voices of the men: all together and each alone, singing to their god.

At midnight Bishop Yefrem stood in the doorway, surrounded by all the congregation holding lighted candles, and proclaimed: "Khristos voskres," and we replied, "Voistine voskres." That is to say, "Christ is risen. Truly risen." Whereupon everyone kissed everyone else.

After more hours of chanting and priest-craft inside the flower-filled church, we were dismissed to our homes as dawn broke over the city; each of us carrying his candle stub and a red-painted egg. All the next day, too, we kissed whomever we met in the street and told them that Christ was risen. This Easter of theirs is a fine, happy holiday and made me, for a little while, think better of the Christmen.

Yet even at this glad season, all was not love and sweet peace in Yaroslav's dvor. Jarl Ragnvald had come up from Aldeigjuborg to keep Easter with his cousin Ingigerd and Eilif, his son. Having been out of touch with Novgorod during the winter months, he had no idea how things now stood. What he found was worse, I imagine, than anything he could have pictured to himself: Harald deep in Yaroslav's confidence, the druzhina divided, Ingigerd balked, Eilif made a fool of, and even the upcoming marriage with Yelisaveta cast in doubt, for that sweet maid was flatly refusing to marry Eilif no matter if they put out her eyes, branded her with irons, or flayed her right down to the bare bones—she loved to imagine herself enduring these ridiculous tortures. Moreover, with an ingenuity worthy of her mother, she was tireless in finding ways to exchange notes with Harald, using me once again as go-between.

Inge's threat to pack her off to her uncle in Pskov had to be abandoned. Yelisaveta broke into a meeting of the Duma one day to cling, weeping, to her father's knees, and Inge, knowing that to interfere with a father's power over his children was a humiliation which even Yaroslav could not brook, pretended that the child had misunderstood her and dropped the matter.

To come back to Ragnvald, he no sooner arrived than he began to abuse his son for sluggishness and cowardice in a voice that could be heard all over the palace. Eilif looked more sullen than ever when he emerged from this parental scolding. But we should have taken no comfort from this; nothing is more dangerous than an angry stupid man.

To me, Ragnvald was frosty, but that was always his manner and so I could gather nothing from it. I assumed Inge told him that I was not and never had been their agent. Whether she went on to tell him of our affair, I am doubtful, and yet she might have—they were very close.

Summer came with long white nights, when the sun, as in Iceland, barely dipped below the horizon. At midnight you could stand on Slavno Hill and count the boats plying the river below.

But even without the cloak of darkness, Inge and I continued our meetings, each more reckless than the last. I spent most of one night crouched naked in the clothes chest when the prince paid an unexpected visit to his wife's bedroom (his usual day was Thor's day). Another time I met him riding to Gorodische as I was riding back, and just had time to turn off into the trees before he recognized me.

Moreover, Inge's appetite for love-making was matched by her contempt—which I did not entirely share—for her husband's intelligence; she had actually begun to make broad references to my youthful vigor in his hearing, as if daring him to suspect us.

For my part, I began to grow weary of being Harald's man by day and

Inge's by night. Time and again I made up my mind to put an end to the business. But always and always I found my way back to her bed.

I can scarcely account for my feelings at this time. Had love made me that weak and foolish? No better than silly Yaroslav himself? Or was it something more sinister—witchcraft or binding-runes? I took that possibility seriously, for Inge knew more about those things than people suspected.

Whatever it was, I yielded the more easily because she still did not question me concerning Harald, nor enlist me in any treachery against him, nor admit to any such thing herself—even though suspicion was piled on suspicion as mysterious 'accidents' began to occur.

One night early in the summer a fire broke out in Harald's dvor while he was lying drunk in bed. His body guards barely got him out alive. A few weeks later he nearly met his death again, this time from poisoning. Someone claiming to be a peasant from the neighboring village of Menevo appeared at his door with a basket of mushrooms (the villagers often did things like this to curry favor). The mushrooms were put into a stew which Harald ate that night. Four days later he began to suffer from cramps, vomiting, diarrhea, and fever.

Yaroslav, who knew everything about mushrooms, recognized the symptoms of poisoning when this was reported to him, and rushed to the dvor in person to investigate. A few mushrooms remained in the basket and his trained eye picked out several that had reddish, wrinkled caps, like little brains—a very noxious variety—mixed up with the others.

Impossible, he said, for country people to have made such a mistake. He, Dag, and I rode straight to Menevo to look for the 'peasant' who had brought them, but the villagers swore that they knew no one answering his description.

There followed some very tense days. Failing to find the culprit, Dag flogged the cook half to death and threw her out. At one point Harald motioned Dag and me to his side and whispered, "If I die, kill her." Meaning, of course, Ingigerd. "I will do it with my own hand," Dag replied, looking hard at me.

Fortunately, the effects of the poison were overcome by Harald's tough constitution, assisted by various herbal concoctions that Yaroslav prepared and fed him with his own hands.

Just as with the ambush, the sickness runes, and the fire, there was no evidence pointing inescapably at Inge, but Dag and Harald believed her guilty all the same. They only differed in how to respond.

Harald was for storming her apartment and hacking off her head. Against this, Dag pleaded for patience. We were already winning the battle for Yaroslav's trust, he said; Ingigerd's increasingly desperate stratagems proved it. And Harald's conquest of Yelisaveta Yaroslavna— her father's darling—would work in our favor, too, even though it had been no part of the original plan. Everything would come to us if only we moved cautiously.

Sterling advice, Harald shot back, except for the fact that he had nearly died three times already; and who could be sure that the next attempt wouldn't succeed?

To this Dag had no good answer.

In private, he pressed me again about Inge. What did I know that I wasn't telling him? he demanded at the top of his lungs. Damn it all, hadn't he ordered me to spy on her? Then how could I have failed to pick up even the smallest hint concerning the fire and the poisoning? He had befriended me and this was how I repaid him! He paced up and down in a fury.

I could only give the same reply as before. "Dag, I swear to you I know nothing. Inge and I never talk about Harald—the subject vexes both of us so much that we leave it alone. Please believe me, Dag. I respect you more than anyone I know. Your anger hurts me."

The strain was beginning to tell on Dag. He was always tight-lipped and irritable now—the old easy manner all but gone. He knew his influence over Harald was wearing thin and he must have wondered sometimes if all this conspiring was worth the effort.

I know I did. Einar Tree-Foot spoke the truth when he said I was like a man caught between two wolves—and I was no longer feeling as cocky about it as I had earlier. What a muddle I was in! Here were Inge and I deceiving both her husband and Harald, while at the same time Harald and her daughter were busy deceiving Inge, with my connivance. Dag, half-convinced I was a traitor, treated me like a stranger, and Harald, with growing truculence, demanded to know why I spent so much time away from him. (I had used Stavko for an alibi so often that it began to embarrass me and I had to rack my brains for new excuses.)

It only required a little imagination to guess whose head was the likeliest of all to roll—and I've always been cursed with too much imagination. I was beginning to sleep poorly—whenever, that is, Inge allowed me to sleep at all.

So passed the summer and the early fall.

You may easily picture, then, with what relief I greeted the messenger whose stumbling, foam-flecked horse carried him into Yaroslav's courtyard one September day at dusk. The animal sank to its knees and died on the spot. Its rider looked about ready to do the same.

Kiev was besieged by a great horde of Pechenegs, he gasped; the garrison was starving, a relieving force under Mstislav was being formed, but Yaroslav, too, must to fly to the rescue of his father's holy city!

It came like the answer to a prayer. To escape, at last, from wretched Novgorod, from women and intrigue! For Harald, for Dag, for all of us, a chance to live like men again and exercise our sword-arms against honest foes—how much better than this wretched life we were leading!

As we gathered round that mud-spattered courier, pressing him for details, I felt as though a great weight had suddenly been lifted from me.

15

TO KIEV!

The courier who brought us the news of Kiev's peril was the servant of one Ugonyay Ekimovich, a boyar of Smolensk. In just eight days he had driven his horse over four hundred versts of forest and swamp.

Yaroslav summoned the whole druzhina to a council of war. Word traveled fast and the great hall was soon overflowing with druzhiniks, while the citizens of Novgorod milled outside.

"It's four weeks now," said the young courier, "that the pagans have besieged the city. They lay waste the land like wolves. They build haystacks of heads. One Kievan got away and brought word to Prince Mstislav at Chernigov. And he sent a rider up the river to Smolensk, where his son Eustaxi rules."

Mstislav, the courier explained, had ordered his son to join him at once in a relief expedition, but also, and most important, to prevent any word of the siege from spreading farther north. On no account was Prince Yaroslav to know anything about it until it was over. Eustaxi made that plain to his boyars. "In order," he said, "that I and my father shall have to ourselves all the glory of delivering Kiev from the Pechenegs."

These words sent a wave of indignation throughout the crowded hall. "But my master," the courier continued, "bears a grudge against Mstislav and so he decided to send me to inform you of it. He asks only that you don't betray him."

The muttering in the hall grew louder, but Yaroslav called for silence and asked how numerous the Pechenegs were and who their leader was.

The youth replied that all of the eight hordes had banded together and were led by Tyrakh Khan himself.

"Tyrakh!" Yaroslav struck the arm of his high-seat. "Is it possible? The very same who sixty years ago cut off my grandfather Svyatoslav's head and used it for a goblet! He must be close on ninety."

"Prince," said the messenger, "I've not yet told all."

"Eh?"

"The trading fleet from Miklagard, sir. The Pechenegs shadowed them all the way up from the coast, not attacking at the cataracts where they were expected, but waiting till the strugi were beached on Kiev's shore and the gates of the city were wide open. At one swoop they caught both the fleet and the city defenseless. The slaughter in those first few minutes was horrible."

Yaroslav started from his chair. "Dear God, my son!"

The courier gazed at the floor. "Nothing was said about him, Prince. He might still be alive."

Vladimir Yaroslavich—Volodya as he was always called—now twelve years old, had gone with the trading fleet on his first embassy to the Imperial City.

Yaroslav sank back in his seat, buried his face in his hands, and groaned, "My son's life in peril and Mstislav—may he dream of the Devil—tries to keep the news of it from me! What is wrong with the man? Has he gone mad?"

"Oh, hardly mad, you simple soul. Say, rather, shrewd and quick to seize the main chance when it's offered."

This was Ingigerd. "His treachery comes as no surprise to me. I never thought him to be the drunken, amiable bear that he likes to seem. He's had his eye on Kiev all along but dared not seize it without a pretext. Now, under guise of liberating it from the Pechenegs, he will enter it a hero. And once installed, my husband, you will never get him out. That's what lies behind this secrecy. You must go there at once and assert your rights to the place."

"Go there!" cried Yaroslav in anguish. "By Saint George, I'll go there! And if a hair of my son's head is harmed, why, I shall have such vengeance— on Tyrakh Khan and on my brother—as never a man had!"

I'd never heard such strong speech from those lips. To defend his child, Yaroslav the mouse could be a lion.

"Under siege these four weeks, you say?" Ingigerd questioned the messenger. "Then they didn't get their crops in?"

"Princess, the autumn rye was just coming ready for the scythe. Tyrakh Khan timed his attack with care. Very little grain was brought inside the city before he struck, and now the Pechenegs have the bulk of it in their own hands. The Kievans will be eating their shoes by now. Unless Prince Mstislav raises the siege they must surrender soon."

Instantly both palace and city fell into a frenzy of activity. Within the hour a galloper was sent flying to Pskov to alert Sudislav, the youngest of the brothers Vladimirovich, to marshal his warriors and sail at once for Kiev. And we hastened to do the same.

In the days that followed, I learned that there is more to war-making than fighting; in fact, fighting may be the least of it. Half the battle is getting there, the other half is finding enough to eat.

With the trading fleet away, Yaroslav's navy was revealed to be woefully small and derelict. Harald's big dragon ship, which had formerly been called Sea Stag but was now re-christened the Saint Olaf (another of Dag's suggestions) was ship-shape and ready to sail. But for the rest of the druzhina Yaroslav had on hand just twenty ships of various types and sizes, and most of them in poor condition.

Transport, however, was not the only problem. The army, even on short rations, must consume a ton of bread and porridge a day. Now, we could not reach Kiev in less than fourteen days of hard rowing, with no stops for foraging, and we should have at least three days' provisions to spare when we got there.

Nothing had been harvested yet around Novgorod. Yaroslav now ordered the peasants into the fields as far as thirty miles from the city. Desperate to be off, the prince allowed time for only one hasty threshing of the grain and none at all for milling. Instead, an assortment of grinding stones was hastily collected with which to grind the rye and oats as we sailed. Astonishingly, in under a week we had our supply of grain—and with it the curses of every toiling, starving peasant in the neighborhood.

During those hectic days of preparation, I nearly succeeded in putting Inge out of my mind, and felt much the better for it. I found myself in the thick of things because Yaroslav seized on this moment to raise Harald to the rank of boyar and make him co-commander with Eilif of the whole druzhina.

Ingigerd fought bitterly against it in the Duma, but, with the backing of the mayor and others of our faction, the prince, for a change, had his way. Of course, to divide the command between two enemies was utter folly. Apart from chasing brigands, this was to be the druzhina's first campaign in a year, and the prospect of action raised everyone's spirits. Particularly Harald's. His energy and optimism were boundless. Even so, he was Harald all the same—thankless and brutal without the smallest awareness of it.

On the night before we were to sail he turned quite casually to Dag— the three of us were supping together in Harald's dvor—and said, "You're not coming with us."

"What did you say?"

"You're not coming."

His voice was husky and he couldn't meet Dag's eyes. I sensed he'd been working up to this for a long time.

"If you like, you can stay here and keep an eye on Ingigerd—sort of thing you're good at. That or go your own way." There was a long silence during which Dag seemed to consider and reject several possible replies. In the end he simply said, "I see," and left the hall. Harald let him go with a shrug.

I couldn't believe what I had just witnessed. As soon as Dag was out of earshot, I exploded:

"Harald, the man saved your life! He's done everything for you!"

"Exactly," he answered coolly. "Done everything. Grateful and all that but one can't be in tutelage forever. I can't breathe around him and that's the long and short of it. I weary of his always being right. And hasn't he used me for his own ends, if the truth be told? Well, all that's over now, friend skald. I won't be used by anyone again. By anyone." He repeated those words, looking straight at me.

Later that night I went searching for Dag and found him, at last, in a tavern that he liked in Vitkova Street, alone with a jug.

"Well, that was short and sweet, wasn't it?" He made a wry face at me as I sat down. "Wine?" He pushed the jug across the table.

"Dag, I know I haven't pleased you, I'm sorry for that. But I only came to this filthy country because of you and I'll gladly leave it for the same reason."

"Don't talk like a fool."

"No, I mean it, I can't bear him any longer, the brutal bastard!"

"You can and will. Stay the course, Odd, the prize is worth it."

"I don't believe that any more. And you—where will you go now?"

"Oh, the world's full of kings. My talents won't go a-begging."

"I don't know what to say."

"Don't say anything. Go along with you now, I'm best left to myself when I drink."

"We'll meet again one day?"

"Of course we will." He put out his hand and gripped mine.

I went to my bed angry that night.

✝

At dawn the druzhina mustered at the riverside: the Swedes, Rus, and Slavs in one group; the Norwegians in another. Even though in theory Harald and Eilif now jointly commanded the whole force, each preferred to surround himself with his own men. There were still, in reality, two druzhinas.

Einar and I stood with the Norwegians, watching slaves trundle our provisions in fifty-pound sacks up the gangway. Fully laden, the Saint Olaf's deck was nearly awash. In a moderate sea she would have shipped water and gone straight to the bottom. Even a sudden squall on Lake Ilmen would be too much for her.

While things were being readied, Harald strode along our front, inspecting us. If the men even noticed Dag's absence they gave no sign of it; it was Harald alone they had eyes for. He knew every one of them by name; knew everything worth knowing about them for praise or blame. Striding along the ranks, a giant among pygmies, his long hair streaming and his moustaches hanging like walrus tusks below his chin, he was beginning to take on that form which one day all the world would recognize: Harald Hardrada—Harald the Ruthless—the Thunderbolt of the North.

"We're on Prince Yaroslav's business," he told them sternly. "Let us give him no cause to regret it."

Touching his thumb to the ax blade of one man, he scowled, "Kolbein Foul-Breath, you couldn't cut your toenails with that. Don't show me your face again until it's sharp." One handsome fellow, whom we called Orm

Peacock because of the care he lavished on his person, had a big bundle of clothes on his back that included a sable coat, two pair of soft leather boots and similar stuff. Harald took the whole bundle from him and tossed it in the river. "We've no room for that costly trash, Peacock. The girls of Kiev must love you in plain soldier's dress or not at all."

Another was doing his best to conceal a small keg under his cloak. That, too, went into the river. "I tell you now, Kolbein Hakonsson—and this goes for the rest of you—we've no room to spare aboard this ship for casks of ale, nor for drunkards either. You'll drink river water and like it until Yaroslav's banner flies from Kiev's wall and if any man disobeys in this there'll be no trial for him, though he be the bravest in my crew, but I will nail his head to the mast and give him no Christian burial."

Other jugs and flasks appeared from under cloaks and inside bedrolls and were quietly laid aside. They knew he was as good as his word. Over the winter he had hanged seven of their mates for rape and four for murder.

"That's better. Now, my boys, attend to this. If ours is the first ship to come in sight of Kiev there'll be a grivna of silver for every man of you out of my own pocket and you may drink yourselves stupid on it once the fighting's over!"

They cheered themselves hoarse.

While this was going on, Eilif was pretending to inspect his men, who joked among themselves and all but ignored him.

Now Yaroslav emerged from the courtyard of his palace, accompanied by Inge, Thordis, and the children. The 'sucking pigs' stood in a row and their father kissed them each on both cheeks and patted their heads, not omitting to kiss Yelisaveta's red-headed dwarf, Nenilushka, too, for luck.

"Fear not my little ones," he said with an attempt at cheerfulness, "we shall bring your brother back to you safe and sound—with God's help. But you must pray for him every night and light a candle to the Virgin every day, you won't forget now, will you? There, there, I know you won't."

Ingigerd stood slightly apart from her brood with only Magnus, as ever, half hidden behind her skirt. Yaroslav kissed her last of all, with great ceremony and tenderness, on her cheeks and lips. He might as well have kissed the door post.

"Yaroslav Vladimirovich," called Harald, "will you do us the honor to use the Saint Olaf as your flagship?"

"Well, ah, yes, why not? Happy to ... fine-looking ship ... stout crew," the Prince blathered, limping toward us.

Our boys whooped and banged their weapons on their shields as the prince had his banner carried before him up the gang-plank. Eilif's men watched in ominous silence.

Harald, continuing his inspection of our weapons and kit, approached Einar and me. Tree-Foot had been up long before dawn sharpening his sword and getting his few possessions together. He needed to get up earlier than the rest of us because his movements lately had become halting and feeble. I'd tried as kindly as I could to dissuade him from coming with us, only to be answered with a bitter stare.

Over the winter he had aged greatly. One day I came upon him sitting on the barracks floor in a daze, not knowing how he got there, and ever since then his words were slurred like a drunken man's and the corner of his mouth drooped. His bright eye had lost its luster. I saw fear and bewilderment in it now. His body was betraying him at last, and he knew it. He showed it by being more prickly than ever.

Stopping before us, Harald frowned. "The old man—," he began, but I cut him off:

"—was formerly one of a brotherhood of warriors the like of which is seen no more, and was standard bearer to Sigvalt, their Jarl. He has forgotten more of war-craft than the rest of us will ever know."

We stared each other down. I was prepared to leave Harald on the spot if he humiliated Einar. He read it in my eyes, I know, and was mindful that he could have no fame without his skald to give it voice. I still had that over him.

"As I was going to say, Tangle-Hair," he replied softly, "the old man is your friend, I know it well. Never fear, old codger,"— he clapped Einar on the shoulder with false good humor—"I expect you don't eat much. We'll squeeze you in somewhere." With these words he passed on, while Einar continued to look straight ahead of him, motionless except for a twitching of his cheek.

That, of course, wasn't what Harald had been going to say. What he did say was cruel enough, though not intentionally so—this was Harald in a good mood, you understand. Having just unburdened himself of Dag, he was feeling generous. Still and all, I had made him back down. With Harald you never knew what that might cost you some day.

Then we raced to man the oars while Bishop Yefrem and his priests held aloft the icons and golden crosses on long staffs and blessed us with perfumed smoke.

We sailed out of Novgorod under two banners, both flying from the Saint Olaf's masthead: one, the trident emblem of the house of Rurik; the other, Harald's own banner. This, like his armor, was a novelty. He'd had it made just lately and boasted (truthfully or not, I don't know) that Yelisaveta had stitched it with her own hands. It showed a black raven on a red ground, and when the wind made it flutter the raven moved its wings. Harald called his banner Land-Waster; it would be well known and much feared throughout our northern land one day.

Along the bank, women waved a last farewell to their men: Ingigerd to Yaroslav (not to me, thank the gods, though I half expected it of her); old Thordis to Einar, touching her apron to her watery eyes (he affected not to notice); and Yelisaveta brazenly to Harald, who returned it with a bold grin. The girl's marriage to Eilif, I should add, which was to have taken place by now—she having just turned fourteen—was indefinitely postponed because she absolutely refused to go through with it.

✝

Our way lay across Lake Ilmen and up the river Lovat which flows into its southern end. This river has a swift current against which we had to battle. Harald, shucking his mail coat and stripping to the waist, pulled an oar with the rest of us and set a pace that we could hardly keep up with. Behind us we could hear Eilif's angry voice cursing his rowers for their sluggishness—the rivalry between the two captains now being reduced to a simple boat race. But we took the lead and never lost it.

It's discouraging how fast your rowing muscles can go soft on you. Though we worked with a will, we still made only about five and thirty versts that first day and by the next morning we could barely straighten our backs. (I should explain that verst is the Rus word for what I reckon is a little less than one of our miles.) We faced two hundred and seventy versts more of this torture before we would cross the watershed to the headwaters of the Dnieper—and we would have to quicken our pace or risk running out of rations short of our goal.

Somehow we did it.

All the ships carried more men than they had oarlocks, so that rowers were able to change off frequently in rotation. Even Yaroslav, not to be outshone by Harald, took his turn on the bench, just as his grandfather Svyatoslav, that fierce heathen warrior-prince, is said to have done. In this way we rowed steadily each day from dawn until pitch darkness overtook us.

For those not rowing there was other work for blistered hands to do—namely, working the grindstones to produce oatmeal for our porridge and rye flour for our bread. Warriors, their arms white with flour up to the elbows, swore that they hadn't joined the druzhina to be housewives!

At night when we camped, our first task was to start a fire and boil the water for the oatmeal and dried beans; next, to heat flat stones in the fire to bake our bread on. Our loaves were often burnt on the outside and half raw within, but we were too tired and hungry to mind.

You might expect that men as tired as we would have no strength left for fighting among ourselves, but so bitter had grown the hatred between Eilif's men and ours that on the very first night a brawl erupted over the choice of a campsite. One man of ours and one of theirs was killed and quite a few on both sides bloodied. From then on curses, taunts, shoving matches, and stone throwing between us were daily occurrences.

If feelings between Harald and Eilif grew more embittered, those between Harald and myself improved. I have already said that he was at his best when he was leading men into battle, and this was even truer (I was forced to admit) now that Dag was out of the picture. Harald did breathe easier. The day's labor was never so grueling that he couldn't joke with us at the end of it, ask me for a bit of a story, get the men talking or singing to take their minds off their blisters and aching bones. Ours was the only part of the camp where laughter was ever heard.

Yaroslav generally took his meals with us and I found to my surprise that there were sides to the prince I hadn't seen before. He could curse—although nothing stronger than 'damn your eyes'; he could laugh at a dirty story; he could even be persuaded to do a bit of a sailors' jig despite his game leg. As the distance lengthened between Ingigerd and him, I saw him undergo a subtle change, becoming less the timid, weak, and foolish man that she believed him to be, and, in some fashion, made of him.

Ah, Ingigerd, what have you done to us men! Whenever she drifted into my thoughts I drove her out with every ounce of will that was in me. How much simpler life was without her.

Once on the Dnieper we were borne along on the swift current that sweeps down to the great sea which the Rus call 'Black,' two thousand versts to the south. Picking up a steady breeze as well, we flew along at three times the speed we had made before.

As we neared our journey's end, we first smelt and then began to see the signs of pillage and destruction. Charred fields, smoldering orchards, whole villages, as well as the dvors of many a rich boyar, burned to the ground; and scattered everywhere the bones of men and beasts, already picked clean by vultures. It appeared from a hasty reconnaissance that many, including even babies, had been burnt, strangled with nooses, or impaled on stakes where they hung until their corpses fell to pieces.

I heard plenty of talk about our enemy. "They're demons from Hell, not men", said one old warrior. "They have the faces of animals," said another. "They eat, sleep, even fuck their women on horseback." Others chimed in: "They neither plow nor sow and their only houses are black tents on wheels. Their dinner is rats and lice, which they wash down with horse's blood. They have no religion except the worship of animals. They dress in sheepskins and their chief weapon is the bow. With these little bows they can drive an arrow through your shield, your ring mail, your leather jerkin, and the shaft will still come half-way out your back."

A little past noon on the thirteenth day of our voyage, we came in sight of the fortified hamlet of Vyshgorod, perched on a height about eight versts above the city. We would use it as a base from which to launch a counter-attack. There was no other suitable stronghold this side of Kiev.

To announce ourselves and give heart to the garrison there, we struck up a rowing chant, which the ships behind us took up also. The chant died in our throats as we drew nearer and saw how the log walls encircling the hamlet bristled with arrows and were in many places black and smoking. Here, too, vultures circled overhead and crows strutted on the ramparts. Save for the cries of carrion birds there was no sound.

16

Devils of
The Steppe

Harald, wanting to have a look round, grounded the Saint Olaf where a steep stairway, carved into the face of the bluff, led up to the citadel. While the rest of the fleet stayed safely out in mid-channel, we leapt down warily onto the narrow beach with our swords drawn.

As we stood at the foot of the steps uncertain what to do, a raven, roosting on the parapet above, gave out a sudden squawk and flapped away. Where it had strutted a solitary face peered cautiously down. Next moment there were shouts from within and the postern gate swung out. Haggard men in battle-stained clothes ran down to meet us.

With Harald in the lead, we climbed the steps and entered the village. Inside, a jumble of tiny cottages crowded right up to the wall. Most were blackened by fire and open to the sky where their thatched roofs had been burnt away. In the lane leading from the postern a raggedy mob of women and children, and even some men of fighting age, reached out bony hands to us. They were as sad a lot of human beings as ever I'd seen. Along every path and in every doorway lay wounded men with hollow, haunted eyes. Such few farm animals as could be seen were skeletons, hardly worth the boiling, though even they would go into the pot soon enough.

Yaroslav, followed by Eilif and the senior druzhiniks, came up behind us. Amid a babble of voices, we were all conducted to Vyshgorod's church—the only building that still had a roof over it. After the sweet, clean air of river and woods the stench here of sweat, piss, and gangrenous flesh was stomach-turning. Among the rows of sick and wounded that stretched the whole length of the darkened nave, lay one figure a little apart from the others, his head pillowed on his saddle and a blood-streaked robe spread over him.

"Eustaxi Mstislavich, is it you?" asked Yaroslav, bending over the body of his nephew.

Though at first sight his face resembled an old man's, so pinched and pale it was, I reckoned his age at no more than thirty. Raising himself on an elbow, he whispered, "Uncle Yaroslav? Thank God."

Any other man than Yaroslav might have answered, "No thanks to you, you wretch!" But not our prince. "Tell me, in God's name, what has happened here," was all he said.

Gritting his teeth against pain, Eustaxi answered, "We men of Smolensk and Chernigov, five hundred horsemen, came here—five? six weeks ago?

We swam our horses across the river and, without stopping to rest or eat, my father led us in a charge straight up to the walls of Kiev."

Yaroslav shook his head sadly. "'Charge!' is the only command Mstislav knows."

"When the enemy caught sight of us they jumped on their horses and galloped away. 'See how they run!' cried my father. 'After them!' They pretended to retreat, drew us on until our horses were exhausted and our column strung out and then suddenly turned on us. In an instant they were all around us, pouring in arrows. One pierced my lung, another pinned my thigh to my saddle. We didn't have a chance." Eustaxi clutched his uncle's arm as a spasm of pain shook him. He and a handful of others, he said between clenched teeth, had escaped and sheltered here—only to starve to death. Foraging parties sent out at night never came back. And every day a heathen band would ride over from their camp to scream insults at them and dare them to come out and fight. "Sometimes"—his voice sank to a whisper—"sometimes they ride up to the walls and spit."

"And you permit this, you dog!" cried Harald, shouldering Yaroslav out of the way. "One skirmish a month ago and since then you've done nothing but skulk in this hole and lick your wounds? No wonder they spit at you. I join them!"

Every head in the place swiveled toward us. Eustaxi groped for his sword; the effort was too great, he rolled back, gasping. "Who the devil are you that talks so brave? If I could stand, damn you ..." A fit of coughing interrupted his words and he spit some blood into a cloth.

"Now, now, my boy," Yaroslav stroked his head. "But your father? Not dead—?"

"I wish to Christ he were! The Wild Bison of Chernigov was taken alive. They brought him here, right under the walls, to show him to us: stripped naked, a wooden yoke across his neck with his arms strapped to the ends of it; his body cut and bleeding from the lash. He cried out, begging us to kill him with an arrow. I ordered it done, but they dragged him out of range at the end of a lasso. He ran, he stumbled, and still they dragged him with his face in the dirt. That was weeks ago. Maybe he is dead by now—I pray he is. But Tyrakh Khan knows his worth in ransom; they'll keep him alive just for that."

Yaroslav could do nothing but shake his head and mutter a prayer.

"But how have you come here, Uncle?," asked Eustaxi. "Who brought word to you, for we didn't—" he stopped short, plainly ashamed of what he'd nearly let slip.

"Yes, I know all about that," said Yaroslav sternly. "One of your people, who meant to do you a harm, has probably saved your lives. His name is no matter."

(I heard the prince say later that the guilty boyar of Smolensk, whom he knew by sight, was lying quite near us among the wounded as he spoke these words.)

"Prince Eustaxi," I asked, "have you not even tried to get a message out?"

"Where to, in God's name? Belgorod and Vasiliev to the south have fallen—at least, we saw smoke on the horizon that way. As for the men of Pereyaslavl, no need to send them word; the bodies of our dead floating down the river was message enough. And they rode up to see what was the matter. They blundered into an ambush exactly as we did. We could hear the sounds of slaughter from here, and there was nothing we could do. Later, a handful of them reached us in the night."

We were all sunk in gloomy silence for some moments. Then Yaroslav burst out, "But there's Izyaslavl and Volhynsk—neither far away and both ruled by warlike princes!"

Eustaxi's jaw set stubbornly. "I obey my father's orders. Those towns, Uncle, are on your side of the river, and you were not to find out—"

"In the name of God!" cried Yaroslav, lifting up his hands, "this is madness!"

"Now then, fellow," said Harald, intentionally not calling him prince or gospodin, "you say the Pechenegs come over daily to harass you? Have they come today?"

Avoiding Harald's eyes, Eustaxi nodded that they had.

"And they'll come again tomorrow?"

A shrug.

"Then we've got no time to waste. They mustn't know we're here. Where can we hide our ships—about twenty, mostly small?"

"Why—nowhere, it's impossible."

"That word comes too easily to your lips, fellow. Nothing is impossible."

"But gospodin Harald," said Yaroslav, "you can see for yourself there's no natural cover along the river bank and not a shed or a barn anywhere."

Harald waved him to silence. "There is one place they won't be seen. We have no choice. Give the order, Prince."

"To do what?"

"Sink them, of course."

"Why, you goddamned fool, you traitor!" Eilif shouldered his way to the front, purple-faced with feigned outrage. Here was his chance, at last. "You see, Yaroslav, what this fool's advice is worth! Sink the ships? Why, he's lost his mind! You'll strip him of his captaincy for this, won't you? By God, he should be whipped and hanged for it! Sink the damned ships?"

"Harald Sigurdsson—?" said Yaroslav plaintively, looking from one man to the other in confusion.

"We'll begin with mine." Harald spoke as if Eilif wasn't there at all. "Tangle-Hair, you see to it. Oars, rigging, provisions, anything portable is to be brought up here, stack it all in the streets if you have to. Then hole her and send her to the bottom."

I confess, I stood frozen like everyone else, not believing he was really serious.

"Body of Christ, do I have to explain it in small words! If we lose surprise we've lost everything. What use are the ships to us? If we lose, we die here, agreed? If we win, we build new ones, it's as simple as that. Obey me in this or I leave you in Eilif's hands, and may God help you! Now, what's it to be?"

"Eilif Ragnvaldsson," said Yaroslav after a long moment's silence, "we shall do as gospodin Harald says."

"But, Prince—"

"At once, Eilif!"

Well, well, thought I, the old dog has learned a new trick; though he would never dare take that tone with Eilif without Harald standing by to shore him up.

Turning back to Eustaxi, Yaroslav said gravely, "Your father's treachery has cost him dear and, if you should die, dearer still. I only pray it does not cost my son's life as well. Now, nephew, as soon as it's dark you will send gallopers to the princes of Izyaslavl and Volhynsk with orders from me to come at once with all their mounted men and as much food as they can carry. And you may as well know that Prince Sudislav of Pskov is on his way here too. From being your father's private adventure this will become such a gathering of brothers as hasn't been seen since our sainted father was alive. That's where all your guile has gotten you."

Eustaxi turned his face away in shame.

For the rest of the day we applied ourselves to the business of scuttling the ships. There was plenty of grumbling from the men—almost amounting to mutiny—but Yaroslav, backed up by Harald, made himself obeyed.

By sundown we carried up to the fort our last remaining sacks of oatmeal, rye, and beans, which Yaroslav insisted on sharing with the local folk and Eustaxi's men, although that left us with only two days' supply at quarter-rations for ourselves. Finally, we had to squeeze our seven hundred men into this tiny place that was already near bursting. Men who were there will tell you that we slept standing up; they hardly exaggerate. Life within these walls would, in a very few days, sink from bad to unbearable; we knew we had no time to waste.

†

At dusk, the prince, with Harald and some others of us, stood on the parapet looking south toward the beleaguered citadel of Kiev, which we could just make out perched on its three hills, a smudge on the horizon. Harald asked Yaroslav how close one might creep to the enemy's camp without danger of being seen. "For I aim to scout them myself tonight," he said.

"But they have the eyes of lynxes," Yaroslav turned an anxious face toward him. "They can spot a man creeping through the grass two versts away. What chance has a giant like you to elude them? I beg you not to risk it. We need you—I need you—too badly."

Harald started to protest when an unfamiliar voice spoke behind us. "There might be a way for a brave man."

We spun around to discover that a Pecheneg warrior had crept up behind us, close enough to touch us, without making the slightest sound. Like all that race, he was short in the legs, his drooping moustache and long hair were glossy black, and his brown high-cheekboned face was scarred with frostbite.

"You remember Kuchug?" He doffed his hat and made a slight bow toward Yaroslav.

"Mstislav's bodyguard, of course!" said the prince. "You remember him, don't you, Harald?"

Harald remembered him all right, and did not look particularly pleased to see him. Kuchug, you recall, had come close to slicing off his head that night when he lost the wrestling match with Mstislav and attacked him with a knife.

"What way, man?" asked Yaroslav, speaking Slavonic, the language which Kuchug had used.

"As my prisoner, prince. Pechenegs often catch Rus hiding in the woods. If they're worth ransoming, they take them back to camp. You, gospodin,"—he spoke to Harald while Yaroslav translated into Norse—"Tear your clothes, rub dirt on your face, I'll cut you a little bit, tie you to my horse's tail, drag you through camp. With God's help we may find Prince Mstislav and make a plan to rescue him. Kuchug is ashamed—he got separated from his master in the rout. Now Kuchug swears by the Blessed Virgin Mary to save him or die."

All this was said without a flicker of emotion in those piercing black eyes of his.

(Kuchug was a Christman. His father, as he later told me, had been one of a handful of Pechenegs who were converted to Christianity by one Bruno von Querfurt, a missionary monk. Bruno had proselytized among the savages twenty years before, until he provoked the khan's anger and was lucky to get away with his life. After this, most of his converts slid back. Those few who didn't were driven out by their fellow-tribesmen.

Kuchug, then a boy of fifteen or so, went with his parents to the court of Vladimir, where he grew up a Christman. After the Grand Prince's death he joined Mstislav's druzhina.)

We adopted Kuchug's plan with one difference. It was perfectly obvious that Harald couldn't go. His outlandish size, for one thing, would have drawn attention. For another, as Yaroslav kept insisting, we needed Harald alive—and the likelihood of anyone returning alive from this escapade was not something you would bet your last grivna on.

So they picked me.

Next morning's dawn found me stumbling behind Kuchug's horse, my clothes in shreds, my arms and chest bleeding from several carefully administered gashes, and my hands tied together with a bowstring.

Though he had lived among the Kievan Rus for more than half his life, Kuchug was proud of his Pecheneg blood and always dressed in the style of his people. He wore a tall fur cap, a caftan of green wool that reached nearly to the ankles, and a pair of thick-soled felt boots. Hanging from his belt on the right side was a quiver; on the left, his saber and his bow, in a case of tooled leather.

Leaving Vyshgorod, we struck south-west for about five versts, then turned eastward so as to meet the river again just north of the city. Along the way, we passed fields of rye, millet, and hay, in which peasants reaped while mounted Pechenegs trotted up and down, striking out with their riding quirts at any who were not brisk enough. In other fields, however, they had simply turned their horses loose to graze and trample the grain. We saw orchards too, that had once borne apples, pears, and cherries—all of them burnt black, like the ones we had passed up-river. Despite this, it was obvious that there was enough grain and pasturage here to feed the eight hordes for weeks while they starved the city into submission. The nomads had no notion of catapults, battering rams, or scaling ladders. If they could not burn the place down with fire arrows, then they were content to wait and let hunger do the job.

Squadrons of Pecheneg cavalry, always on the move, kept the whole citadel under observation, so that escape was impossible, while the defenders had to rush continually from place to place to guard against sudden attack. As we came within view of the city, a war party was assaulting a stretch of wooden wall, trying to set it afire by dragging bundles of burning faggots up to the foot of it, while the defenders fought back with arrows, stones, pots of boiling water, and quicklime.

Our way took us through the ruins of what had been the podol, or merchants' quarter, of the town. Like the Market Side at Novgorod, it had no wall, and its inhabitants in time of danger were expected to take shelter within the citadel. But this time the attack had been too sudden. Every shop-house was razed to the ground and the wreckage of their contents lay everywhere. Amidst the debris were many bodies—some mere skeletons, others with tatters of flesh still clinging to the bone. Perhaps these had been tortured longer before being allowed to die—tortured in full view of the citadel, of course, where their comrades could see them and hear their screams. Was one of those mutilated remnants young Volodya?

Beyond the podol, the ground rose steeply to a flat wooded hill-top south of the citadel, where the Pechenegs had their encampment. Kuchug had already made several nighttime sorties to steal a little food or an unguarded horse, but he hadn't dared penetrate to the center of the camp as we now proposed to do.

As we approached, he turned in his saddle, screamed something at me in his native gibberish, and, touching his riding quirt to his horse's flank, jerked me off my feet and dragged me up the slope over sharp stones and brambles.

Just when I'd eaten as much dust as I could stomach, he reined up and dismounted, and, cutting me loose, slashed me across the back with his quirt and kicked me for good measure.

"Dammit not so hard!" I burst out in Slavonic.

Ignoring my cry (for a true steppe-dweller would not have known a word of that language), he pointed to a scrawny poplar tree nearby and, handing me a hatchet that hung from his saddle-bow, indicated that I should cut it down for firewood.

While I chopped, he hobbled and unsaddled his mare and sat down on the sheepskin-covered saddle to watch me. Everywhere around us Pechenegs swarmed. They had made a great haul of loot from the captured merchant boats; they swaggered about with flagons of Greek wine to their lips and bolts of silk wrapped around them and trailing in the dirt. By every campfire, too, were heaps of other loot and weeping women, bruised and disheveled.

Being a fast riding war band, these Pechenegs had left their lumbering ox-drawn tents far behind them on the steppe. There were, however, several luxurious tents of silk which must house the lesser khans and their master, Tyrakh. His was plainly the large white one, visible from where we were, beside whose entrance his horse-tail standard was fixed in the ground.

And tethered by a lasso to that standard-pole crouched the unmistakable figure of Mstislav: bloody, filthy, naked, and still supporting the galling yoke on his neck. Every Pecheneg who passed by either kicked him, struck him in the face with his quirt, or spat on him. To these injuries he made so little answer that I feared he must be near death. Kuchug walked past him, hoping to catch his eye and whisper a word of courage, but though the eyes were partly open, they gave no sign of awareness. So as not to betray himself, the faithful druzhinik was forced to spit upon his master as the others did.

Only once during the hours that I watched him did someone come and push a bowl of something in his face—just enough nourishment, I guessed, to keep him alive for more days of fun.

As for the other captives, they were imprisoned in a large pen—hundreds of naked bodies heaped one atop the other, the ones on the bottom surely dead already, and the others not far from it.

I was just trimming the limbs from the poplar tree when a young Pecheneg in a make-shift coat of yellow silk, clutching a flagon of wine in one hand and his quirt in the other, sauntered up to Kuchug and, pointing the quirt at me, screamed something at him. Instantly a circle of bystanders formed around the two men, all shouting at once and gesticulating, with many curious stares directed at me.

Presently, over comes Yellow Coat to me, cuts me across the knuckles with his quirt, making me drop the hatchet, and almost in the same motion gives me a blow across the face. Then here comes Kuchug, with a look of fury, right behind him, with his own quirt upraised. If I expected him to apply it to my attacker, I was disappointed. He struck me himself, every bit as hard as Yellow Coat. After that they took turns aiming insults at each other and blows at me, encouraged by the shouts of the bystanders. If only, I lamented, Harald had gone on this mission as originally intended; the thought of him being horse-whipped was so very appealing.

Just as I was thinking that I'd had enough of this and was wondering whether to grab for the hatchet or make a dash for the river, Yellow Coat throws down his quirt and draws his saber. I gave myself up for dead then, but I'd forgotten Kuchug's swift hand. In less time than it takes to tell it, Yellow Coat was flopping like a fish on the ground, his right arm at some distance from the rest of him. The bystanders slapped their thighs, stamped on their hats, and roared with laughter. Kuchug put an end to their fun with a thrust through the fellow's heart.

As the laughter subsided, there arrived on the scene an important personage—a khan perhaps, to judge from his fine coat of scale armor, jeweled sword belt, and spiked helmet. He sent the onlookers scurrying with a wave of the arm and turned on Kuchug.

Black Odin, thought I, here's an end to both of us! He's bound to discover that Kuchug has no friends nor kinsmen here and belongs to no horde.

But that wasn't what happened at all. After a few words between them, Spiked Helmet comes over to have a look at me, prods Yellow Coat with the toe of his boot, yawns and strolls off.

Afterward, when we were safely away, I learned from Kuchug what it had all been about. Yellow Coat, he explained, had tried to claim me as one of his own slaves and demanded that Kuchug give him up.

"Nobody minded your killing him?"

"Oh, I think nobody liked that fellow anyway, always picking fights."

"And the khan, or whatever he was, didn't ask who you were?"

"I told him a story," he shrugged. "A lot of these Pecheneg are not so very smart; it comes of drinking too much horse's blood."

But that was later.

As Spiked Helmet departed, Kuchug screamed and gestured to me that I was to drag the body of Yellow Coat by its heels to the bluff that overlooked the river and fling it down. He himself marched along beside me, swinging his arms and strutting like a bantam rooster—and not omitting to flick me with his quirt every few steps.

"Enjoying yourself, aren't you, you bastard," I swore at him under my breath.

Pechenegs we passed grinned and saluted him, but he, with his chin tilted to the sky, paid them no attention. I, however, with my eyes on the ground, noticed something along the way that intrigued me very much and occupied my thoughts for the rest of the day.

The time that remained until nightfall passed uneventfully. Leaving me tied hand and foot, Kuchug trotted off to take his turn at shooting arrows into the city. His shafts, however, delivered not fire but fiery words. Yaroslav and two or three others who could write had been up half the night writing out dozens of copies of a message to the Kievans, announcing his arrival with reinforcements and exhorting them in God's name to hold out just a few days longer. He printed this message on strips of birch-bark, which he rolled around each of Kuchug's arrows. We could only hope that some would be found and read.

At last, the sun went down, leaving the glow of a thousand cookfires to illumine the scene. Round them warriors squatted, their faces ruddy in the fire-light. While baskets of bread were carried round by slaves from fire to fire, each warrior—or those I could see, anyway—reached under his pony's saddle to pull out strips of meat, made tender by heat and horse-sweat. Soon the odor of rancid meat and fermented mare's milk—their favorite drink—mingled with the smells of horse dung, wood smoke, and unwashed bodies.

Supper was followed by more hours of carousing, punctuated by the screams of captive women. The savages milled about, drinking deeply, laughing, quarreling, capering to the music (if you could call it that) of drums and cymbals, until, thoroughly drunk, they rolled up in their sheepskins and fell heavily asleep. All, that is, but those who were detailed for sentry duty. Of these were half a dozen who guarded the tent of Tyrakh Khan, and, at the same time, kept an eye on his royal prisoner.

No one had taken Mstislav inside or even covered his nakedness with a blanket against the frigid night. What a sad end for Mstislav of the Loud Laugh, I thought—even if he was a military ass and a traitor to the pact he had made with his brother.

Time now to slip away to Vyshgorod. What we had learned so far was discouraging: the enemy's force, though unruly and disorganized, was large, well fed, and in a mood to stay. Mstislav was alive—barely—but it seemed impossible that we could get him away from his captors or prevent his being killed instantly if we launched an attack on the camp.

"To the river," Kuchug motioned with his head.

Our plan was to pick our way along the edge of the bluff, then back through the deserted ruins of the podol, and away to the north, following the shore and swimming, if necessary, to avoid patrols.

But first, I wanted a closer look at that discovery of mine; I'd had only a glimpse of it earlier in the day. Half hidden by bushes at the bottom of a small ravine was the mouth of a cave.

"Kuchug," I whispered, pointing down into the dark cleft, "you know this ground. Are there more caves here like that one?"

"Many. Come away, leave it."

"Why, what's the matter?"

"Crazy old men in there—dead men, too. Maybe ghosts, I think. Leave it alone."

Now, I'm no more fond of ghosts than the next man, but my curiosity was aroused.

"Let's have a look."

"What for?"

"Because I've taken a drubbing all day for nothing unless there's some advantage here for us." A vague notion had occurred to me of somehow smuggling our men into these caves for a surprise attack.

I took his arm but he drew back. "Too narrow, no good for steppe-people. Come away, hurry!"

"Not yet. Stay here, I won't be long. Lend me your sword."

17

the caves

Clinging to roots and brush, I eased myself down the side of the ravine. The night was dark, the bottom of the ravine darker still; but it was when I put my head into that cave's mouth that I felt darkness envelop me like a black sack.

A quavering inner voice pleaded to go back, but no— just a little farther—a little farther … The floor took a sudden dip, I lost my footing and slid down on my backside in an avalanche of pebbles. When I finally came to rest, I lay still, my heart beating like mad. From the echoing clicks of the falling stones I sensed a large space around me.

Off to my right something stirred. The scuffling of feet? Tightening my grip on Kuchug's saber, I crept in that direction. Again the scuffle of feet—surely human—rapidly retreating. Did whoever it was fear me more than I did him?

"Ya drug," I called softly in Slavonic, "I'm a friend. Show yourself."

But there was only the echo of my own voice. Then, more stirrings: soft steps, an indrawn breath, the rustle of cloth. Whoever they were, they surrounded me now. Why didn't they speak? For a swift instant I was in Pohjola again, in the bowels of Louhi's Copper Mountain with its buried horrors. The hairs on my neck stood up. I would have run away except that I had lost all sense of direction. I crouched down, feeling the cold sweat run down my back.

"In Christ's name, stranger," came a voice nearly at my elbow, making me jump, "you are welcome if you come in peace."

Flint scraped against steel; a candle blazed; then another and another ... Standing in the yellow pools of light, were white faced men, wrapped in dark robes.

The one who had spoken held up his candle, allowing me to see his face. It was covered by an immense white beard that began below the eyes and rippled over his chest right down to the knotted rope that served him for a belt.

"I am Feodosy, a servant of God and the abbot of these humble brothers," he said. "We are all poor monks here; you will find little to eat, but you are welcome to what we have."

Feodosy? Didn't I know that name? Father Dmitri had mentioned a Feodosy of the Caves in our catechism class and read us something by him. Yes, that was it—he was the one who warned against sharing your bowl with a heretic for fear of pollution. Well, never mind, I thought. If only he hates the Pechenegs half as much as he does the Catholics.

"Who are you, stranger, and what do you seek in Pechersky Lavra— the Monastery of the Caves?" It was a deep, not unpleasant voice.

Quickly gathering my thoughts, I answered that I was a druzhinik of Yaroslav the Wise.

A current of excitement ran through the shrouded figures around me. "The prince here!" they whispered. "How? When?"

Briefly I told of our arrival and explained our position. "I was sent to scout the camp and chanced to see the entrance to your cavern. I have no plan, but hope somehow to turn it to our advantage."

"Ah," said Feodosy, "I hardly think so. We are but humble soldiers of Christ here—our enemies are temptation, pride, and lust."

"And demons, Father," struck in one of the monks helpfully, "don't forget the demons."

"I wasn't forgetting—"

"Demons, is it?" I said in sudden irritation. "There are your demons!" I thrust my saber into the blackness overhead. "You must know what's going on up there—has it occurred to you that you might help?"

"But we are helping," replied Feodosy, offended. "We pray without cease for the deliverance of Kiev."

"Oh, yes, of course—that."

"You give no credit to prayer?"

"Prayer is best combined with action, Father Feodosy; there may be other ways of helping."

"May there?"

"How large is this place?"

"Why, large enough to afford each monk the solitude he craves. Altogether many caves reached by many tunnels—some of them natural, most dug by ourselves and by the saintly hermits who lived and died here before us."

"Take me through them, Father, and as we go we shall both of us pray for inspiration."

And so, with Feodosy and a few of the more sociable brethren leading the way, I crawled along dripping, niter-encrusted tunnels that led from one tiny cave to another. Within most of them, faintly limned by a candle flickering before an icon, knelt a monk—shaggy, bone-thin, and rapt in contemplation of the holy mysteries. Everywhere, soft sibilants of prayer whispered along stone corridors.

The extent of this underground city was astonishing. The monastery numbered only about fifty souls, but each one had his den at the end of some twisting passageway, dug by himself, in order to be removed as far as possible from his fellows. Hours passed, or so it seemed, while we groped our way down one black tunnel after another.

"Perhaps you have seen enough?" Feodosy suggested at last.

I said I supposed so. I had to admit that the notion of smuggling in fighting men was a foolish one; they could too easily be trapped here and starved into surrender.

With an uncanny sense of direction the abbot began to lead us back to our starting point. When we came to a place where a hard-packed mound of dirt seemed to offer a place to sit, I begged a moment to rest.

Agitated murmurs stirred among the brethren.

"Please," said Feodosy sternly, "not to sit there. It is where Brother Timofeo buried himself."

"Buried himself, did he?" cried I, leaping straight up.

"His one desire was to be deader than the rest of us," replied Feodosy. "Deader?"

"We war against the body, gospodin druzhinik, as you do against your bitterest foe. Yet even in this a limit must be set. A monk, like anyone else, may fall victim to the sin of pride. I fear there was a tincture of it in

Brother Timofeo. He refused all nourishment while heaping dirt upon himself, a little more each day, until at length, being nearly entombed, he gave up the ghost."

They were all entombed, as far as I could see, and no better off than a flock of ghosts. There flashed through my mind the painful memory of how Kalf Slender-Leg and I had quarreled that day in Nidaros when he tried to convert me to a hermit's life, using almost Feodosy's exact words.

"You spend your whole lives down here, Feodosy, never seeing the sun, never feeling the rain?"

"God must be sought in solitude and quiet," he replied. "A quiet which has been sadly shattered in these past weeks."

"It seems quiet enough to me."

"Oh, yes, at night, when the pagans are asleep. But in the daytime we hear the drumming of their horses' hoofs above our heads."

"And shouts, Father," added the helpful monk again, "don't forget shouts."

"Shouts too," said Feodosy patiently, "though faintly."

"You hear them? I swear I will never say a another word against prayer, gospodin abbot, for mine has just been answered!"

"Eh? How so?"

"Like flint against steel your words have struck a spark in me. Listen. I have something to propose to you—a sacrifice, a very great one for men who prize silence as much as you do, but one that will win you the undying gratitude of your prince. Imagine that it is his voice you hear now, not mine."

And I laid before them the stratagem that had just then taken shape in my mind. When I finished, Feodosy and his fellow monks looked uneasily at one another.

"Brother Nikita won't go along," said one, with a shake of his head.

"It will kill Brother Gennady," said another.

"Pah!" said Feodosy testily. "If the sound of his own singing hasn't killed Brother Gennady already, neither will this."

"There's no warrant in scripture for such a thing," a third monk warned.

"But you're wrong, Brother Vasili," Feodosy answered, "just think a moment. Joshua at the battle of Jericho! Why, it's nearly the same thing, don't you agree, druzhinik?"

146

"Why, yes, Father, now you say so, just about identical—I should have thought of it myself, by God!" I made a mental note to ask someone who this Joshua was.

"Of course," said Feodosy, "I shall compel no brother against his will. But to strike a blow for our prince and our Faith! And to picture the expressions on those heathen faces!" He began to smile and then to laugh out loud—a sound those dismal walls must have heard but seldom.

"Then you'll do it?"

He embraced me, planting a woolly kiss on each cheek. "Tell the prince we are his men!"

The other monks kissed me in turn, calling me 'God's angel of deliverance'—which made me feel damned queer; nor would they let me go without sharing a bit of moldy bread and water with them.

Back in the outer cavern, which was now ablaze with banks of candles, I was presented to the whole crew, who had gathered from their isolated cells to pray and break bread together.

Feodosy, kneeling before a great carved crucifix that stood over against one wall, asked God for his blessing on our enterprise. Afterwards, he offered me a drink from his bowl and we sat for a while working over the details of my scheme. He would accomplish his part in three days, four at the most, he promised, and would send word by one of the brothers when he was ready.

I would never have expected to like this fellow, who, had he known me for what I truly was, would surely not be sharing his water bowl with me. But in the flesh I found him kindly, patient, and good-humored; not at all the ranting fanatic I would have supposed from the words that Dmitri read to us. What is more full of surprises than Man? I began to like Feodosy despite the fact that I could no more comprehend his manner of life than I could interpret the dreams of a fish.

Outside again, I filled my lungs with fresh night air and found Kuchug perched at the edge of the ravine, exactly where I had left him. "Now, let's be off, friend Kuchug," I said. "Tonight has been worth all the pounding my poor shoulders have taken."

18

AN ARMY
OF GHOSTS

It was a long hike back to Vyshgorod, and late at night before we reached it. I roused Harald from his sleep and described my adventures to him, sketching a rough map of the Pecheneg camp with some idea of the caves and tunnels beneath it. When I was done, he burst out laughing to think of starveling monks saving Kiev with such an absurd trick, and he promised me a bonus of twenty silver grivny if the plan succeeded.

"And if it doesn't?"

"In that case, Tangle-Hair, surrender to the first Pecheneg you meet and beg to be his slave; you'll live longer and happier that way than if you show your face to me again. Now go get some sleep, you look about done in."

Some hours later, after I'd slept a little and Kuchug had gently washed my wounds and doctored them with some concoction of his, Yaroslav convened his war council. We met in the church, where Eustaxi lay, and Kuchug and I reported to the assembly all that we had seen. I couldn't avoid mention of the sad state of the prisoners and the great number of dead.

"And my son?" the prince asked, tight-throated with dread.

"We saw nothing of him. I'm sorry. But many may have gotten to safety inside the citadel."

"Yes, yes, of course, of course they may." How desperately he wanted to believe it.

"The main thing," I said, "is that the Pechenegs are eating through the countryside like a plague of locusts, and what they don't eat they burn. Unless we drive them off soon, Kiev will be a city of corpses."

"Then there's nothing more to say," said Harald, "we attack at once."

"As Mstislav did?" Eilif laughed harshly. "We all see what that came to. Yaroslav Vladimirovich, don't listen to these two crack-brained children. Take the advice of seasoned men. It's plain that we can do nothing until Sudislav and the other princes arrive."

Harald turned on them hotly, "Prince, give no ear to cowards! Sudislav might be as much as ten days behind us. As for the other two, we don't know if the couriers we sent even got through. Meanwhile our rations are nearly gone. In another day we'll all be starving. No. We must raise the siege now, and do it in a way that will put the fear of God into these savages for years to come."

"Of course," sneered Eilif, "you'll tell us how you plan to do that."

"With pleasure, Eilif. With the help of certain allies of ours, seven hundred brave druzhiniks will be as good as seven thousand. Now, attend all of you to my plan—" (Not for the last time did Harald lay claim to a stratagem of mine.) When he was done, and his words had been translated for those Rus and Slavs who spoke no Norse, there were grunts of satisfaction around the room. The idea pleased them.

Eilif, shamed and desperate, swore, by Christ, that neither he nor a single one of his Swedes would waste their lives in this folly!

"In that case Eilif Ragnvaldsson," cried Yaroslav in a fury, "I strip you of your rank, in God's name I do, and—and I order you from my sight!"

Shocked silence.

What an effect this bracing military air was having on our prince. At home, under his wife's withering glance, he would never have dared.

Eilif knew that too. "You what? Strip me of my rank? Why you pathetic, weak-minded, old cripple, the princess will have the balls off you for this—I mean if you've got any ..."

Harald sent him staggering across the aisle with a single blow to the jaw. As he rose on wobbly legs and drew his sword, two of his own men pinioned his arms and dragged him, choking with rage, from the church.

Of course, it was easy to say later that we should have killed him then, when we had the chance. The next morning he was nowhere to be found within the walls of Vyshgorod.

Now there followed an anxious time of waiting.

Regularly each morning a band of Pechenegs came screaming over the plain, to ride round and round our walls until they tired of launching arrows and insults. During these assaults only Eustaxi's men were allowed to show themselves on the ramparts, while the rest of us, by Harald's order, crouched out of sight.

We were hungry all the time now. Water from a well within the fort was the only thing we had in abundance. We were reduced to eating the last of the cats and dogs and all but two of the remaining horses. Inside Kiev, I kept reminding myself, it must be even worse.

A day, a night, another day crept by, while we stewed and fretted. Harald and Yaroslav began to give me searching looks. Had I led them into making fools of themselves? I put on a bold face, but doubt gnawed at me. Had Feodosy and his crew of lunatics sunk back into their pious torpor as soon as I departed?

But the next night—our fifth in Vyshgorod—brought a messenger to say that all was in readiness. Yaroslav ordered us all on our knees while he thanked Christ and a host of saints for near an hour. Kuchug and I slipped away unnoticed and spent the time more profitably readying our gear.

Finally, our little army, with a surge of battle joy that made us forget our empty bellies, moved to attack.

Harald and Yaroslav set out together at the head of the Norwegians and the bravest of the Rus warriors. They would be the spearhead, aimed straight at Tyrakh Khan's silken tent.

The Swedes, Eilif's former men, were now commanded by a certain Helgi Whale-Belly, a druzhinik they'd elected from among themselves. He was ordered to lead his men around to the west of the city and, as soon as he heard the sound of battle on his left, to attack the camp at its farther end, free the prisoners who were penned up there, scatter the horses, and fight his way to us. The Swedes received these orders in silence.

Harald had pleaded with Yaroslav to stay back, but the prince would not be dissuaded from leading the main thrust. He would leave to no other's hands, he swore, the sacred duty of cutting his poor brother's bonds. Among his motives was no doubt an element of sweet revenge—that brawny, boastful Mstislav, who had bullied him since childhood, should have to owe his life to his despised and crippled brother.

Wrapping our weapons in our cloaks for silence, we advanced along the river bank and through the ruins of the podol to that point where the ground begins to rise. We saw no Pecheneg pickets anywhere; weeks of drinking and gorging had taken its toll of discipline.

The prince, in spite of his age and his club foot, drove himself to keep pace with Harald's long strides. But what Yaroslav could do, Einar Tree-Foot could not. The hardships of the past few days had been too great for his already failing strength; it was impossible that he could hobble on his crutch from Vyshgorod to Kiev.

"We leave this place in the hands of a true and tested warrior, Tree-Foot," I had told him, trying not to let pity show in my voice. "If we fail, you'll organize the defense of Vyshgorod."

"Aye," he answered. There was so much desolation in that single word.

It was near dawn by the time we were in position—time for me, Kuchug, and the monk who had brought us Feodosy's message to slip into the river. Wading armpit deep through the icy water, we watched for the glimmer of a candle flame on the shadowy face of the bluff. Feodosy had said there was a cave mouth there, about half the way up, from which the monks were accustomed to lower a bucket to haul up their drinking water.

The signal light winked on and off. We reached the spot and found a knotted rope waiting for us. Hand over hand, with all our paraphernalia tied to our backs, we climbed the bluff.

Feodosy, who met us at the top, betrayed momentary alarm at the sight of Kuchug in his barbarous costume. Then, with unmistakable pride, the abbot showed us what his people had accomplished in this short time—a prodigy of digging—incredible, considering the frailty of their undernourished bodies, and the fact that they only dared work during the daytime when sounds underfoot would go unnoticed amid the bustle of the camp. These monks had the instincts of moles. Apart from psalm-singing, excavation was their chief joy. Now they had pushed their tunnels still farther and in dozens of places dug narrow shafts upwards to within a foot of the surface.

Undoing our packs, we distributed amongst them the pots and pans that we'd collected from all the kitchens of Vyshgorod, the hunting horns, the tubes of birch bark, and lastly Yaroslav's own brazen war trumpet, freshly blessed and sprinkled with holy water. With just such an instrument (I now knew from inquiring of the prince) had that Hebrew viking Joshua brought down the walls of Jericho. The camp of Tyrakh Khan had no stone walls to fall, yet we hoped to rival his feat nonetheless.

"By the way, Feodosy," I asked, "has a man been to visit you anytime in the past three days—a Swede, about thirty, thick featured, with his hair in his eyes?"

"We have seen no such person."

Where in Hel's Hall could he be? My greatest fear was that, knowing our plan, Eilif would find some way to make it fail.

The monks, with all their noise-making gear, went to their stations. Kuchug crept out of the cave at the bottom of the little ravine, scrambled noiselessly up the side, and strolled as slow and easy as you please toward the khan's tent. I climbed up behind him just far enough to see him go. This was his own idea—to stand beside his master from the first moment of the attack and defend him with his life until we reached them.

The starry sky was fading into grey. Somewhere a horse snorted and shook its head. Here and there a sleeping body stirred. Drawing my head down, I waited the few moments it would take Kuchug to reach his destination; then I put Yaroslav's trumpet to my lips.

Picture a field of slumbering men flying straight into the air—for that is what happened when the trumpet's bray shattered the silence and was followed next moment by the clashing of pots, the squeal of hunting horns, and the most frightful hooing and wooing beneath their feet. Ghosts, trolls—whatever it is that a Pecheneg fears—by this they thought themselves assailed. There was instantaneous panic.

"God and Saint George!" rang Yaroslav's voice in the distance. The sun, just rising, picked out his trident and Harald's raven as they gained the high ground and soared above the heads of the terrified Pechenegs. On the heels of their standard-bearers came the two leaders themselves and all their Rus and Norwegian fighters deployed in the 'swine array'— the wedge-shaped semblance of a pig, with overlapping shields for the hide and spears for the bristles.

Slinging the trumpet over my back, I boosted myself out of the ravine and dashed after Kuchug. All around me was indescribable confusion. Men ran and stumbled this way and that, not knowing where to turn, while their frightened animals reared and plunged.

I found Kuchug, true to his word, standing guard over his master—all alone, for the khan's guards had fled. A moment later Harald and Yaroslav came pounding up. While the druzhiniks formed a wall of spears around the tent, Harald and I slashed through the white silk and stepped inside.

We found the great khan, abandoned even by his women, crouching naked on the floor and moaning with terror. By pure good luck one of the underground shafts from which the ghostly sounds issued was exactly beneath his feet.

Now, part of my plan was to take Tyrakh prisoner, if we were lucky enough to catch him, for he would be more useful to us alive than dead. I imagined it would be a simple matter to truss up a ninety year old scarecrow and throw him over my shoulder. No one had bothered to tell me that Tyrakh Khan weighed close to three hundred pounds. His belly was huge, his breasts pendulous like a woman's, his hairless chins quivered.

As soon as he saw us, I think he realized that he was the victim of some kind of trick and that it was only the Rus, after all, that he had to deal with. For he lumbered to his feet and, unarmed as he was, flung himself at us.

Ramming his bald head into the pit of Harald's stomach, he tossed him as a bull tosses a terrier. This to Harald the giant! As he charged through the tent flap I leapt on his back, locked my arms around his fat neck and held on for dear life. It took five of us, finally, to bring him down. Meanwhile some of our men caught two loose ponies by their bridles, threw saddles on them, and, with lassos tied the Khan's bulbous ankles to the two inside stirrups; thus he lay on his back with his legs in the air between the horses.

By now, Mstislav was on his feet, supported by Kuchug and Yaroslav, each under one of his stiffened arms. The Wild Bison of Chernigov gazed dumbly at his brother as though at an angel just flown down from the sky. All along the parapet of Kiev's citadel figures appeared, pointing to us and cheering.

But our victory was still far from sure. We had gotten in—now we must get out. The ghostly noises were growing fainter as the monks, for whom trumpeting and screaming were not regular pastimes, began to tire. At the same time, the Pechenegs were already somewhat recovered from the first shock. Even worse, those at the western end of camp, who, being beyond reach of the monks' tunnels, had heard no ghostly sounds at all, were streaming in our direction to see what all the commotion was about.

And the Swedes who should have taken them in the flank and scattered them? We listened in vain for their war-cries.

"Close ranks around the prince!" shouted Harald. "Fall back to the podol."

But it was a steep drop down to the level of the riverside and the enemy was pressing us hard. By this time, some of them had gotten mounted and were putting their bows to use. Their volleys rained down on us, splintering our shields and rattling on our helmets. It was only because I'd had the foresight to put on three mail shirts that I was not killed half a dozen times.

Brave Kuchug was not so lucky. An arrow drove through his teeth and came out at the base of his skull with a gush of blood. As he fell, Mstislav sagged and Yaroslav had to support his brother's whole weight alone. With one arm around his thick waist he struggled to keep him on his feet while he held his shield over both their heads. Doggedly he went on, asking no help of anyone, until a Rus druzhinik, seeing him stumble, ran to help him.

By now, we had jumped, slid, and tumbled down to the riverbank, but in the process our solid shield-wall was broken up, leaving gaps where the enemy could rush in. Where I was, a band of them, desperate to rescue their khan, charged into us swinging sabers and maces. At the cost of many brave men's lives we beat them back. But another band, mounted on their sure-footed ponies, had taken a different way down, slipped around our right flank, and now barred our way to the citadel. We were hemmed in right, left, and front, with our backs to the river. Where were the shit-eating Swedes!

Then, hearing a rasping cry behind me, I looked around to see Einar Tree-Foot galloping towards us along the river's edge on a nag that was as thin and mangy as himself. His sword was in his hand, the reins were in his mouth, on his legless side the empty stirrup danced on the end of its leather.

He came on as in a dream, slowly—and slowly a Pecheneg archer marked him and drew back the feathered arrow to his jaw. Einar toppled from the saddle, the arrow deep in his side. But as he fell, his foot caught in the stirrup and the terrified horse plunged into our midst, dragging him with it. As he came within reach of my sword, I slashed at the leather and cut him loose.

I knelt down, covering him with my shield, as the roar and rush of battle, suspended for that frozen moment, broke in on me again.

"Tree-Foot!"

"Aye," he croaked. "Tree-Foot's not—not the man to lie low when a mate's in trouble. Eilif's turned the Swedes around, heading back to Vyshgorod. I seen 'em from the wall. He's left you to die."

"Then, we'll die together, Jomsviking—take my hand!"

I hauled him to his feet and got his arm around my shoulder. I wasn't far from Harald and shouted to him that we were betrayed. I doubt he heard me, though, for just then a great shout went up from the walls of the city.

Hundreds of paces behind and above us, the great gate swung open and a lone figure on a white horse came flying down the slope that descends from the citadel to the riverbank. For a few breathless moments he was all alone, heading at a dead run straight for the Pecheneg band that blocked our retreat. And something that he held cradled in his arm—I thought at first it was a shield—flashed golden in the rising sun. The white horse, struck in the chest with an arrow, fell to its knees and the rider pitched forward—surely to his death—in a swirl of flashing sabers. But now behind him the Kievans, screaming like berserkers, poured through the gate after him. Seeing this, our courage rose and our strength redoubled. We and the Kievans struggled towards each other, trampling the Pechenegs down between us. The blood lust rose in my chest. I screamed my father's battle cry and swung my ax right and left and felt the crunch of bone under its blade.

As we linked hands, I glimpsed again, above the sea of bodies, that heroic rider; realized, that it was the boy Volodya! He had mounted a Pecheneg pony and still clutched to his chest his golden 'shield, which was, I saw now, a great gilded icon of Saint George.

Led by Volodya and backed by the Kievans, we made a fighting retreat up the slope. As the last of us passed within, the gate swung shut in the faces of the Pechenegs, who howled with fury and sent flight after flight of arrows against it. I leaned against a wall, my legs trembling, chest heaving. With an edge of my tunic I wiped sweat and Pecheneg blood from my eyes.

The folk of Kiev mobbed us. Men and women, young and old; some fell on their knees before Yaroslav while others stretched out their hands to touch him, and all of them cried his name, hailing him, as they had once hailed his father, 'Velikiy Knyaz—Grand Prince'.

Mstislav—naked, filthy, and bloody—was not even recognized.

Young Volodya, wearing a mail shirt several sizes too big for him and dragging a man's sword from his belt, pushed through the crowd toward his father. Like everyone here, he was pinch-faced and haggard, but otherwise unhurt. Looking at him, it was easy to see the lineaments of the warrior he would one day be—the high forehead and piercing gray eyes, the strong jaw, which owed more to Ingigerd than to Yaroslav. The meeting of father and son amidst the wild cheering of the crowd was wonderfully moving. Tears streamed down both their faces as they embraced.

"My eagle, my young falcon," cried Yaroslav, breathlessly, "what madness seized you? You could have been—he's only a child—who permitted this?" He didn't know whether to be glad that his son was alive or furious with the guards who had obeyed the boy's command to open the gate. "Ah, but God himself held his hand over you, didn't he, and Saint George shielded your breast!"

That much was certainly true; the heavy oaken board was shaggy with arrows.

"We found your messages," answered his son. "I did the only thing I could think of. I knew that our people would fight like madmen to rescue both me and the icon. Father, I return your city of Kiev to you, undefiled by even one pagan foot."

The crowd went mad, seeing in this brave and serious boy the image of his grandfather.

But I could not give myself completely to joy. A victory that cost the life of Einar Tree-Foot seemed almost too dearly bought for me. He was still breathing as I laid him down beside the gate and wondered if I dared cut out the arrow head, which was so deep. But he reached around with his left hand and wrenched the barbed shaft straight out. "You feed your hirdmen well, Jarl," he cackled aloud, "see how much fat clings to the tip."

Where were his wits wandering? Was he young again on some battlefield of long ago? One of those vanished warriors who made grim, laconic jokes at the moment of their death?

"Einar, it's me, Odd."

"Odd? Young Odd—?" Letting the arrow slip from his fingers, he gripped my shoulder and drew himself up till his face was close to mine. "Einar Tree-Foot's done what he longed to do—die with steel in him. Won't the Valkyries carry me to Valhalla now? " It was his one fear, that he would die a peaceful death and be nothing but a squeaking ghost in Hel's gloomy hall.

"But Tree-Foot," I said, "these bastards have made us into Christmen, and now they say we can't go to Christ's mansion and Odin's mead-hall both."

"Eh? Rubbish! Didn't that scrawny priest tell how Christ was pierced in his side with a spear?

"He did."

"Well, by the Raven, then he's earned his right to sup at Odin's table too! Ha, ha ..."

The laugh became a rattle in his throat; a shudder ran along his limbs; his grip on me loosened. So died my friend. An Age, I do believe, died with him.

"Tangle-Hair!" came Harald's voice from the parapet. "My fine fiery poet! Get you up here at once and stand beside me as a skald should. Hah! What a day! What a victory! What glorious poetry you'll make of it!"

With a bitter taste in my mouth, I left Einar for a while to go up on the wall. There I found Harald, Yaroslav and his son, and Mstislav, looking more dead than alive.

The fat khan, his back in shreds from the dragging he'd suffered, was slumped like a flour sack over the edge of the parapet. His groans were like music to us. A slave-woman of the town who had lived with the Pechenegs and knew their language was fetched to act as interpreter. Harald spoke in Norse to me, I translated his words into Slavonic for her, and she, in turn, shouted them in Pecheneg to the khan's warriors, who were gathered in their hundreds at the foot of the wall. In this cumbersome fashion Harald harangued the enemy.

He demanded first that the lesser khans come forward to parlay with him. When they appeared, he told them he would return their master in exchange for all the prisoners they held. At this Yaroslav looked up in surprise. Harald, in typical fashion, had not thought it worth his while to confer with his own prince before parlaying with the enemy.

Below, after a brief conference, the khans agreed to his terms, and pretty soon the surviving captives from Chernigov, Smolensk, and Pereyaslavl were shepherded up the slope, those who could walk carrying those who couldn't. The gate opened to admit them but the Kievans watched them enter in stony silence. How could they be fed in a city already starving?

When he saw that the survivors were safely inside, Harald spoke again through the interpreter, saying that we would give them back their khan only in exchange for a hundred of their nobles, to be handed over at once.

The Pechenegs spat on the ground and glowered at us but eventually the hundred 'nobles' appeared marching up the slope. They lay down their weapons as they entered the gate. Our druzhiniks had all they could do to keep the townsfolk from tearing them to pieces.

(In my opinion they were not really nobles at all, but rather the poorest of the Pechenegs dressed up in fine clothes and costly armor, and ordered to sacrifice themselves for their betters. How would we know the difference?)

Then Harald laughed at the khans and mocked them: "You fools! It's true what all the world says, that the Pechenegs are the stupidest of men! Did you imagine that Grand Prince Yaroslav of Kiev would ever consent to give back the murderer of his grandfather? Now, watch and you will see how we deal with him. Kraki, the loan of your axe."

Kraki, one of his bodyguards, handed him the weapon.

I had never before seen done what Harald did then, although my father had described it to me once, on one of our wild nighttime rambles: the ancient ritual slaughter of the 'blood eagle'.

Tyrakh screamed just once as Harald, standing behind him, brought the axe head whistling down and split his spine lengthwise. Wrenching the axe out he struck twice again until the body was opened all down the back from the base of the neck to the tail bone. We were all spattered with his blood.

Then, tossing the axe aside, he put his hands into the crevice, grasped the ribs, and, with a cracking of bone, wrenched the two halves wide apart. Into the cavity he thrust his arms and pulled out the lungs, which he spread across the dead man's shoulders so as to resemble the wings of a bird. Gouts of blood dripped from his fingers.

Volodya turned away and was sick, while Yaroslav and many another looked pale around the gills. But in Mstislav's dull eye there flickered a gleam of satisfaction.

Taking up the axe again, Harald lopped off the Khan's head and tossed it casually to me, telling me to keep it safe for he had a use for it.

"And now," cried Harald, "let us see if this headless bird can fly to its roost." And lifting the mangled carcass up by its legs, he tipped it over the edge. It hit the ground with a sound like wet slops tossed from a window. The Pechenegs drew back and gazed in horror at the bloody mess. Harald had given these cruel men a lesson in savagery that surpassed anything they knew. They were more than beaten; they were shaken down to the soles of their feet.

"This," he shouted at them, "is how Northmen deal with the Pechenegs and always will!" And he spat at them.

Throughout the Pecheneg camp now arose a shrill keening, growing louder as more and more took up the cry. The great khan was dead.

Nothing could be done now until he was wailed over for many days and finally buried with his horses and his women, in a mound by the bank of the Dnieper far to the south. Meanwhile a murderous struggle over the succession would begin at once among the lesser khans, who were all his sons or grandsons by various wives and concubines. Much blood would flow before one of them emerged victorious.

"Grand Prince, look there—" said a Rus warrior to Yaroslav, pointing toward the west. We all looked and saw a dust cloud, which soon grew into a line of horsemen, hundreds of them, racing over the plain. The Pechenegs ran in terror, leaving behind everything but the remains of their khan. And this time it was not the wily feigned retreat for which they were so famous, but the genuine thing.

Within minutes not a live Pecheneg could be seen from the walls of Kiev.

"Our cursed luck!" said Bryacheslav, Prince of Volhynsk, to Pozvizd, Prince of Izyaslavl, as they reined in their sweating mounts. "To have come all this way and missed the fun!"

19

A SKULL AND OTHER MATTERS

After the flight of the Pechenegs, Harald, Yaroslav, and I rode back across the littered plain to fetch Eustaxi from Vyshgorod and unite him with his father. We took armed men with us, as we were uncertain what sort of reception to expect from the Swedes.

We ought not to have worried. They mobbed Harald as he rode through the gate, holding onto his stirrup, calling him 'Jarl' and 'Boyar', and begging his forgiveness. Helgi Whale-Belly held up Eilif's head on the point of a spear.

"He lied to us, Jarl Harald," pleaded Helgi. "He came out of the woods, where he'd been hiding, just as we were making ready to attack the camp. He called us fools, for we'd be massacred, he said, while you and your men plundered the khan's tent and made off with all the treasure. Well, we didn't know what to think, for it's plain you've always favored your own men over us. He convinced us to stay back and wait for you to be killed. Pardon us, Harald, we were too hasty. See, we've punished the liar as he deserved. Now let us be your men. One druzhina, one captain!" These last words were taken up as a chant by all the others crowding around.

Harald looked grim; I had an idea what he was thinking. We had only ourselves to blame for this. Allowing the Norwegians to be a guard within the guard had been a mistake from the beginning, it was easy to see that now.

To the Swedes' entreaty Harald replied only, "You'll oblige me by helping the people of Vyshgorod to bury their dead and repair their houses."

Thinking this to mean they were forgiven, they rushed to obey.

We proceeded to the church to see Eustaxi. He was feverish and seemed weaker than he had been the day before, but he understood us when we told him of our victory, and he was anxious to see his father. We carried him to Kiev.

It would be hard to say which of the two looked more pitiful. Mstislav lay in bed in the bishop's house while healing-women plastered him from head to toe with moss and mud, and others massaged his shoulders. I was there and saw their faces—father and son, each so full of pain at seeing the other's condition, and neither admitting to being hurt himself. We shooed the women out and left them alone. What words passed between them, no one would ever know.

✝

Throughout the remainder of the day the necessaries were seen to. By that I mean bringing into the city whatever food could be found before the wolves made off with it, and disposing of the dead before they poisoned the air. Of these, the Christians, including about fifty of Harald's men, were buried all together in a common grave, to which, in sorrow, I added Einar's slight remains, laying his cross-shaped sword on his breast so that, whether bound for Heaven or Valhalla, he would be ready. As an offering to the ghosts of our dead, the hundred 'noble' prisoners were variously burnt, impaled, used for archery practice, sawn limb from limb, and dragged to death by horses while the good people of Kiev howled curses and, for a little while at least, forgot their empty bellies. We flung the bodies into the Dnieper. Rus towns and nomad wagon-camps from here to the Black Sea would watch those swollen corpses floating by and rejoice or grieve accordingly.

Late in the afternoon, towers of purple cloud swept up from the south as if by command and poured out a drenching rain that scoured the battlefield clean.

✝

During the days that followed, I plunged into constant activity. With the foragers I combed the fields, with the huntsmen I prowled the forests, and waded into the streams with the fishermen. Of game and fish we found sufficient, but of grain and fruits there was little. Still, if we could not do much for the Kievans' bellies, something, at least, could be done for their souls. On the morning following our victory a solemn thanksgiving mass was held in the open air where all could attend. The four sons of Vladimir the Great knelt side by side before a make-shift altar: Pozvizd and Bryacheslav, both strong men and handsome; Yaroslav, bearing himself with a palpable air of pride, for, despite his lameness and his bookish soul, he had shown real bravery in battle; and kneeling beside him a pathetic and chastened Mstislav.

Abbot Feodosy and his monks were sent for by Yaroslav—I carried the invitation myself. Those of them who agreed to come up (which were by no means all) emerged blinking like moles into the light. Yaroslav met Feodosy at the gate to the citadel, knelt at his feet, kissed him, and personally led him inside to the wild cheering of the populace.

That same evening a victory feast was held in the palace. We called it a feast, although there was scarcely a drop to drink of wine or ale. I chanted two victory odes, which I had composed in haste that very afternoon; one praising Harald and the other Yaroslav. Harald presented me with my twenty silver grivny, while Yaroslav was so pleased with his poem that he promised me a horse from his own stables and a falcon from his mews as soon as we returned to Novgorod.

When it came time for the drinking of toasts, we were embarrassed, as I have said above, by the lack of strong drink. But Harald summoned his cup-bearer anyway. That youth produced, with a flourish, a round white bowl, filled it with wine, and proffered it to Yaroslav. It was, of course, a skull.

I had watched Harald earlier in the day when he sawed the cap off above the eyebrows, scooped out the brains, peeled away the scalp, and dried the bone over a slow fire. The wine was what Christmen call the blood of their Lord—a jar of which the bishop of Kiev had hoarded in secret. Harald, with his usual directness, threatened to chop the man's hands off if he didn't hand it over.

Yaroslav, for some reason thinking that it was Eilif's skull, recoiled; but we assured him that it belonged to none other than his enemy, Tyrakh Khan.

"Drink, Grand Prince," said Harald, bowing low, "and pay the debt of blood owed to your grandfather Svyatoslav's ghost."

Yaroslav looked as if he really would rather not, but took a small sip and passed the bowl to Mstislav (who by now was recovered enough to sit at table). With a bearish growl, he tipped back his head and drained it at a gulp. "Never was wine sweeter, by God! Fill her again!" he roared.

He held the last bowlful to the pale lips of Eustaxi, his dear son, who lay on a pallet beside the bench, so weak that he could scarce lift his head. The wine ran down his cheek.

If Mstislav's son was a sorry sight, Yaroslav's was a proud one. Volodya's heroism was on every Kievan's lips. When their mayor was killed early in the siege, said the bishop, it was this lad of twelve who took command of the defenses, refusing to hear of surrender, and eating never a mouthful more than the poorest of his men. "And at the end! Only a heart inspired by God could have dared such a deed as he did!" the bishop cried, clasping his hands together.

While his praises were being sung, the boy kept his eyes fixed on the floor and blushed. How splendid he looked in his dark blue caftan; his scarlet cloak, trimmed with gold and fastened with a ruby clasp; his boots of soft yellow leather; his tall sable hat. It was the costume he had worn for his audience with the emperor of the Greeks.

Yaroslav gazed on his son with fond, proud eyes as though unable to believe that he had fathered this image of perfection. And the thought occurred to me—surely, for the first time in my young life—that I would most likely have sons someday and that I would give anything in the world to have one like Vladimir Yaroslavich.

(What pain it is, now in my old age, to think how soon fate would make him hate me; and how one day, not many years later, we would face each other in bitter war, he on the deck of his warship and I commanding the flame cannons that guarded the harbor of Miklagard.)

"Hallo, Odd Tangle-Hair, my friend!" came a voice behind me. "You here, too? By God, is good to see you, ha, ha!"

He had grown so thin that I barely recognized Stavko Ulanovich as he bounded up to me, as usual speaking, chuckling, and salivating all at once. I hadn't known that he was traveling with the convoy. He embraced me with one arm, the other was in a sling.

"You're wounded."

"Ah. Is nothing, I am lucky. Was bloody murder, my friend, when they jumped us. And me having to protect not only myself but fifteen screaming women. Beauties they were. Cost me fortune. Now poor things are skin and bone; I could not give 'em away. Well, not to complain. Scrawny woman better than none at all, eh? Ha, ha! I've got 'em locked up. You come around whenever you want and help yourself."

✝

To return to the Swedes, Harald rightly argued that they were spoiled beyond recovery and that men even once guilty of disobedience on the battlefield could never be trusted again. They made matters worse for themselves by looting houses in the town, brawling in public, and raping a number of women. Kiev to them was just another captured city and they felt free to treat it so.

Harald had the solution.

When the following Sunday came round, all the druzhiniks were ordered to attend a special mass for the dead. Yaroslav was insistent that the Swedes be given a last chance to confess and take holy communion, even if it was all for the sake of a trap. When it came their turn, they entered the cathedral, stacking their arms outside. When they came out again it was to find their arms gone and a cordon of Rus warriors surrounding them. We cut down every one of them while the Kievans looked on in dismay.

No doubt this was another example of Harald's faithlessness, but this time, in my opinion, justified. Yaroslav later pretended to be shocked by the deed, though in fact he had agreed.

The day of the Swedish massacre happened also to be Harald's seventeenth birthday. I, myself, turned twenty a week later. Prince Eustaxi would have been twenty-seven in the same month had he lived; but, after clinging to life for so many weeks, he died quietly in the night while his father slept beside him.

Mstislav was laid low by this. He had stayed on in Kiev only because his son was too weak to be moved. Now, sorrowing, he made ready to take him home for burial. It was a sad remnant of his once proud army that straggled out of Kiev on a bleak October morning. What had begun as a bold, if underhanded, grab for power ended as a funeral cortege.

Had Yaroslav wanted then and there to scrap the treaty with his half-brother and declare himself Grand Prince of all Rus (as he was already being called), who could have faulted him? But, despite Harald's urging, Yaroslav would not break his Christian oath just because his rival was a beaten man. Whether 'Yaroslav the Wise' would be better called 'Yaroslav the Fool', I leave to others to decide.

✝

By the end of October, the prince was eager to return to the comforts of his familial hearth. He had already sent the Novgorod merchants back to the city with news of our victory and of Harald's promotion to command of the druzhina. (The true version of Eilif's death was covered up to spare Jarl Ragnvald's feelings.) For our transport he commandeered twenty-five strugi, promising to return them to their owners next spring. But the common people, when they got wind of this, came crowding round the palace to beg their prince not to abandon them. When he came out and tried to reason with them, they drowned his words with shouts, and actually menaced him. The horrors of the Pecheneg raid were still too fresh in their minds. Their prince must spend the winter with them, they insisted—he and his miraculous son and the giant captain of his druzhina. They needed this time for forging weapons, drilling the militia, and rebuilding their herd of cavalry horses. If Yaroslav tried to desert them now, as God was their witness, they would burn all his ships!

And, at last, though he longed to return to his books, his comforts, and, most of all, to the arms of his loving and faithful wife, Yaroslav yielded.

Now, Harald, too, was anxious to be quit of Kiev and go home to take more sweet, stolen kisses from Yelisaveta, but like it or not he must stay with his prince. Which meant that I would be staying, too. Of the three of us, only I was content. I'd succeeded in pushing Inge and everything to do with her far to the back of my mind. That had cost me an effort and I was in no hurry now to go home and face it all again.

20

I SWEAR A GREAT OATH

The winter passed pleasantly enough. I devoted much of it to improving my Slavonic with the assistance of a girl from the town whom I slept with.

And I spent much time in the company of young Volodya. He too was happy to be staying in Kiev. Novgorod, with his mother, nurse, and tutor, held no charms for him, while here were chances for danger and adventure. The Pechenegs disappointed him by never once showing their faces, but still there was tracking and hunting, skating, skiing, and sleigh-riding to occupy him—all of which he was keen on.

Harald often invited himself along on these outings. From the start he patronized the boy, pretending they were great chums while never missing a chance to show him the 'correct' way to draw a bowstring, to build a camp fire, to launch a falcon (which Harald himself had not known before a year ago). Volodya bore all this patiently enough, but when Harald boasted to him one day, "You shall soon have me for a brother-in-law, young'un, what d'you say to that?" the boy regarded him silently for a moment and replied:

"Eilif once said the same thing to me, friend Harald—those very words—and look at him now."

"What?" Harald spluttered, "Why, damn you—!"

Volodya turned his back and marched away, leaving the captain of the druzhina fuming.

What led up to this boast of Harald's was the following. The previous night Yaroslav had drunk rather deeper than he was used to and was in an expansive mood. (Barrels of wine and ale had, by now, been brought in from the towns upriver.) As we all sat talking after supper, he turned to Harald suddenly and said:

"Look here, Harald Sigurdsson—been meaning to bring this up, waiting for the proper moment. You needn't answer right away but give it a thinking over, will you? I mean to say, Eilif's dead now, isn't he, God help his soul, and so his betrothal to my Yelisaveta—well, that's obvious, isn't it? But still I favor the idea of uniting the captain of the druzhina to my family by a marriage. Now, I know what you're going to say—she is a bit wild, feuds with her mother and that sort of thing, but she's young, she'll settle down, and she is a lovely thing to look at, now you must admit that. Of course, Ingigerd has it in for you a bit, hasn't she? Oh, I notice things, you know, though really I don't know why. She has her moods and quirks. Well, I suppose, married to a man so much older than herself, and Novgorod's a gloomy place, I'm the first to admit it. Sometimes, you know, I think I should have been a monk, I crave the solitary life. But we princes have our duty, like it or not. We must father more princes to take our place—and what a prince I have fathered, eh? What a young lion!" He embraced his son, who sat quietly beside him, and kissed his cheeks. "Now, what was I saying—oh yes, your marriage to Yelisaveta. We'll bring Ingigerd around to it, just you let me handle that part of it. But here I am running ahead of myself and don't even know if you favor the match or not." He paused and looked at Harald expectantly.

"You do me great honor, Prince," replied Harald gravely. "Though I have only a passing acquaintance with your daughter, she seems to me a virtuous and good-hearted girl, as befits the child of such a father. With your permission I will begin my suit the very day we return to Novgorod, and furthermore I will make it my business to gain the friendship of the Lady Ingigerd, whose dislike of me I find both painful and mystifying."

He avoided my eyes for fear he would burst out laughing in the old man's face.

Ye gods, I thought, if only Dag were here! This smooth piece of work is worthy of the master himself!

Inside him I knew that Harald was shouting with glee, and, as soon as Yaroslav had limped off to bed, he did precisely that: shouted, pranced, and drank until dawn in a state of mind that seemed equal parts joy and madness.

Without his knowledge, Yaroslav's words had had an effect on me, too. As I said, I had succeeded pretty well over the winter in driving Inge from my thoughts. Novgorod and its intrigues seemed very far away, and the question of Inge's part in those various attacks on Harald was no more to me than a sort of weary perplexity, when I allowed myself to think of it at all. But the first breeze of spring carried the scent of her perfume on it and seductive memories invaded my waking and my sleep: of Inge's skin, slick with sweat, in the steam bath; of the nervous excitement before each tryst; of late nights sipping wine before her fire; of rolling in her bed while good Saint Irene, veil over face, saw nothing.

In short, I itched for her again. Could I, I wondered, give all that up for mere prudence sake? It was Yaroslav who decided the question for me, because the offer of his daughter to Harald meant that Dag's strategy, even without Dag to guide it, was bearing fruit. What I'd taken on faith so far, I could see happening now. Harald, backed by all the resources of a rich and doting father-in-law, reclaiming Norway from the Danes, installing Yelisaveta as his queen, and sending me home to Iceland a rich and influential man, able to take vengeance at last on the murderers of my family.

I must do nothing to jeopardize that. Let Inge be as innocent as an angel, it no longer mattered. Now, more than ever, loving her could only bring me to grief. Her daughter's betrothal to the hated Harald would provoke a domestic crisis beyond anything that poor, fond Yaroslav could imagine. I knew Inge that well, at least. And when it came, I had better be clearly on one side or the other, because the fence that I had straddled up till now would be flattened at the first assault. There was no middle ground any more.

No! I told myself. If I ever loved her, I do no more. My allegiance goes where my interest lies. The business between us, whatever it meant for her or for me, is over. On the first day that I set foot in Yaroslav's dvor I will tell her so. By Christ and Odin I swear it.

How strong, how resolute I felt, having sworn this great oath! How easy when a thousand versts lay between us.

✝

April. The ice broke up in the Dnieper. The Kievans, who, as far as I could see, had done remarkably little all this time in the way of forging weapons or drilling their militia, reluctantly gave us back our liberty.

Prince Yaroslav had done nothing all winter long but moon about 'his Lady', forced to bear the burden of government on her frail shoulders these many months. For her sake he had lit candles by the armload and worried himself sick with imaginary fears.

Now, in our fleet of borrowed strugi he made the men bend to their oars just as hard as when we were racing the other direction to Kiev's rescue. Harald, as I have said, was equally hot to be home: to claim his bride and drive Ingigerd insane with rage. What a consummation of his desires!

And now I, too, was ready. Like a man who has made up his mind to bear an ordeal—to have a rotten tooth pulled or an arrow cut out of his hide—let it come now, I thought. Let there be no more waiting.

Our swift ships devoured the miles to Novgorod.

21

YELISAVETA BETHROTHED

The willows that grew by the Volkhov were green with new buds while grey ice floes still bobbed in the water. The subjects of 'My Lord Novgorod the Great' jostled one another on the banks, straddled tree limbs, and leaned far over the railing of the painted bridge.

To the thunder of their hurrahs the leading strug tied up to the palace jetty, and their prince, with his splendid young son beside him, hurried down the gangplank. On their heels came Harald and I, leading the Norwegian and Rus druzhiniks, all mingled happily together now. One druzhina, one captain.

Within the palace yard we splashed ankle-deep through the spring mud and halted by the foot of the stairs as Inge came down to meet us. Standing on the bottom step, so as not to soil her shoes, she made the smallest bow to her husband that decency demanded and said, "Yaroslav Vladimirovich, I thank God to see you safely home."

How strange to hear that voice again—I'd forgotten how low and warm it was, even when—as now—there was little feeling in her words; and again to be reminded of that certain way she had of lifting her chin, and how the corners of her mouth turned slightly downward when she was serious—that and so much more, impossible to put into words: so familiar, and yet I felt as though I were seeing it all for the first time.

She offered her cheek for the obligatory kisses. But Yaroslav's cheerful countenance clouded over as he took a step nearer her; and I saw why. Her cheeks were hollow and there were dark circles under her eyes. She had always been slim, but she was much too thin now, her pale skin stretched tight over the planes of her face. And her whole bearing was stiff and unnatural, as if only a great effort of the will was keeping her upright. What was the matter with her? Was she ill?

Yaroslav, all sympathy and self-reproach, patted her hand while he called upon God to see what a saint, what a martyr, he had for a wife. With a look of impatience, she withdrew her hand from his anxious grasp and addressed Harald instead, saying: "Boyar, I congratulate you on your new rank and position in our household. Your victory over the accursed pagans would astonish us if we were not already accustomed to expect miracles from you." This speech was prettily spoken—almost convincing, if you didn't know how they hated each other. But if she had meant by it to lure Harald into bragging at her husband's expense, he disappointed her.

"Not my victory, Princess," he came back just as smoothly; "my part in it was only to carry out my lord's orders."

They were both, in fact, being uncommonly polite. Why?

She turned now to me. "And Odd—Thorkelsson, was it?—forgive me, I've no head for names." She favored me with the polite smile one gives to strangers. But before she looked away, her eyes held mine for just a moment longer. They were sick and desperate eyes. I mumbled some reply, I don't remember what. Fury, haughtiness, false smiles and lying words—all those I had expected, but not this. It took me up short.

Meantime Volodya, the young hero, was being mobbed by his younger brothers and sisters who hung on his arms and legs in transports of excitement. Only Yelisaveta took no notice of him; her glance was for Harald alone. And in a twinkling she and he were hurrying out of sight around the corner of the building. Behind the prince and his lady, we trooped up the stairs to the vestibule and from there into the great hall. Everywhere, I looked around hopefully for Dag but, of course, did not find him. I hadn't really expected to. Harald had driven away for good the shrewdest and most loyal counselor he would ever have. I found instead Thordis, sitting by the oven with her sewing basket. I told her straight out that Einar Tree-Foot was dead. Her wrinkled old face seemed to crumple like an empty wineskin, but, true northern woman that she was, she asked only if he had shown courage, and when I said he had, she nodded and bent again to her needle. If there were tears later, no one saw them.

Soon after this, Inge beckoned her old nurse to accompany her, and the two women disappeared through the passageway into the seclusion of the tower.

I, too, after having spent so many days and nights without respite in the company of Harald and Yaroslav, craved a little solitude; and I had much to think about. I slipped out of the dvor unobserved and walked to the tavern in Vitkova Street that had been Dag's favorite. The tavern keeper, who knew me slightly, started in at once with idle questions and ignorant opinions about Kievans and Pechenegs, only ceasing when I turned to the wall with my mug of ale. I drank steadily; without pleasure, but only hoping to numb my brain, for I was suffering agonies of indecision. I must—I would—break with Inge if possible, this very day, as I had sworn to. Yet, even as I formed the thought, I felt my nerve weaken. Could I be so harsh to this frail creature?

✝

Sundown. Time for the feasting to begin. With an unsteady step I made my way back to the palace. To my surprise, there were scores of unfamiliar faces in the hall—Swedes from the Lake Malar district to judge by their accent. What were they doing here? The answer lay with a newcomer at court, a man not much older than myself, by the name of Yngvar Eymundsson. He sat near the head of the table with Harald and me. He was Ingigerd's nephew, he told us, and had just lately come over with nine ships and four hundred fighting men.

Harald bristled on hearing this, naturally suspecting that this kinsman was Ingigerd's candidate for Eilif's replacement. He attacked him with bullying questions: Why was he here? How long was he staying? Was he aware that he was addressing the captain of the druzhina? To all of which Yngvar replied, with a frank and open smile, that he felt privileged to be sitting next to a personage of so high a rank, that he hadn't any plans really except to seek fortune and adventure, and that, for the moment, his intention was to study the languages spoken in this part of the world, considering that knowledge to be of the greatest usefulness to a traveler in strange lands.

"Yes, well," muttered Harald, disarmed for the moment, but still suspicious, "then you want to talk to my skald here. He pitches the local gibberish by the shovelful, I never saw the like."

With that remark he dismissed us, and leaned across the table to whisper something to Yelisaveta, who was seated facing him. This, in itself, was a remarkable change in affairs: in the past, Inge had always sat the pair so far apart that they could scarcely see each other, let alone converse; had she lost that power now? Or the will to use it, which amounts to the same thing?

I was willing to be distracted from my thoughts and fell into pleasant conversation with Yngvar on the pitfalls of Slavonic, which is a devilish hard language to learn because the words come at you all jumbled up and you can say a thing four or five different ways without changing the sense of it. I recommended to him my practice of studying in bed with a local girl. He laughed and said he would begin at once.

Notwithstanding his suspicions of Yngvar, tonight was Harald's night, and how he relished it! He struck a fierce pose while I sang the tale of his deeds, and beamed with self-satisfaction as the skull of Tyrakh Khan was passed around from hand to hand. All throughout dinner, in fact, his expression resembled that of a cat who has caught a mouse under its paw and anticipates the pleasure of killing it slowly. This was because he knew something that the rest of us did not.

Presently Yaroslav called for silence. Silence being, as usual, beyond his power to command, he settled for some lessening of the racket, and began in his halting, rambling way—he was rather drunk besides—to say something about Harald, and then about Yelisaveta, and wasn't it too bad about Eilif Ragnvaldsson ... As his meaning began to be perceived, the room suddenly got very still indeed—which made the prince falter at the sound of his own voice.

"Yes, well, as I say, ah, Eilif being dead, God keep his soul, yes, and my beauty, my Yelisaveta, being ripe for wedding and bedding, eh? Ha, ha—"

Hot-Eyed Freya's girdle, but she was ripe! I'd been noticing her all evening. As Inge sickened, in equal measure had her daughter bloomed. Eight months had turned Yelisaveta into a woman. Surely, those were not the breasts of a maid of fourteen swelling under her gown, nor those the curvaceous hips of a virgin. Gone from her face was the last of its little-girl roundness; I was suddenly aware how much there was of Ingigerd in it.

"And so I, ah, well—when I made Harald Sigurdsson the captain of my druzhina, I gave him leave to sue for my daughter's hand in marriage. And it seems that he has wasted no time but has done so with the greatest dispatch, just as he pursues all his affairs, by God! And my daughter, with a like promptness, has accepted him. Ah, so there it is. The two of them gave me their glad tidings but an hour ago."

Across the table Harald's and Yelisaveta's eyes met and flashed with wicked joy, as if to say, "We have wounded the dragon to her death!"

"So then," Yaroslav's speech lurched to its conclusion, "since she herself is willing, why, I can see nothing in the way of, well, and what d'you say to it my dear,"—Ingigerd had come into the hall only moments before and taken her seat without a word to anyone—"for a mother's wishes must be consulted too, dear me, yes. Only, it all happened so quickly, don't you see?"

Harald's bold gaze shifted to Inge and, in a voice dripping with sarcasm, he said, "Princess, you would not begrudge your daughter the chance to wed her one true love, would you? You of all people?"

He couldn't resist turning the knife. But if his aim was to provoke an outburst of screaming rage he was cheated of it. She sat statue-still, seeming hardly to breathe. "Husband," she said very softly, "I should have thought a public feast not the proper setting for a family council, but I yield, as always, to your wisdom. The union of our daughter with Harald Sigurdsson has much to recommend it, yet we should not hurry the consummation of it. Let them spend some months together in courtship—until the New Year, say. And if then they are still of the same mind, why, how could I, or anyone, object?"

The prince heaved a loud sigh of relief and took a long pull at his ale horn.

But Yelisaveta demanded shrilly, "Till the New Year? Till September? And it being only April now? Why, mother, aren't you anxious to see your grandchildren? The girls will all look like me and the boys like Harald. Won't that please you? And how you'll love to dance them on your knees, won't you, mother?" She threw back her long hair and laughed.

"Yes, well—" said Yaroslav hurriedly, "time enough later to set the date. Now, in God's name, let us have merriment!" He tipped Harald a wink as if to say, "You see, I told you there'd be no trouble about it."

Yelisaveta ran to embrace her father, kissing his cheek and mussing his hair. After that, she and Harald danced together for an hour without stopping and everyone stood back to watch how he swung her through the air as lightly as if she were a straw doll.

Ingigerd did not stay to watch.

Her food untouched, she rose to leave. Yaroslav, with the hopeful expression of a devoted hound, clung to her hand, plainly begging to be taken into her bed. I saw her touch her forehead and wince. Full of apology he let her go.

The party lasted nearly until dawn, with much drinking and the customary dirty jokes and songs with which we celebrate these happy occasions.

✝

When I awoke the next afternoon, though my head throbbed and my stomach was sour, I determined to see Inge that day without fail and deliver a parting speech that I had been rehearsing all the way from Kiev. Yesterday's moment of weakness was banished. Her pitiful condition had taken me by surprise, that was all. Of course, I would gentle the tone a bit from what I'd planned on. I was not a savage, after all. I was no Harald.

He, however, had other plans for me. He wanted to spend a few days at his country estate and, as on other occasions, conscripted me with the men of his bodyguard to attend him. There was no appeal from these invitations. We went down by river because of the mud being still too deep for horseback riding. Yelisaveta was not one of the party. Now that they were practically man and wife, said Harald, it was high time the girl learned that a man's amusements are his own business and he comes and goes as he likes.

On the second day of our carouse, Harald barked at me, "God damn it, Tangle-Hair, what ails you? You're no amusement for me at all. Are you in love? That must be it. Well, for Christ's sake, take your long face out of here, hump the poor girl, whoever she is, and get it out of your system. When I see you next I expect to find you in a better humor."

So back went I to Novgorod, rowing myself in a small boat, not minding the slowness of my progress, because I knew what I would find when I returned. What must happen would happen tonight. Of that there could be no doubt.

✝

The late afternoon sun was just going down behind Slavno Hill as I tied up my rowboat to the prince's dock. Passing through the courtyard gate, I walked quickly around the back to the men's latrine, glancing guiltily behind me (from old habit) as I went.

There was someone there. I retreated behind a corner of the stable and waited for him to leave. All right, now—no! Here came two others. One of them grunted over the trench for what seemed like an hour. Gone at last. Good, no one coming. Now, quickly!

I went straight to the 'message tree'—the maple sapling beside the latrine where Putscha would by now have tied the bit of thread for me to find. My heart thumped with dread and desire all at the same time. How would I begin? My speech had flown from my head entirely. Never mind, I would find the words when the moment came. Kind but stern. No nonsense. First, she must tell me the truth, the absolute truth, about her schemes against Harald. Once she had done that, well then I would ... Where was it? Where was the thread?

I touched every twig within the dwarf's reach but found nothing. Could a bird have taken it for its nest? But that had never happened before. More likely a breeze had shaken it loose. It couldn't have floated far—I knelt down and begin to pick at the sparse blades of grass around the sapling. Nothing.

What in Hel's Hall was wrong with the woman? Didn't she want to see me? Of all possibilities, I had never even considered this one. True, my feelings had changed, but I had reasons. What reason could she have?—Yngvar! That must be it. I marked him down as Harald's replacement—damn it, he was mine! Don't be an ass—her own nephew? Back to the grass, look again. My fingers scrabbled in the ground. Where was it?

"Lose something, druzhinik?"

"Prince!"

My heart somersaulted into my mouth. He must have it. Had he caught Putscha tying it? Had he flogged the truth of him? Black-Browed Odin defend me! For a long, long moment we stared at each other in silence.

"So, it's you, Odd Thorvaldsson. I thought it might have been. Wasn't sure, though. Until now."

"Prince, I—"

"Glimpsed you from the window. But at that distance, well, my eyes aren't what they were—

"I can explain—"

Still pretty sharp at close hand, though. What was it, a button? Bothersome things are always coming off. Here, maybe I can spot it for you."

"What? Oh, yes, yes, my button—but I don't think it's here. No, please, Prince, spare your knees, it doesn't matter, really."

"Well, if you're sure?"

"Quite sure. Thank you, though. Thank you, sir."

He faced the trench and pissed. I wiped my sleeve across my forehead.

"Funny you being here, Odd Thorvaldsson. Isn't Harald still visiting his estate?"

"I was unwell, Prince. I came back early."

"What was it, touch of fever? It's all these spring mists and stagnant water, you know. Perhaps I could make you up a drink of—"

"No, no, no, no, no. Thank you. Decent night's sleep and I'll be fine. Going to do that right now."

"I see. Well, I'll say good night, then."

"Good night, Prince."

He hoisted his trousers and began to limp away—then turned and came back. "I say, since I've found you here, I may as well ask you now."

"Anything, anything, ask away!"

"Eh? Only meant to say that tomorrow's my name day. Saint George, you know. Twenty-third of April. Small celebration, nothing much. To tell the truth, last week's banquet has rather hurt me in my larder. So, short rations, I'm afraid, but we're used to that, we old soldiers, aren't we? Eh? Ha, ha."

"Yes, indeed, Prince, yes we are!"

"I've sent round for Harald to come back too, if it's convenient for him, but I especially wanted you to join us. To be frank, it's on account of my Lady. Not herself lately. No, not a bit like her old self. Blessed if I know what's ailing her. Needs some cheering up. Doesn't seem to want my company much, though." He shook his head. "But your way with a story! Well, it might be just the thing, don't you see? Better than a dose of physic. Will you come and do your best? If you're feeling up to scratch, I mean."

"Absolutely, Prince, you can count on me!"

"Well, damned grateful to you. I say, Odd Thorvaldsson, you won't let me forget about that horse and falcon I promised you?"

"No Sir, I won't. No indeed."

"Yes—well then, ah, till tomorrow?" He limped away; a small man, round-shouldered.

22

PUTSCHA BREAKS
his WORD

St. George's day. Church occupied the morning and in the afternoon we dined. It was said that in the old days whenever Vladimir the Great celebrated his name day he would invite every soul in Kiev, from the highest to the lowest, to dine royally with him in his mead-hall. His son, at the best of times, was not so generous as this. The fare, as promised, was skimpy.

Both in church and at table I stole glances at Inge. She looked no better than before; worse, if anything. Yaroslav fussed over her endlessly, squeezing her hands and putting morsels of food to her lips, all the while reproaching himself for tiring her. She honored these attentions with such hateful looks that I expected her any moment to shriek and claw his eyes out. To her children she was merely indifferent. In fact, the only signs of affection I witnessed from her that whole evening was a kiss bestowed on the head of Putscha, who stood, as always, at her elbow; and, now and then, a melting look at little Magnus, who crouched over his plate like some timorous mouse, with his little shoulders hunched and his head pulled in between them as far as it could go. Olaf's bastard had reached the age of nine while we were away at the wars. Unlike Yelisaveta, the months had not improved him; he was still as sad and sorry as on the first day I saw him.

Harald and his companions had arrived back just in time for the prince's celebration, bursting into the hall with a great show of noisy joviality as the meat was being carved. Throughout the meal and the drinking that followed, Yelisaveta waited on her husband-to-be as though she were one of his slaves. Her servility was rewarded with an occasional grunt of appreciation, which seemed to be enough for her. She looked happy.

As soon as the plates were cleared away, Yaroslav, pretending that he had just now thought of it, invited me to entertain the company with a story. I tried my best with the tale of the giantess Kraka who fell in love with a shepherd lad, but disconcerted by Inge's cold unblinking eyes, I made a hash of it—starting and stopping, fumbling for words, losing my way. The moment I finished, she murmured a faint thank you and left the table, without a parting word to her husband or anyone else. This time the prince made no move to follow her, but only stared glumly at his plate.

The party broke up soon afterward. Yaroslav limped off to the cold comfort of his books, while his daughter sneaked away with Harald to find some cozy place for love-making. Yngvar hung about for a while after most of the others had gone, and we exchanged a few words. I had the feeling he was working himself up to ask me something, but if so, he changed his mind. With an exaggerated yawn and stretch he went off to sleep.

Leaving me alone with my thoughts.

I felt balked and frustrated. I simply didn't know what to make of Inge in her present mood. Did she want our affair to end like this? All right then, damn her, that was fine with me too! I banged my empty mug on the table to punctuate this thought, and was about to stalk off to my sleeping bench when Putscha appeared suddenly out of nowhere.

Perhaps he had slipped back into the hall after his mistress left, or, perhaps, had hidden in some dark corner all this time, waiting to catch me alone. Touching his finger to his lips, he beckoned me to follow him. I had no friendly feelings for this vainglorious little manikin, who swaggered about with his ridiculous toy sword and his great bunch of keys. But, sensing that it must have to do with Inge, I obeyed. He led me through a side door and into the long corridor that ran the length of the palace, connecting a series of little rooms. Choosing one that was empty, he motioned me inside and carefully shut the door after him. There was among the sparse furniture a foot-stool, on which he indicated I should sit so that my head was level with his. I have already remarked upon this head, with its crisp silver curls and handsome features. But the face was more lined than I had remembered it, and the eyes weary.

"Well, Putscha, say whatever it is and be quick." I determined to take a brisk tone with him and let none of my uncertain feelings show.

"Haraldsskald, sir, lend ear, please, for begging," he began in a halting Norse that was even more painful to the ear than Stavko's. "Not like Putscha beg, eh? But am with shoulders holding—no—carrying—ah—"

"Speak Slavonic, man, I can follow you."

With an expression of relief, he switched to his native tongue. His voice, like every dwarf's, was thin and reedy.

"Gospodin, I bear a heavy load on these small shoulders of mine. From that day last fall when the merchants returned from Kiev to report Eilif's death and trumpet Harald's praises, my mistress began to sicken. You understand me, you have seen her. She scarcely sleeps or eats, weeps for hours on end, or flies into sudden rages; is dead to everyone but Magnus. Him she hugs to her bosom, when she thinks no one is watching, and drenches with her tears.

"Whole days she spends on her knees, imploring the Virgin and Saint Irene to pity her. Other times"—his voice dropped to a whisper—"she goes out to the villages, attended by no one but myself, where certain old women dwell. She tells them her dreams and together they look for omens in drops of blood, and do other things best not to speak of, even in private."

"Witchcraft? Hah!" I couldn't hold back a bitter laugh. "How fortunate that her husband let a few of those crones escape the noose!"

"You make a joke of it, gospodin?" said the dwarf icily. I motioned him to go on. "Yes, well—all the months you were away, your name was always on her lips. This is the truth I'm telling you, not flattery. 'When Odd comes back all will be right. Odd will defend me from my enemies.' That was how she talked."

"Well, damn it all, Putscha, here I am—where is she?"

"As the time of your return drew nearer, she began to suffer terrors: you've been so long away, and constantly in Harald's company; what if your feelings toward her have changed? She can't bring herself to test you and learn that they have. Forgive her weakness, gospodin; she's a woman after all."

This was close enough to the truth that it sent a tremor through me:

could these witches of hers have seen into my thoughts? But I said aloud, with true feeling, that it was a sad thing to see a proud woman brought down to this.

He gave me a sorrowful nod. "Imagine an apple, gospodin," he said, "with a worm in its core. Imagine that worm eating and boring, day and night, never ceasing, but consuming more and more of the healthy fruit until, in the end, nothing remains but a hollow rind. From the outside you would at first notice nothing."

"Hmm. And by the worm you mean her passion for a certain dead saint who loved God more than he loved her? That's at the root of all this, isn't it?"

"It might be. Or it might be her passion for a certain young poet. Or maybe, somehow, both at once. Who can understand women?" A tear appeared in the corner of his eye. He seized my hand with his small ones and said, "Go to her, gospodin, for only you can give her joy again, if anyone can. Go tonight, I beg you, before she—before she does herself a harm. You understand what I'm saying? I'm afraid for her, I would not be here otherwise."

"What? Putscha, you're imagining things."

"No, gospodin, I do not imagine. She has poison; I was with her when she bought it. I don't know from one day to the next if I will see her alive. It's turning me old, gospodin. What will become of Putscha if my Lady dies? I'm hated here; they will drive me away, kill me!"

So this was what he really feared, and I could well believe it. I answered him earnestly, "Putscha, I don't desire Ingigerd's death any more than you do. She's a woman of great intelligence and spirit—I only wish she used them to better purpose."

The dwarf looked not entirely reassured by my words; he had hoped for something stronger.

"I've meant to see her since I came back; could it be arranged for tonight?"

"I will see to it, gospodin"

"Whatever I say to her, Putscha, will be between the two of us alone. You get my meaning?"

"But, gospodin, I always sit in the corner …"

"Not tonight, little man."

He scowled at me. By her own preference and despite my grumbling there was scarcely a meeting between Inge and me that he had not been a silent witness to. I never understood her mind in this. And Putscha knew very well that I disliked him for it.

"Make up your mind, dwarf, I'm putting on no more performances for you. Keep clear of her chamber or else. Agreed?"

"You've no right—!"

"Agreed?"

A lengthy pause, a sigh. "If you insist."

"Good. Now see that the tower door is left unbarred and I will need nothing more from you—you understand me?"

"It will be as you say." He turned to go.

"Putscha," I called after him, "I will do my best to ease her pain."

"Thank you, gospodin. God will bless you, I'm sure." With these words he bowed himself out the door.

It was still too early to enter the tower without risk of meeting someone—the children, or Thordis, or some servant—on the stairs, so I went back into the hall to wait and ponder what I'd heard.

Poor Ingigerd. I had no joy nor comfort for her—and I felt none myself. To be honest, I dreaded this meeting, now more than ever because of what Putscha had said. Still it must be done. I would make it plain to her that our intrigue must end; that, though I had loved her, I was Harald's sworn man and intended to remain so; that I hoped we could part with a promise to remain friends and not betray one another. That was the gist of it, anyway.

When, at last, deep night descended, I drank down what was left in someone's half empty ale horn and headed for that heavy door at the end of the hall which no one might pass without the permission of the prince or princess. As the dwarf had promised, it was unbarred and unguarded.

I crept up the spiral stairway, which I had trod so often before, and with each step felt my courage leak away. I made myself remember last spring: the enormous relief I had felt to be quit of Novgorod; and how clearly I had come to see Ingigerd for the Queen Spider that she was, entangling in her web me, Yaroslav, Harald, little Magnus—making us all unwilling partners in her private misery.

Now I stood hesitating before her door. Kind but firm, I commanded myself like an officer instructing a nervous recruit. Don't touch her, say your piece, and leave.

I knocked. Then, hearing no sound, gave the door a push. The chamber was lit only by the candle flames that flickered before the icons, and a hazy moonshine that sifted through the quartz window pane. But even if it had been black as pitch I could have found my way to her bed with ease, I knew that room so well.

She lay upon the bed, fully dressed, one arm thrown across her eyes, the other hanging limp over the edge. On the floor, beneath her curving fingers, a bit of glittering glass caught my eye. I stooped and picked up a little stoppered flask half full of some liquid. A cold shiver went through me. "Inge!" I grasped her chin and shook her hard.

Her eyelids fluttered. "Odd? Is it you?"

"What have you done, Inge?"

"Is it really you?"

"Princess," (there must be no more 'Inge's I reminded myself) "what is this for? Have you lost your mind?"

"My mind? Yes, I think so," she replied in a small voice. "If only that were all. I've lost everything, Odd—my pride, my power, everything. I've lost even the courage to die, though I long to die. I've tried and tried to drink the poison—Oh, Odd help me to die if you do nothing else for me!"

Fending her off with one hand, I pulled the stopper with my teeth and emptied the contents of the flask on the floor; it gave off a strong, sweetish odor. There was a jug, too, on the table beside her bed, but it contained only a little wine, doubtless to mix the poison in. She must have drunk a fair amount of it for courage and then passed out.

"I'm glad to have put a stop to this foolishness, anyway."

"Are you? Are you truly? Then I've not lost everything after all." Holding my face between her two hands she stared into my eyes. "You haven't turned against me? You swear it?"

"Princess, listen to me—"

"No, don't answer me with words—words are liars. If you love me give me back my life, darling Odd, make love to me as you used to." She put her arms around my neck.

"No, Princess, I—"

I tried to pull away from her embrace, but she drew me down on her, clawing up her skirt and fumbling with the drawstring of my breeches. I tried—oh, believe it, you sour-faced Christmen who will judge me—I tried, but I was helpless. I would happily blame it on magic, on incantations mumbled over a lock of my hair, on binding runes hidden among my clothes: but witchcraft or not, the craving for her overwhelmed me. I cursed myself and kissed her.

She made love with a desperate fury—twisting, plunging, crying out, and lifting me with her to a pitch beyond anything we had known before. No time now for 'the decencies': the painted eyes of Saint Irene, unveiled at last, grew wide with wonder, I don't doubt, and saw more—oh, much more—than a saint should.

Afterward, we lay still together, and it felt as though I held a wraith in my arms, there was so little substance to her. With my fingertips I could feel every bump of her spine. The worm-eaten apple; a body consuming itself. And yet a body that held such power over me. What was I to do now?

"Christ! I've missed you, she breathed in my ear. So many months. This was like the first time again, wasn't it? Better, even."

"Yes." It was the simple truth.

Just then a small sound—an in-drawn breath or the rustle of cloth—came from the shadows across the room. Inge felt me stiffen.

"It's only Putscha," she whispered. "He must have come in while I was asleep. Never mind—you know he's seen it all before, and you've nothing to be modest about, my darling."

"Damn the little spy, I'll wring his neck for him!"

"Odd, don't. What's the matter—" I was half out of bed with Inge doing her best to restrain me. "Putscha," she cried, "you've angered my friend. Get out and leave us alone!"

At that, the odious little liar darted across the room—the top of his curly head outlined for an instant against the window pane—and ran out the door, slamming it behind him. I'd never known him move so fast. I let Inge draw me back into bed. I would settle with the dwarf later.

"And now, my darling," whispered Inge, when I was reasonably calm again, "now that I'm sure of your love, I have the courage to ask a great favor of you."

This was the moment. "Inge, I also have—"

"No, Odd, hear me out." There was an unmistakable edge of command in that low voice. "I've never asked of you anything but to make me feel like a woman, which you have done—with some pleasure to yourself, too, I think. Now, I ask you for one thing more. Oh, God, in my mind I've made this speech a thousand times, and now that you're really here, my courage almost fails me."

"Then stop before you go too far."

"No, I must speak! The insolence of Harald Sigurdsson has become unendurable to me. He is a serpent that strangles me in its coils. He hoodwinks my husband, he corrupts my daughter, he conspires against my foster son, and all the while mocks me to my face! This is what I ask of you, Odd Tangle-Hair: rid me of that monstrosity, that freak, that troll! Every death I devised for him stupid Eilif has bungled: ambush, spells, poison, fire—why do you look at me so? Surely, you guessed."

Aye, surely I did. While denying it to everyone, in my inmost heart I had known she was guilty. Still, to hear it from her own lips like that winded me like a blow to the belly.

"Only do this one thing for me, Odd, just this one thing," She pressed herself against me, speaking urgently. "I have nowhere else to turn. Shall I get on my knees? I will if you want. I beg you, Odd Tangle-Hair, bring me Harald's mocking tongue, bring me his leering eyes, bring me his scheming brain hot from his skull—kill him, kill him, kill him!"

She was screaming: the shrill scream of madness. Having lived for most of my life on familiar terms with madness, I knew it when I met it.

I clapped a hand over her mouth. "Stop it! You'll wake the whole palace."

"I don't care, I don't care!" She tore my hand away and beat her fists against me. "I don't care if I wake the dead, I'll be among them soon enough! I swear by the Living Christ, I'll get more poison, I'll drink it in front of you, die at your feet if you refuse me!"

One last time I tried reason. "Inge, why do you inflict this torment on yourself? When Magnus grows up let him fight for his throne the way his father did and good luck to him; no one owes him more than that. Meanwhile, let Harald have your daughter—God knows they deserve each other. He only wants to go home to Norway, he's no threat to you here."

"Liar! D'you think I'm as big a fool as my husband? Oh, no. I've known Harald's every word and movement, and yours and Dag's too, almost from the day you arrived here. I know how you schemed with the mayor. I know how you plotted to break the influence of my cousin and me, wipe out the Swedes, and give power back to the boyars, those puking sots!"

I opened my mouth but no words came out. She gave me a pitying look. "Why, nothing easier, poor darling. When you had your attack of 'honor' and refused to be bought, well, Stavko Ulanovich and I had to make other arrangements, that's all. You know he sold Harald slave girls, and at such a good price! It so happens that one of those charming girls—I won't tell you which—understands Norse—not much, but enough. Oh, if only you could see your face, my dear. Yes, a woman—a mere girl, in fact—who was nothing to Harald and the rest of you but a creature who poured your ale, mopped up when you puked, and fell obediently on her back for your pleasure—that this girl had ears to hear and a tongue to tell. So there was no need after all for you to spy on him. I had a different part reserved for you, Odd: to be the dagger in my hand if every other means failed. Who stands closer to him than you do? At night when he lies in his drunken sleep—the point of your dagger at his throat— one thrust. It will be easy. And you hate him as much as I do, don't try to deny it."

"Then it was only for this, our love-making, you evil bitch? Great Odin, how you must have laughed at me—the young fool that I was!"

"Let go, you're hurting me!"

Hurting her! What pain sears like the pain of injured pride? I sank my fingers into her thin arm. Love, if there was any left in me, died then; I spat it out like bad food.

"Odd, please. That wasn't the only reason. I do love you. In Christ's name I swear it. You can't blame me for using you; aren't you using Harald? Listen to me now, I know what you want and I won't send you away any poorer than he would. Whatever you expect from him, I'll double it. A chest of gold? A city? A province to rule? Return to Iceland? Christ, I'll make you king of the filthy place! Or better than all that, stay here with me." She wound her fingers in my hair, her voice wheedled. "How much longer can my husband live? Perhaps he's nearer death than anyone thinks..."

"No, Inge, I won't have his blood on my hands, nor anyone else's—not for your sake."

"Then, by Christ, it'll be your blood that flows!" Instantly she was transformed into a snarling cat. She shoved me away from her. "Don't think you can stand against me, young Odd Tangle-Hair, you're not man enough for that!"

"Am I not? Well, if that's all you think of me, I'll be on my way." Some small voice of reason in me warned, Putscha knows you're here and he's devoted to her. Get out before you do kill her, she isn't worth hanging for. I reached for my breeches.

"No, please, I didn't mean it!" She clutched my hand, covering it with kisses. "Forgive me, I don't know what I'm saying. Pity me. Can't you see I'm desperate?" She clung, trembling, to my shoulder.

And somewhere I did find pity for her. It was in this same rose-scented room that we'd first spoken. That fragrance which always lingered here brought back a rush of memories—of a grand lady, gracious, wise, and generous. She had shown me my face in her mirror and we had smiled. But even then the invisible worm was eating, boring into her flesh, reducing her at last to this: a woman driven insane by her extravagant loves and hates.

And madness made her deadly. Loving her no longer, I could now see good reason to fear her. In the space of a few minutes she had threatened to kill herself, Harald, Yaroslav, and me; and she meant it—me, perhaps, especially, for I knew too many of her secrets. She could contrive my death in a thousand ways, while what could I do to her? I uttered a silent prayer to Odin All-Father, who is the patron god of liars as much as he is of warriors and poets.

I said: "Hush, Inge, don't cry. I'll be Harald's murderer if you wish it, but only for love of you, don't shame me with some cheap reward. You'll have his head, I promise you. Hush and listen now. It's not as easy as you think. Your spy must have told you how well-guarded he is. He's suspicious of everyone, even me. I'll have to pick the moment carefully. Can you be patient a little longer?"

"In God's name, do you mean it?" She wiped a hand across her tear-streaked face. "You aren't saying it to deceive me? Swear it by the Holy Cross."

"By the Holy Cross, I swear it."

"Say, 'May my soul be damned for all eternity if I'm lying'."

This, too, I repeated. (And, reader, before you condemn me for an oath-breaker, remember please that it was never my idea to be a Christman.)

"Oh, Odd, I do love you! Stay with me tonight!"

She began again to caress me, but even with Odin's help I couldn't bring myself to that again. And then suddenly her head fell back against the pillow. She was asleep.

While she slept, my thoughts raced. I was in an intolerable predicament. As long as Harald stayed on in Gardariki there was the very great likelihood that either Ingigerd would succeed in killing him, or he her, or that both of them would turn on me. I could not breathe easy until Harald was safe on the throne of Norway. Somehow, I must bring that about. I must step into Dag Hringsson's shoes and accomplish what that smooth courtier couldn't. And soon. But how?

And then I had it!

Thank you, Odin, father of all inspiration! What an ass I've been not to see it sooner; it's the only thing we can do. And with luck I can be there and back before midsummer. I'll set off this very night!

I eased myself out of bed. Inge had curled up against my chest; as I moved away she sighed in her sleep and rolled on her back with an arm outflung.

I stood a moment looking at her: her golden hair spilling over the pillow, the straight strong line of her nose, her lips slightly parted, her breasts gently rising and falling. I thought her still the most beautiful woman I had ever seen. Beautiful, clever, strong—there was so much in her to admire, and all of it squandered, all turned to viciousness and lies. Sorrow struggled with anger in my heart and neither could gain the upper hand.

But the spell with which she had bound me was broken for good and all. I had said none of the things to her that I'd planned to; it was too late for that now. If she would kill herself then she would. I could not be a hostage for her life. There was nothing to do now but go, and I had much still to accomplish before daybreak. I dressed quickly and let myself out. But on my way down the spiral stair whom should I meet but Putscha coming up. The sight of the little traitor infuriated me all over again.

"What now, you toad, sneaking back to your hidey-hole already, are you? Eh, owl-eyes? You couldn't keep your word, could you, little half-man? I should have sped you on your way with the point of my sword up your ass!"

His face wore an expression that I would have called dumb amazement if I hadn't known better. But, then, hadn't he learnt the art of lying from the Mistress of Lies herself? With a great sense of satisfaction I kicked him downstairs, not caring if his screams roused the whole palace. But he didn't cry out.

I left him sprawled on the bottom step, open-mouthed and staring.

23

A SECRET
MISSION

Once I'd made up my mind to get away, I couldn't go fast enough. I ran across Gotland Yard to our barracks, where I knew Harald intended to spend the night. I found him there playing dice with a few of our men, although it was nearly dawn.

"Where've you been all the night? I never saw such a fellow as you, Tangle-Hair, for popping up at strange hours. Don't stand in the doorway, man, you'll let in the cold."

He was drunk and in a foul mood; probably because he was losing.

"No, Harald, you come out. I need to talk to you alone."

Another of the gamblers, who was also one of his bodyguards, held him by the sleeve and gave him a warning look.

"Bah!" he said, lurching to his feet and knocking over his stool, "when the day comes that I have to fear my own skald's dagger you can cut me up and sell me for horsemeat."

It was a chilly night and the two of us stood shivering together outside the door as I explained my idea to him.

"What? Stupidest damned thing I ever heard! What you want is a pail of cold water over your head, you've drunk too much. Obviously, the jarls can't invite me back to Norway if they still think I'm dead; it doesn't take great brains to figure that out. But why should they take your word for my being alive and well in Gardariki? It's a case of the truth being too fantastic. Besides, they don't know you from a tree stump. Now if it were Dag ..." He checked himself, remembering too late why, of course, it wasn't Dag.

"Now look here, Tangle-Hair," he jabbed me with a forefinger. "I aim to make Yaroslav dower his daughter with horses, arms, and gold enough to equip an army ten times the size of Olaf's. Then will be the time to think about going home. Why put my enemies on their guard now. Stop thinking so much—it's making you weak-minded."

He turned to go back in. This was going to be harder than I'd thought. Harald had no reason to share my urgent desire to get out of Novgorod and I, of course, dared not tell him my reason—to put an end to the impossible situation I found myself in.

"No, but wait, Harald." I held him back with a hand on his arm. "Think. It's not too soon to test the water. We've had no news of home for more than a year. Who knows what state the country's in? At least let me find that out, and if the time seems right I'll make your case to the jarls. Give me your signet ring to convince them that I am who I say, and fifty gold ounces—part to pay my passage, the rest as earnest money for the jarls with a promise of more to come if they side with us."

He stood hesitating with one hand on the door latch and looked at me so hard that my nerve began to fail.

"What are you up to, Tangle-Hair? What aren't you telling me? Why this sudden desire to visit Norway with a bag of my gold?"

If he wouldn't be persuaded by good sense, then I must try nonsense. "I don't like to talk about it, Harald," I said in a low voice, "but you know that I come from a family that's gifted in dreams and visions. I had a dream the other night, as I dozed by the oven. First I saw the Tronder jarls hanging garlands on a tall oak tree and kneeling before it. Then I saw two snails, slimy white things, a bigger one and a smaller one. They crawled into a fire which sprang up from the roots of the tree and there they turned black and shriveled away to nothing. Now I think that the oak tree, Harald, is you, and the snails are Ingigerd and Magnus."

"Oak tree, eh? Snails? I like that. You wouldn't be making it up would you?"

I gave him a reproachful look. "You know there's a sacred bond of trust between lord and skald. If my word isn't good enough for you, say so and I won't trouble you again."

"Dammit, did I say I didn't trust you? Don't be putting words in my mouth!"

"Then I have your leave?"

"I didn't say that either. When would you be back?"

"By Midsummer's day if all goes well."

"I have a mind to wed Elisif then."

"Norway would be a splendid wedding present, and you'd still have Yaroslav's gold to repay yourself with."

"Aye, that's true. Come inside, dammit, don't make me stand out here freezing. Fifty gold pieces d'you say? I've just lost more than that to these cheating bastards." He indicated with a scowl his companions. "I've no more on me."

"I expect they'd loan it back to you."

"And you want me to gamble it on your coming back?"

"You've gambled it away once already."

"Got an answer for everything, haven't you? All right," he smiled slowly. "Done."

With some reluctance on the part of his friends, the coins were handed over and collected in a big leather wallet into which he also dropped the signet ring from his finger.

"Now, friend Odd, just one thing more before you go galloping off. It occurs to me that the trouble with your plan is that the jarls are not made to commit themselves openly to me. They can change their minds, keep the gold, and swear they never laid eyes on you. No. They must declare for me in front of witnesses or not at all."

"But you can't expect them to do that in Norway before you and your army arrive."

"Exactly. So they must do it here."

"Here? In Novgorod?"

"In a public audience before the prince and princess—especially the princess. You tell them that, Tangle-Hair, and tell them also that the purpose of their mission must be kept secret until I say the word. I want to surprise the Swedish bitch and her puppy. What a sight that will be!"

My heart sank, for it seemed utterly improbable that the jarls would consent to make so long a journey. But there was no backing out of it now.

"All right, then. I'll take a fast horse from the stable and I'm off to Aldeigjuborg. It shouldn't be hard to find a west-bound merchant ship there this time of year."

"Hold on. What am I supposed to say when people notice you're gone?"

"Anything but the truth. Oh, and one other thing—get rid of all your females and buy new ones, and not from Stavko Ulanovich."

I left him puzzling over that.

✝

On a summer's evening four weeks later I sailed into Nidaros harbor aboard a merchant ship out of Gotland. I had thought Nidaros such a magnificent place when I first saw it, fresh from Iceland. It came as a shock to realize what a mean little village it was compared to Lord Novgorod the Great.

Two years ago, my crew and I had spent the winter at an inn (more precisely, a brothel) presided over by Bergthora Grimsdottir—a big, homely woman, both tough and tender-hearted. During that year, I had, against my will, fought in the Battle of Stiklestad, where King Olaf met his death and where I first laid eyes on young Harald.

Entering the inn yard now, I beheld Bergthora's ample backside as she bent over to draw water from the well. I crept up behind her, grabbed her round the waist, and kissed her neck. She uttered a scream and threw her arms in the air, and followed this with kisses and hugs till I scarcely had breath left in me.

No need to recount all the questions she peppered me with nor my answers, of which I doubt she believed the half. To the question of what brought me back, I said only that I had a little business to transact for my master. "Now, Bergthora, where's that rogue, Stig No one's-Son? Inside pinching the girls and drinking up all your profits, I'll wager. He and I quarreled and parted company I'm ashamed to say. I'd like nothing better than to make it up with him. Come on, let's surprise him."

"What, him?" She squeezed out a tight little smile. "Oh, he never came back. Never thought he would, not Stig." She turned her head away, not wanting me to see the tear in her eye.

"Never—? Why, then, he's the damndest fool in all the world! Oh, but he'll come rolling home to you one day yet, Bergthora, don't you worry. Now, Kalf Slender-Leg's still here, isn't he?—how I've missed him!"

A large teardrop rolled down her cheek. "Gone away too."

"What, back to Iceland?"

"No, not there. T'was not long after you sailed when he stole away one morning early—we were all still abed—with his little bundle of belongings on his back. I know it on account of he was seen at the waterfront—no one could mistake him hobbling on his crutch, dragging his useless leg behind him. They say he took passage on a ship bound across the sea for Frankland. You know, I came to love him like a son; and one who'd always stay by me—not a rover like you and Stig. But it weren't so. On two legs or one you're all alike, you men.

"He left me a purse of silver, though—t'was all he had left in the world—with a note that deacon Poppo read to me, saying how an angel of the Lord came to him in his sleep and bade him go on pilgrimage and walk in Our Savior's steps. That was all, except begging me to pray for him every day just as he would for me. Walk to Jerusalem! That poor boy as could scarcely walk at all!"

Bergthora was Christian, though she never let that get in the way of business. But Kalf—Kalf my boyhood friend, closer to me than a blood brother—had become consumed with the Faith. He joined Olaf's army and was crippled in the battle. His piety led to a painful breach between us, though in the end we forgave each other. How pleased he would be if he knew I'd been baptized!

✝

I stayed that night at the inn, with Bergthora hovering over me the whole time, cutting choice slices of meat off the spit for me, filling my ale horn, and offering the pick of her girls. And each of us tried to put on a cheerful face for the other, but it was hard.

I was happy to get away next morning and be about my business. I hired a horse in the town and asked directions to the farmstead of Jarl Haarek of Tjotta. Haarek was a slippery character who had once been Olaf's man but then betrayed him to Canute, King of Denmark, England and now Norway too. Soon after Olaf's death at Stiklestad, though, smelling a change in the wind, he became one of the first to trumpet the martyred king's sainthood. Skeptical at first, Haarek heard me out and, after a short rumination, sent riders to summon Kalv Arnesson, Thorir Hound, and half a dozen others, who, like himself, had been quick to shed Olaf's blood and even quicker to regret it once they got a taste of Danish rule.

To this assembly, I recounted, in my most high-flown skaldic manner, how Harald Sigurdsson had been carried half dead from the bloody field of Stiklestad, and how, after recovering his strength, he had followed in his saintly brother's footsteps to the land of the Rus. There he was at this very moment—wealthy, powerful, and held in the highest esteem by Prince Yaroslav the Wise and his excellent wife.

"Nevertheless," I said with feeling, "in spite of his comfortable situation and against the wishes of the prince and princess, who long to keep him with them, he thinks only of returning to his native land and uniting it under his banner in a rising against the Danes."

I knew that my own future, just as much as Harald's, depended on my eloquence, and so I put my whole heart into it. "With God's help and yours," I concluded, brandishing my fist in the air, "Harald Sigurdsson Haarek will one day sit on Norway's throne, a worthy successor to his sainted brother!"

But these jarls were shrewd men, not easily swayed. Instead of the cheers and table-pounding that I had hoped for, there were questions testing me on details of the battle which only someone close to Harald and Olaf could have known. My answers were chewed over in long stretches of silence. Finally they asked to see the signet ring with Harald's initial on it and they passed it around from hand to hand, studying it thoughtfully.

Really, my argument was a strong one. It was taken for granted that none but Olaf's kin could ever rule Norway, and Harald—brave, capable, a proven warrior, the very incarnation of Olaf—was plainly to be preferred to the weak and immature Magnus. Of course, that argument could cut two ways. The jarls were not so sure that they wanted a strong king who would tax their peasants and curtail their liberties. The ultimate persuader was money. Every mercenary captain is expected to line his pockets, but Harald had a positive genius for it. Even half his fortune—which was the figure I mentioned—would be enough to keep these jarls fat and drunk for the rest of their days.

On what terms would he return? they asked. I replied coolly, as if it were the most natural thing in the world, "Harald, wishes to be invited by a deputation of you in Novgorod. You understand that without oaths publicly taken he places himself in danger. The expenses of your journey"—here I dropped my wallet full of gold on the table, artfully allowing the coins to spill out—"he insists on paying himself." (Their eyes grew wide.) "The city of Novgorod, I may add, has not its equal anywhere in the world. Every sort of pleasure can be tasted there. And you would, of course, be the guests of the prince and princess, than whom there is no pleasanter couple to be found in all Christendom. The crown must be offered to Harald in their presence, he insists on this point, though he asks you to keep your mission secret until the final moment, when he himself will break the news to them gently—they are such a sweet and sentimental couple and prone to floods of tears."

✝

We sailed out of Trondheimfjord in three well-built ships, each carrying three of the jarls with their retinues and baggage. The most precious item of baggage was the narrow circlet of gold that had once sat on Olaf's brow. A brave Norwegian had snatched it right from under the Danes' noses and had kept it safely hidden all this time.

We had a favoring wind all the way and Midsummer's day found us crossing Lake Ladoga on the last leg of our journey. I'd hoped to sail straight past Aldeigjuborg in order to escape the notice of Ragnvald, but the jarls insisted on stopping here to rest and stretch themselves before going on. I had passed through the town on my outward journey unobserved, but it was impossible that this large entourage could fail to draw attention to itself. And sure enough, here came Jarl Ragnvald, hurrying down to the pier with expressions of delight. He greeted me like an old friend and insisted on bringing us to his hall, where he set every one flying about to produce a feast that very night.

Naturally, he said, his curiosity was piqued as to his guests' object in visiting Gardariki. A secret? How extraordinary! Well, he would inquire no more about it—diplomacy was too deep a matter for his simple nature—but would only beg to have the pleasure of our company for a few days before we completed our journey. The noble jarls would find his ale vats overflowing, his larder well-stocked, and they would insult him if they did not treat his possessions entirely as their own.

This was a side of Ragnvald I was seeing for the first time. Fawning humility, it appeared, was as much a part of his nature as overbearing pride. Either way, I didn't trust him, and the prospect of delay made me frantic. But my Norwegians were delighted; they loved being groveled to. After three maddening days of this, I commandeered a small boat and went ahead by myself to prepare the way, after getting their promise to follow me within the next day or two.

It was midnight, although the midsummer sun still hung in the treetops, when I entered the courtyard of Harald's dvor. From the hall drifted the sound of laughter and snatches of song. I pounded on the door until a servant answered.

"Tell gospodin Harald," I said, "that his skald hails him King of Norway!"

A moment passed, followed by the din of many voices shouting at once. Harald, his face flushed with drink and his clothes disheveled, came to the door. His bodyguards, in similar condition, crowded round us.

"You've come back, by God!" said Harald.

"Didn't you think I would?"

"Frankly, no."

"I'm sorry to hear it. You may have a better opinion of me when I tell you that the Tronder jarls are only a day's sail away and have pledged themselves to give you Olaf's crown—Your Highness."

"Hurrah for Odd Haraldsskald! Hurrah for Harald and Norway!" a chorus of voices rang out.

I was lifted up and carried inside, toasted and cheered, and made to recount every detail of my mission to these happy men, who would soon now be going home to their farms and families.

In the midst of this noisy excitement, though, Harald, who should have been the happiest of all, was strangely quiet and looked at me from time to time in a way that I didn't quite like.

"Does something here displease you, King?" I asked him, while the others carried on drunkenly among themselves.

"Not a bit, Tangle-Hair, I'm well pleased with your success and mean to reward you for it. It's only that I must think precisely what reward will suit you."

I had learned from experience that Harald was to be feared when he screamed or when he spoke very, very softly. He spoke softly now.

"I expect you haven't heard much of the news from Novgorod," he went on. "We had a bit of excitement some weeks back."

"I would like to hear about it."

"Oh, you will. Just days after you left in such a rush, what d'you suppose happens to our gracious Lady Ingigerd? She takes deathly ill with the belly ache, fever, and fainting; her nails turn blue and her tongue turns grey; and she can scarcely breathe. Mind you, I'm only repeating the court gossip—not being one of those who are invited to the princess' bedside. Yaroslav, so I'm told, sends for the physician, the physician sends for the priest, and somebody sends for Ragnvald. And all of them wail and wring their hands for about two weeks while she lies near death. Now, it's said that when they first found her there was a flask in her hand with a few drops of some rather nasty liquid still in it. Queer business, don't you think?"

While he spoke his eyes never strayed from mine. I returned his gaze steadily and managed (I hoped) to sound only mildly interested. "Now you mention it, Ragnvald did say something to me about her being down with a touch of fever early in the summer. Is she recovered?"

"Not much, according to Yaroslav. We never see her. She takes her meals in her chamber with no company but her dwarf, and seldom shows her face to anyone else. A great improvement as far as I'm concerned." He uttered a sharp bark of laughter—and still those eyes searched mine.

"And what does she say about the bottle of p—liquid?"

"Of what?"

"The liquid, the stuff you just mentioned."

"Oh, that. Remedy for headache given her by her old nurse; it seems the recipe got a bit muddled. Anyway, that's the public story. Elisif thinks she tried to kill herself and only wishes she hadn't botched it. What d'you say to that, Tangle-Hair?"

"King, I don't say anything to it."

He took a swallow of ale and drew his sleeve across his mouth, then stared at me in silence for a time. "No, of course not. Why should you? Boring story anyway. Come on, drink up!"

We drank until the sun was high and then lay down to sleep. Later in the afternoon, Harald informed me that he was going to pay a call on Yaroslav and I could join him if I cared to, or not, if I didn't. I could see no reason for hanging back and so rode with him along the river to the city. It should have been a pleasant ride since the day was not too hot and the summer foliage was in its glory. But all the way there, Harald was grimly silent and ignored my attempts at conversation.

We found Yaroslav in his study, surrounded by dusty volumes, by tangled scrolls that rolled in confusion across the floor, and by sheaves of maps piled on all the tables and chairs. With his hair sticking up at all angles and his clothes looking as though he had not changed them in days, the prince appeared more than usually distracted.

"Gospodin Harald! Or, Son-in-Law as I may nearly call you now—eh? A pleasure to see you. And Tangle-Hair, too! Back so soon? I had the idea that Iceland was much farther...wasn't that what you said, Harald? Well, never mind. All went well, did it? Your inheritance, I mean? Delighted to hear it."

But his smile quickly faded as he took in the cluttered room with a sweep of his arm. "You see before you, my friends, a man perplexed; torn by sorrow and satisfaction all at once. What's that, Odd? Harald didn't tell you? Well, well. A messenger, you see, arrived from Chernigov not many days after you left to report the sad news that poor Mstislav was dead. While hunting wild horses on the steppe, his mount stumbled and fell on top of him. God help his soul. He always did ride like a madman. What a week that was—my Lady near death from that ghastly medicine and then Mstislav on top of that! Honestly, I wonder I didn't lose my wits.

"Anyway, that's all past. But his death leaves me now indisputably the Velikiy Knyaz—the Grand Prince of all Rus according to the understanding that we had. The other princes, all my brothers and half-brothers, have already taken their oath to me. Gratifying and all that, of course, but truthfully it would have meant more to me ten years ago than it does today. It means moving the court to Kiev, though I'm far more comfortable here. And then there's the expense—my Lady will insist on refurbishing the old palace top to bottom—you remember the state it was in. And there's the question of what to do about Novgorod. Wouldn't dream of letting anyone but my young eagle govern it, but I fear my Volodya's still too young for the job, don't you think?" He didn't pause for a reply. "Of course, my Lady carries on like a mad woman when I mention my doubts and hesitations to her, but we can't let the women bully us, can we?"—this with a wink at Harald—"What I've agreed to for the moment is to send her nephew Yngvar off to Tmutorakan with his warriors and from there on to Serkland, just to show them my banner, for that was all part of Mstislav's domain. The young fellow couldn't be happier. Tells me that he's ready to set out almost any moment—but don't let an old man rattle on like this, what have you two come to see me about?"

Harald tugged at his drooping mustaches and repeated my news. He added that he wanted to settle Yelisaveta's dowry and marry her without delay before they left for Norway.

Yaroslav greeted this with the expected noises of surprise, but far from being grieved, as I thought he might be at the prospect of losing his captain so soon, he seemed actually relieved and congratulated Harald warmly. "Although," he added in a confiding way, "I don't know that any man ought to be congratulated on being made a king, for it's a hard and thankless job. You've been a godsend to me, Harald Sigurdsson, upon my soul you have, but my Lady has been after me day and night to deprive you of your rank, to send Yelisaveta away, to make you swear an oath to defend little Magnus. Really, it distracts a man from his books and cogitations—especially when I have all these other things on my mind. So perhaps it's best after all, your going back to Norway."

The good old man; he spoke his true mind. Harald, in the end, was just too much bother for him. "Now as for my pretty Yelisaveta," he went on, "God in Heaven, I shall miss her smiling face! Yet to see her Queen of Norway: there's something to gladden a father's heart! And you, Odd Thorvaldsson, you'll be leaving us too, I expect."

"I had thought to," I answered, with an eye on Harald, "if I'm still wanted."

"Well, why ever not?" he exclaimed. "Why, you'd be an ornament to any king's court with your recitations and poems and whatnot—wouldn't he, Harald?"

"Indeed. A man of many devices is our friend Odd."

Yaroslav blinked in surprise: Harald's tone was like ice. "Yes, well—," sensing tension in the air, he fumbled for words, "we needn't keep you, Odd. Harald and I must settle all sorts of matters if he's to carry off my daughter so soon. Until later—?"

24

PRAISE THE DAY
AT NIGHTFALL

There's an old verse that runs:

> *Praise the day at nightfall,*
> *A woman when she's dead,*
> *A sword proven,*
> *A maiden married,*
> *Ice you've crossed,*
> *Ale you've drunk.*

In other words, don't deceive yourself with pleasant expectations, for nothing in life is certain.

All that day and the next I spent loitering about the palace, hourly expecting to see the jarls' ships sailing into view, and in the meantime brooding over Harald, who continued to treat me like a stranger. Me, who had just laid the crown of Norway in his lap! Damn the fellow! What was eating at him? On the third day, as I was just about ready to go back to Aldeigjuborg and kidnap my jarls, they arrived. A crowd of on-lookers gathered to watch the three sleek dragons empty their bellies of warriors. While war horns brayed, they marched through the wide gate of Yaroslav's dvor.

I noticed that the jarls were all dressed in new cloaks of silk brocade trimmed with sable, and tall hats in the Rus fashion; obviously presents from their generous host, the Jarl of Aldeigjuborg. I was a little worried to see that Ragnvald himself was with them; and more than a little, when a moment later who should come striding through the gate, arms swinging, head high, but Dag Hringsson. Harald, at my side, saw him at the same time I did and flinched as though he'd seen a ghost. Dag saluted us jauntily and went straight on up the stairs.

In short order, Bishop Yefrem was sent for as well as Dyuk the mayor, who arrived with a dozen of the highest ranking Rus boyars and an honor guard of the town militia. Also present were Yngvar and a few of his men, all armed. Inside the crowded hall, Harald and I took our places to the left of Yaroslav's throne, together with as many of our Norwegians as could be squeezed in, all of them prepared to burst their lungs cheering for their new king.

When all were assembled, Yaroslav welcomed the jarls with a typically wandering speech in which he provoked some nervous laughter by comparing Saint Olaf to Saint Vladimir with respect to the extraordinary sinfulness that often precedes great conversions.

Meanwhile, I studied Inge, who sat beside him, her backbone straight as a spear, her face a perfect mask. She had come into the hall from the tower, accompanied by Putscha, her children, and Old Thordis. She took small cautious steps, leaning on the arm of one of her maids, while Putscha, the bantam cock as ever, made a great to-do of clearing the way for her. Why had she made the effort, sick as she was, just to witness her own humiliation? Ragnvald approached and spoke to her in a low voice. I thought I saw a quick smile cross her lips.

I shifted my attention to the others. On her right hand stood Volodya, Yelisaveta, the younger children with Thordis, and at the tail end Magnus, doing his best to be invisible. He pulled at his earlobe, twisted his fingers, and raised his eyes from the floor only to cast agonized looks at Ingigerd. Someone, I noticed, had at least put decent clothes on him for a change.

Kalv Arnesson, the jarls' spokesman, a brawny man with bushy blond whiskers and a commanding voice, made reply to Yaroslav's speech with one equally long, in which he managed to say practically nothing at all. Those in the audience who knew no Norse were beginning to shuffle their feet.

At last, amidst a solemn hush, a cushion bearing the golden circlet was handed to Jarl Kalv who advanced at a slow and impressive pace towards us. This was the climax. Within the next few moments Norway would have a king. Harald stepped forward, his fingers reached for it, nearly touched it—but Kalv turned aside from him, to the left, and knelt before Magnus! The hall erupted with gasps and a confusion of angry voices. Yelisaveta, with a stricken look, ran to stand by Harald, who stared bug-eyed as Magnus put out two trembling hands to take the crown from the jarl. What colossal treachery was this!

"We repent us," Kalv's big voice sounded above the rumble of excitement in the hall, "of the slaying of Olaf our King and we hereby make amends to his son. We affirm, each and all of us, the justice of our choice: the son of Saint Olaf has the blood of the Ynglings in his veins, the son of Sigurd Sow does not. Grand Prince Jarizleif Valdemarsson," (thus he Norsed Yaroslav's name) "we beg you to give your fosterling into our care."

While Yaroslav stammered, Ingigerd came suddenly to life. Looking severely at the jarl, she said in a ringing voice, "Ask it rather of me, Kalv Arnesson! Can I entrust a defenseless boy to the very murderers of his father? I love this child as if he were born of my own womb. Can my heart bear the anguish of parting from him? I am loathe, Kalv Arnesson, to give him up to you. And yet—and yet—(she paused for effect) the throne of Norway is his birthright, which I ought not to deny him. You jarls of Norway, I command each of you singly to step forward and kiss the Gospels while you swear true faith and allegiance to Magnus Olafsson. And Kalv Arnesson, I require you to adopt him as your own foster son. Furthermore, I warn you that I send him well-guarded by the trustiest of our retinue, who will die before they desert him. Those, Kalv Arnesson and all of you, are our terms. I say 'our', being confident that my husband, the Grand Prince, agrees with me in every detail."

It was the old Inge's voice, strong and clear, and brooking no opposition. The Grand Prince's head wobbled in dazed agreement.

Her words had the sound of being well-rehearsed. After all, she and Ragnvald had had a full week since our arrival to plan this counter-stroke. Or, perhaps, longer? Had Ragnvald been alerted even before our ships reached his harbor? Had someone informed him? And was it someone with a personal score to settle? Was it Dag Hringsson? I couldn't imagine how it was done, but damn me if I didn't see his hand in this!

At that moment, the selfsame Dag was taking his place with the jarls to swear his oath of allegiance before Magnus. Dag, as I might have predicted, had landed on his feet.

Ingigerd, leaving her chair, went and stood behind Magnus and placed her hands on his shoulders (whether to steady herself or him was hard to say). She watched as the jewel-encrusted Gospel book was taken up and kissed by each of the men in turn. Knowing what a fortune I had promised the jarls on Harald's behalf, I could only conclude that she had beggared herself to surpass it.

Now Kalv Arnesson turned to us and bellowed, "All you men of Norway, acclaim your new king or never see your homes again! If you are for Magnus, cross over and stand by me."

The Norwegians looked at Kalv, they looked at Harald, they looked at one another, they shifted their feet uneasily.

"You see, Kalv Arnesson?" Harald sneered. "Here's loyalty! Here's good faith! Look at 'em—they know who's the rightful king in this room!"

But one man went and stood by Kalv.

Then another.

When the third man stepped forward, Harald tried to drag him back, but while he struggled with him two others crossed over. Then the formation dissolved entirely. In a mass they crossed over to Kalv's side and, clashing their swords against their shields, hailed Magnus as their new king. Finally, only I and six others, shiftless men who were not greatly liked by their comrades, remained with Harald. I could see I was in bad company.

"Tangle-Hair!" It was Dag's voice. "Come over, you'll be welcome among us."

But I stood hesitating. Why should Magnus welcome me? Skalds a-plenty, not tainted by Harald's service, would be competing for his favor. He might even despise me, for it's a rare thing that a skald deserts his lord for any reason short of death.

Nonetheless, I almost took that step.

But at that moment Inge flung out her arm at Harald and shrieked with crazed laughter, "Harald Sigurdsson, you too must swear allegiance to your king, God damn you—you upstart, you thrall, you pig farmer's son! Crawl to him, water his feet with your tears, plead for your very life! Beggar! Murderer! Seducer of little girls! You refuse? Then take your shameless face from my hall and let the earth swallow you up, if it has the stomach for you! By God, you'll live in Hell as surely as Olaf lives in Heaven!" Her voice was cracked, her breath came in sobs.

But Harald was every bit her equal in fury. Words burst from him like red hot stones from a volcano's mouth: "Whore! Adulteress!"

"Eh?" said Yaroslav, who had gone unnoticed for some minutes now. "What does the captain of my druzhina say?"

I felt the blood drain from my heart.

Shoving men left and right, Harald plunged through the crowd to stand face to face with the Grand Prince. "Yaroslav Vladimirovich, God only knows how many men your wife has slept with—half the druzhina would not surprise me—but I know for a fact that Odd Thorvaldsson, whom I called a friend, has plowed her furrow a hundred times— the two of them laughing at you and me all the while!"

"Liar! Filthy liar," screamed Ingigerd.

"Will you call your own daughter a liar, Princess? Eight weeks ago her dwarf, Nenilushka, went to your apartment looking for her father. She entered your chamber but, seeing you asleep, she was just turning to go when who should come walking in but our good friend, Tangle-Hair! The girl was afraid and hid herself in her father's place. All that she witnessed—my lusty skald pounding away on you fit to break his breeches, she told next morning to her mistress, your daughter; and she came straight to me with it!"

My thoughts raced back to that night. It was the daughter in the room with us! And Putscha really hadn't known why I was angry with him when I met him on the stair.

No sooner had Harald finished speaking, than Putscha, his handsome features twisted in rage, drew his wooden sword and ran at his daughter. But before he could harm her, Harald caught him by the scruff of his neck, lifted him high in the air, and flung him down on his head. Nenilushka, with a cry, rushed over to him. The scene that followed, in which she tried to tend her injured father while he did his best to thrash her with his toy weapon, and both of them so puny and deformed that neither one could subdue the other—this scene, I say, was found by many in the audience to be so droll that, despite the high drama of the moment, they laughed out loud. Harald put an end to it by banging their two curly heads together and kicking each in a different direction.

At the same time, Inge demanded of her husband, "Yaroslav, will you permit this elongated freak to slander me on no better grounds than the ravings of a simpleton?"

"Simple she is," Harald shot back. "She barely understood what she had seen but, by God, she did not make it up!"

"But the whole thing's absurd, outrageous!" stammered Yaroslav. "My wife and young Odd? I warn you, gospodin Harald, if you're pulling my beard, you shall feel my anger. What proof have you?"

"Torture, Grand Prince—torture will provide all the proof you need. Put them to the trial of water and the trial of hot iron. Start with that little abomination, Putscha. Look at him, his guilty knowledge is written all over his face. Then Thordis, the nurse—there were no secrets kept from that troll-hag." A feeble cry escaped the old woman's lips. "And if that doesn't satisfy you, then here, here is one whose word you can't doubt. This one here, whom we both called friend, my own skald. Torture Odd Tangle-Hair. And when you've squeezed everything out of him, you have my leave to hang him!"

With a blood red haze before my eyes, I drew my sword and charged at him. I was nearly on him when two of his men tackled me. While they held my arms, Harald hit me in the face and drove his other fist into my stomach. I dropped to the floor gasping and he kicked me two or three times in the kidneys for good measure.

I describe the rest of this scene with a detachment I did not feel at the time.

The bishop had looked as stunned as everyone else by Harald's words, but in a twinkling he saw his chance to deal a death blow to the princess. Yefrem was of a boyar family and he shared their hatred of Ingigerd.

"Fornication!" he thundered. "Fornication, Grand Prince, is a sin which only God is fit to judge. Yaroslav Vladimirovich, why has your wife gone more than a year without conceiving? It is because she uses magic to avoid bearing her lover's child and so cannot bear yours! You are too lenient with her, Grand Prince, and always have been. If you had beaten her as a husband ought, you would not find yourself betrayed by her now—by her, I say, never mind this foolish youth,"—touching me with his shoe—"for it is always the woman, tainted with the sin of Eve, who is most abandoned to lust and corruption!"

With a groan, Yaroslav shrank back in his throne.

Sensing that he'd hit the mark, Yefrem soared higher. Ingigerd and

I had made a special point, he cried, to fornicate on Easter Sunday, on Epiphany, and other holy days. We had used positions which God intended only for brute animals, and had done other lewd things which a Christian could not decently name. (What a fertile imagination this bishop had! He was only guessing, of course, but he was doing pretty well.) "And the crowning blasphemy, Prince, is that she stood godmother to her lover at his baptism. O, Woman"—he turned his fiery eye on her—"were you so sated with fornication that you must spice it with incest! Yaroslav, are you a faithful son of the Church, and do you submit yourself to Her authority in all things touching on morals?"

The prince could only nod.

"Then, you must—must, I say, check the anger that swells in your bosom; stifle the sense of outrage which urges you to draw your sword and strike off this Bathsheba's head. It is a hard thing, I know, but I ask it of no ordinary man. You must leave her to be judged by God alone—that is, by His representative on earth—His anointed bishop!"

At this, there were shouts of approval from the boyars in the hall. Yaroslav looked like he was ready to faint. He had no desire to slay his wife with his own hands; he hadn't the nerve for it. Now the bishop offered him a way to let his cowardice look like strength.

"As—you say, Bishop," he assented in a voice barely audible.

Then for the first time I saw fear in Inge's eyes.

"Now Yaroslav, see here." It was Ragnvald, jowls a-quiver, shouldering the bishop aside. He looked frightened, and with good reason. What would become of him if his cousin Ingigerd fell from grace? "In God's name, let us not be hasty here—"

He got no farther than that for now Dyuk bustled forward, commanding his militiamen to seize Ingigerd and take her to the convent of St Mary's outside the city. "The rest of you arrest the dwarf and him"—he pointed at me—"and lock 'em up in the jail."

But now Yngvar and his Swedes—Ingigerd's countrymen—made their presence felt. They would kill to defend her.

"Back away, you men!" ordered the mayor, drawing his sword. "We've slaughtered Swedes in Novgorod before now." His boyars, too, reached for their swords.

"In God's name," croaked Yaroslav, "no bloodshed, I beg you. If my wife and Odd Thorvaldsson are innocent they have nothing to fear."

Reluctantly, the Swedes stood back.

"Thank you, Grand Prince," said Dyuk. "I expected no less from Yaroslav the Wise. Take them away."

Harald's eyes met mine as my jailers hauled me to my feet. Not a glimmer of apology in them. I expected none. His own hopes in ruins, what more natural than that he should want to bring down the rest of us out of sheer malice. I remembered Einar Tree-Foot's words to me: You're in a cage with two wolves who want to tear each other to pieces; mind they don't rend you instead.

What pained me even more than Harald's treachery was the face Volodya turned to me—cheeks burning with shame, and tears in his eyes, though he fought them back: because I, his mother's lover, had betrayed his friendship and cheapened his honor. And I had. There was no denying it and no room for pardon. Someday, if I lived long enough, he would come to kill me.

My last sight as they dragged me away was of little Magnus, looking lost and bewildered, his lopsided crown held up by one large ear, and flanked by the nine rapacious jarls, any one of whom could have made a mouthful of the child.

As for the Tronder jarls, they appeared delighted, and why not? Not only had they gotten a king and made a great deal of money on the side, but they had been treated to an absolutely cracking good show. Nothing this entertaining had ever happened in Nidaros!

25

ON TRIAL

The Rus jail is a unique structure, consisting of a single high-walled wooden cell with a small barred window in it but no door. It is entered by climbing a ladder to the top—speeded by the point of the jailer's spear—and lifting up one side of a heavy iron grating, about four foot square, that covers an opening in the middle of the flat roof. A prop placed underneath the grating allows just enough room for a body to squeeze through. The drop to the floor is eight or nine feet.

First I and then Putscha landed hard on the straw-covered floor. The vacant-eyed wretches who were our fellow prisoners (two skeleton-thin men and a woman with her filthy child) barely looked up as we thudded into their midst.

The jailer dropped the grate and fastened it with an iron bolt. He pressed his ugly face against the bars. "Take your ease, gentlemen," he chuckled. "Being as it's summer you'll be tolerable cozy, unless it rains. In winter they always dies within a day or two. As to vittles, a pan of gruel is sent in through the little window down there and the slops go out the same way—and not a great amount of difference between 'em, ha, ha! Good day to you."

The place of our confinement was not Yaroslav's jail (he had one on the palace grounds) but My Lord Novgorod's own, maintained for the city by the mayor and his men. It stood in the Nerev End, close by Dyuk's house. A dozen of the Novgorod militia had marched us here and now stood guard outside.

My situation, from whatever angle I considered it, was grim. At the very least, I would be tortured into admitting my affair with Inge. But more likely I would never live that long. Ragnvald, of course, would want me dead. His Swedish countrymen had backed off today, but he, with his deep purse, would soon screw up their courage. And then there were the Norwegians. Little Magnus now had an army at his command and he was devoted to his foster-mother; he would not want me to slander her in court. Either group, and most likely both together, could overpower the Novgorod militia.

Putscha said nothing but his eyes followed me as I paced the cell. It was anger, not fear, that had the upper hand with me. Harald had violated the bond between a lord and his skald. Without a thought, he threw away my life for the sake of his grudge against Ingigerd. That made me his enemy. If I lived—if I lived—I would kill him. Where Ingigerd and Eilif had failed, I would succeed. We Icelanders are patient men when it comes to vengeance.

The little patch of sky overhead darkened gradually to the deeper blue of a midsummer's night. Outside, Dyuk's militiamen still kept guard. Putscha turned his face to the wall and slept. I could not. Who would strike at me first? How would it come? Finally, I must have drifted into sleep.

Towards morning, we were roused by the bump of the ladder against the wall and the creak of the jailer's steps. His face came in view again as he propped the grating up and lowered a knotted rope ladder which he fastened with a hook. If we would not climb up of our own will, he said, he would send the guards down to persuade us.

Moments later, the dwarf and I stood together in the dark street, ringed by armed men. Nearby a cock crowed. Presently, the mayor, leading a fresh company of militia, arrived to take charge of us.

After much time and temper were lost in a fruitless search for the manacles and leg-irons (it was hard to keep these items from being stolen by boyars who used them on their private prisoners) we were marched up Sherkova Street to the northern slope of the citadel where Saint Sophia's thirteen lofty spires stood out black against the sky.

Close by the cathedral was the bishop's palace, a large and handsome dvor not much inferior to Yaroslav's own. Filling up the broad expanse in front of it were several hundred armed men—the combined forces of the Rus boyars and the city militia. They were here to see the detested Ingigerd paid back at last for her foreign, high-handed ways, and to make sure that no one—not even Yaroslav himself—interfered to save her. More Rus fighters lined the river bank below the citadel and guarded the nearer end of the bridge against an attack from the outlanders' quarter.

There was a surge of excitement in the crowd when we came in view. Dyuk was greeted with cheers. Some shouts were aimed at me—mostly inquiring how the princess was in bed. There seemed to be more raillery than real anger in them. But it was different with Putscha; the jeers aimed at Ingigerd's lackey were vicious. He stolidly ignored them.

Meanwhile, on the farther bank of the river, another army was forming, made up of the jarls' retinues and Yngvar's Swedish warriors. Yngvar must, of course, defend his kinswoman; and the jarls must support Magnus, who was devoted to Ingigerd. So, with much shouting and trumpeting of war-horns, they were mustering at the market end of the bridge. This day looked likely to end in bloodshed.

Flanked by the mayor and his guards, Putscha and I mounted the outer stair of Bishop Yefrem's palace and entered into a large audience room. There, at one end, raised on a dais, stood the Bishop's high-backed throne. The man himself had not yet made an appearance, but his priests and deacons were ranged in their tonsured rows on either side of his seat and nearby a scribe crouched, stylus in hand, over a little writing desk.

Harald, Yelisaveta and Nenilushka occupied a space before the dais which was reserved for the witnesses and defendants. The simple-minded girl started up a piteous shrieking as soon as she saw her father. She would have run to him if Yelisaveta hadn't yanked her back by the hair of her head and slapped her face.

Putscha did not once look at her.

To me it was the sight of Harald that made my heart nearly burst in my chest. Unarmed as I was, I fought to get at him. It was only the mayor's guards who kept me from losing my life then and there. Held fast by them, I could only scream "betrayer" and "bastard" at him across the room.

Outside, what had been a confused murmur of voices now rose in angry shouts and cat-calls. The princess and her women were arriving on mule-back from the convent. Ingigerd had no friend in this crowd. On the arm of her cousin Ragnvald, she made a stately entrance—dressed for a banquet, not an inquisition, in a gown of red silk with a jeweled tiara on her head. Her stark, impassive features and slightly protruding eyes resembled more the painted face on an icon than anything merely human. She was not here to play the penitent, that much was certain. In her train followed her cup-bearer, her groom, Father Dmitri, several nuns from the convent and, last of all, Old Thordis, who alone looked plainly terrified.

With the addition of Inge and her entourage, the room was full to bursting. Some moments later, the bishop entered from a side chamber and took his seat upon his throne.

"Yefrem, where is my husband?" Inge accosted him at once. "For I recognize no judge but him."

"What you recognize is no matter to me, Princess," the bishop answered her sharply. "Your husband is too heartsore even to lay eyes on you. He has sent us word that he will not come at all today. Now sit down on that bench and curb your tongue."

Pleasantries out of the way, Yefrem plunged straight into the examination of witnesses. Nenilushka was summoned first. With wailing and wild looks, the girl was dragged by Harald himself to the foot of the throne.

In her own words, demanded Yefrem, looking down on her from his great height like Almighty God himself, what had she witnessed on the night in question? Could she point to the two persons she had seen? Could she describe for him their indecent acts and lewd speech?

But the poor girl, made even more idiotic by fear, only howled until Yefrem, with an angry wave of the hand, dismissed her. "Let it be recorded," he said, "that the testimony of the dwarf, Nenilushka Putschavna, was communicated in private to her mistress, the Lady Yelisaveta Yaroslavna, whose account of it, already taken on oath, we do accept without question."

The scribe at his desk scratched away furiously.

Then, smoothing his features into some sickening imitation of sweetness, the bishop fixed his eye on Ingigerd and said, "Before hearing testimony of any other persons in this case, we are moved by the example of Our Savior, who forgave Mary Magdalene the harlot, to turn to our daughter, Ingigerd, and entreat her, here in the sight of all, to prostrate herself before God, and, watering the ground with her tears, to make full and public confession of her most hideous sins."

Ingigerd, by way of answer, spat out the single word, "Eunuch!"

In the moment of uneasy silence that followed this exchange of sentiments, the rumble of the crowd milling outside sounded louder and more ominous. Yefrem's small eyes darted to the door, to the window. He dabbed at his brow which was suddenly damp with sweat. Could it be that our bishop was not a physically brave man?

To be truthful, I was not feeling very brave myself, anticipating that I would be the next one summoned to the foot of the throne. Even if no one stuck a knife in me between now and then, I was sure that I would not be allowed to simply give my testimony. Words meant nothing if they weren't extracted by torture.

But, no, it was Putscha who was wanted next.

"The princess's dog," sneered Yefrem, leaning forward in his seat with his hand on his knee. "The evil assistant in all her depravity. Already bearing God's curse upon your body, you plunged with her into every species of crime, did you not? Nothing was concealed from you. You can tell us much about her fornication with the outlander, Odd Thorvaldsson, and other sins just as vile, can't you? Show him the knout."

The flogger, a burly fellow in the mayor's retinue, stepped forward. In his hand he held a thick staff to which was attached, by a swivel-ring, three feet of knotted rawhide, which had been boiled in milk to give it the hardness of metal. He drew it lovingly across his palm. I reckoned he could cut the hide off a bison with half a dozen strokes of that murderous flail.

"Strip him!" cried the bishop.

The dwarf's jacket and shirt were ripped down the back, exposing the bunched muscles of his powerful torso. A militiaman stooped over to make a whipping platform of his back, while another lifted Putscha up and spread-eagled him in such a way that the 'platform' could grip the dwarf's wrists over his shoulders. The flogger took up his position behind them and massaged his arm.

The first blow opened a gash from shoulder to waist. And so did the next one, and the next; each stroke skillfully aimed at a different spot. After the fifth, the bishop asked whether Putscha had ever witnessed a secret meeting between the princess and any man, be it me or another.

The dwarf was mute.

After the eighth stroke the question was repeated.

By now, Putscha's back was a bloody red mess, and drops of his blood spattered the floor, the dais, and all the nearer bystanders. Still he would not answer. The flogging continued, nine strokes, ten ... The little man bore it with unbelievable fortitude. Not a single groan escaped him, although his daughter howled louder at every blow. After the twelfth the flogger looked questioningly at the bishop as if to say, Another might kill him.

Yefrem nodded and Putscha was allowed to slide to the floor. A guard dragged him back to the prisoner's dock, leaving a sticky, red smear on the floor, and dropped him at my feet. He was conscious enough to show me a twisted smile: blood flowed from his lips and tongue which he had chewed to shreds.

Throughout this ordeal, Inge had watched the suffering of her servant without a flicker of emotion. After all, was not his misshapen little body fashioned by God to be her footstool? And does one weep for a footstool?

"We will return to the dwarf later," said the bishop.

My turn now, thought I. And it will be worth the beating to confess—not to my affair with Inge but to Dyuk's intrigue with Harald. After Inge's attempt on Harald's life, you recall, Dag had decided to reach out to the boyar faction that hated her, and I volunteered to arrange the first meeting. Since then, there had been several more. Oh, I had things to confess about the mayor and Harald that Yaroslav would hear with great displeasure. Their hatred of the princess seemed to have driven this rather obvious point clear out of their heads. Dyuk might weather the storm but for Harald, at least, it would mean banishment from Gardariki. Without either Norwegian or Swedish fighters to support him, Harald was now powerless and useless.

But my moment was not yet.

"Fetch the woman, Thordis," the bishop commanded. A pair of guards dragged her from Ingigerd's side.

"Now then, Thordis Helgasdottir," said Yefrem, making his voice mild, though without disguising the menace in it, "answer me truthfully, as you love God, and no harm will come to you. Have you been a companion to the Princess Ingigerd from her babyhood until this day?"

"Yes," she answered in a whisper.

"And are you her chief confidante in all things whatsoever?"

Thordis hesitated. In the silence, sounds of battle could be heard outside. The mayor, followed by several of his men, raced out the front door and down the stairs. I observed the bishop mop his brow again.

"Answer me, woman, I warn you. Have you not been a partner in all her depravities? And are you not, moreover, skilled in all manner of potions and charms, both of the sort that sicken and the sort that bind? Are you not, in fact, a witch?"

That fearful word, as good as a death sentence.

The bishop was after more than just adultery. If it could be proved that Ingigerd had had commerce with a witch, she would suffer a far nastier fate than dragging out her life behind convent walls. Probably, Yefrem was mistaken as far as Thordis was concerned, but that wouldn't save the old woman from torture. Only Inge could do that by confessing her visits to the village babushkas.

"No, may the Virgin help me!"

"Virgin, is it? And why should the Blessed Virgin help you? Flog her!"

"Lady!" Thordis shrieked, twisting her body to look at her mistress.

I looked too. Could Inge watch this and not pity the woman who had dressed, bathed, fed, and played with her from infancy? But Thordis, like Putscha, existed only to serve her, and there was no limit fixed to this service but death. The thing that was incredible to me was that *they* believed it as much as she did, for both of them could have saved themselves by testifying against her.

Like the dwarf, the old woman was stripped to the waist and spread-eagled on the guard's broad back. Again the knout whistled and cracked. Her body stiffened, she gave out a cry like a tortured house cat.

I can scarcely account for what I did then. After all, she was only a woman and no kin of mine, and if her own mistress wouldn't save her, why should I? But somehow I seemed to feel the cold breath of Einar Tree-Foot on my neck. He had cared for her—or anyway, she for him.

"Stop it, Bishop," I shouted. "Let her go, she had nothing to do with any of it. I will tell you what Nenilushka saw that night."

"Yefrem!" Inge made a sudden dash to the dais, getting there ahead of me. "Now I must speak! To save this young idiot from his folly," she indicated me with a shaking forefinger, "I have kept silent because I feel in part to blame for his attack on me. You see, we happened to be talking one evening, quite innocently, when this brainless boy, misunderstanding a careless word of mine, took it as an invitation to go farther. Absurd, but he is a vain youth, as anyone can see. That night, the night Nenilushka was in my chamber—not hiding, as they allege, but prattling to me about something or other in her childish way while she waited for her father— this young man burst in, stinking of strong ale, shut the door behind him and overpowered me, ripping off my shift, and forcing himself between my legs. Nenilushka, may heaven bless her, rushed out the door to find help. Seeing this, Odd became frightened and ran away. A moment later Putscha came in to say that he'd just passed Odd on the stairs and that the brute had knocked him down. Now you have the truth of what Nenilushka saw; such a sight as to rob the poor thing of the little brain she had. Small wonder if her account of it is so muddled. Who could think for one instant that I would take this sorry fellow for a lover? I have told you all the truth, now. Order the rapist to hold his filthy tongue and release my nurse at once."

"Lord Bishop," interrupted the flogger, "pardon my clumsiness. The old woman is dead."

I goggled at Inge. In my slight experience of life I had never known a woman, and scarcely a man, to be so bold a liar. But before I could find voice to answer her, another did: "Bitch! Whore!" Yelisaveta screeched, "Rape, d'you say? No man need rape you! Tell us, mother, did Olaf rape you or wasn't it the other way round?"

In the wink of an eye mother and daughter were on the floor, clawing and pummeling each other as they rolled over and over in a tangle of skirts and long hair. Militiamen and deacons together barely managed to drag them apart. Their clothing torn and their faces scratched, they thrashed and bared their teeth. If either of them had worn a knife, as women often do, one of them surely would have lain bleeding out her life on the floor.

Now everyone was up and shouting. Here came purple-faced Ragnvald rushing to the dais, demanding, "Put Odd to the torture, Bishop! Make him confess to attacking my cousin. You hesitate because it would leave you with no case for adultery. Well, here's what we do to molesters of noblewomen women in my city!"

He thrust at my belly with his dagger, but a militiaman struck his arm aside and others stepped between us. The Jarl of Aldeigjuborg shook his fist and screamed, "I'll have his life before the sun sets, you see if I don't!"

"No, Jarl, that's a pleasure I've promised myself." This was Harald. He towered over us, holding in his hand the knout, which he had taken from the flogger. As Ragnvald turned, Harald struck at his legs, knocking them out from under him. In his pain the jarl dropped his dagger and scuttled as fast as he could out of harm's way.

Now Harald and I were face to face and I could do no more than spit at him. He laughed. "Let's see if you're half the man Putscha was." The knout slashed down across my left shoulder. I felt the shock of that blow all the way to the soles of my feet.

Tears sprang to my eyes, I swallowed hard and braced myself for another blow, but at that moment the door flew open and a breathless militiaman stumbled in, crying, "The Swedes and Norwegians have crossed the river! We're routed. The mayor says to get away—the princess under guard to his dvor, the skald and the dwarf back to the jail!"

"You milk-sucking babies," roared Harald, "must I do everything for you!" He took one more cut at my face with the knout, but his aim was off. The guard at my side staggered away, clutching the place where his ear had been. Flinging the knout away and drawing his long sword, he raced for the door. Even without a horde of warriors at his back Harald was formidable.

"Out through the kitchen to the back stair!" cried Bishop Yefrem, and showed us the way by being the first to bolt in that direction. The mayor's guards herded us behind him while the flogger applied his knout to our backs.

26

LYUDMILA

Hurrying us through streets that were thick with fighters, the mayor's men returned Putscha and me to the jail, and formed a cordon around it.

I can scarcely describe my feelings. As much as the blow that Harald dealt me seared my flesh, Inge's words burned still hotter in my brain. Her betrayal was the more unforgivable. Harald was goaded by anger and humiliation which any man may feel. But she! From the very start she'd done nothing but lie to me, and now, just as coolly, lied about me.

As I paced my cell in silent rage, I barely noticed the shouting and clash of arms that sounded nearby—now approaching, now receding, then again coming nearer. It was about twilight that the street directly outside the jail erupted in fighting between the Rus and the hated outlanders. Torches flared, bodies lurched back and forth across the narrow field of vision afforded by our window, and the night rang with shouts.

The glimmering of a chance to escape this wooden prison released me from the prison of my thoughts. Here, at least, was something I could grapple with. "Putscha! Get up!"

He lay, as he had for hours, on his stomach, with his arms outspread; his back livid and oozing blood.

"Let me be."

"No, listen. We must run for it now while the guards are busy defending themselves; we won't get a second chance. Here, stand on my shoulders. Your hand is small enough to reach up between the bars of the grating and pull out the bolt. Then lift up the grate and throw down the rope ladder."

"I can't move, I tell you!"

From outside came the footsteps of more men running, and the clangor of arms grew louder.

"Up you get, little man—scream all you like, you won't be heard above the noise outside."

Scream he did, as I jerked him to his feet and swung him up in the air with a hand under each arm.

"Never mind the pain."

"What d'you know about pain?" he hissed between clenched teeth.

"Now, now. If it were Ingigerd here instead of me, she'd be standing on *your* shoulders and you'd be thanking her for the privilege. Feet on my shoulders, now. All right, I've got your ankles." His height added to mine—and neither of us tall—just barely brought his fingers in reach of the bars. "Can you get your hand between them?"

He sucked his breath between his teeth and grunted against the pain. A mere Norseman would have screamed the house down.

"Good fellow! Can you feel the bolt?"

"I have it but it won't come."

"Putscha, look out, a torch! Push it away, man!"

"Can't, too far—"

A flaming brand had landed on the grating. Someone—Swede or Norwegian—meant to cook us. An ember drifted down onto the straw-covered floor, just beyond the reach of my foot.

"The bolt, Putscha, as you hope to live, pull harder!"

A wisp of smoke curled upwards from the straw.

"No—no—wait, I have it!"

"Right. Feet in my hands, now, I'm going to lift you straight up. That's it, knees on the ledge, keep low or they'll see you from the street. Can you see the rope anywhere?"

With my hands free, I turned to stamping out the fire—only to send bits of flaming straw whirling in all directions. With a rush and crackle the floor burst into flame in a dozen places at once. In a flash of memory, I was back in my father's house, our enemies screaming outside, the roof collapsing in flames, my mother's hair burning, the flames scorching my feet …

My blood turned to water. I screamed and screamed again. "The rope, the rope, hurry, damn you!"

But, instead, the dwarf glared down at me from his safe perch, his bloody lips twisted in a sneer. "Burn, is it? I, Putscha, could take twelve strokes of the knout for all you cared. Twelve strokes, outlander, there's burning for you. Why shouldn't I let you burn?"

I danced amid the leaping flames. Seeking escape too, were the roaches and rats—whole tribes of them hidden in the straw. They climbed my legs, crawled under my shirt, and clung to my back.

"For pity's sake, Putscha, don't do this to me!"

"What, won't you call me 'little man,'? I do love to be so addressed."

"I'm sorry."

"Oh, I'm sure your sorry now. Oh, yes."

"Please, please, Putschaaa!"

"'Please' is it? I don't reckon there are many you've said that to." He squinted at me against the rising smoke. "Shall I let you live, then? Well, brave druzhinik, here's your rope."

I leapt for it and climbed with the strength that only terror lends us; I and pounds of frenzied rats who sank their claws into me. But my cell-mates I could not carry. The woman, her screaming baby under her arm, hung on my belt. I kicked her away—I was long past caring for any human being but myself. I reached the top with the seat of my pants scorched. The rats and other vermin departed at once for safer havens.

All around me buildings flared and the air was thick with flying ash, to which was added the smoke that billowed up from our cell. I could hear the screams of those wretches we had left below.

"Putscha, you filthy little brute, I'll pay you back for this!" On hands and knees, I made a grab for him, intending to push him back into the flames.

"Hands off!" he warned, backing away with his tiny fists raised in self-defense.

I grabbed for his throat but missed.

"You aren't safe yet, Haraldsskald. Where will you go, eh? Where will you hide so your master doesn't find you?" Again, with an acrobat's quickness, he dodged out of reach. "But I know a place where we can lie low. Food and shelter, anything you like—"

Smoke stung my eyes, the wooden planks under my hands and knees were hot. This was senseless; I could never catch him up here.

"Follow me if you dare!" He made a running jump from the roof. Whether to strangle him or accept his promise of safety amounted to the same decision: I must follow.

Balancing on the narrow ledge, I looked below me. The street was littered with bodies. Warriors hacked and slashed at each other, though it was impossible to see in the cluttered air who was who.

Putscha was disappearing down the street. I jumped and landed running. Dashing this way and that with me hot on his heels, he threaded a maze of back streets—past blazing houses, past mobs of battling men—until we came out at last on the verge of the wild land beyond Lyudin End.

"Stop and let us rest a minute," I gasped. "Where are you taking me?"

"I'm not taking you anywhere; follow or don't, it's all the same to me."

"Are all footstools as bad-tempered as you, Putscha, or does it take a princess' heel marks on your rump to make you so high and mighty?"

"Mightier than you, anyway; 'Putscha pleeease,' he mimicked me."

I grabbed for his throat again but he danced out of reach, laughing, and took off downhill into a ravine choked with brambles. They must have torn his raw skin cruelly but he never slowed his pace.

All that dark blue night we pushed our way through woods and marsh, stopping only to drink water in greedy gulps from a brook. As the sky lightened, we arrived at a clearing in the woods. In the center of it stood a tiny hut built all of sticks with a roof of bundled twigs. Tethered before the door a solitary goat cropped the grass.

"It's to this you bring me—?"

The dwarf drew himself up to his full height and made a face like a thundercloud at me. "Hold your tongue, outlander! The Princess Ingigerd was not too proud to visit my mother—not once but often."

"Your mother?"

"And see you address her respectfully. Lyudmila Ilyavna is her name. She was born beside the far-off Volga, and the blood of Rus, Slav, and Royal Khazar is mingled in her veins. If you are polite, she will help you. If not, she will eat you up."

"Eat me! I've run all this way to meet a troll hag?"

"Silence, I say!"

At these words the bearskin that served the cabin for a door was pushed aside by a thin hand and a woman stepped into the light. I had expected the mother of a dwarf to be a dwarf; my imagination had already conjured up some evil, shrunken thing like Old Louhi of Pohjola.

But Lyudmila Ilyavna was as tall as I.

She had been a beautiful woman once and was still a handsome one. Her hair, in which wild flowers were twined, fell in two snow white plaits to her waist. They framed a face that was finely shaped and uncommonly smooth for a woman of sixty winters or more. It was more like the face of a maiden, except that the blooming color had faded from it as if from an old fabric washed too often. Her lips, too, lacked of redness, though they were full and rounded. Her eyes were as pale as water.

"My child—? Ahh, what has happened to you!"

She ran and knelt before the dwarf, pressing his head to her bosom. (A bosom, I could not help but notice, that was ample and of a certain firmness.)

"Who is guilty of this? Speak, my darling."

Seeing them together, I had to remind myself that Putscha was a middle-aged man with a grown daughter of his own and not, rather, some unnaturally grey-headed little boy.

He recited all the events that had led up to our escape.

"And our poor, dear princess," she asked, "has she escaped as well?"

"Mother, I know not if she's alive or dead."

"And Nenilushka?"

"May she dream of the Devil! I have no daughter anymore!"

"Oh, no, you can't mean that! It's pain that makes you talk so."

Still embracing him, though carefully so as not to hurt him, she turned angrily to me. "And you, my princess's lover—why were you not flogged? Of course, they hesitate to punish a Northman. No, they scarcely dare raise a hand against you, while they beat my poor child nearly to death because of what he is."

Mindful of Putscha's warning, I answered as politely as I could: "Good woman, you are hasty. I was betrayed by my own master and ill-used—it grieves me to say so—by that princess you admire. As for your son, he would not be here if I'd not helped him to escape. I beg you to shelter me for just a night or two."

She looked doubtful. "Darling Putscha," she said, tenderly kissing his forehead, "I will send him away if you wish it."

"He can stay," answered the dwarf sullenly, "provided he makes no more allusions to a person's size or a person's office."

"You have my word on it, little—er, gospodin Putscha," I said.

We made a cozy party inside the tiny hut. Leaves, berries, and herbs of every sort hung in bunches from the roof together with such familiar stuff as garlic and toadstools. Picking from here and there, she mixed ingredients in a mortar and pounded them to a paste which she applied gently to her son's back. She allowed me to take one finger of the stuff for my wounded shoulder, and it did numb the pain.

While she was occupied, I had a look round and saw that there were neither icons, candles, nor crucifix on the walls. Putscha might be a Christian—at least, he regularly attended mass with the Princess—but his mother plainly was not.

"And now drink this, my darling, and sleep," she said, holding a cup of something to his lips. Where had I met that sickly sweet smell before? Ingigerd's poison! Though hers was, no doubt, a more potent mixture.

In a few minutes the dwarf was snoring loudly.

"Outlander, you may take a drop too, if you like."

"Not just now, thank you." I wasn't so sure of her that I would let her drug me.

"Then it's time I milked the goat. You'll excuse me."

"I'll come along."

"Please yourself."

She sat on a three-legged milking stool and began to pull the teats in a steady rhythm. I sat cross-legged on the grass beside her.

"Lyudmila Ilyavna, your son told me that Ingigerd used to visit certain old women in the villages, but that was a blind, wasn't it. It's you who are the witch she comes to for charms and potions."

Her eyes filled with fear. She said, "I did not like to give her so much of the sleeping drug, but she wouldn't be put off. You must believe me, gospodin ..."

"Don't be afraid, woman, I'm no hanger of witches. I leave that to the Christmen. I cleave to the old ways, as you do."

A brindled cat materialized and began to rub against her legs in hope of getting some of the milk. She squeezed a stream into its mouth.

"I have some little knowledge of herbals," she said carefully. "Putscha makes too much of it."

"You don't eat your guests?"

"No," she smiled, "I don't." Her dimpling cheeks looked very girlish.

"What was his father? If a stranger may ask."

"You mean, don't you, was his father a dwarf? The answer is no; the dwarfs are all in my lineage. His father was a Rus warrior, Churillo Igorevich, by name. He was as tall as an oak and ruddy as the sun. A fighter and trader who fared all the way to the Volga, from where he brought me back as his bride."

"To live here in the forest?"

"No, gospodin, to live in Novgorod in a fine wooden house with red shutters and a red rooster on the door. I loved that house. I was still very young. My handsome Churillo enlisted in the druzhina and was greatly prized for his strength and courage.

"Then one day old Vladimir, who was still Grand Prince then, decreed that all the Rus must turn Christian. My husband was one of those few who refused. There was fighting in the streets when the soldiers came from Kiev, and we fled, first to his village, and finally—to escape the whispering of our neighbors—to this lonely spot. I had already given birth to a daughter and here I bore a son—both dwarfs. As I said, they are common in my family, we don't know why. After the second one— Putscha—was born, my husband hanged himself one night from the elm tree yonder, believing that he was cursed by Vladimir's new god."

"Ah, Lyudmila, what feelings, what memories of my own family, your words stir in me. My father too fought against the Christmen and was driven mad by them. And Putscha knows all this?"

"He guesses. From childhood on, he has done everything to harden and strengthen himself. Jumping, tumbling, lifting huge stones by the hour. All to be the son his father wanted. But in his own mind it is never enough."

And so, I thought, he struts about with his chest stuck out and his little wooden sword in his belt. I sighed inwardly. It would be harder to dislike him now.

"You said there was a daughter, too."

"Famine and pestilence carried her off some fifteen years ago. It's just as well. She and her brother behaved as man and wife, you see, since neither could find another dwarf to mate with. Poor Nenilushka was their child. It was during that famine that Putscha sold himself and his little daughter into the princess' service. We never could have survived otherwise.

224

"My clever Putscha became the princess's eyes and ears. And Nenilushka was given to Yelisaveta, who was still a baby then, to be her dolly—one that walked and talked! There seemed nothing against it at the time. And, as the two girls grew up, we hoped that Nenilushka's weak mind would preserve her from court intrigues. We were wrong."

"Your family has born too many misfortunes, ma'am."

"No more than most. Anyway, what is life for heathens but misfortune?"

"Aye, that's true enough." Then, in a few words, I sketched my own history and told her of my vow to go home one day and kill my enemies.

"Then I wish you good luck, gospodin. Meanwhile, in such a hard world as this should we not take our pleasure where we find it?"

"To be sure."

Having finished with the goat, she sat with her hands folded in her lap. Those pale-as-water eyes regarded me gravely under their long white lashes. A red flush rose up her throat and touched her cheeks with color.

"Gospodin Odd, I am not young but would you—?"

"I would with pleasure, Lyudmila Ilyavna."

She led the way to a shadowy glade beyond sight of the house, in case her son should awaken sooner than expected. I never had a more tender lover than this white-haired woman. She was like cool water to my wounded spirit. Afterwards, I lay with my head in her lap and let her search my hair for lice.

"I can see why they call you Tangle-Hair," she said.

"You know my nick-name? What else do you know? Did Ingigerd ever talk about me?—not that I care."

She smiled at that. "What a vain young man you are! Even while you hate her, you want to hear compliments. Well, she said you were as ugly as a tchernobog. What d'you think of that?"

"Hmpf. Did she say nothing good about me at all?"

"I'll not give away her secrets, even to please you, my friend. I'll only say, dear Tangle-Hair, that she didn't exaggerate." Lyudmila touched me between the legs.

Late in the afternoon Putscha awoke and we three shared a meager dinner of porridge and goat cheese. With the last few drops of thin beer that remained, Lyudmila poured a libation to the domovoi, the guardian spirits, of the house.

Later, as we talked, I said, "I must get back into Novgorod, there's a man there I've sworn to kill."

"What a great many you have sworn to kill, gospodin Odd," Lyudmila laughed.

Putscha looked at us in puzzlement a moment; then began to rail at me: "You'll be putting your neck in the noose if you do—and mine and my mother's besides. You're no match for bloody Harald. He'll flog you until you confess how you got away and where you hid."

"You shame me, Putscha Churillovich," I answered truthfully. "I confess that I have not the fortitude of a dwarf." (His chest swelled with pride.) "But I must manage it somehow. Lyudmila, can you sew me a shirt of invisibility such as old tales tell of?"

"No," she answered, "but I can do something that will serve nearly as well, if you agree to it. The men of the Volga wear their hair and mark their bodies in a peculiar way, or, at least, did so when I was a girl. I decorated Churillo when we first met because he admired it so; he claimed it doubled his natural ferocity. If you'll permit me, your closest friend won't know you when I've finished."

My transformation occupied most of four days.

First, for an hour, she honed the blade of a long, thin knife with which she shaved off my beard until only two long moustaches hung down. Following that, she shaved my scalp, leaving just a horse-tail of hair sprouting from the middle of it, which she tied up in a knot. This took all of an evening.

"Tomorrow," she said, "I will go into the woods to find the berries I need."

She was away all the next day while I endured Putscha's boasting and haughty looks. When she returned, more hours were spent in pounding and grinding her ingredients and still more in sharpening a sparrow's wing-bone to a needle point.

"Tomorrow morning," she said, "when the light is strong."

In the cool of the morning I sat outside on the milking stool with my shirt off. She began with the fingers of my right hand, dipping her needle in the little bowl of blue ooze that she had mixed, and pricking my skin with it.

By end of day she had covered both my arms from fingertips to shoulder with a tracery of whorls and spirals that wound in and out without beginning or end.

"Amazing!" I exclaimed, spreading my fingers and holding my arms out before me. "And I'll take good care not to wash until the need for disguise is past."

"Oh, don't bother yourself about that," said she.

"Eh?"

Putscha let out a snort of laughter.

That night I felt feverish and my skin burned and itched; and the next day I did nothing while Lyudmila doctored me with various ointments and assured me that this was all quite normal. On the following day, feeling much improved, I rose early and made ready to walk back to Novgorod.

"Those fine clothes might give you away though, mightn't they?" she said thoughtfully. I was still dressed for Harald's coronation in my very best hat, tunic, shoes, and jewelry, everything fastened with silver and trimmed with fur.

"I've saved my husband's old things."

"Mother!" Putscha looked shocked.

"Hush! Do you want him to be caught?"

"Give me your man's clothes, Lyudmila," I said, "and take these of mine in return."

"Why, that's kindly of you, Odd." She went to a tiny chest that sat in a corner of the hut and took out the clothes, all carefully folded.

Without delay I put on her husband's well-worn boots, wide trousers, sleeveless tunic (which showed off my beautiful new arms), and broad belt of plain leather with a big buckle of tarnished brass. Around my neck I fastened his torque of twisted wrought iron with a Thor's hammer pendant.

"His sword and shield I cannot give you," she said, "they are buried with him. But here is his broad-ax. It has chopped nothing but firewood these many years. May it taste the blood of your enemies."

"I'm in your debt again."

"Let us all be still for a moment now," she said. "It's a good custom to be silent before someone sets out on a journey."

We sat for a few moments, gazing silently at the floor. Then, "Good bye, my friend," she said, rising and kissing me on both cheeks. "And wear this, its power is great." She hung an amulet of carved bone around my neck.

I returned her kisses more warmly than one is accustomed to do with old women. But she was like no other I had known.

27

ÐAG AÐVISES

I tramped the woods for most of that day before reaching the outskirts of the city. As I drew near, the smell of smoke filled my nostrils and I began to notice signs of devastation all around me. Whole streets had been ransacked and burned out. Here and there people stood about or sat in silent groups or else wearily picked through the smoldering wreckage of their homes.

The Novgorodtsi are no strangers to fire. Hardly a month passes without some conflagration, and the people, patient and resigned, always set to work at once clearing and rebuilding. But this felt different. The faces I saw were grim and vengeful. Every man or youth I passed was armed and many, too, were bloodied. A bitter civil war had been waged here with steel and fire. At the moment all seemed quiet; who could say for how long?

I followed Yanina Street through the Nerev End towards the river, passing on my way the jail, or what remained of it. The painted bridge, at least, was intact, although I had to talk my way past suspicious guards at either end of it. The Market Side had fared only a little better than the Saint Sophia side. Yaroslav's dvor was unscathed except for blackened stretches of the palisade. Undamaged, too, were the Norwegian barracks, but those of the Swedes' together with the great merchant warehouses in Gotland Court were a complete loss. In the Court scores of wounded druzhiniks sat or lay stretched out on their cloaks—some of them gambling or drinking; most doing nothing. I felt their eyes on me as I picked my way among them to the Norwegians' quarters.

There one of Harald's former men—a fellow who knew me well—lounged in the doorway, gnawing a mutton bone. He looked straight into my eyes and asked me my name and business.

I swallowed hard and replied "Churillo Igorevich," in Rus-accented Norse. "I look for Harald, the giant."

"Gone," he sneered. "Cleared out."

My heart sank. "Gone where? Who might know?"

The fellow gave a shrug. "Wait here."

A moment later who should appear in the doorway but Dag Hringsson. I should have seen his hand in this all along!

"And who might you be?" he asked.

A moment later, he stood laughing and scratching his head in astonishment when, out of earshot of the others, I revealed myself.

"Damn my eyes! Well, one thing's sure: we can't call you Tangle-Hair anymore."

"Walk with me along the river," I said, "we have things to talk about."

He grimaced with pain and touched his thigh which was tightly bandaged. Leaning on a stick, he limped along beside me. I asked how he came to be here and what had happened.

"What happened is that the Swedes and Norwegians fought the Novgorodtsi until the whole place turned into one big bonfire. Many were killed on both sides—one of them our friend the mayor. Now it's a stand-off—they on their bank of the river, we on ours. And all for the sake of rescuing the fair Ingigerd—and you too, I might add. You have a lot of friends among Harald's men."

"Rescuing me or killing me to keep me quiet? Someone tried to roast Putscha and me in our cell."

"Ah, well, that was suggested by Ragnvald, though I opposed it—much too fond of you for that; and feeling a bit guilty, too, if you must know. I owe you an apology, Odd. I'm the one who spoiled your party. After Harald dismissed me, you see, I sailed home to Stavangerfjord, where my lands are. It so happened that I was in the neighborhood the day that you and the jarls put into the fjord for food and fresh water on your way south. Any fleet of unknown dragon ships is cause for alarm to the local people and so they ran to tell me. I got there in time to see you at a distance without being seen. Now, where could you and the Tronder jarls be going, I asked myself, if not to Novgorod for some purpose involving Harald?

"To say it short, I followed you to Aldeigjuborg in my own ship. There I lay low until you got fed up with waiting and took yourself off to Novgorod. Then Ragnvald and I went to work on the jarls. Not that I have great hopes for little Magnus as a king, mind you, but that's of no importance for the moment. Anyway, I came here with the jarls and kept out of sight in a house that Ragnvald keeps in the town."

"But damn it, Dag," I protested, "it's you who got me here in the first place with the promise that Harald would be king of Norway someday. Your parting words to me were 'stay the course'. And then you turn right around and do this! I call it unfriendly of you."

"Yes, yes but how could I have known that a chance to do him harm would come along so soon? I couldn't let that pass, now could I? Come, you'd have done the same thing yourself."

I supposed I would have. "All right, I bear you no grudge."

"I'm glad of it, my friend." He clapped me on the shoulder. "Anyway, I ask you to believe that I did everything I could to save you. While Yngvar and his Swedes recaptured lovely Ingigerd from her guards, I made straight for the bishop's palace with Jarl Kalv and his men. There we ran up against Harald with a few Rus, holding the stairs. He and I faced each other with drawn swords at last. I tried with all the strength and skill in me to kill him, and he likewise. Neither of us succeeded, but he left me this leg for a souvenir. He and his comrades beat a retreat when we found the back stairs and got around behind them, though by that time the mayor's militiamen had carried you off.

"After that, the fight shifted back and forth across the river. Men of ours reported seeing Harald everywhere in the town, hunting for Norwegians, like so many rabbits, to punish them for deserting to Magnus. The boyars' army crossed the river in boats and sacked the warehouses. In revenge, Ragnvald organized a raid on their side to burn down their houses—and the jail, too, I've no doubt. I hope it will console you to learn that he didn't come back alive. Anyway, you saved yourself. Tell me all about it."

I described the trial and my escape.

"So Ragnvald tried to stab you and Harald to flog you? Have you learned something about fishing on both sides of the stream, my boy?

Store it up as a lesson for the future. And, being lucky enough to escape with a whole skin, you've come back in this colorful get-up? Why?"

"Can't you guess? But Fate has cheated me. When did he leave, where would he have gone?"

"Ah, I see. All I can tell you is that when order was restored, Yaroslav safe on his throne, and Inge at her husband's side again—for the old fool believes her lies—Harald found himself suddenly without friends. The jarls were out for his blood by order of Magnus; he could hardly go back to Yaroslav after calling his wife a whore; and even the boyars, whose cause he took up, had no use for him. To them he was, after all, just another greedy outlander.

"The very next day, his betrothal to Yelisaveta was called off, he was stripped of his rank and lands, and ordered to take himself far away. Which he did, four days ago, with a handful men whom he bribed or bullied into going with him. All we know is that they sneaked off in the middle of the night with a string of Yaroslav's best horses. By now he could be anywhere. He's a beaten man, Odd—for the moment anyway."

None of this surprised me, but I would not give up so easily. "Yelisaveta knows where he is, by God, I'll wring it out of her!"

"How? By breaking into her bed chamber at night? My boy, you have a positive genius for self-destruction."

I sank down on the river bank and put my head in my hands. "Dag, I'm tired of losing, tired of running, tired of starting over, tired of being cheated of my revenge. My luck is hopeless. I think I will drown myself."

"Now look," he said, easing himself down beside me, "stow that. Anyone as fearsome to look at as you are shouldn't be talking such talk. And, as for Harald, he's not the boy to stay hidden for long. That great carcass? Just give him time. You'll have your chance yet. In the meantime, though, you really have to get clear of Novgorod, unless you plan to spend the rest of your life in disguise. Yaroslav has put a price of fifty grivny on your head."

"But where shall I go?"

"Not easy to say. For one thing, you've no money left. Harald ran off with everything he could carry, including your savings. In his mind you owed it to him. I'd urge you to come back to Norway with King Magnus and me, but we may be here for weeks yet and you need to do something before that. Have you no ideas at all?"

"None."

"Well, now look, here's a thought. The boyars have made Yaroslav agree to cut down the number of Swedish mercenaries in the city—which, in fact, the old boy doesn't mind doing; you know Yaroslav—fewer mouths to feed. The first to go will be Yngvar and his men—off to the Volga and Serkland to claim it for the new Grand Prince.

"Yes, Yaroslav said something about that."

"Why not go with them, Odd? Pull an oar, bash some skulls—best thing for you! Who knows, you might come back rich. Tell him you know the Volga blindfolded—Jesu, you look like you do. By the time he finds out you're an impostor it'll be too late to do anything about."

"Except kill me for raping his aunt."

"Oh, Yngvar's got more sense than that. You just tell him the truth, I don't think he has any illusions about Ingigerd. Besides, he likes you."

"The last person you said that about was Harald."

"Did I? Why, I never—, I mean—" He looked at me and I looked at him, and we began to chuckle, and then to laugh out loud, and then to roar, helplessly, till our sides ached. People in the street stopped and smiled in spite of themselves. Still howling like a couple of madmen, we went reeling down the street arm in arm in search of the nearest tavern.

28

YNGVAR'S DOOM

Four days later, a flotilla of dragons and strugi pulled away from Yaroslav's dock and pointed south. On a rowing bench in the flag-ship, straining with his shipmates against the Volkhov's rushing current, sat Churillo Igorevich. Well, it seemed like a good idea, the way Dag put it; and only Black-browed Odin sees the ends of things.

Yngvar stood in the stern, his yellow hair streaming in the breeze and his hand resting lightly on the tiller stick. He gave a wave of his arm to the small crowd who had come to see us off. Among them were the Grand Prince and Princess with Putscha by her side. The dwarf had walked into the palace the day before, as bold as you please (Dag told me) and spouting some lie about where he'd spent the past week.

The 'sucking pigs' were there—but not their nurse; no, not old Thordis. The children didn't appear to miss her. The younger ones skipped up and down the dock, whooping and playing at pirates. A year ago young Prince Volodya would have joined in with them; now the hero of Kiev kept a proper demeanor. Yelisaveta, too, stood apart from the rest, seemingly enclosed by a wall of despair that neither sight nor sound could pierce. One could only guess at her thoughts, but surely here was another Ingigerd in the making. Magnus was there, even in his king's regalia still managing to look like a lost waif. Ringing him like so many mountains stood the Tronder jarls—big of bone, loud of voice, and greedy of heart.

Dag was there. He had bought me a change of clothes, a mail shirt, and a sword and dagger. He was a fine man, Dag. Brave, generous, and quick-witted. I never saw him again. The wound in his leg festered, so I heard long afterwards and he died of it. I think he already knew he was a dead man that day when we laughed together.

Of all those gathered on the riverbank this bright, brisk morning, only Dag and Putscha knew my true identity. Yaroslav and Ingigerd had seen me walk right past them, close enough to touch, without a flicker of recognition. The same with Yngvar when I offered myself as a guide to the Volga country.

I pulled at my oar and watched the figures on the bank grow smaller. In my mind's eye I saw another youth: short, dark, tangle-haired, his head humming with dreams of adventure, his heart high with hope; saw him warping his ship out of Nidaros harbor with a grin and a wave as his men churned the water with their oars.

"Yngvar Eymundsson," I murmured, "with all my heart I wish you better fortune than that other youth has found."

✝

Churillo Igorevich had only a brief existence. When we were a week gone from Novgorod, I revealed myself to Yngvar and explained the truth concerning Ingigerd and me. At home, I suppose, we would have had to fight, but out here all that seemed far away.

"So," he grinned, "I lose a guide but I gain a skald—not a bad exchange."

Unhappily, it was a very bad exchange, as things turned out.

Yngvar's plan was more ambitious than the one Yaroslav had conceived. In earlier days, the lower Volga had often been visited by the Rus. For more than a generation, however, there had been no contact because of the continual movement of new and ever more savage tribes across the steppe. Yngvar vowed that we would dip our helmets in the Volga and drink of its waters. He wanted to see if the region was still as rich in gold as it was rumored to be and whether the river was safe once again for merchant ships.

His idea was to follow it from its source to the point where it enters the Khazar Sea; then to coast along the western shore of that sea and return to Tmutorakan by a river route, if there was one; otherwise by foot.

From Tmutorakan it would be an easy voyage round the peninsula of Chersonesos to the mouth of the Dnieper and home.

The force he commanded was not a large one. It consisted of his seven dragon ships with about three hundred Swedes to man them, and eight strugi carrying about the same number of merchants and adventurers recruited from the streets of Novgorod.

You may have heard somewhat of Yngvar's famous expedition to Serkland. A liar by the name of Ketil-Garda, who wasn't even there, invented a fabulous account of it which has spread far and wide. According to him, we spent our first winter at the court of a beautiful queen, whom our leader instructed in the Christian faith. Later, we slew a giant and carried away his foot, which we afterwards used to lure a dragon from its hoard of gold. And much other nonsense besides.

If only the truth were so amusing.

Our route took us from Lake Ilmen up the Lovat to the Valdai hills where, instead of portaging to the Dnieper as one would if he were going on to Kiev, we portaged to the Volga, which also rises here. That river is big beyond imagining and unpredictable besides. In some places giant tributaries flow into it and the water runs deep and fast. Elsewhere the channel, though broad, is so shallow that even our flat-bottomed strugi had to be dragged over the stony bed.

Now and then we passed Rus villages. At each one, Yngvar stopped and made a speech to the assembled warriors (some of the older ones with scalp-locks and arms tattooed like mine), informing them that they had now the good fortune to be subjects of Grand Prince Yaroslav the Wise of Kiev, and that they must swear allegiance to him (Yngvar) as the Grand Prince's representative. Some repeated the oath with laughing and foolery; some wandered off; some just stood and stared. Yngvar fumed, but there was nothing he could do.

Spring, summer, and fall we followed the Volga, stopping often to hunt and gather fruits and berries along the way. After a while we encountered no more Rus, but Volga Bulgars instead, whom we sometimes surprised watering their ponies at the river bank. In answer to our questions they invariably pointed downstream and bade us continue to the mouth of the river, where we would find the place we sought—the rich and far-famed city of Atil. There we would be treated as honored guests, they said, and could pass the winter amidst every kind of luxury.

We pressed on. Atil, we knew, had been the capital of the once mighty Khazar empire. The city had fallen to Grand Prince Svyatoslav, long ago, when he warred against that people. Despite its capture on that occasion, we saw no reason to doubt that it flourished still.

But all we found was a desolate ruin, haunted by wolves and ghosts. The Rus had savaged the city so badly that survivors, if there were any, fled away and never returned. (I was one day to befriend a Khazar warrior in Golden Miklagard, Moses the Hawk, who knew his homeland only from the tales his old father told. When I described to him this scene of desolation, even that fierce, hard-bitten man shed a tear.) Perhaps our Bulgar informants up-river were ignorant of all this. Or, more likely, they simply lied to be rid of us.

Though we were angry and disappointed, we set about to explore the ruins of the khagan's stone-built palace, which lay on an island in the middle of the shallow river. Here, we had been told, he kept his twenty-five wives, his hundred concubines, and the four thousand warriors of his druzhina. It was hard to see all that in the toppled wreckage that lay before us.

Elsewhere we found traces of what seemed to have been churches for Christians, Saracens, and Jews. The Khazars, themselves, practiced the Jewish religion, though it was remembered of them that they tolerated all religions equally. Now all were equally laid low.

We had hardly arrived at Atil and were debating whether to go on or not, when winter struck like a man with a knife. We awoke one morning to find our ships frozen fast in the river. Now we could go neither forward nor back but must make do with what little shelter the derelict city offered, while we cursed old Svyatoslav for his unrivaled stupidity.

Being an Icelander, I thought I knew about cold. But this was a cold so bitter that crows fell dead from the sky; a cold that cracked stones and split tree trunks; a cold that turned your beard rock hard and made icicles of the water dripping from your nose; a cold in which you feared to lower your breeches long enough to shit; a cold sharp enough, when the wind howled across the estuary flats, to peel the hide off you. I wore three fur coats, the inmost with the fur against my body. I wore felt boots, over which I pulled a pair made of horse-hide and lined with bearskin. Fur leggings, mittens and a hat completed my outfit. I was so bundled up I could hardly walk, and still I was cold.

We would surely have died if it hadn't been for the Oghuz. These men—whom, at first sight, I took to be Pechenegs—were a tribe of nomads, swarthy and bow-legged with jet black eyes and heavy beards, who pitched their leather tents in the ruins of the city. One old man amongst them could speak the Slavonic tongue tolerably well and he conveyed Yngvar's speech to the rest of them, explaining that we were servants of the great Rus Khan in the West.

Much to our astonishment they hailed us as friends, declaring that they were allies of the Rus from long ago when the two peoples made war together against the Khazars. In short, they befriended us, and all through that winter shared with us their food, their tents, and their precious fur coats. Even so, frostbite claimed many noses, toes, and privates, and the smell of gangrene was ever present.

But we endured. Most of us.

✝

The coming of spring brought with it great shoals of fish, heading up-river to spawn. We ate them till our bellies bulged and salted them by the hundredweight to take with us. Then, saying goodbye to the Oghuz, we sailed out of the Volga into the Khazar Sea.

Taking two young Oghuz along as guides, we coasted south, looking for the mouth of the Terek river where a Rus town, called Semender, was said to be. We reached the Terek after several days and, for once, were happily surprised. There really was a town there, and a thriving one at that. The people of Semender owned Mstislav to be their overlord, though they had never seen him, and when Yngvar told them that that man's noble brother now ruled in his stead, they received us kindly.

We felt now that we had accomplished the first part of our mission and should think of returning. Our plans were changed, however, by the arrival of envoys from a certain Shah Malik. This man, though an Oghuz by birth, ruled over the Saracen Emirate of Gand in the land of Kwarizm, which lies at the southern end of the sea. He was, said his envoys, raising rebellion against the dynasty of the Ghaznawids, who oppressed his country, and, in view of the old alliance between Oghuz and Rus, the Emir felt he had a claim on Semender's help, and ours too. They promised that we would be well rewarded just as soon as Allah allowed their Emir to gallop his horse over the bodies of the Ghaznawid dogs.

Yngvar leapt at the chance to earn glory for himself in battle, as well as putting the Oghuz in Yaroslav's debt. So it came about that at the head of a fleet of twenty ships, our own and those of Semender, he set sail for the Kwarizmian shore.

Our campaign, so bravely begun, ended as a sorry tale of treachery and bad luck. Let it be enough to say that Shah Malik had no stomach for a real fight and only hoped to frighten his overlords with a show of force. When that failed, he informed us that our services were no longer wanted and closed his gate in our faces.

Some of the Semender warriors went home, the rest enlisted under Yngvar, for he, refusing to be cheated of his booty and fame, spent the summer raiding the coast of Kwarizm and plundering many a rich harbor—until one night our luck deserted us.

A storm demolished all our ships as they lay exposed on the beach. When we appealed to our erstwhile ally for shelter, we were answered with arrows. There was nothing to do but march back along the coast to Semender, carrying on our backs as much of our plunder as we had been able to salvage.

Our route took us around the eastern spur of an enormous mountain range whose snow-capped peaks touched the clouds. On the lower slopes, sheep grazed and villages clung to jutting crags of rock. Between these mountains and the sea was only a narrow pass, rocky and rough, and affording many places for ambush.

Day after day we pushed on over the sun-scorched ground, leaving a trail of jewelry, coin, and other costly trash behind us. We were meat for the eagles. Some were picked off by the arrows of marauding Albani mountaineers, others succumbed to a bloody flux in the bowels. Yngvar died of this one night, calling on Christ to save his soul.

Not long after that, near a pestilential Saracen town called al-Bab, the Emir of that place, one Mansur bin Maymun, invited the leaders of our band to parlay with him. After Yngvar's death I was chosen as one of several leaders by the men. While he entertained us, his warriors fell upon the main body of our men, hemmed in between the mountains and the sea, and cut down every last one. We survivors were thrown into chains. And that is how, for the second time in my life, I became a slave.

It was Mansur's idea to give us away as gifts to the neighboring emirs and chieftains with whom he wanted to have good relations. Tall yellow-haired men were prized by these rather short, rather dark people. I, however, being short and dark myself, was not considered worth giving away. And so, one by one, I saw my comrades disappear.

Slavery was more galling to me now than my experience of it in Finland had ever been. There, I was the captain of a crew who looked to me to lead them. Here, I was alone, with no one to be brave for. I dreamt of escape at first, but by degrees I sank into a state of hopelessness from which there was no brave and beautiful Ainikki to rouse me.

The only profit I derived from the endless drudgery of hauling water and wood to the Emir's kitchen, was that I learned somewhat of the Greek tongue. Among the slaves of Mansur's household was a Greek sea captain—a leather-skinned man by the name of Leonidas. His ship had been seized by pirates on the Black Sea, and for years he had been traded from pillar to post until finally washing up here.

For three years he and I were chained together in the slave barracks each night. Since we had no language in common and he absolutely refused to learn mine, I was forced to learn his. Along with his language I learned, too, that I was a 'barbarian': a lower form of life than himself, though, he grudgingly admitted, cleverer than others he had known. What he loved to talk about most were the great seaports that he had spent his life sailing amongst: Sinope, Trebizond, Cherson, but, above all, the great, the incomparable City of Constantine. In a tone of awe he would describe its miles of soaring battlements, its church whose dome was like the vault of heaven, its hoard of priceless relics among which were the Virgin's robe, Moses' staff, the head of John the Baptist, the foot of Saint Paul—the list went on and on.

Leonidas and I became close despite our contrary natures. To my mind he was a braggart and a liar—telling things about this Constantinople so fantastic that none but a fool would believe them. From his point of view, I was a most unsatisfying partner in the 'Greek wrestling' that he urged upon me night after night and to which, from sheer loneliness, I sometimes gave way.

He was a quarrelsome man, too, and often we would argue about the most trifling things, only to make up again later. We had quarreled one night about something or other, I forget what, and kept up a row until the other slaves pelted us with their shoes. Leonidas turned his back to me and I to him and so we lay angrily until we fell asleep.

In the morning when Mansur's overseer banged on his brass pot to awaken us, Leonidas lay dead beside me, without a mark on his body. He had complained the previous day of a gripping pain in his jaw and arm; it had made him worse-tempered than usual. But how could a man die of that?

And it seems to me that I went mad for a time, though I don't remember clearly; that I began to weep and to beat on his chest with my fists, and wouldn't leave off until the steward drove me away with blows and curses. I speak of it now only to show how just a single Greek can corrupt a Northman's spirit. Imagine, then, the effect of a city full of them! After Leonidas's death, I sank into such a state of melancholy that the Emir lost patience with me and sold me for a few coppers to a leather tanner in the town. The tanner passed me on to a wool dyer, who traded me to a butcher, who sold me to a quarryman. The quarryman used me to pay off a gambling debt that he owed to an itinerant merchant, a Turk by the name of Murad.

The very devil of a man.

Murad's business consisted in selling cheap goods made in the coastal towns to the tribesman who dwelt deep in those mighty mountains that hung above us. He used me as a beast of burden, to carry his tinker's pack up mountain paths so steep that even the mules could not manage them. And how he loved to use the rod on me!

Once, and still near the beginning of my time with him, I felt that I could not stand one more beating and decided to kill myself by falling off a high rock ledge. But the pack on my back broke my fall and all I got were bruises. For punishment, Murad branded me with an X on my chest.

As savagely as he was accustomed to beat his mules, so he beat me. And after a time I became, like the mules, stupid, stolid, and mean.

29

RETURNED FROM
THE DEAD

The Rus have a saying: 'Day after day as the rain falls, week after week as the grass grows, year after year as the river flows'.

Sluggish and bitter on the tongue, the waters of my life crept by for four long years.

It was now the spring of the year 1037 (as Catholics count the years; Greeks and Rus would call it the six thousand-five hundred-and-forty-sixth year from the Creation of the world, and the Mohammedans, the four hundred-and-fifteenth from the flight of their Prophet). I was twenty-five years old and felt a hundred. I had long ago ceased to hope.

But my master's business prospered. So much so, in fact, that he was able to purchase some quite beautiful girls, captives in a raid of one mountain tribe upon another, and with this valuable cargo and several camels to carry his other goods, he joined the great caravan that came each spring up the western shore of our sea. The caravan brought horses and spices from Arabia, steel from Damascus, pistachio nuts and dried fruits from Persia, and every sort of beautiful and costly trifle from the workshops of Kwarizm. I could scarcely picture to myself the country from which it had started. As to its destination, my fellow slaves were as ignorant as I, and our masters did not see fit to enlighten us.

With the soaring mountains on our left, we headed west, gradually turning to the north until the tallest peaks were lost to view. Our way was across the open steppe. Crossing that endless expanse of grass and stony barrens was, to me, exactly like being adrift at sea. The sun told me we were making westward, but how far we were to the north or south I had no clear idea.

Still, as day followed day, I began to suspect that I knew our destination. I tried not to hope, for fear I was mistaken, but the closer we approached the more unbearable was my anticipation.

As we approached the city wall, acres of young fruit trees bloomed and green ears of grain bowed in the wind, where I remembered only charred stubble, corpses, and vultures. But it was still the same citadel that looked down from its heights upon the wide Dnieper. Kiev! My unsuspecting master had brought me to within an inch of freedom.

We halted at a caravanserai on the left bank. As the hour was already late, the Saracens faced east to say their evening prayers while we slaves, released from the long coffle-chain, saw to watering the camels and performing all the other business of setting up camp.

Later, after chewing my few scraps of dinner, I was manacled, as always, and my slave collar was attached by a short chain to a camel's hind leg—an arrangement which the camel resented as much as I. That night I could not close my eyes. My brain was in a fever. Somehow, somehow I would find a way to escape. If I didn't, then I deserved to die a dog's death.

The next morning, our masters mounted their horses and camels, loaded us slaves with bundles of trade-goods, and drove us through the waist-high water at the ford, where the mid-channel island lies.

Once beyond this wooded island, I could see the podol sprawled along the river bank: risen from its ashes, and once again a noisy, lively jumble of shop-houses, tents, stalls, and pens for animals and slaves. The river bank, moreover, was thick with strugi—fifty hulls at least, with workmen crawling over them like ants, hammering, scraping, tarring, to make them ship-shape. The time was early June and this was a part of the great trading convoy making ready for its yearly voyage to Golden Miklagard—New Rome, New Jerusalem, Constantine's great city.

A space had been reserved in the busiest part of the market for our caravan. Scarcely were we installed than hordes of customers crowded round us. My master's string of girls were set out for inspection on a low platform built of planks. I, too, mounted the platform—not as merchandise, but to carry my master's stool, fan, and parasol, for the day was a hot one.

A stream of buyers passed before us while Murad and his fellows kept up a constant sing-song chant, advertising the quality and price of this girl and that one. I was standing by his stool, fanning him listlessly while my eyes drank in every detail of the scene before me, when I saw a face I knew! Five years had not changed it: the same pushed-up nose, the same bulging eyes, the same greasy braids weighted at the tips with lead balls. He was examining a young girl of my master's string, pinching her jaw between thumb and forefinger and peering into her mouth while tears ran down her cheeks.

"Stavko!" I hissed.

He gave a start and looked up to see who spoke.

In Norse I said, "Stavko, it's me!" I was nearly close enough to touch him; I stretched out my hand. "In God's name, buy me!"

"Strong back, sir, good legs." Murad, smelling a sale, sprang from his stool and propelled me forward, going into his pitch in the Arabic-Turkic-Slavonic pidgin that all the merchants spoke. "Simple-minded, but I've taught him to fear the rod. Give you a good day's work." He thumped my chest with his fist. "Good health, last you for years."

Stavko's eyes looked straight into mine. He seemed to hesitate a moment, then frowned. "No. I buy only females; how much for girl?"

They bargained over her while I watched in despair. Stavko knew me. He knew me, damn his eyes!

"Get back, you!" Murad noticed how I stared at them and shoved me away.

I cannot describe the torment that racked me for the rest of that day. Truly, I was abandoned—By Odin All-Father, by the White Christ, even by Stavko Ulanovich, the slaver. Might they all rot! I would make one more try for freedom and if I died, so be it.

I had a plan.

At dusk, Murad and his friends covered their stalls and drove their slaves back into the river, loaded down with the unsold goods which they would guard over-night in the caravanserai. I was lucky in that I had only the stool, umbrella, and fan to carry.

We were at the island now, midstream; Murad, on his camel riding ahead of me, not looking back; the leafy branch of a tree between us. I let go the umbrella and other things, sank under water and swam until my lungs were ready to burst. Ten or a dozen breaths would bring me opposite the cave's mouth, high up on the bank, where Kuchug and I had climbed up the rope that night long ago; the entrance to the Monastery of the Caves. Father Feodosy and his monks—they would remember me, and would surely redeem a Christian from slavery to the Infidel. How thankful I was at that moment to be a Christman!

But as I came up gasping for air, the men of the caravan were already upon me, the long legs of the camels churning the water all around. Murad, with a guttural curse, leaned low from his saddle and slashed at me with his long rod. I covered my face with my arms and howled.

The next day he woke me with a kick and told me that I was to be sold; furthermore, if he could find no one to offer even one copper penny for me he would kill me and throw my body to the dogs.

This time, when we forded the river, he attached a chain to my iron collar and dragged me behind him. I was half drowned, half throttled, by the time we reached the bank.

All that day I stood in my rags beneath the blistering sun. A few customers paused to thumb my muscles or look at my teeth. Each time this happened I screamed and rattled my chains like a madman to frighten them away; and the more Murad cursed me the louder I screamed and flung myself about. If only he were true to his word I need not see another sunrise!

But nearly at the day's end a man with the costume and bearing of a boyar, put a silver coin in Murad's palm and instructed his servant to lead me away by my chain. I screamed, I gibbered, I dug my heels in the ground. No use. The servant was stronger than I was. My new owner never looked back, never slowed his pace. We mounted Borichev Slope and went in through the citadel gate. My little store of strength exhausted, I gave up struggling, and trotted at the end of my leash, my arms hanging loose and my head jerking up and down.

Everywhere we passed, building sites swarmed with workmen where fine houses and churches were rising. We stopped, at last, before a single-storied log house that lay off a narrow lane. The door opened to my owner's knock and I was dragged inside. The room had only one occupant. Resting his elbows on a table and with a toothsome smile lighting up his face, sat Stavko Ulanovich.

"Well done, gospodin Boris," he said to the man who had bought me. "You will have your house back again by evening with many thanks."

With a doubtful look at me, Boris and his servant left us alone.

"Odd Tangle-Hair, let me embrace you!" Like an affectionate dog on its hind legs he pawed me, eyes brilliant with happiness, spittle flying. "How you do look!" he cried in his wretched Norse. "Ribs sticking out, body black as Ethiopian's, hair and beard filthy, everywhere sores, flea bites, lash marks on shoulders—" he appraised all my defects with the thoroughness of his trade. "Dear friend, what has happened to you?"

I shook him off, my throat aching with tears and anger. "Why not yesterday, you bastard?"

"Please, do not spoil joyous moment. Yesterday was not safe to know you; today is. That's all."

"Why this man's house?"

"Because my shop too well known, I do business always in Kiev these days. All will be clear in time, ha, ha."

"All of what?"

"What do you think of city now? Big changes, eh? Hustle and bustle!" It seemed he had no intention of answering my questions. "Grand Prince has such plans for new capital! Stone cathedral, can you believe? And triumphal gate to rival Miklagard itself. What times these are! Only last year, those devils of Pechenegs attack city again. Again Yaroslav rushes to defense, but this time is Vladimir, the young eagle, who commands druzhina under his father's proud eyes. Since then, Grand Prince and Princess make Kiev their capital while son rules Novgorod—"

"Shut up, man! Give me food and drink, before I faint."

"Ach! Stupid of me! You are starving, is plain to see. Only, damned inconvenient—servants all let go for today."

He began an aimless search of the room which produced nothing in the way of food. Three doors gave access to other rooms. Two of these he opened; one he did not. Disappearing through the second one, he soon returned, wreathed with smiles and holding out a pail of beer and a round of cheese.

"Slowly, my friend, slowly, you make yourself sick."

"More!"

He watched me in silence for a time; then began again in a hesitant manner:

"Odd Thorvaldsson, please to pay attention. I am speaking now as agent, once again, of Grand Princess Ingigerd. She, ah, has favor to ask of you." He watched me closely to gauge the effect of his words.

"Ingigerd? Who owns me, you or she?"

"Owns you?" He rolled his eyes—incredulous, astonished. "Owns? Good God, what a thing to say! No one owns you, my poor friend; we are simply delighted to see you returned, so to speak, from dead."

"Then get this off me."

I hooked a finger in my iron collar from which the chain hung down my back.

He cursed himself for a heartless wretch—he had not seen it under my beard; could I forgive him?

It was a common type of lock; he tried two or three of his own keys and found one that fit it. Removing the collar, he lightly touched my skin where it was rubbed raw. Gravely, with none of his customary foolishness, he said in a low voice, "You are much changed, my friend."

"Bath and a haircut, I'll be all right."

"Not just that, something else. Your eyes: they were never so cold. Last time I saw you, there was still—excuse me for saying—some little bit of boy in you. I don't see now. Where has gone that boy?"

"He died, Stavko Ulanovich. Beatings killed him; hunger."

"So? And what remains?"

"What you see, nothing more."

"Here, sit down, tell me your story."

"My story? I hardly remember it. I slipped out of Novgorod aboard Yngvar Eymundsson's ship—"

"Princess's nephew helped you escape!"

"He knew nothing about it, though that can't matter to anyone now. He fattened the crows long ago. They all did. They were brave men. Be sure and tell that to the slandering bitch when you see her."

Stavko seemed to cringe and fell into a fit of coughing. "Perhaps God has spared you for reason, Odd Tangle-Hair."

"If it's to tear out the throats of the ones who betrayed me I'll thank him for it."

This time he couldn't restrain a desperate glance at the one door that he had not opened.

I spoke to it in a loud voice: "Ingigerd, your Man of Affairs is on the point of shitting in his pants he is so nervous. You want to talk to me? Come out where I can see you."

There was a pause, and then the door swung open.

Serene, cool, the lips faintly smiling—she was not the screaming virago I had last set eyes on, but looked as she had on that first day when she summoned me to her chamber—all easy charm and pleasantry. Her waist might be a little thicker, her face a little fuller (she was forty and some now), but still as beautiful—as achingly beautiful— as ever. Her dress was very plain and she wore no jewelry. Was she afraid to be recognized coming here?

"I won't need you any longer, Stavko," she said. "Leave us."

"Princess, is that—?"

"It will be all right."

He bowed himself out the door.

She sat down on the only other chair in the room, removed her head cloth and shook out her yellow hair. There was a long silence, which I waited for her to break.

"Slandering bitch? Really, Odd, that's uncivil of you."

I made no reply. After a moment, she continued, "Poor Yngvar. We couldn't imagine what had happened, you're the first survivor to come back. Of course, the Grand Prince will have to be told—he's been very worried—but your name needn't be mentioned. How did my nephew die?"

"Puking and praying. I'll spare you the poetic touches."

"I always admired your poetry."

"You're looking well, Inge. Sleeping all right? Appetite good?"

"Quite good, thank you. But you, my poor Odd—what you've been through! I had my people search the rubble for days to see whether you still lived—"

"And to slit my throat if I did."

She waved her hand impatiently. "You've no right to talk like that to me, Odd. To give you a warrior's burial, is what I meant to say. But when it seemed you had escaped death I prayed for you, wherever you might be. Was it awful, Odd?" She leaned towards me, her eyes full of tender concern.

"I don't know. Compared to having my privates cut off for raping a princess, it wasn't bad, really."

"It's cruel of you to say that. I had to protect myself."

"Of course. And everything's smoothed over now, is it?"

"Yes", she said. Her husband was actually a changed man. As blindly devoted to her as ever, but no more the bookish recluse. He was busy day and night now with his Greek architects and his builders—with the pleasing consequence that she rarely had to endure his company. She kept in close touch with Magnus, whose rule over Norway appeared secure; he had grown into a fine young man, loved by his subjects. For herself, she was, at least, no longer plagued by seditious boyars and meddlesome bishops. The mayor of Kiev was her own creature and, as for Yefrem, he had vacated his bishopric quite suddenly and his replacement was a very pliable priest.

"I congratulate you on your good fortune, Princess. And Putscha? Lurking in the next room with his ear to the wall, I suppose? Come out, little spy, and say hello to your old prison mate!"

"Alas," she said, lowering her eyes, "dear Putscha Churillovich hanged himself soon after our trial. He became despondent when his daughter suffered a rather grisly accident. Somehow the foolish child got into the mews and frightened the birds—you know how high-strung they are—especially a pair of young eagles who were still quite wild. We heard her screams; I suppose she couldn't find her way out in the dark. By the time we beat the birds off she was quite horribly gashed and died the next day. Putscha didn't long outlive her. It was all very sad. One of the eagles broke a wing and had to be destroyed."

"By God, you chill my blood, Inge. The dwarf was devoted to you, he never would have betrayed you. Tell me, Princess, whose back do you stand on now?"

"I don't think I care for your question, gospodin."

"No? Well, here's another. What have you done with his mother?"

"Who—?"

"His mother, god damn you!"

"Why, I know nothing of her. I shall send at once to Novgorod to have her found and provided for."

"Liar. Lyudmila Ilyavna was the wise-woman who sold you potions and amulets. You've got rid of her, too, haven't you? I can see it in your face. You've done away with them all; except Thordis—the bishop's torturer spared you the trouble of killing her. So now there's no one left who really knows what we did together—no one, that is, but me. Why are we sitting here, chatting like old mates, Inge? Have I drunk poison with my ale? Are you here to watch my death agony?"

"Stavko was right, you are changed." Just for an instant her eyes turned cold: a murderer's eyes. "I liked the old Odd better."

"You ought to—he was a fool."

"Perhaps a little," she smiled. "Be easy, Odd Tangle-Hair, I'm not here to kill you. I can see you've had a harder fate than you deserved. Four years has it been? By Christ, I see ten, at least, carved on your face. I am here to repay you for them."

"You haven't got money enough."

"Oh, money is the least of it, although you shall have plenty of that too. Enough to return to Iceland in magnificent style, shall we say? And King Magnus, if I ask him, will do as much as Harald would have done to help you avenge the murder of your family."

With a sudden stab of feeling, I realized how faint had grown my memory of all that. My family? My enemies? I had scarcely thought of them in years—

"Odd, are you listening to me? Money, I said, will be the least of your rewards. The greatest will be satisfaction.

"What are you talking about?"

"I want a man killed."

"What man?"

"Harald. I know where he is." She looked at me hard.

"Go on."

"You take it that calmly? Have four years erased the memory of how he betrayed you, kicked you, took a whip to you? Your sworn lord!"

"I said, go on."

"All right. Last fall, after four and a half years of silence, he announced himself. A man claiming to be a merchant of Novgorod stopped here on his way home from Miklagard and delivered a casket of jewels—sapphires, pearls, rubies, priceless stuff—a present, he was instructed to say For the Grand Prince of all Rus from Harald of Miklagard as a token of friendship and alliance past and to come. The impudence of him! And more rich gifts are promised. How he comes by such wealth the messenger could not, or would not, say. He claimed that both the jewels and his instructions were conveyed to him by a go-between, who told him nothing more than the message he was to deliver. Harald, it seems, is playing a little game with us; and my fool of a husband is half persuaded already that he never heard him call me whore to my face."

"He knows the shortest way to Yaroslav's heart."

"For a fact. But there's worse than that. With the jewels came a packet of letters—by mistake—they were intended for my daughter. Poems again, sheaves of them, declaring his love. Love! What can that monstrosity know of love? And all written in such a scrawl—my little Svyatoslav makes his letters better than that. I suppose he's learned to write himself, not having you to do it for him anymore."

"A wasted effort, since you intercepted them."

"That was luck. There'll be others, or have been already, for all I know."

"And Yelisaveta still unmarried at—what?—eighteen? And living here?"

Inge flung out her arm. "She lives in Novgorod with her brother, who is too good to think ill of her and lets her do as she pleases. It's an impossible situation. She refuses to wed anyone but Harald, and her father is too tender-hearted to compel her. And until the little idiot either marries or becomes a nun, we can't find husbands for her sisters without the whole family being a laughing stock. Christ! I would cut out her heart with these hands if I could. It's as well that a thousand versts lie between us. But that will all change when you, my dear, return from Miklagard with Harald's head. Mind you, there must be no room for doubt whose head it is, you must pickle it in brine in a well-tarred cask. When I throw it at her feet, Yelisaveta will sing a tune more to my liking."

"By the Raven, Lady, you make me shudder; you're madder than ever."

"Say what you like of me, my dear,"—her voice steady and even—"but tell me the truth: could you kill him?"

"Inge, why do you worry yourself about Harald now. Magnus is safe on his throne, isn't he?"

"He'll never be safe on the throne while that monster lives. I'll ask you again: can you kill him?"

"These past years have cut deep into my strength, I don't know how much will come back."

"No, no, don't speak so, you can do it, I know you can. You'll play David to his Goliath, by God!"

"I'll play what?"

"Oh, never mind, you false Christian, it's not important. But you'll do it? You agree?"

"Princess, I'm a little confused. Why are you asking me to do this? Surely you can find assassins in Kiev."

"Oh yes, I have plenty of druzhiniks who are brave enough, or stupid enough, to face Harald in a fight and lose their lives. But not one who has such reason to hate him as you do, not one who knows his tricks as well as you do, not one who's as resourceful as you are, for it will need wiles more than brawn to lay Harald low. Just to find your way in that huge city takes more brain than any of my men have. Will you do it?"

"Commit murder for you? Why should I?"

"I don't understand you, Odd. I'm sending you to do what you've dreamt of for four long years, and proposing to pay you well for it. Is that so hard to accept?"

"What d'you know about my dreams, damn you! Harald was not the only one who betrayed me. At least, he showed me an honest face; I knew what he was when I joined him. But you—you played me like a fish, and you're trying to do it still. Yes, I want Harald's life—among others, but how do you know, Inge, which one of you I'll take my revenge on first?"

She dismissed this with a wave of her hand. "Yes, yes, I told lies, what of it? How else can a woman make her way in the world? Much was at stake."

"Meaning your neck? And what if I should take that white neck between my two hands now and crack it?"

"Then you would be a very great fool indeed! You really don't understand, do you? You think it's a sort of big village, Miklagard. You imagine you have only to stroll along the cow path once or twice to meet everyone there. You have no conception of the thing. Imagine a hundred Kievs side by side and that is still not the half of it."

"You've been there?"

"I've heard."

"One may hear many things." I thought of the tales Leonidas had told me.

"What's more, an ordinary outlander can't stray from one small corner of the city except in the company of a palace official, and even that is not granted to most. Without credentials, decent clothes, money for bribes and the like you'll never get close enough to Harald to spit at him. You'll starve to death in some gutter and be swept out with the rest of the garbage."

"Harald made his way."

"Harald left with a great deal of our money. So will you, if you take my help. I propose to send you as an ambassador, with decent clothes and a retinue of servants; I will even give you real business to transact. That will get you into the palace and into the houses of important men. Someone there will know our Harald. Anyone as rich as he doesn't go unnoticed. The rest I leave to you. So, Odd, you must decide. Would you rather kill Harald or me? You can't manage both. If it's me you want, well, here I am, alone with you—you'll never have a better chance. Go on."

My slave collar with its chain lay on the floor by my foot. In one swift motion I scooped it up, looped the chain around her neck, and pulled her to me.

"Stop! Stop it! Are you mad?"

I began slowly to tighten it. She beat my shoulders with her fists.

I twisted harder.

Her eyes were huge with fear; her nails dug into my wrists. "In the name of God," she croaked, "don't kill the woman who loves you!"

I loosened the chain enough to let her draw a rasping breath. Her heart pounded against my chest. She pressed her lips to my cheek.

"Do you remember the first time you made love to me, Odd? Do you? And can you guess how I've missed you, how much I despise all the others? Let me live, Odd. This needn't be the end for us. Let me go—"

I let the chain clatter to the floor.

"Darling Odd, I knew you couldn't—"

With all the strength I had, I drove my fist into her face. She staggered back against the table by the wall, pressing a hand to her mouth.

"Mad dog!" she hissed. "You think I came unguarded? There are men outside. You won't get a dozen steps—!"

"Aye, Inge, but you cannot cut off my head and have Harald's too. You said it yourself. Now it's you who must choose: which one of us do you hate the most?"

She stared at me speechless.

"Come, Princess, which is it to be?"

"Harald," she whispered.

I hit her again. She reeled against the cupboard on the wall, bringing down all the crockery with a crash.

"Not me?"

"Harald!"

"Are you sure?" I kicked the table away and came at her.

"HARALD! HARALD! Break my bones, God damn you, if that's your price, I'll pay it!"

Rage blew like a gale in my chest. I should have killed her, you will say. Had it been Harald in my place, he wouldn't have hesitated a second. But I lowered my hands.

Inge struggled to master herself. When she spoke again her voice was steady. "You will bring back the head. You will collect five thousand silver grivny from Stavko. Five thousand! And then you will leave Gardariki and never come back. You understand? Christ, if only you had taken Ragnvald's instead of my cousin's bribe in the first place, what a lot of trouble you'd have saved us all! Well? Do you agree to my terms?"

"I agree to go. As to terms, I'll leave you to worry about that. Have money, clothes, arms, and whatever documents I need sent round to Stavko's. I will travel under the name of Churillo Igorevich."

She startled.

"You know that name, don't you, Inge? The husband of sweet Lyudmila, whom you claim not to have known. Good-bye, murderer."

†

Stavko's shop-house was in the podol; I had no difficulty in getting directions. I lay up there for a week, during which time I did little besides sleep and eat. By week's end I was, in outward appearance, already much improved. But in my spirit—just as once before in my life, when I escaped the flaming ruin of my home—the unseen wounds were slower to heal.

Waking and sleeping, Murad haunted my thoughts. Hardly a night passed but I awoke with my heart pounding, feeling his rod on my back. And, by day, bouts of melancholy alternated with bouts of anger. I fear I was poor company for the genial Stavko. Of course, he offered me the freedom of his women but, strange to say, I had no appetite for them and, though I tried, I could do nothing—which frightened me and made me feel even worse.

One day at dusk I said, "I'm going out, Stavko Ulanovich. I have some business to attend to."

He jumped up and put his back to the door. "Please, my friend, better you stay put until fleet sails. Would be very embarrassing for princess if you should be recognized."

"Lend me a long cloak and get out of my way."

"Tell me what business, I take care of it for you."

"The cloak, Stavko!" I took a menacing step toward him.

"Yes, yes, don't get angry. But I warn you, Odd Tangle-Hair, stay out of trouble."

"No trouble, Stavko." I had already stolen a knife from his kitchen and hidden it under my shirt.

I walked at a leisurely pace through the crowded market, stopping now and then to examine some item for sale, until I came to the place where the Saracens had their stalls. They were just closing up for the night.

"Murad Bey—"

He looked around sharply.

"It's me, your former slave. See how my fortunes have risen in only one week!" I smiled at him.

He eyed me mistrustfully: What did I want?

"I bear a message to you from my new master—the gentleman who bought me, you remember. He has some choice boys to sell, young beauties fit for castrating, he offers you the pick of them."

No. He squinted, trying to read my eyes. He was going to pray now, he might look at them tomorrow.

"Too bad," I shrugged, "they're Christian children and stolen, he's anxious to get them off his hands, you understand. Someone else will buy them tonight."

I turned to go.

"Wait," he called after me, "where does he keep them?"

"Just along there, not far." I jerked my thumb toward a warren of shop-houses and narrow alleys up by the citadel slope.

He was tempted, uncertain what to do. I tried to take his elbow, but he drew back. "No, no, I go nowhere with you—"

"Then die here!"

Holding out my cloak for cover, I shoved the knife into his heart. He never made a sound. I let him down gently and propped him in a sitting position against the wheel of a push-cart. It was over in an instant.

I knew he wore his key around his neck—the one with which he locked the manacles, the leg-irons, and the collars that prevented his merchandise from strolling away. I cut it loose and tossed it up onto the platform among the slaves. That should keep everyone busy for a while.

Shucking off the cloak, I slipped into the swirling crowd, taking my time, not running nor looking back, while shouts and alarms rose behind me.

"No trouble, you said!" Stavko stepped out from behind a coppersmith's booth and gripped my arm tightly. "That was very foolish act, my friend."

We moved up the lane side by side, looking as innocent as a couple of deacons.

"Risking mission just to pay off private grudge. What if all slaves acted like you? My God, where would we be then?"

"I know where you'd be."

"Now, now, now, such talk between comrades." He shot me a reproachful look.

"Follow me again and I'll kill you."

"Really, Odd Tangle-Hair. I only keep friendly eye on you—these are my orders. Luckily for us all, convoy sails tomorrow. Up on citadel they have just sighted smoke-signal from Vyshgorod: Novgorod fleet is passing it now. So! What shall we do, last night in Kiev? For Rus, only way to begin long journey is in state of drunkenness, is not so with you? Come along home now, we finish cask of mead together, there's good fellow."

But I soon found Stavko's company tiresome and went early to sleep. A sleep in which I plunged my knife again and again into a heart which sometimes was Murad's, and sometimes was Harald's, and sometimes Inge's.

30

STAVKO SUPPOSES

The trading fleet from Novgorod had doubled the number of strugi to nearly one hundred and the podol now presented a scene of even more bustling activity as merchants, sailors, and porters jostled each other along the crowded riverfront. Human chains stretched from the warehouses to the water's edge as, from hand to hand, were passed the precious furs of Gardariki, the kegs of honey, and the great wheels of wax, enough for all the candles in Christendom.

And slaves. Miklagard devoured slaves. The best-looking of the women were destined for the city's brothels, of which it had as many as it had churches. The strongest of the men were fated to sweat out their short lives in the furnace rooms beneath the great bath-houses, where the lowliest citizen of Miklagard could waste his day in princely splendor.

And then there were the little boys—the luckiest of the lot, really. First, of course, there was the terror of the knife, the pain, the mortifying wound. But for those who survived the removal of their manhood, and were ambitious besides, there lay open boundless opportunities to exercise their subtle talents. The imperial eunuchs—as I would one day learn to my sorrow— were among the most powerful men in the state, and most were 'barbarians' by birth.

Among all this human cattle were Stavko's recent purchases: twenty-six good-looking females, some of them purchased from my late master, the rest picked up here and there. He licked his lips anticipating the day when they would stand on the auction block in Miklagard.

Besides making money for himself though, Stavko had another mission: to keep an eye on me

From my belt hung a purse heavy with gold; in it, too, was a letter naming me gospodin Churillo Igorevich, boyar and envoy of Yaroslav the Wise, Grand Prince of Rus. It asked the favor of an imperial audience for the purpose of contracting a marriage between the eldest of Yaroslav's daughters—a marvel of beauty, prudence, and affability—and some lucky Greek princeling.

Needless to say, all this had been concocted by Ingigerd without 'Wise' Yaroslav being any the wiser. She counted on rumor of my business reaching Harald, wherever he might be, and bringing him out in the open. Then all I had to do was kill him.

Simple.

The strug that Stavko and I had bought places in was a vessel of about fifty feet in length and nine or ten in the beam, carved, as all the Rus ships are, from a single enormous tree trunk, without deck or keel. The only additional timber she carried were a mast and rudder, rowing benches, and strakes added to the sides to give her more freeboard. Twenty rowers sat on the benches and an equal number wedged themselves in amongst the cargo to wait their turn at the oars. No room here for passengers who didn't like to work. Or to fight. Every man aboard carried arms and looked as though they could use them.

From up and down the line came cries of "Ready to cast off!" Ingigerd's new archbishop, resplendent in robes of white and gold, blessed our fleet while colored smoke from the censers drifted over the water and a deep-voiced chorus chanted hymns.

"Cast off!" cried one hundred steersmen, and the shore rang with answering cries of "God keep you!" as two thousand oars churned the water. If all went well, we would sight the walls of Miklagard in six weeks' time.

In the late afternoon I took two hours at the oar, then, drowsy in the heat, propped myself against a pile of furs and lay my head on my folded arms. Stavko, beside me, plucked at the strings of a gusli and tried to make me join him in a sailors' song. He gave up after a while and turned to better-humored shipmates.

A younger, a different, Odd would have sung, would have felt his heart lift at the surge of the boat when the oars dipped, would have turned his smiling face to the sun's warmth and the gusting wind.

That Odd was gone; a stone lay in the place where his heart had been. And I neither could nor even wished to be the old Odd again. The old Odd was too full of hopes, too fond of life. If I was to face Harald and kill him, cold hate must fill me up like water filling a skin bag, flowing into every fold and wrinkle, pressing out fear.

We ended our journey that day at the little hilltop fort of Vitichev, here to join the boats from Pereyeslavl and the other down-river towns. Vitichev had been a smoldering heap of sticks when Harald and I had ridden down to inspect it after the raising of the Pecheneg siege. Rebuilt now and defended by miles of wooden ramparts that snaked across the landscape, it stood guard once again over the line that divides forest and farm from steppe: the tilth of Christmen from the grassy haunt of the heathen. All beyond this point was new to me.

The steppe-grass stands as high as your head and, when the wind blows through it, it stirs in long ripples that sweep from horizon to horizon. In all this wide expanse the only thing made by man is the occasional tumulus—a brown hillock against the sky—of some proud Pecheneg chieftain, who sleeps in death with his women and his horses. Here herds of bison, and antelope graze. They are food for the wolves, who play the part of sharks in this grassy sea.

Ten uneventful days slid by. But on the last of them, as it drew toward evening, a murmur of sound reached our ears, beginning like the distant echo of the sea in a conch shell, then growing steadily until it became the groaning of a giant.

"The cataracts," said Stavko, with a weary shake of his head. "We anchor close as possible tonight and tomorrow run all in single day. Go early to sleep. Tomorrow will be hardest day of your life."

The Dnieper cataracts are seven sets of granite ledges that rise out of the river like whales' backs, spanning a length of seventy miles from beginning to end. The short June night passed quickly and the sun was scarcely up as we approached the first of them. The Rus call it Essupi, which means 'Do Not Sleep'. With a sudden, sickening jolt the current caught us and flung us at a wall of solid stone around which the water boiled in foaming eddies, throwing up a mist as dense as fog.

"Into the river, the starboard side!" our steersman shouted, his words barely audible above the roar.

Standing waist deep in the foaming water, we formed a human barrier between the rocky ledge and our hull, clinging to the low gunwale while we planted our heels in the sandy bottom until our legs were numb with cold and quaking with exhaustion. As we struggled on the starboard side, the men opposite steadied the strug with long poles to prevent her swinging out into the middle of the river where more jagged rocks waited to break her in splinters.

We were nearly around the ledge when Stavko, who was straining beside me, lost his footing. In an instant the suck of the water tumbled him over and pulled him down head first between the hull and the bottom. One foot kicked in the air.

What a simple thing to let him die, I thought, this creature of Ingigerd's. I'm sure to regret it if I don't. But with this idea barely formed in my mind, I reached down and hauled him up choking and gasping, and, with the help of a shipmate, boosted him over the gunwale.

The second and third cataracts were passed in the same way as the first. Stavko, soon recovered from his dunking, again fought the crashing waters with the rest of us. The noise made speech impossible but he shot me a questioning look and nodded his head in thanks. I think we were both wondering the same thing.

Just when I thought my arms and legs could do no more, the terrible thunder of Nenasytets, 'The Insatiable', assailed our ears. This, the fourth cataract, was the biggest and most fearsome of them all, consisting of twelve high ridges with murderous whirlpools between them.

Ships and men were no match for The Insatiable; here we must portage. With the strugi hauled up on shore and unloaded, we partly dragged, partly carried both ships and cargo over a distance of about nine versts under a relentless sun. Naturally, we put the slaves to work but there were not enough of them to do it alone. The air shimmered, the grass snared our feet, and dust filled our throats. Thanks to my years of slavery, I was more accustomed than most to toiling in fierce heat, but many a strong man fainted dead away before we were through.

"Over there!" shouted someone, pointing. On the horizon a thin column of smoke stood out against the vast white sky. A Pecheneg band had seen us and were signaling to their comrades. Although the common opinion among the Rus was that the savages were too cowed to try anything so soon after their latest defeat at the hands of Yaroslav and his son, nonetheless we posted flankers until all the boats were safely back in the water.

Cataracts five and six were passed with relative ease. At the seventh and last, which the Rus call Strukun, or 'Rusher', the river narrows and takes a sharp bend to the right. Here the banks rise up to a height of fifty feet, forming a narrow gorge, where the current is very fast and likely to dash you against the side if you aren't careful. The Rus boatmen, even as skillful as they are, never get through it without loss. The strug just ahead of us careened into the wall and capsized, spilling out cargo and crew. And we, swept along willy-nilly, could do nothing to help them.

Beyond the gorge the current slows as the river widens into a broad and shallow ford.

We raced out of the chute into a storm of arrows. Two strugi ahead of us were stopped dead in the water, their crews battling to throw back the Pecheneg cavalry that swarmed about them, shooting arrows and leaping from their saddles right into the ships.

Besides those in the water, other bowmen lined the banks, catching us in a deadly crossfire. Men toppled, clawing at shafts in their chests. I was out of the fight before I could even draw my sword. An arrow pierced my right shoulder with a tremendous smack and knocked me to the deck.

Looking dazedly about me, I saw Stavko fighting in the bow. A Pecheneg thrust at him with his lance. Dodging sideways and seizing it in one hand, he yanked the man from his saddle and hewed off his arm. At the same moment another savage took a cut at him with his saber. He parried the blow and drove his sword into the fellow's side. This slave dealer, I realized, was no shirker in a fight. If it ever came to blows between us he would not be an easy man to deal with.

Meanwhile more strugi came hurtling out of the gorge until our attackers, seeing the advantage in numbers turn against them, broke off suddenly and galloped away.

It wasn't much of a battle, really; there hadn't been above two hundred of the savages. In years gone by, said the old hands, we might have met twice or three times that number. Something was happening on the steppe, some obscure movement of tribes, some shift of power that we aliens could scarcely guess at.

My wound was attended to by an elderly Rus who had healing-wit the equal of a woman's. He drew the arrow and bound up my shoulder while Stavko held me down, and remarked cheerily that he thought it would heal up nicely unless, of course, the arrow was poisoned, in which case the wound would turn black and he would have to do me the favor of taking off my whole arm in order to save my life. With those encouraging words he turned his attention to another, who was spouting blood all over the deck.

I ground my teeth and cursed my evil luck.

As that day's fiery sun went down, we approached a long wooded island that split the broad river like a ship's prow. The Rus call it Khortitsa, and when it comes in view they cheer and break into rowdy song, because danger is all behind them now.

Upon this island there stands an ancient oak tree, many feet in girth. And here the Rus, though all of them profess the Christian faith, perform an ancient ceremony in which they peg arrows in the ground in a large circle around the tree and, within this circle, sacrifice cocks and sprinkle the blood on the roots. It is their way of giving thanks for having survived the double perils of the rapids and the steppe warriors. When the ceremony was done, we threw ourselves down wherever there was a patch of grass and slept for many hours.

Altogether we spent three days on the island, given over to burying our dead, re-packing loosened cargo, and hunting the deer, which are plentiful here. One evening, Stavko tore himself away from the company of his girls long enough to discover me sitting alone in the shade of a tree by the water's edge.

Dark thoughts troubled my mind. Thoughts of foolish choices made, of wrong paths taken, of years squandered in futility, while at home my enemies slept peacefully in their beds and my dead kin waited un-avenged in their tombs. Ingigerd's promise had wakened these slumbering memories to life. The thousands of miles that separated me from my home weighed on me as though I were tethered to the end of some immense chain, too long, too heavy, to drag any farther.

I wanted no company, not his anyway, and gave him no sign of welcome.

"How is wound today, Churillo Igorevich?"

He always accompanied the use of my false name with such great winks of his eye as might have aroused the suspicions of a tree stump.

"It's all right. There was no poison."

"I rejoice to hear!"

He went on for a time, smiling inanely, while he inquired as to my appetite, my digestion, my sleep, and my limp prick. I was close to laying hands on him.

"And now just one more question, my friend. Why you saved me from drowning?"

I turned away with a shrug.

"No, answer, please. For I understand quite well that you detest my manners, my occupation, and my regard for princess, whom you consider enemy. You suspect I am here to spy on you, no? Or maybe worse?"

"It's crossed my mind."

"Then why save my life?"

"I often do things I live to regret."

"Tch, tch. Even generous act must be rounded off with insult. From you, Odd Tangle-Hair, always insults. Still, deeds speak for themselves, no? So I thank you—and I confess now to playing little trick on you: I slip in the river on purpose."

"On purpose! What in Hel's Hall did you do that for?"

"Just to see where we stand with each other, my friend. To see if anything at all remains of that young Odd that you say is dead. Someday I might need to know that, who can tell?"

"It was a fool's trick."

"Maybe. But I slip in that very spot once, years ago, and survive without anyone's help. Of course, I am not such a young man anymore!" Chuckling, he slapped his stomach.

"Don't think you've learned anything by it. Next time I'll be sure to let you drown."

"Ah, well, we shall see. Now, my friend, can we talk about your mission?"

"You're here. Talk away."

"Yes, well ..." He settled himself beside me and leaned his back against my tree. "Princess is optimist, I am not. Friend Odd, you were willing to save my life—no, no, too late to deny it—maybe now I return favor, eh? Give up this mission, my friend, while you still can."

"I thought you were Ingigerd's man."

"Is only because I like you, Odd Thorvaldsson, I really do, though God alone knows why."

"You think I won't find Harald?"

"On contrary, I fear opposite: that you will find him in very strong position with plenty protection around him."

Suddenly he had my full attention. "Stavko Ulanovich, what do you know that you haven't told Ingigerd?"

"Me? I know nothing. Only speculate on certain observations I have made. For instance, that merchant that Harald sent to Kiev with gift for Grand Prince. Did you ever hear the like of it? Send a fellow off with fortune in jewels in his hands and expect him to deliver as ordered and come back with note of receipt? That would require very strong bond between these men—stronger even than greed, and few things, my friend, are stronger than greed. Now, I ask myself, what could that bond be: blood-brotherhood? Or maybe code of warrior band to which both men belong? For that fellow did deliver jewels and he is returning to Harald."

"How d'you know so?"

"Follow my eye, he's just over there."

"What!"

"Ssh! Just look."

I looked to my left and saw, some twenty paces distant, the solitary figure of a well-dressed young man seated upon a mossy rock. His mouth was set in a frown as he honed the edge of a long-handled ax with careful strokes of a whetstone.

"Well, let's just have a little talk with him—" I tried to rise but Stavko squeezed my bandaged shoulder.

"Ach! Careful!"

"You see. Not ready for a fight, my friend, which is likely to be what you'll get if you accost him in your bad humor. Besides, I have talked to him already. You are interested?"

I nodded.

"Then sit still and listen. Very mysterious fellow, this one. Not Novgorod merchant as he claimed to be; I take my oath on that, I know every one of them. This man's face I never saw before last autumn when he came to Kiev with strugi returning from Miklagard. He would say only that he had been approached by someone who asked him to deliver this small fortune in jewels on way home as favor for man he had never met. This was his ridiculous story."

"That much I know already, Stavko."

"Be patient, friend Odd. Princess smells a lie and, wishing opinion of myself, arranges for dinner where I may observe him. I can tell her only that he is impostor."

"What kept her from seizing the fellow then and there and flogging the truth out of him? It couldn't have been her tender heart?"

"Please!" He held up his hand as if to say, No more jibes, thank you, at the woman I admire with all my hard heart and greedy soul. "Maybe foolish, but we decide to watch him instead. Few days later, when Novgorod ships set out for home, this man goes with them. Plainly, he does not realize what a mistake he has made, giving to mother letters intended for daughter. Princess sends a druzhinik to follow him, but he goes quickly from Novgorod to Aldeigjuborg, takes ship for Sweden, and there we lose him. Yet now is here again! Stranger and stranger."

Stavko drew his knife from his boot and began to clean his nails.

"Well, don't stop there, man. If he's not what he claims to be, what is he?"

"You have heard, perhaps, of Varangian Guard? It is elite regiment in emperor's army, created over fifty years ago when Vladimir the Great gave thousands of his mercenaries—Swedes and Norwegians mostly—as gift to Emperor Basil. Ever since that time, only Northmen can join it. These Varangians, they are pampered, well-paid, loyal; stand day and night with long-handled axes on shoulder, ready to obey emperor's command, and his alone. And that man is one of them."

"How d'you know so?"

"I recognize him yesterday, make myself agreeable to him—you know my nature—offer him good price on girl, pour him some wine. I say nothing about meeting him in Kiev. We spoke only few words at that dinner and he was too drunk to remember. So this time, when I ask, just casually, who he is, he tells truth. Strangely enough, he is Icelander like you. Name is Ulf Ospaksson. Perhaps you know the name?"

I shook my head.

"Anyway, he has been home on leave to settle some family business and now is returning to regiment of Guards. Of course, I do not ask about Harald, not to rouse suspicion, but I bet you anything that where we find this fellow we will find also Harald. Who else but fellow Guardsman could be trusted to deliver that valuable present and those private letters?"

"Interesting, Stavko. I see a flaw in your argument, though. If the reputation of these Guardsmen is as great as you say it is, and Harald, as we know, is not bashful—well, why all the secrecy, then? According to the princess, he signed himself merely 'Harald of Miklagard'. I should think he'd want his emissary to make much of it, not conceal it."

"Is puzzling, I admit. But look now—when was Harald ever content to take orders from another? Wherever he is, he must command, no? Now what if he has not quite reached that rank yet; some other Northman is higher than he. But he feels it, feels it almost in grasp. So. Now he only teases us with just little peeks, makes us wonder and worry: where is he? What is he up to? Until, finally, moment comes when he is ready to step from shadows, show himself to us, Harald the Magnificent! Eh? What d'you think of that?"

"I suppose it could be."

"I would rather be wrong, believe me. Maybe Harald is willing to fight you man to man, but maybe not. Maybe his Varangian comrades are willing to let you leave city after you kill him—but maybe not. This mission already foolish, in my opinion. Now is plain suicide. Is Harald's life worth so much to you?"

"I'll know that when I stand face to face with him, Stavko."

✝

Four days rowing from Khortitsa brought us to the Dnieper delta, where we spent a day putting up masts and rigging and attaching rudders in order to transform these river boats into sea-faring vessels. Three or four weeks of sailing still lay ahead of us. For the first time now, we were beyond the sight of land—never a comfortable feeling at best, and made less so by the way these clumsy ships rolled and yawed in the waves. Twenty-two days later (and most of them stormy) we made landfall at the mouth of the Bosporus. This is a strait more than twenty-five versts long, through which the Black Sea (or Pontus as the Greeks call it) empties itself into the little Sea of Marmora. At the far end of it stands the City of Constantine—Golden Miklagard .

That night no one slept.

Sitting round our campfires, the old hands nudged each other and winked, savoring beforehand the delights that tomorrow promised.

We would take steam-baths, said one to me, in a vaulted palace of stone. "And not such stone as you've ever seen, mate, but smooth, with a sheen to it like polished steel, and glowing with every color of the rainbow!"

We would have our pick of beautiful women, said another, and would eat rare dishes and drink the finest wines until our bellies burst—and all at the emperor's expense! "For I'll have you to know," said he, "that this Emperor Michael, or Romanos, or whoever he is—for they come and go so fast lately that it taxes a man's mind just to keep up with 'em—but this emperor anyway, just like his ancestors, treats the Rus with respect, and so he should, by God! Three times—in our grandfathers' day, and their fathers', and their fathers'—we Rus sailed against the City and though we never breached her walls (those God-built walls, impossible!), still, we scared those old emperors into giving us fairer conditions of trade than any other folk can boast of, be they Bulgar, Saracen, or Venetian!"

"Aye," struck in the first man, "they're cowards at heart, these Greeks, not proper men like us. It's plain they fear the Rus. Just see how they make us live outside the walls, across the bay, and can't go over into the City proper except in batches of fifty, without our arms, and always with some poncy little Greek from the palace dancing round us."

"Basil was no coward, though," said Stavko; "he that blinded ten thousand Bulgars and made them find their own way home!"

"Well, but where's his like today?" replied the other. "They're ruled by weaklings and women now, or worse—men without balls! Don't tell me!"

He brought his hand down, *thwack!* on his knee, and that seemed to close the debate. There was a chorus of aye's all around and then the talk went back to the excellence of the wine and the women. About that there was no disagreement at all.

31

GOLDEN MIKLAGARD

Morning comes dark, wet, and blustery. We weigh anchor at dawn and row, five ships abreast, along the European shore, letting the swift current do most of the work. As the channel narrows, low wooded hills come into view on either hand, thickly grown with oak, pine and black cypress. The current sweeps us past fishermen's' cottages, white-washed and thatched, each one perched on its own little cove along this snaggle-toothed coast. As we draw nearer to the city, scattered houses collect in drowsy villages and these grow into bustling towns. And now grander buildings appear at intervals: princely villas and silent monasteries, lifting up their red-tiled heads above strong, encircling walls. Soon the strait is thick with vessels of every size and description, darting this way and that on their various errands.

But we are not the lads to make way for anyone. We are the Rus!

On we sweep, rank after rank, still five abreast and holding to our course, with oars rising and dipping in perfect time to the booming notes of the oarsmen's song.

Boats that are not quick enough to yield the right of way are swamped in our wake. Their passengers shout curses—from a safe distance. We ignore them.

We are the Rus.

And it must seem doubtful to those gazing at us from shore whether we have come to trade or to fight.

My shoulder being still too painful for rowing, I stand in the prow with Stavko. Only one rank of strugi precedes ours. Of these, the middle one is captained by Vyshata Ostromirovich, a crusty old boyar who is the commodore of our fleet, and responsible for dealing with the Greek authorities. We are not yet in sight of the city when three warships appear, beating up the channel towards us.

"Imperial dromons," says Stavko with a hint of borrowed pride. "How would feel to have ship like that under your feet, eh, Churillo?"

They are more than twice the length of the biggest of our strugi and broader in the beam. Two hundred oars in double banks propel them and each ship has also a pair of masts rigged with sloping three-cornered sails. Emblazoned on the sails in black and gold is the eagle of New Rome. And something else I have never seen before: their prows end in massive bronze beaks that cut the water like plowshares, flinging up sheets of white spray as they come on.

"Will there be trouble?"

"No, no, no. Is only escort. Every year same thing. They must look us over, count us, tally up value of cargo, write it all down—not once, but three, four times, this copy here, that copy there."

"Why?"

"Why? Because they're Greeks, that's why."

The two flanking ships swing out to right and left, athwart the current and drop anchors, barring our way. The middle ship draws alongside Vyshata's and throws out grappling lines. The strug backs water furiously and passes the order down the line—which still does not save us from collisions and tangled oars as our fleet slows to a halt.

The dromon towers over the strug. Her gunwales are crowded with archers and javelin men, all in conical helmets and hauberks of iron scales. Her deck bristles with catapults and with slender, bronze tubes mounted on swivels, whose open mouths are fashioned to resemble the heads of roaring lions. I take them at first sight for trumpets and wonder aloud why no one sounds them.

"Pray you never hear their music," Stavko says, crossing himself, "is roar of hell-fire."

The lion-headed 'trumpets' direct their glittering eyes at Vyshata's deck. A rope ladder is let down, by which the boyar mounts. The dromon's captain, reclining on a couch before his cabin, rises and permits his orderly to drape a plum-colored cloak around his gilded corselet. And Vyshata, that proud old warrior, kneels before this man!

"Stavko, how many ships like that do they have?" I whisper without taking my eyes from the scene before us.

"You're asking me? Maybe two hundred, maybe twenty, maybe not that many. No one gets close enough to military harbor to see. Is only one of many well-kept secrets here: secret of silk, secret of throne that floats in air, secret of those accursed fire-tubes—secret of their power. Is it still as great as in Basil Bulgar-Slayer's reign? Or is only mummers' show now, all masks and pretending? Who can say? Miklagard is city built on secrets, Churillo Igorevich. Mystery is her strength."

It is late afternoon before we begin to move again. The dromons come about (despite their enormous size they handle smartly) and lead us the last few miles to the harbor of Saint Mamas, where our quarters await us. Stavko leaves me to go aft and look after his human cargo.

Alone, I sink again into that mood of doubt and discontent that never leaves me for long. My thoughts circle uselessly round and round the same few questions: have I done right to come here? Am I fated to die here, far from my home with my vengeance still unsatisfied? If only I might have a dream or a sign to guide me, but my father's ghost has been silent for a very long time. Is he angry with me?

Then, as I stand lost in gloomy thought, the starboard shore falls away sharply to form a deep bay and, at the same moment, the setting sun breaks through the clouds in a blaze of molten orange. Spread out before me across the sparkling water is a sight dazzling to the eyes: a series of rising terraces clothed in marble, acres of it—walls, columns, arches, steps, piled one atop the other and everywhere crowned with golden domes, touched to sudden life by the fire from above.

It is all true, those boasts of Leonidas's, that sneer of Ingigerd's. But no one's words could have prepared me for this, just as no words of mine are big enough for it now. The sight of it comes like rain to my barren spirit. Curiosity and wonder—feelings I have forgotten I possessed—stir in me again like seeds in the damp earth. To walk those avenues, to enter those cool marble towers and hear the whisper of silk along their secret corridors ...

"Aye, Tangle-Hair," says a voice within, "but, for all that, don't forget what you must do here. In one of these gleaming piles you will find Harald—or he'll find you. Make no plans to outlive that day."

POST-SCRIPTUM

I vowed I would not spend two nights under the old man's roof. In fact, three whole weeks passed by and the beginning of the fourth found me still at work—cramped, inky, and sore-eyed.

During these weeks, a change had gradually come over me. It began, I think, when I learned to my astonishment that Odd was baptized; it progressed as he described to me the expedition against the Pechenegs, where he hit on that ingenious alliance with the monks; and, after that, when he told of all the wrongs done him by Ingigerd and Harald.

I was scarcely aware of this transformation, however, until my brother Gizur, acting as bishop in our father's absence, made an unexpected appearance, accompanied by our mother.

Odd and I had been working since sun-up. The sun was now at his highest when the door flew open with a bang and Gizur stormed in, his face as dark as a thundercloud.

"Found you at last! God's belly, what a day! We've ridden round the district for hours hunting for this godforsaken little cranny. Mother is exhausted; she would come along, although I need no help for what I mean to do. Collect your things, Teit, you're coming home."

I was like someone deep in a dream who is suddenly startled awake; I clung to the shreds of it.

"No, Gizur, not yet. He's just now sailing into the harbor of Golden

Miklagard to search out his enemy, Harald. And, Odd, you stayed in Miklagard, didn't you, and rose to fame and fortune."

"Miklagard?" sneered Gizur. "Then he's the only Icelander who ever went there and came back poor. What, no silk-lined cloak, fellow, no jeweled scabbard, no belt of silver links? Perhaps you'd like to tell us why you choose to live in squalor."

I had asked Odd the same question once, with the same sneer in my voice. He had frowned and turned his head away then, but not before I saw the pain in his eyes. And after all these many weeks with him, I still did not know the answer.

"Speak up fellow," said Gizur, "or has your flood of words suddenly run dry?"

"I have my reasons, priest, they don't concern you." Odd spoke quietly, but his black brows drew together.

Gizur, as he often does, began to fume and sputter.

Meanwhile my mother, with a pained expression on her face, had gone poking all about the room, blackening her fingertip on a sooty wall, sniffing at the pantry. "When was the last time you had a proper meal, Teit?"

"I don't know; yesterday there was some porridge, I think."

"When was the last time you had a wash, for that matter?" said Gizur, returning to the attack. You smell like a goat. And so does your friend here—his customary condition, no doubt, living no better than an animal."

"Gizur, have a care," I warned. "Don't judge him by what he is now. In his time he was a great skald, a brave warrior, the secret lover of the Grand Princess of Novgorod. You must address him as gospodin Odd."

"Gospo—what? My ears must be deceiving me; did I just hear you praise a man for being an adulterer? You, who are so much purer in heart than all the rest of us put together!"

"Not praise him—but you must understand that he was ensnared by a sensuous and vengeful woman. The first time he lay with her she—"

"Enough! Stop at once before you pollute our mother's ears! What have you been learning in this pagan hell-hole?"

"You're too hasty, brother. He's not quite a pagan, as we all thought, not really. He was baptized—admittedly by the Greek rite, but still, that counts for something."

"Not with me it doesn't. Listen, Teit, you have a responsibility to the family; you aren't just anyone's son. What would our flock think of us if it should ever get about where you've been and what you've been doing? Or does the family's position mean nothing to you anymore?"

"Ask that of our father, Gizur, this was his idea. He ordered me to record Odd's story."

"Well, his eccentricities must be borne with, but not yours. He told you to spend two or three weeks? Very well, you've had the three. But not a day more. Now, for the last time, Teit, are you ready to leave?"

"No, Gizur, I'm not!" I was astonished at these words of mine. Where did they come from? "Gizur, rant as much as you please, I'll leave when my task is done and not a minute sooner. What I'm recording now is exactly the part of Odd's saga that concerns King Harald of Norway. Alas, we were sadly deceived about that man. Granted he was a brave warrior, but in every other way detestable. I know that won't please father but it's the truth."

"I don't care if it's the truth or not!" shouted my brother. He turned on Odd: "Now, look you, you've done some mischief to Teit. I can hardly believe I'm speaking to the same boy. If there's magic in this, you had better watch out, my friend. I'm warning you, there's the drowning pool for people like you. Or, you might just find your house burned down around your ears one fine day!"

"Gizur, in the name of God," I cried, " don't *you* be a house-burner! Yes, Odd's a blasphemer, but he's shown me something of life that I can never learn at home, things I ought to know. I think father understood that when he brought me here. I'll be a better priest for it—if I decide to be one."

"If?" said Gizur with a stunned expression. "If, he says! I've had enough! Give me that book and all the loose sheets; these, at least, I will burn, and then, brother of mine, I will drag you home by your ears!"

But at that point our mother said firmly, "No, Gizur, I forbid it. Your father gave his blessing to this enterprise, for whatever reason, and you shall burn nothing before he returns from Rome."

He glared at her, but backed down a step. "All right, but Teit is leaving with us now and that's flat." He took me by the arm but I shook him off. Again he laid hands on me and in a sudden flash of anger—it shames me to say it—I hit him on the chin with all my strength and knocked him down. He sprawled on the floor with his cassock up around his knees.

There was shocked silence.

Odd was half out of his seat, with his hand on the hilt of his dagger. His eyes searched me from top to toe as though seeing me for the first time—or so it felt—and the hint of a smile touched his lips. I can scarcely describe my own feelings: horror and thrilling excitement all at once.

Gizur got slowly to his feet and touched his mouth, where a trickle of blood was starting. In a husky voice he said, "Well, brother, let us thank God you didn't have a sword or an ax in your fist or I would be lying dead in this filthy straw. He stabbed his finger at Odd: "For this we have you to thank!"

Odd's gaze swung from me to Gizur and back to me again. "You do amaze me Teit Isleifsson," he said, "I didn't suspect I had let such fighter into my house." He sank back slowly onto his bench. "And now I'm going to tell you something: go home with your brother."

"What? No, Odd, I won't be bullied. I was bullied into coming here when I didn't want to. I won't be bullied into leaving."

"Go home, Teit," Odd said again. "Obey your brother. If you stay I'll not speak another word to you."

"Why, Odd Tangle-Hair? You don't fear the likes of Gizur?"

"Oh, but I do," he said softly. "He doesn't threaten lightly, your brother, and I'm too old to survive another house-burning. My father turned cowardly at my age. It's in the blood. Now go and leave me in peace."

I, who had not cried since boyhood, felt hot tears on my cheeks. Silently, I went at once and gathered up all my papers and stuffed them into my satchel. I didn't say good bye when I went out the door, and didn't look back.

I thought sorrowfully to myself: Farewell Odd Tangle-Hair that was. I will never walk the streets of Golden Miklagard with you now. And farewell Odd that is. You will sink into decrepitude and madness, like your father before you, and not a soul will mark your passing.

But then I thought: No! Impossible. I don't accept it! God will not let this happen—you hear me, Odd Thorvaldsson? With God's help we'll manage it somehow. We aren't done with each other yet, you and I.

✝

AUTHOR'S NOTE

The tenth to eleventh century was the Age of Conversion for northern and eastern Europe, which until that time had been almost untouched by Christianity. Saints Olaf and Vladimir[1] stand out as major figures in that momentous process. Unfortunately, the written sources for this age are often little better than works of fiction themselves[2].

Among the major characters, Odd, Stig, Stavko, Putscha, Einar Tree-Foot, and Dag are fictitious. The historical characters are as follows:

Teit Isleifsson, Odd's amanuensis, grew up to become the greatest Icelandic scholar of his generation. Turning the family seat of Skalholt into a school, throughout a long lifetime he taught Latin and theology to the grandsons of viking warriors. It is only my fancy, however, that his father Bishop Isleif contemplated writing a biography of Harald. It would be another two centuries before Snorri Sturluson and his contemporaries composed biographical sagas of the Norwegian kings.

Yaroslav the Wise, as he is depicted in the Russian Primary Chronicle, is noted for his piety, his learning, his promotion of education, and his fondness for the company of monks. His personality is conveyed best by comparison with his brother, Mstislav. The latter, according to the Chronicle, was strong, brave, ruddy-faced, boisterous and generous—qualities which are never imputed to Yaroslav. We read there also that the prince had a deformed foot—a fact which has been confirmed by examination of his skeleton, entombed in the Church of the Holy Wisdom in Kiev.

Of Ingigerd the Chronicle relates nothing but the bare fact of her death in A.D. 1050, four years before that of her husband. Far more interesting are the Scandinavian sources. In one, *The Tale of Eymund*, the Princess appears as willful, fearless, and conspiratorial; capable of plotting the assassination of a traitorous captain of the druzhina. While her attempts on Harald's life are fictitious (as far as we know), they are, at least, not out of character. Ingigerd is depicted, with her daughters Yelisaveta and Anna, in the murals which decorate the interior of Yaroslav's Church of the Holy Wisdom in Kiev, but the stylized Byzantine portrait displays her true features as little as it reveals her secret thoughts.

Jarl Ragnvald and his son Eilif are historical (though it is only my notion that the former was loathsome and the latter stupid). It would seem that the concentration of power in the hands of Ingigerd, Ragnvald, and Eilif, backed by their foreign mercenaries, constituted a sort of Swedish 'mafia' at court. The growing preferment of Harald, culminating in his receiving joint command of the druzhina with Eilif, must have gone down hard with them.

The plot of *The Ice Queen* springs from the constellation of Ingigerd-Yaroslav-Harald-Magnus-Yelisaveta: all historical figures, and yet no contemporary source gives a believable interpretation of the relationships among them. For the present attempt I claim nothing more than psychological plausibility.

Since Harald's gigantic stature is, to my mind, so much a factor in the way others react to him, it is worth noting that references to it in the Icelandic sources are many and clear. For comparison's sake we may note that Tsar Peter the Great, whose diet was, if anything, less wholesome than a Norseman's, attained a height of six feet seven inches, was immensely strong, and was at age eleven mistaken by a stranger at court for a sixteen year old.

I note a few other particular points below.

The embassy of the Tronder jarls seeking Magnus for their King is factual (excluding, of course, Odd's part in it) and coincides pretty nearly with Harald's departure from Novgorod. It is not hard to see a connection between the two events. Cheated of the crown he believed himself entitled to, Harald was forced to seek his fortune elsewhere. His career in Miklagard is narrated in *The Guardsman*, the next volume of this series.

The question of what language, or languages, the Rus spoke in Yaroslav's day cannot be decided with certainty. Russian scholars have generally sought to eliminate the Norse element in Rus culture, while Westerners have perhaps exaggerated it. It is well-known that the Vikings, wherever in Europe they settled, quickly abandoned their language for that of the people they lived amongst. To take the best known instance, it is unlikely that William the Conqueror and his Norman (that is, Northman) knights, in 1066, still spoke their native Danish. Why should the same not be true for the Rus, whose forefathers, according to the traditional account, came with Rurik the Dane in the eighth century to rule over the Slavs? On the other hand, Yaroslav's mother was Scandinavian; his wife, of course, spoke Norse as her mother tongue; and, in general, the prince surrounded himself with Swedish expatriates, with whom surely he could converse. For my purposes, I have taken the middle ground: that while Slavonic was the general language of the court, Yaroslav and his family, as well as other Rurikids like Mstislav, were bilingual. Beyond that narrow circle, some Rus perhaps spoke Norse poorly and most of them not at all. All scholars are agreed that by the generation following Yaroslav's, at latest, the Norse language was entirely extinguished in Russia.

Odd's ruse involving the Monastery of the Caves never happened, but it might have. The right bank of the Dnieper south of Kiev is honeycombed with caves and miles of narrow intersecting tunnels, some unexplored to this day. Here, from the eleventh century onward, monks turned their backs on the world and here, after death, their mummified remains were laid to rest. From such beginnings Pechersky Lavra (the Monastery of the Caves) grew to become one of the holiest shrines of Russian Orthodoxy.

Regarding Harald's gory execution of the Pecheneg chieftain, some scholars have doubted that the ritual execution known as the 'blood eagle' ever existed outside the fervid imaginations of Icelandic saga writers.

Yngvar Eymundsson's disastrous expedition to the Caspian Sea is historical and well-documented. While the details in The Saga of Yngvar Wide-Farer are mostly fantasy, there exists a unique monument to the expedition: twenty-six inscribed memorial stones from Sweden which were erected in honor of local men who (to quote from one of them), "Went out far, valiantly, after gold, and gave meat to the eagles in the south, in Serkland." We learn from the stones that the men hailed mostly from the Lake Malar region of Sweden and that roughly half were married men who left wives and children behind to mourn them. All sources agree that young Yngvar himself died. It appears that no one (excepting, of course, Odd) came back alive. The expedition's date, its precise route, and purpose continue to be debated; I have chosen one possible version out of several and have telescoped the chronology a bit.

The Dnieper cataracts disappeared when hydro-electric dams constructed in the 1930's raised the level of the river. Luckily, we have a Byzantine source which describes the passage of these rapids in vivid detail. In more recent times too, the Dnieper Cossacks used to shoot the rapids in vessels that differed little from the ancient strugi.

FOOTNOTES

[1] I have preferred to use the familiar Russian form of his name instead of the Ukrainian Volodymyr, which is undoubtedly more authentic. Either way, the nickname is Volodya.

[2] Our principal Scandinavian source is the 13th century Icelandic historian Snorri Sturluson. He wrote biographies of the kings of Norway in a work entitled *Heimskringla*. It can be read online at Project Gutenberg. (www.gutenberg.org). Click on "The Saga of Olaf Haraldson" and "The Saga of Harald Hardrada." The principal Russian source is the Primary Chronicle. It can be read online at the University of Toronto's Electronic Library of Ukrainian Literature (www.utoronto.ca/elul/English/218/PVL-selections.pdf). These two works are indispensable, and yet both also contain a great deal of pious myth-making.

ABOUT the AUTHOR

As a boy, Bruce Macbain spent his days reading history and historical fiction and eventually acquired a master's degree in Classical Studies and a doctorate in Ancient History. As an assistant professor of Classics, he taught courses in Late Antiquity and Roman religion and published a few impenetrable scholarly monographs, which almost no one read. He eventually left academe and turned to teaching English as a second language, a field he was trained in while serving as a Peace Corps Volunteer in Borneo in the 1960s.

Macbain is also the author of historical mysteries set in ancient Rome, (*Roman Games*, 2010, and *The Bull Slayer*, 2013) featuring Pliny the Younger as his protagonist. Following *Odin's Child*, *The Ice Queen* is the second in his Viking series, *The Odd Tangle-Hair Saga*,

CPSIA information can be obtained at www.ICGtesting.com
Printed in the USA
LVOW♯ls0459211015

459125LV00002B/3/P